Reviews of Legacy's Path

June Chapko has created yet another book that entertains but also serves as a catalyst for creating our own legacy. Throughout our lives, we often wonder "What am I here for?", "What difference can I make?". Prepare yourself a cup (no, better make that a full pot) of your favorite tea (or coffee) and join the folks from Mary Ludwig's estate sale as the answers for each of them are revealed. Yours may be too!

Donnella Looger

I read the first book in this author's Legacy Series and couldn't put it down. You get to know and love the characters and watch a legacy being handed down. I love the bonus recipes from the friends I've gotten to know. I'm happy Legacy's Path is filled with more adventures, drama, love, and healing. Meeting new characters increased the friendships I had from book one. This Texas author has used her God-given talent to change lives through the story. I look forward to book 3 and beyond.

Sam Newton

In Legacy's path, the author takes us along with each of her characters, those from Book One, The Estate Sale, and new, lovable ones in this book; to discover more about the path Mary Ludwig's legacy has them on. Be prepared with tissues as you experience drama, love, forgiveness and healing, with each turn of the page. June's style of writing brings the story to life.

Kathleen Garcia

Legacy's Path is the continuation of June Chapko's eloquent and moving The Estate Sale. Just as Mary's loved ones grow in spirit in executing her final wishes, so the reader will be blessed by this sensitive and inspirational tale of love and lessons learned.

Nancy Christy

Legacy's Path

The Legacy Series: Book Two

Legacy's Path

❦

The Legacy Series: Book Two

JUNE CHAPKO

Chapko, June
Legacy's Path
The Legacy Series: Book TWO
First Edition

Publishing services provided by 40 Day Publishing
www.40DayPublishing.com

Contact the author at Amazon.com/author/junechapko
www.facebook.com/teatimewithjune/
junesteacuptreasures.com/

Front and back book covers by Thompson Printing Solutions

This book was printed in the United States of America.

Acknowledgments

It's been said writing is a lonely business and I find that to be true, but without the support of special people, this book would not exist.

I appreciate my husband, Nick, for allowing me to pursue my desire to get this book finished. His willingness to eat frozen dinners, have me disappear to the office cave for hours into the night, and mumble conversations with my characters, was a true sacrifice.

I'm grateful to my Mary inspiration, Charlotte Bain, and my Granddaughter, Harleigh Garcia, for modeling their hands on the cover to symbolize the passing down of a legacy.

My beta readers, Donnella Looger, Hal Carson, and LaVerne Stanley, did awesome editing work. They worked tirelessly to help make this book the very best it can be

My daughters, Kathleen Garcia, and Susan Smith, supported me when I was discouraged and pushed me to get it done!

A huge thank you goes to all my past and future readers, including members of Brookhill Baptist Church and Book Buddies Book Club of Universal City, for continued nudging to hurry up and finish writing book two.

I thank God for guiding me throughout this past year as I poured my heart into Legacy's Path.

Chapter One

The jet engines roared as the plane lifted higher and higher before leveling off where Brian Hills spotted billowed clouds beneath. He loved airplanes and having worked at Boeing as a project negotiator for twenty years, he'd had his share of flight time. Brian's late wife, Cassie, and his daughter, Kat, accompanied him frequently until Cassie died in a car accident almost five years ago. Now, here he was, flying from England with Betty, his new bride, and Kat, back to San Antonio, Texas, to begin a new life. He was working on his book, "Miracles in Flight", a book about life, God, and miracles coming true. He felt blessed at this moment, suspended between heaven and earth. God gave him another chance at love.

Betty leaned across her husband's chest to glance out the oval-shaped glass. "Brian, the sunrise looks like a dream."

He set his cheek lightly next to hers, patted her back tenderly and swallowed the lump in his throat. "Having you as my wife is a dream."

"I love you, Brian." She kissed his cheek. "Look, aren't the colors mesmerizing?"

"Yeah, and your blue eyes mesmerize me more," he teased.

"You're being silly now, but I love it."

Brian looked over Betty's shoulders to see if Kat was awake and noticed she had ear buds on. "I guess Kat is tuned out to our amazement over the sunrise and clouds."

"Let her be, she probably wants to not think about returning home just yet. The wedding and excitement of being in England kept her occupied these past two weeks. Now it's back to the real world of school and life."

Brian glanced in Kat's direction again. "I'm just glad they found and arrested Jared. Hopefully he's been indicted and put away. I wish we could have gotten charges on him for stalking Kat, but the attempted armed burglary should keep him locked up."

"Don't think about it. I know it upsets her, but it does the same thing to you. Let's talk happy stuff and enjoy the remainder of our trip home."

"You're right, Betty. Sorry." He put his arm around her and pulled her close.

***

Kat remained still, hearing snippets of conversation between her Dad and Betty. The music flowing through her earbuds had stopped but she wasn't ready for conversation. She felt frozen in time and thought it the best place to be at the moment. Kat savored memories of the two weeks in England and dreaded returning to whatever waited back in Texas. School would begin next month, her final year before getting her marketing degree and then deciding what to do with it.

Kat kept her eyes closed, listening to passengers coughing lightly, soft air-conditioning fans, and occasional call-button pings. What would their life be like at home, now that Dad and Betty were married and living in the same house Kat's mom occupied before she died? It'd be painful to see Betty cooking in Cassie's kitchen, making the bed in her mom's bedroom or just being there when Kat came home. Now that she was back home, thanks to being stalked at school, she'd have to face the reality that Dad had moved on with his life. Maybe she needed to do the same. One more year. If she could finish school, find employment and then find her own place, things would be different. She loved her Dad, and was very fond of Betty. They both have a new future ahead. She needed a fresh start, too.

Kat felt a jab as someone bumped into her arm. Startled, her eyes flew open. A child and his dad were making their way to the restroom. No apology. Not even a glance. She sat up and removed the buds from her ears.

"Did you have a nice snooze?" Betty asked softly.

"It helped, but it'll be great to be in my own bed tonight."

"I know what you mean. The trip was extraordinary," Betty offered, "but I'm with you, it'll be nice to get home."

"Didn't Emily look beautiful?"

"She did," Kat said, turning to look at Betty, "and you were beautiful, too."

"Oh, thank you, Kat. You're sweet to say that."

"I mean it. You and Dad really looked awesome. I loved your dress and you looked so happy. You both did."

Betty took hold of Kat's hand and squeezed. "I'm happy and want you to be, too."

"No worries there. I just hope I'll find someone to love."

"Kat, I told my dad once that I wanted to find someone to love me the way he loved my mother. He said, 'You will, when the time is right.'"

Kat looked over to her Dad and back to Betty, then smiled. "I guess the time isn't right for me just yet."

The flight attendant rolled her cart to a stopping point beside Kat. "Would you like a drink?"

"Thanks, I'll have orange juice."

Betty ordered coffee for Brian, who had dozed off, and tea for herself.

"How long before we arrive at JFK airport?" Kat asked the attendant.

"About four more hours."

"Thanks."

Betty chuckled. "Don't think about the time, it goes slower when you do. We'll be home and you'll be tucked in by ten tonight."

Kat relaxed as she drank her orange juice and was glad Betty was sitting next to her. She liked her humor and felt comfortable with her. She's not Mom, but I like having her here.

***

Brian put the key in the lock and opened the front door. "Home at last," he said tiredly.

Kat was the first one in and couldn't wait to jump into bed. She dragged one of her suitcases up the stairs to her bedroom, calling out "Goodnight, newlyweds," as she disappeared around the corner.

"Goodnight..." Brian began but Kat was gone before he finished. He turned to Betty as they both stood on the porch. He picked her up and carried her across the threshold. "Welcome home, Mrs. Hills." He kissed her before she could say a word. Setting her down gently, he pulled her close and held her in silence.

"Brian," she started, but his lips stopped any words from forming.

They broke the embrace. "The door," Betty motioned.

He turned, realizing the front door was still open and two suitcases sat on the porch.

They both laughed as he retrieved them and locked the door.

"Want some coffee?" she asked, making her way to the kitchen.

"No, I want my wife to come sit with me and tell me she's happy."

Betty gladly accepted the offer and lay down on the sofa with her head in his lap. "I am happy, Brian. I've waited for you all my life. My Dad told me God would bring my love when the time was right."

"And it was perfect for me. God knew I needed you in my life...and Kat's life."

"I hope she'll allow me to get close to her. I mean, I know she likes me and she's happy for us. I just want to be there for her."

"She will, Betty. Kat has a lot to process and work through. She does like you a lot, so I know it's only a matter of time. Just be patient and let her come to you."

Brian stroked Betty's hair. He loved the soft, honey strands wound around his fingers, and the warm glow in the dim light. He watched as she closed her eyes and dozed off. Brian placed one arm under her back and the other under her knees, slowly rising, and carried her upstairs. She stirred when one step creaked, gave him a small grin and put one arm around his neck.

"I love you," she whispered.

"I love you, more."

***

The jarring phone woke Kat. She grabbed the bedside extension. "Hello?" That's funny, no one there. Probably a wrong number. She looked at the clock, although the sunlight streaming through the bedroom window told her it was mid-morning. Yep, almost ten-thirty. Must be jet lag. Closing her eyes, she knew there would be no more sleep for her now. "Stupid phone," she scolded. Kat slowly made her way to the shower. Might as well face the day and maybe I'll sleep well tonight. She woke up several times during the night, a little disoriented, but then realized she was back in her Queen Anne bed. Last year was an awesome year. After attending the estate sale of Mary Ludwig, she and her dad were beneficiaries of fantastic gifts. Kat looked at the old rocker she bought at that sale and could still remember the excitement of finding out Mary also included the bedroom set with the purchase of the rocker. That was the sale of a lifetime. She smiled to herself, thinking what a fantastic woman Mary must have been and wished she had known her. Okay, enough daydreaming. Maybe I'll fix breakfast…if no one's up yet. She grabbed her jeans and a loose-fitting top, then headed to the shower.

***

Betty roamed around the kitchen, trying to be quiet. Brian was still asleep, and she guessed Kat was, too. The tea was steeping and Betty sat at the kitchen island, looking around. She'd been here many times before the wedding and had helped Kat prepare meals. This was different, strange. Now it was Betty's kitchen. She knew Brian must remember his late wife, cooking meals, preparing coffee, and just mulling around. Would it bother him seeing Betty doing the same? Would it bother Kat? She hoped not.

Betty hoped to put her personal touches here and there, slowly transforming it into a new environment that blended them all together as a family. Time…it would take time. Tears formed as she strained the tea into her cup. She wondered if Cassie drank tea. A tear escaped but she brushed it away. She hoped Cassie was a coffee drinker.

Brian came up behind Betty and put his arms around his wife. Betty jumped, and then turned to receive a morning kiss. "How's my bride this morning?"

"She's fine. Are you ready for caffeine?"

"Excellent idea. I thought maybe we'd go to IHOP for breakfast. What'd you think?"

***

"Rita, I was about to hang up," Kat said. "Hope I didn't call at a bad time. Good. Yes we got home late Monday night, and I think I slept most of yesterday. How are the sculpture classes going? I'm anxious to hear." Kat listened as Rita shared a few highlights of the summer session of Rita's Artsy Kids, the classes she taught for inner-city children. Rita received a huge art collection from the estate sale of Mary Ludwig last year. Since then, she was able to sell some and use the money to start classes to help kids feel loved and accepted. Kat admired Rita so much. She was a strong woman and only twenty-eight, just six years older than her.

"That's great, Rita. Would you have time this afternoon to get some tea somewhere? Awesome, I'll meet you at Madhatter's Tea Room at two."

Kat felt so unsettled. She thought her future was all mapped out. She'd get her marketing degree and work for a company as a meeting, convention, and event planner. She got her negotiating skills from her dad and loved the prospect of coordinating events. That was before Jared, before he began stalking her. Even though he was in jail right now for burglary, there was no guarantee he'd stay there. She didn't feel safe. Even now, out in public, she scanned crowds to see if he was there. It seemed she was always looking over her shoulder. Kat didn't want to burden her Dad or Betty with her fears. They were so happy together, and the double wedding in England with Emily and Seth was beautiful. No, she wouldn't say anything to them. Kat could talk to Rita though.

"Hey, Kat," Brian called up the stairs to his daughter. "Betty and

I are going to see a movie. Want to come along?"

"Thanks, Dad, but I'm meeting Rita for tea," she answered, poking her head over the stair rail. "I'll be fine, go and have fun."

"Okay, love you."

"Ditto," she said, blowing a kiss down the stairs.

***

"Rita, I can't believe your sculpture class for kids has more than doubled in size. You must be thrilled," Kat said, sipping her tea. "Madhatter's isn't too busy, glad we chose two o'clock."

"I am excited, Kat. I actually had to split the kids into three small groups. I chose one from each group to be the guide. We change guides every month to give all of them a chance to hone leadership skills."

"What an awesome idea. You're so creative."

Rita cradled her hands around her teacup, ignoring the handle. "One of the girls, she's thirteen, won a prize in the local showing. Her mom, who is a single parent, cried."

"Aww, how sweet. See all the good you're doing."

"We've been at it only six months, so it'll be exciting to celebrate a year. By the way, how are you adjusting since getting back from jet-setting to England and seeing your dad and Betty get married? Did the double wedding with Seth and Emily go off without a hitch? Pun intended," Rita said, laughing.

"It was an experience I'll never forget. The brides were beautiful, grooms handsome, and being a bridesmaid made me feel special."

"You are special. I hope you brought photos."

"I have some on my phone I'll show you, but I'd like to talk to you about something else first."

"Oh?" Rita said, raising one eyebrow. "What's up?"

Kat looked around the room to make sure no one was listening. "The thing is, I'm not sure what to do now."

"What do you mean? You're going back to college for your senior year, aren't you?"

"Dad expects me to and I know I need my degree, but...."

"But what?" Rita said, puzzled.

Kat was quiet, twisting a napkin around her finger, searching for words that made sense. "Ever since the episode of Jared's stalking me, his getting arrested and now not knowing what will happen with him, I'm confused and scared."

"He's still in jail, right?"

"As far as I know, but he could bond out again. I feel him nearby all the time and yet when I look around, he's not there."

"You should talk to your dad."

"I don't want to dump this on him. He's still honeymooning. Besides, he'd tell me what I already know."

"What?"

"God is always with me and watching over me."

"Do you believe that?"

"Of course, but...."

"But what?"

"I need certainty. I need to know Jared is not going to suddenly show up. I don't even know why he chose to stalk me. If I knew the reason, maybe I could do something to discourage him."

"Kat, one thing I know is certainty in this life isn't a given. Jared may or may not show up one day. You can't put your life on hold thinking you'll have a guarantee he won't. What will you do? Lock yourself in the house and never come out? You don't have total security there either."

Kat looked into Rita's eyes and then exhaled. "You're right, I'm sounding paranoid."

Rita moved her teacup aside and took Kat's hand in hers. "I remember when I was with your family this past Christmas, your dad shared with me about having a heart for Jesus to reside in."

Kat nodded her head. "Yes, it was after he read his poem about making room for Jesus in your heart."

"Exactly, and I know He resides in your heart. The thing is, God doesn't give us a spirit of fear. Fear can't live in the same heart where Jesus resides. 2 Timothy 1:7 would be a great Bible verse to memorize."

Kat's eyes widened and the corners of her mouth curved upward. "Oh, Rita, thank you. You're right and I'll do that."

Rita patted her friend's hand and added, "Plus, I'm here for you, too."

"I know. I'm so happy we both went to the estate sale last summer. We may never have met otherwise."

"Oh, I don't know. God brings people together for a purpose. He always has a plan and there are no surprises for Him."

Kat looked at her watch. "Yikes, it's almost four. I promised to fix dinner tonight, and I need to run by the store. Why don't you join us? We're having spaghetti, garlic bread and salad."

"May I have a raincheck? I actually have a date." Rita laughed.

"Really?" Kat asked with excitement in her eyes.

"Don't look so surprised," Rita teased. "I do occasionally get out for fun."

"Who is it, someone I know?"

"His name is Ron Davis and you don't know him. He's a friend I've known since doing art in the area. He's involved with the Blue Star

Art Center."

"I remember your mentioning him when telling us about the great offer to move to the studio apartment. I'm really glad for you, Rita."

"It's just a date. We've done things together with other people occasionally, but this is the first date alone."

"You'll have to fill me in on the details tomorrow." Kat stood, gathered her keys and cross-body bag. "I'm sorry, but I have to go. Thanks for listening."

Rita rose and hugged her friend. "I need to get moving, too. You're welcome, and if you need to talk anytime, you know where to find me."

"I'll remember. Can I drop you off at your place before I head home? I know the trolley's close by, but I'd like to."

"Sure, it'll shave a little time and give me extra minutes to make myself date-worthy." Rita laughed.

"You're gorgeous, Rita, and Ron should appreciate how special you are."

"May I quote you?" she asked, getting into Kat's VW.

***

Rita looked in the bathroom mirror after stepping out of the shower. "'Gorgeous,' Kat says. Humph! I would say tweaky," she spoke to her reflection. Not quite blonde, streaks of auburn here and there, and a smidgen of tree-looking roots at the crown of her head. Crinkles around the eyes, dimple on the chin instead of cute ones in the cheeks. A small childhood mishap-bump at the top of her nose, and odd-shaped earlobes. Definitely tweaky. Ron never seemed to notice her tweakiness or, if he did, never acted like it was important. The ringtone on her phone played Call Me. She answered after seeing

Ron's name displayed.

"Hi, Ron, yeah, I'm having a terrific day. Just had tea with a friend and now I'm trying to determine what to wear tonight. You're funny. Of course I know I'm going out with you. Sure, I'll be ready. Seven o'clock sharp. You're still not telling me where we're going? Okay, then I'm not telling you what I'm wearing." She laughed. "See you later."

Rita enjoyed being with Ron. His sense of humor kept her in good spirits, his good looks made her proud to be seen with him, and he always treated her like a lady. She loved how he prayed before they began their meal. Yes, he was a good man. When she was with him, she never thought about her childhood and how her parents rejected her. Rita had shared with Betty the traumatic event of their packing up and moving, taking the mobile home and disappearing while she was at school. But it was a memory she preferred to keep buried. Kat wasn't even privy to such a depressing story.

"Okay, gorgeous, time for a nice hot cup of tea. Seven o'clock will be here soon enough," she said to no one but herself.

***

Brian Hills sat quietly in his study. Since getting home from England and having this week to readjust, he knew it was almost time to return to Boeing and resume his work schedule. Today, he mentally walked through the past month, bathing himself in the memory of his wedding and the honeymoon. Seth and Emily out-did themselves in providing a beautiful venue for both of their weddings. How many couples get to experience the English countryside, horseback rides, strolls through English gardens and visits to a castle? How many couples take their twenty-two year old daughter on their honeymoon, he chuckled to himself.

He wondered how Kat felt watching Betty become his wife. Was she happy or were feelings of defensiveness for her mother going on? Brian knew his daughter was happy he found someone to love. She was always telling him he should get out and look for happiness. Kat seemed to like Betty a lot and yet....flying home, she acted a little distant, maybe due to all the activity. They'd kept her busy in the days following the wedding. Emily arranged for her to attend concerts and tea rooms and even go horseback riding.

No, there was something going on with Kat and he hoped she would confide in him. Maybe she's lonely. She had friends at the college in San Marcos. School begins in a couple weeks so she'll probably make new ones. It'll be different, though, not living on campus this year. Cassie knew how to handle situations like this. She could talk to Kat and work things out. But she's not here, she's dead. He felt a cold brush of air swoop across the back of his neck. Looking around, he forced himself to refocus.

A glance at the clock brought him back to thinking about life now, not the past. Betty would be in soon from her meeting with a client whose book was due out soon. It reminded him he needed to get back to work on his book. Maybe they could go to the Wimberley Writer's Cabin, the cottage Betty received from Mary at the estate sale last year. He smiled to himself, proud he had come up with a plan. Now he needed to convince Betty. Maybe they could talk about what's bothering Kat, if there was something. It could just be his imagination.

***

Ron Davis couldn't stop thinking about Rita. Since taking her home after their date tonight, he realized there was a lot more to her than sculpture talent and good looks. He had known her for several years, and helped get some of her work recognized in the Southtown Arts District. Their friendship never went any further than group outings with friends or coffee to discuss work. He wasn't really sure what prompted him to ask her out the other day. It just seemed natural somehow. The look in her eyes when he suggested...ugh...he hated how that sounded...when he invited... her out for dinner, stirred him. Her brown eyes sparkled with what he felt was affection. Dinner was terrific and Rita seemed relaxed. Ron wondered if the change from fond friendship to a date would be awkward, but it didn't seem so to him. Now the big question is where do we go from here? A second date certainly. He hoped she was thinking similar thoughts.

Ron tossed his keys on the bar and slid off his shoes. He noticed the phone's beeping with a message. Not now. He wanted to kick back and think about Rita without anything edging its way into his thoughts. Coffee seemed the perfect companion right now. He set the Keurig and as soon as it filled his mug, he settled in the recliner with the footrest up. The jangling phone made him jump. He looked at the clock. Almost eleven. Who for name's sake would be calling at this hour?

***

Kat decided on the spur of the moment to stop at the coffee shop on her way home from registering at UTSA. She parked near the entrance to have a clear view of customers coming and going. This was her usual method of determining whether to go in or not, regardless of where she was. Even at the university, she stayed put until she was sure Jared wasn't anywhere nearby. Just thinking his name gave her shivers. Kat knew this was no way to live; but for now, at least, it was how she'd have to do things. Hopefully, there would come a time when her carefree days returned.

She got out and locked the car, went in, and ordered her Caramel Macchiato. She gave a false name for them to write on the cup; just in case he was somewhere she couldn't spot him. She wanted to feel normal, a student having coffee where other students hung out. They called her faux name, she picked up her coffee, and sat where the door was visible. She exhaled.

Having settled entrance for her senior year, it was time to get serious about the direction of her future. Next summer she planned to intern somewhere, so she needed to busy herself with lining it up. She hoped to find something out of state, away from him.

Kat studied the faces of those in the room. Many people were around her age, a grandmother with two young children happily enjoying a huge cookie, and a man in a business suit who seemed out of place. One guy bent over his laptop with his back to Kat. She stared intently trying to see what he looked like. For a moment her heart raced. He turned toward the door as a young woman entered and headed toward him. They embraced and then she went to the counter to order.

Kat settled down and sipped her coffee, wishing she was waiting for someone to meet up with her. The dates she'd had up till now were very casual; movies, dinner, a few concerts, and bowling. She hated bowling and never went out with Charlie again. Of course, she could have told him how she felt, but didn't want to hurt his feelings. He was in love with the maroon ball and swinging it down the alley, getting strike after strike. Then he attempted to teach her how to accomplish it. She didn't like how he brushed against her as he stood behind her demonstrating how to swing. When he reached her dorm, she rushed out of his car and into her room without even saying goodnight. It all seemed silly now as she thought about it, but she was three years younger and a bit naïve about dating.

It'd be fun to date someone who cared about things she enjoyed; to attend a concert or go horseback riding together. Since her experience in England and getting to ride Oliver, she found a love and freedom. Oliver was a free spirit indeed and knew where he wanted to go. After frequent rides, and before leaving, they rode as a team. Maybe she would try to get in some riding here in San Antonio. She chuckled to herself. When would she have time once she was back in school and summer reserved for internship?

Time. She looked at her watch, realizing it was getting late, and she wanted to get home before dark. She made a quick call to her dad as she made her way to the car, letting him know she was on her way. Kat couldn't stop thinking she would never outgrow her need to feel safe. But then, does anyone?

***

Betty and Brian settled on the sofa in the living room, with mugs of coffee. "Kat is on her way home. Before she gets here, I wanted to talk to you concerning her," Brian blurted out.

"Is something wrong?"

"That's the thing, I feel like there is, but can't identify anything in particular. She seems a bit distant or distracted. She isn't my Kat lately."

"Has she said anything or given any hints?"

"No, and I was hoping you might have an idea. Did she say anything to you on the airplane or after we arrived home?"

"We really didn't talk much on the plane. Come to think of it, she was a bit quiet."

"Yeah, and has been all last week and most of this one, too. I guess she'd tell me...us, if Jared were anywhere around. Maybe I should call the detective and find out what the status is."

"Wouldn't hurt. But better yet, why don't you and Kat have a father-daughter evening and spend time with each other. You and I have been pretty wrapped up together."

Brian set his coffee on the end table and pulled Betty close. "You're my bride, we're supposed to be wrapped up together," he teased, planting a kiss on her lips.

She kissed him back, and then became serious. "You don't think our togetherness is the problem, do you?"

"I gave it a thought at first, but she's thrilled you're in my life. I know she cares a lot for you. No, I don't think we are the problem."

Betty heard the car in the driveway. "She's home. Why don't I find something to do while the two of you have time together?" she said, patting his shoulder as she stood.

"Thanks, Honey. I love you."

"You better, I'm making banana pudding tomorrow."

Brian got up and headed to the door as Betty disappeared upstairs. The front door opened and Kat looked a bit startled when she came face to face with her dad.

"Hi, Dad, I wasn't expecting you to meet me at the door."

"We heard the car and I thought I'd greet my favorite daughter."

"I'm your only daughter, Dad." She laughed.

He hugged her and suggested coffee or iced tea.

"I just had coffee so I'm fine."

"Well, I'm having a refill. Want to sit and talk a while?"

"Sure, give me a minute to change clothes. I need comfy right now. Where's Betty?"

"She had some paperwork to do upstairs, so I thought I'd stay out of her way," Brian laughed, filling his mug.

JUNE CHAPKO

"Okay, I'll be back in a minute."

How do I approach the topic without just asking what was bothering her? Brian remembered how Cassie used to get him to open up when he was concerned about work or something going on in his mind. She approached him softly, making him feel loved, knowing he was in a safe zone. She wouldn't ridicule, blame or brush his concerns aside. Cassie had a knack for drawing him into conversation. He asked her about it once. She told him she always prayed before discussing things with those she loved. He bowed his head quickly and asked God to help him create a safe zone for Kat, a place where she would want to open up to him.

Betty sat in front of her computer, but her mind was downstairs with Brian and Kat. She knew Brian was in deep water trying to help his daughter find her way. Betty wanted to help, but this was something he would have to work through and she didn't want to be a wedge between them. Whatever was going on, she prayed God would help Brian to unveil it and figure out how to help her. Of course, it would have to be a two-way conversation. Apparently, this is the first real difficulty Brian has had to work through with his daughter since losing his wife.

"Please, Lord, help the two of them to be honest with each other," Betty prayed.

***

Kat picked up the ringing phone as she entered the kitchen. Her dad was putting out macaroon cookies. "Hello...hello?" she said into the phone. "That's odd," she said to her dad. "The caller ID says private number and no one said anything. This makes the third no-answer call I've had since we came home."

"It's probably a wrong number, and they're too embarrassed to say anything. Don't take it personally, it's our landline."

Kat hung up the phone and took a cookie as she sat across from Brian at the breakfast bar. "I don't like calls where no one says anything. They remind me of a dumb scary movie I saw years ago. Turned out the calls were coming from inside the house." She visibly shuddered.

"Well, unless Betty is prank calling us, it was just a wrong number." Brian reached across to take her hand. "I'm here and you don't have anything to worry about."

She looked into her dad's eyes. He meant it. He was her hero and would defend her against anything. She felt a droplet slide down her cheek. "Dad, I don't know what to do," she cried. Once the tears started, they wouldn't stop.

Brian made his way around the bar and wrapped Kat in his arms. He stroked her hair as she sobbed. "You can tell me whatever is going on, Baby. I'm here to help you get through it."

"I didn't want to bother you or Betty. You're still on your honeymoon, and I don't want to burden you with stuff. I don't know how to put it into words. I'm confused about what to do with my life, always watching for Jared to show up; and I feel a little like a third wheel with those I'm around."

"First of all, you're important to me and Betty as well. You're not bothering us by sharing your feelings or telling us what's going on in your life. We're here for you. We can talk about what you want to do after you receive your degree. Nothing is set in stone. As far as Jared is concerned, we'll contact the detective tomorrow and see what's going on. What do you mean you feel like a third wheel?"

Kat turned her gaze from her dad to the uneaten cookie, not wanting to look him in the eye. "I see you and Betty finding each other. Seth and Emily are living a fantastic life in England and Rita is dating. I have no one. I feel like I don't belong anywhere. I'm not even carrying out Mary's legacy since the estate sale. I don't know how or what to do."

"It's all in God's timing, Baby."

"That's what Betty said one evening some time ago."

"It's true. Look how long she waited for Mr. Right." He placed his finger under her chin and turned her face to him. "You're looking at him." He grinned.

"Daddy, you always could make me laugh," she said, sniveling her runny nose and drying her moist eyes. "You waited too, though, and I'm happy for both of you. But I don't want to be hanging around all the time."

"Don't worry. Once you're back at school, you'll meet new friends and we'll probably never get to see you. Be patient."

"Thanks, Daddy. Now what about him?"

"In the morning I'll see if Detective Winters is available to talk and update us."

Kat hugged her dad and grabbed her cookie. "I need some milk with this."

"That's my girl. Back to her old self. I'll have half a cup of coffee with you."

***

Detective Raymond Winters sat at his well-worn wooden desk in the cramped corner of the police station. He hoped Brian Hills and his daughter, Kat, didn't think the work station was an indication of his qualifications. "Please excuse the lack of space," he said, noticing Brian's eyes take in the surroundings. "We're having some remodeling done and for now, this is home for me." He laughed.

"Not a problem," Brian said, taking a seat on the hard oak chair next to his daughter. "We're just glad you had time to meet with us. Kat and I are hoping you can update us on what's happening with Jared Orlov."

"After you called, I checked with the jail, but you may not be pleased with what I found."

Kat's eyes widened and she gripped her dad's arm.

"Why? What's happened?" Brian asked, patting his daughter's hand.

"It seems Jared's attorney presented evidence showing there was no gun in his client's possession at the time of the attempted burglary. Since no entrance was made to the building, he was released with time served."

"What?" Kat shouted, attracting attention from a detective on the opposite side of the room.

"He could have disposed of the gun," Brian suggested.

"Trust me," the detective said, "they searched for it. Even though the witness indicated he thought a gun was present, he didn't actually see one with his own eyes."

"Where is he now?" Kat asked with a shaky voice.

Detective Winters took his time answering. He knew the fragile state the young woman was in because of Jared's stalking her. "Sometimes the justice system doesn't operate the way we hope it will, but in this situation there was no other recourse but to release him."

"Where is he?" Brian echoed Kat's question.

The detective looked straight at Brian. "We. Don't. Know."

Kat began to cry and leaned against her dad.

Detective Winters slid a box of tissues to the edge of his desk.

"I'm sorry, really I am. If it were within my control, I'd have him locked up for a long time. He's trouble...." Brian's glare stopped him from elaborating further.

"I tell you what. I'll do everything in my power to find him, and I promise to let you know the moment I do." The detective stood, extending his hand, indicating their meeting was over.

Brian rose, helping his frantic daughter to her feet. He shook the detective's hand and thanked him for his time. *Lord, only You can provide Kat with the comfort she needs right now.*

Chapter Two

Betty walked into the old house she'd lived in for so many years, still filled with her past. She came to think and make decisions about what to do with stuff. After Mary's estate sale last year, thoughts floated around Betty's mind concerning her own collections and possessions. She never married until now and at almost fifty years-old, there would be no children to hand things down to. Brian's daughter, Kat, certainly wouldn't be interested in any of it. She has her mother's things. The china cabinets filled to over-flowing with other estate-sale treasures, knick-knacks all over the place, and photo frames with pictures of people she didn't even know. Betty bought them because she loved antique frames and couldn't make herself throw away the photos. Why would anyone sell pictures of family members? She removed one from the cabinet and examined the woman's face. Genteel features, long grey hair, and tiny lips. They stood out because of their smallness. Betty wondered what her name was. Maybe Loretta? She would make a sweet Loretta. Placing the photo back in the cabinet, Betty was suddenly overcome with a sadness she couldn't explain. There were so many forgotten elderly people and no one will hear their stories or know the history of their lives.

Mary Ludwig was fortunate at age ninety-seven; her story was told through her generosity and would live on through those who knew her well. Others, like those blessed at the sale, discovered a legacy they didn't know existed and will carry it forward. But what about the rest, the ones having long since passed on, with heirs' selling their photos? Who will tell their story? Betty winced, but thankful God brought Brian into her life. Still, there was heaviness in her heart that weighed her down. *I have so many material things but their value doesn't matter in eternity.* Since losing her childhood home in a fire, all family memorabilia was gone. A scripture came to mind. "What is more, I consider everything a loss because of the surpassing worth of knowing Christ Jesus my Lord, for whose sake I have lost all things...."

Betty took out her cell phone and called Brian. No answer. He and Kat must still be talking with the detective. She hung up and grabbed her handbag. Betty knew she must get home and talk to him, hoping he'd agree with what she wanted to do. Locking the door, she suddenly realized the heaviness had left her heart. Hoping Brian would be home when she arrived, Betty started the car with a sense of urgency, leaving the driveway a bit faster than normal.

***

Brian drove toward home slowly, trying to allow his daughter to compose herself after getting the devastating news from Detective Winters, about Jared Orlov's disappearing. *How could they not know where he is? Right now, he needed to set aside his own anger about the situation and focus on helping Kat handle this. It was his job as her father to protect and watch out for her welfare. He couldn't do it if he was consumed with anger. Pray.*

"Kat, let's stop somewhere for ice cream." Silence. "How about Dairy Queen?" More silence. "Coffee?"

"Dad, please, I just want to go home. I know what you're trying to do, but you don't have to treat me like a little girl who was bullied

24

at school."

"Well, you're still my little girl regardless how old you get. And, in a way, you have been bullied. His being released from jail and the police not knowing where he is, that's bullying."

"Yeah, I guess you're right, a little. I hate not knowing where he is. It scares me."

Brian picked up his speed a little, heading toward their house. "We'll go home. Betty should be back from her old place and we can all talk about what to do next."

***

Betty looked into her husband's eyes. "It's not possible," she stated a little too loudly. "How can they not know his whereabouts?"

The three sat around the dining table in their normal discussion mode. Betty was prepared to talk about her old house and the wonderful thing she wanted to do. When Brian and Kat returned, filling her in on the situation with Jared, she couldn't believe her ears. She tossed her thoughts aside and became involved in processing the news of Kat's stalker.

"We have already prayed through this thing, and we all trust God to watch and protect," Betty offered. "But, there are some practical things we can do to make you feel safe," she said, looking at Kat.

"Like what?"

"We need to change our home phone number, and then set both Brian's and my phone number as a one-button emergency contact."

"That's a great idea, Betty," Brian said. "Something else too. I'll go with you to the college, Kat, and talk with the administrator. I think it's important they know about this."

She gave her dad the bullying conversation look, but agreed. "I guess we should."

Betty continued, focusing on Kat. "For now, it would be a good idea for you to let us know if you're running late, stuck in traffic or stopping for coffee after school."

"I don't want all this to alarm you," Brian cautioned while giving her the warmest smile he had in his daddy repertoire for scared daughters. "This is all part of making sure I'm being the protector God planned for me to be."

"Thanks, I know, and I do feel protected. By both of you."

Brian stood, followed by his wife, and they formed a protective circle around Kat.

She put an arm around Betty and her dad, listening as he led them in a prayer.

***

The late night phone call took Ron Davis by surprise. No one ever attempted to reach him after nine. Except for wrong numbers. The call from his brother, Jake, not only surprised but devastated him as well. Mom has cancer. It's aggressive. You should come now. Guilt crept in the moment he hung up the phone. How long has it been? She lived just hours away near Dallas. He had no valid excuse for staying away. He loved his mother. He loved Jake. Ron left home, went to college and found himself caught up in making a living. A darn good living. He loved the world of abstract art and the people he met in the field. He spent time in Austin working his way into forming a community of artists. Ron was instrumental in introducing new artistic forms and then he discovered Blue Star Arts in San Antonio. He never left.

Jake, just two years younger, never moved away, preferring the more subdued town of Mesquite. He was always on hand if Mom needed help with anything. Since Dad's heart attack took him when Ron was in Austin, Jake stepped up and watched out for her. Ron helped financially and went home for Christmas every year. Well, almost every year. He missed the last one because he wanted to finish up a project involving the San Antonio Riverwalk. The time he had spent with the people whose art was now prominently displayed at various points along the Riverwalk Extension had certainly been well-spent but at the loss of time with his family.

His headlights caught the Mesquite sign. Twenty miles. He should have left earlier, but he wanted to see Rita and let her know he'd be gone a few days. Turned out, he couldn't reach her anyway, although he did leave her a message. Now it would be after ten before he'd arrive. I'll call her in the morning.

Ron searched his mind frantically trying to recall the last time he was with his mom...two Christmas's ago. He and Jake took her to the Gaylord Hotel in Grapevine to see the spectacular winter displays. She almost danced with the snowmen, happy and excited. He hadn't seen his mom so filled with joy in all his life. Cancer. Why didn't Jake call him before now? How long does she have? He should have called her. More guilt.

***

Rita finally located her missing phone. Foolishly, she had left it at Rita's Artsy Kids, after cleaning the area to make room for a large display. Last night, tired from the physical labor, bending and reaching, she locked up and headed back to her apartment without making sure her phone was in her pocket. Now, back in the studio, she spotted the blinking red light, advising her of a missed call, and of course it had to be from Ron. She slapped her leg, punishing herself for leaving the phone behind. His message wasn't happy news. He just found out from his brother in Mesquite...Mom...cancer...be back soon. Brother? Rita didn't know he had a brother. At least she couldn't recall Ron's mentioning one. She hoped things weren't too bad with his mom. He said he'd call again. Rita paused and prayed for him and his family.

She took stock of her late evening rearrangement of the studio and decided it would work. The kids would each have a space to display their projects when parents' night rolled around at the end of September. The after school class was smaller than the summer ones she offered. It had been a hectic time from June until last week. Having only a week to get things in place took much of her time, but she still managed to have tea with Kat and a date with Ron.

Rita was still concerned about her friend and hoped Kat opened up to her dad. Her college classes begin next week, so maybe that will help her mind focus on something besides Jared, and the other issues filling her head.

She smiled thinking about her date with Ron. He was such a gentleman, a little quirky, but she felt proud to be with him. She loved his newsboy cap, which suited him perfectly and gave him a boyish look. Her smile sombered as she thought how he must be hurting right now.

After checking the storeroom to be sure her random bits and pieces of sculpture were in their proper bins, Rita decided to head back home and put finishing touches on the first star she was working on for the Blue Star Arts Center. Well, the rough draft touches anyway. Her design took longer than she thought, but it had to be perfect. Phone? In pocket! She locked up and walked the two blocks to her place. The air felt different tonight. Maybe fall will come in during September like it should. Ha, that's a laugh...it's Texas after all.

She'd most likely be using the air-conditioning through Thanksgiving.

The thought of Thanksgiving reminded her of last year. Blanca's husband, Carlos, died after his truck flipped. Her daughter, Briana, took it so hard but then seemed to pick up her life after the tragedy. Faith in God and Blanca's support helped her through it. She's finishing college with plans to go into the mission field as a teacher. What a blessing they attended the estate sale and found a way to carry out Mary's legacy.

Rita hoped this Thanksgiving would be tragedy-free. Ron's face came into her thoughts. She wondered how close he and his mom are. Memories of the relationship Rita had with her own mother started to creep in. Not a place she wanted to go. The tug in her heart was pulling her there when the phone rang.

"Hi Ron, I've been praying for your family, how are you doing? That's good." Rita listened as Ron explained the situation. She just found out about the colon cancer last week and didn't want to worry Ron until she knew more details. Jake decided to call him anyway so they could all hear the prognosis together. "Thanks for telling me. I'll keep praying. Do you know when you're coming back? Okay, take care."

***

Ron ended his call to Rita, wishing he were there instead of here, sitting on the porch dealing with his mother's cancer...future. He wondered how long she knew something was wrong before seeing the doctor. Lillian Davis never was a woman to burden others with her ailments. When he arrived, she acted like everything was fine and other than looking a bit tired, seemed her normal self. All the way from San Antonio, Ron pictured her frail and ashen, but she was quite the opposite. Maybe Jake was dramatizing things.

He went back inside to talk with Jake. Maybe Mom's asleep. He found Jake watching the news on TV and joined him. "Where's Mom, sleeping?"

"Yeah."

"Jake, she doesn't look sick. What exactly did her doctor say?"

"He told us she has stage four colon cancer."

"And?"

"Isn't that enough? I kind of lost it after the word cancer and don't remember what else except she needs surgery as soon as possible. It's scheduled for next Monday."

"I'm glad she agreed to surgery right away instead of waiting."

"Me too," Jake said, staring at the commercial on TV.

Ron noticed Jake didn't look his way. "What's up? You don't seem present in the room. What's going on in that head?"

"Nothing."

Ron leaned in to talk face to face with his younger brother. "Spit it out, Jake. What's wrong? Is there more you're not telling me?"

Jake finally met Ron's eyes. "Money. Mom never had to work. Dad's insurance dwindles daily, and her Social Security check goes for bills and living expenses."

"Money? How long has money been an issue? What about their savings?"

"Taxes had to be paid on the house and her homeowner's insurance went up again. I know you sent money occasionally, but if you were more connected with us, Mom might have told you."

"Whoa, Little Brother, maybe I haven't been able to be here, but the money I sent should have helped cover most of those expenses. If more was needed, y'all should have said something."

"You know how she is, keeps things in. The problem at hand is where do we find money for the surgery and chemo treatments? She'll be unable to do much for herself, and we can't afford to bring someone in. I can't be here all the time. I have a job you know."

"Okay, I see where this is going. Little Brother has been the one to stay near Mom and watch out for her. Commendable. And I'm the bad seed because I left town to seek my proverbial fortune."

Jake rose from the recliner and jammed his hands in his pockets. Trying to maintain his composure, he took a deep breath, exhaling slowly. "Ron, I don't regret my choice to stay here, and I'm not condemning you for leaving to pursue your dream. I just don't want to lose Mom. I'm afraid if we can't afford the treatment she'll need...well, you know."

A shroud of guilt draped over Ron, silencing him. I should have been here. I should have asked questions. How he hated the word should. He always told people not to let others "should" on them. Right now, he hated himself. He stood, reaching his arm around his brother's shoulders.

"That's what I like to see," Lillian said, slipping unexpectedly into the living room, "My two boys together. I've missed that."

Both men turned, startled. "How long have you been standing there?" Jake asked.

Ron let his arm fall from Jake's shoulder and went over to hug her. "Hi, Mom, did you sleep?"

She hugged her firstborn ferociously as his arms enclosed her small frame. "I caught enough winks for now. Don't want to sleep too much or I'll be awake all night."

"Let's sit down, Mom. Jake and I have been talking, and I think it needs to be a three-way conversation." The look on her face told Ron she overheard them. Guilt again.

"Does anyone want coffee?" Jake asked.

"I'll have some," Ron agreed, turning to his Mom. "You?"

"No thanks, Sweetie, I had a cup earlier."

Jake headed to the kitchen while Ron helped his Mom get comfortable in her rocking chair, the one her grandfather made. Lillian had told both of her sons how the creaking lulled them to sleep each time she had rocked them in it. His heart stirred with love for this woman.

Jake returned with two mugs of steaming Southern Pecan, set them on the coffee table and took a seat. He picked up the remote and silenced the car salesman on TV. He looked at his brother and then his Mom. Jake wondered how they were going to work this out. He certainly didn't have a bulging wallet or stocks earning huge profits. Did Ron? If not, the future didn't look too promising.

"I told the doctor I'd go ahead with the surgery next week. I'll have time to take care of some things and find someone to help out for a short time until I get on my feet."

"Mom, we need to talk." Jake said.

Lillian looked at her sons and saw concern in their eyes. It broke her heart and if she could erase the pain of the last few months, she would in a heartbeat. It took courage for her to tell Jake the extent of her illness. She didn't want him fretting and worrying. He always looked out for her and helped keep things going. After their dad died a couple years ago, things fell apart for Lillian. She didn't know much about their finances...Albert always took care of it. His job at the airport provided a decent income and insurance, but then she had to tell Jake about her financial situation. He tried to be there for her, even took time off work helping through those devastating days. Ron wasn't around much, except at Christmas or he would stop by when in town for an art show. He sent money but Lillian suspected it was more from guilt than generosity. Not that Ron was selfish or tight with his money; he just always focused on his career.

"Mom, I know I haven't been around much," Ron said bluntly. "It's been hard to get away this year. I really wanted to come Christmas."

"I know. It's okay," Lillian assured. "I know you care and would be here if you could. I raised both you boys to become independent and live your own lives. Your aspirations took you to San Antonio. Jake made his life here. But you're both young. I see you marrying, having children and giving me grandchildren someday. This colon cancer is simply a bump in my road and I won't allow it to move in and change your lives."

"We," Jake interrupted, pointing his finger first at Ron, then himself, "plan to be involved in this and anything else we need to handle for you."

"Jake's right, if money is an issue, we'll find it. You're going to get the best care there is and you'll be back on your feet, feeling sassy, in no time. We don't want you worrying about anything except getting through this and healing."

"I love you both. Your dad would be proud of how you turned out. And look, we're all together now, let's enjoy the time we have. How about a game of Scrabble?"

"Mom, we have to talk about some things. Ron needs to know the scope of your cancer."

Ron jerked his head toward his brother with raised eyebrows. "There's more?"

"Now, now, don't get all worked up," Lillian said, "we can discuss it later."

Ron stood and paced from the chair to the hallway and back before speaking. "No Scrabble, no TV, no nothing until I hear everything. I want to know what else is involved and until I do, none of us is leaving this room."

Jake finally broke the silence. "It appears the cancer has metastasized to her liver."

No one spoke. Lillian seemed to sink into the wood of the rocker. Ron stared blankly at his sibling. Jake put his head in his hands, covering his ears as though to block out the words he just spoke.

"I don't feel like playing Scrabble anymore. I'm going to lie down," Lillian said softly.

Chapter Three

Jared Orlov walked slowly through the rain to his second floor apartment. He didn't mind getting wet. The sound of downpours seemed lonely; fitting for a guy with an estranged family and an outcast at the university. His entire life was a downpour. It was as if the whole world dumped buckets on him and left him out to dry. Today his car broke down leaving him to walk the two miles home. Reaching the entrance he stepped inside. His shoes were soaked and the tee shirt stuck to his skin. Jared climbed the stairs rather than take the elevator to avoid running into anyone. His mind was focused on how to get his car fixed. It never failed but one thing after another went wrong. Maybe he's worthless after all; enough people told him that throughout his life. He needed a hot shower, dry clothes, and then he'd make a call.

Getting his car running was priority. He called his half-brother again and left another message. Gus and Jared had different fathers. Jared's dad was okay. He tried to provide and even helped him get into the University. But he gave up on him at the first sign of trouble. His Mom did too. Jared and Gus got along decently and he came to Jared's rescue once in a while. He bailed him out last year after the tire slashing in San Marcos. The whole thing went south...he thought the car belonged to Kat's boyfriend. Turned out, she didn't have one. The guy he kept seeing was a friend of another girl living in the dorm. Stupid mistake. Jared wanted to apologize but she's so afraid of him now he can't get near her.

His phone vibrated on the table. It was Gus. Finally. "Hey, I've been trying to find you. My car is down...again. Can you pick me up and have a look? Great, thanks. I'll wait out front. Later." He disconnected and shoved the phone in his back pocket, deciding to check out the left-over pizza in the fridge. Twenty minutes till Gus shows up. He's a mechanic; he'll fix my car.

***

Gus slammed the hood down, jerked the red mechanics rag from his back pocket, wiping the grease from his stained hands before dabbing at his rain-soaked neck. "Looks like I'll need to tow it. Could be an easy fix or not. Won't know till I get it back to the shop."

Jared frowned. "I was hoping you'd get it going here. Another day without my car," he said resting his hand on the dull finish.

"Hey, I can only do so much in a rain-drenched parking lot. Besides, I have a brake job waiting for me to finish. I'll try to get you up and running by tomorrow afternoon and give you a call."

"I guess. Can you drop me off?"

"Sure, let me get this thing hooked up and we'll be on our way."

"I need to get a couple things out first."

"No problem," Gus agreed as he began preparing to hook the charger up. "By the way, did you ever find that gal you were looking for? You know the one at the University?"

Jared flinched at the reminder. "Sort of," he said, pulling some papers from the front seat.

"What does that mean? Either you did or you didn't."

"It means I know where to find her, but haven't actually done anything about it yet."

Gus shook his head and grinned. "I guess that makes sense."

Changing the subject he asked, "You ready for me to hook it up?"

"Let's get it going," Jared hollered, opening the truck door that proclaimed, Gus Mancheck, Master Mechanic, in bright Gold Lettering. "I really need my car by tomorrow night. I can't deliver pizzas on foot."

"If it's something simple you'll have it in plenty of time. It may be the fuel filter is clogged up, or any number of things. Did you have gas in it?" Gus laughed.

"Hilarious. I might be a pizza delivery guy, but I'm smart enough to not run out of gas."

They plowed through a huge puddle and pulled to the curb at Jared's apartment. He opened the door and jumped down from the truck, barely avoiding the chasm of water. "Call me as soon as it's ready to go."

"You got money to pay for it?" Gus teased.

"You'll get your money, don't worry," he called out as he slammed the door shut. Jared watched Gus slosh out of the same puddle and disappear from sight, before he headed upstairs. He felt the papers in his pocket and decided to try calling her number again.

***

Gus was glad to see the rain stop. He hated towing a vehicle in blinding rain and flooded streets. So much can go wrong. He maneuvered his truck into the yard over to the bay. He wanted to get it unhooked so they could get started on diagnosing the trouble. His mechanic, Charles, was finishing the Chevy brake job, so Gus would put him on this right away. He didn't want Jared missing work. He knew Jared had money his dad gave him, so getting paid wasn't an issue. He only wished his half-brother would get his life on track. Getting kicked out of the University was a major blow, but even that could be fixed if he would just make the effort. The last fiasco with getting arrested was more than his parents could handle. They gave him a hefty sum of money and told him to make a life for himself. Luckily, he was released due to lack of evidence, so he slid through unscathed. He needs to forget that girl. Gus had a business to run and couldn't be sticking his nose in Jared's love life.

He pulled the car into the bay, unhooked it and gave his mechanic the key. "Charles, we need to get my brother's car diagnosed and fixed by tomorrow afternoon if possible. Check out the fuel filter. If that's not the problem, we'll look at the ignition. Let me know."

"I'll get right on it."

***

Lillian tossed back and forth on her queen-size bed feeling lonelier right now than the day she buried her husband. Jake blurted out the truth to Ron and made it real. She was going to die. Before long Lillian would join Albert in the plot reserved for her at Laurel Cemetery. She wasn't afraid to die. Years ago, both she and Albert came to know Jesus and knew they would spend eternity in heaven. Her concern now was on her sons. They both were starting out their adult lives and while they took different paths, life was good. Jake loves his job as hotel manager and Ron relishes the arts. Lillian wanted so much for them; marriage, children, and of course for them to live out their salvation. She wanted to live to see grandchildren. Now the boys couldn't seem to agree or come together on how to handle their mother's life...or death.

She heard the bedroom door slip open quietly then close. Lillian didn't want to worry them longer so she lifted her legs over the side and made her way back to the boys. I guess we do need to talk about the elephant in the room.

"Hi Mom," Jake said, pouring himself a glass of iced tea. "Hope I didn't wake you. I just wanted to make sure you were okay."

"I wasn't asleep. A lot of things are going on in my head and I needed space to sort them out." She sat down at the dining room table. "Where's your brother?"

"He went outside. I think he's on the phone, something to do with work."

"When he comes in we need to talk about the obvious."

Jake looked at his mother and saw the determined set of her jaw. He knew what the obvious was. "You want me to go get him?"

"No, he'll be in soon enough. I will take a glass of that tea though."

"Oops, sorry, Mom, I should have asked when you came in." He pulled a tall glass from the cabinet, filled it with ice and poured the last of the tea from the pitcher. "I'll make more in a bit," he said, handing Lillian the glass.

"Thank you, Jake."

Ron strolled in from the side door and saw his mom and brother looking serious. "Okay, what did I miss?"

***

"Brian, you're home early. It's not even seven," Betty squealed, throwing her arms around her husband. "Are you hungry? We have leftovers I can reheat."

Hugging his bride, Brian kissed her breathlessly before she unleashed herself from his hold. "Kat's upstairs, studying," she said, winking.

"Does that mean I can't kiss my wife?" he teased.

"Not at all, I only wanted you to be aware," she laughed. "You didn't answer my question. Are you hungry?"

"Sorry, I was distracted by a gorgeous woman. No, I ate about four, but I would love a cup of coffee."

"Coming right up." Betty put a K-cup in the brewer and continued. "When you've had a chance to unwind, I'd like for you, me and Kat to have a discussion."

"What about? Not Jared, I hope."

"No, it's something exciting. Brian, I can't wait to share what I want to do. It has to do with Mary's legacy and the three of us."

"You've got my attention. Tell me more."

"Not yet. I want Kat to be in on it, too. She'll be done in about half an hour," Betty said, handing Brian his coffee. "Why don't you take a shower and by the time you're done and relaxed, Kat will be finished. I'm so excited. Did I mention I was excited?"

"Yes, but you didn't have to. I can see it all over your face. Your eyes sparkle, those soft cheeks are rosy, and you're bouncing around like a school girl."

Betty nudged him with her elbow before he headed up the stairs. "I'll take that as a compliment," she called after him.

***

Jared stretched out on his futon; feeling relaxed since Gus called saying his car would be ready in the morning. The fuel filter was the problem. Guess I wasn't paying attention to maintenance. He laughed thinking of Gus's description of it: looks like a muddy birdhouse. He even checked it out for other maintenance issues. So much for car trouble, tomorrow he'd be riding proud again.

Jared finally figured out why he couldn't get through to Kat by phone. The recorded message said, "You have reached a number which is no longer in service. Please check the number and try again."

She must have changed it. How can I apologize if I can't connect with her? He knew where she lived so writing a letter, sending flowers, or just a card, were options. Truth was, he didn't want anything in writing or traceable. He was already on the cops' radar and didn't need stalking added to his trouble. Well, he already had that before although they couldn't prove he actually stalked her. Then again, maybe he had been a little obsessive. Ever since the day in the University library, he couldn't get Kat out of his mind. He didn't even get a chance to know her. To this day he couldn't figure why he blurted out, oh, you're one of those, after her saying she was a Christian. Thinking back, maybe she thought he meant beer or alcohol, instead of coffee or a soft drink. Jared hated alcohol. His uncle made a believer out of him years back. If he could reach his foot up high enough, he'd give himself a good hard kick in the pants. He'd give most anything right now to rewind the clock and start over. He'd have to find a way to reach her.

***

"Let me get this straight," Brian puzzled, "you want to sell your house and use the money to make a movie about lonely seniors?"

"Well, when you put it that way it sounds ridiculous." Betty pouted. "You left out a lot."

"Dad," Kat chimed in, "you're not listening. There's more to it."

"Thanks." Betty smiled in Kat's direction. "I've outlined what I want to do, so let me go over it one thing at a time. First, of course, is to sell the house and a lot of things in it. I'd like to bring some pieces here," she said, looking hesitantly at Brian first, then Kat. "I have a few special items I want to keep."

"Of course, this is your home." Brian nodded.

"What happens after the house is sold?" Kat asked.

41

"I plan to begin checking with organizations, nursing homes, assisted living, and places where seniors are found. I want to locate those who have no family and may feel abandoned." Betty pulled out a silver picture frame with a photo of the woman who caught her attention when she was at the house. "I know nothing about this lady. I bought the frame from an auction house years ago, but couldn't bring myself to throw away the photo. The other day when I was at my house, I suddenly realized there are many seniors whose stories will never be known because they're alone. They've outlived family and friends. I want to find them and make their lives count."

"Betty, I understand your attachment, since you have no family," Brian began, "but you're suggesting something that's near impossible."

"Don't discourage me, Brian. I know it will be difficult, but nothing is impossible. God will help me and I'm depending on both of you to help me."

"Kat got up from the sofa and put her arms around Betty's neck. "I'm in. Just tell me how I can help." She turned her head slightly, still hugging Betty, "and I know Dad will join us, right, Dad?"

Brian slapped both knees, stood and joined them in a group hug. "Sure, we'll figure it out one piece at a time. You'll need to give us direction, honey, because the vision is in your head. It'll be up to you to make sure we get it into ours."

They all laughed and set plans in motion to put the house up for sale. "That was the easy part," Betty offered. "I'll give Lane Jennings a call. He's the realtor from the estate sale group, and I know he'll be happy to list it."

"Brilliant idea," Brian agreed. "I'll go with you tomorrow afternoon to the house and we'll mark whatever you intend to move over here."

***

Kat couldn't keep her mind off Betty's idea about filming the lives of seniors who seem forgotten. She wanted to help and while sitting in class, remembered a guy at church. Clay something. He talked about having been an extern with a film company in San Antonio. Wish I had paid closer attention when he was sharing in our small group. She couldn't remember his last name. Maybe I can approach him Sunday and find out more of what he actually does. Who knows, he just might be able to help.

Class ended with Kat still in her thoughts. She was the last one to leave and as she approached the door, Professor Evans called her name. She turned. "Yes, Professor Evans?"

"I just wanted you to know that I'll be hovering when you leave the campus. Since your dad came up to fill us in a couple weeks ago, I felt I should be around when you're by yourself. May I walk you to your car?"

Kat smiled. "That's nice of you, Professor, but I'm fine. I try to be aware of the people around me, and lock my doors the moment I get in. I appreciate the thought."

"Okay, if you're sure," he said.

"I'm sure." Kat thought he looked a bit disappointed. "I'll see you in class tomorrow," she said, turning to go down the steps toward the parking lot. Wow, just what I need...a stalker and now a hoverer.

***

Jared was happy to be delivering pizzas again. Getting his car back today in running condition was good timing. His delivery was of all places, just two streets over from Kat's. Did he dare try to make it over there and risk a late delivery? His boss would flip out if a

43

customer called in complaining, wanting to know where their pizza was. He decided to make the delivery first, and then whiz by her house. Pretty dumb idea...no chance I'd even talk to her...she'd probably call the cops. Three minutes after he dropped off the pizza to the customer who never tipped more than a dollar, he found himself driving past her house. Her car was there. Big deal, now what? He hurried on to get the next pizza delivered before heading back for more orders. At least he knew she was around. Jared figured she transferred back to UTSA. He found his way to Hildebrand Street and started looking for the next delivery address. I need to do something to redeem myself. Maybe I can get back in school, find a decent job, start going to church...hey, Kat attends church, of that he was sure. He could look for churches in her area and begin visiting. Brilliant.

***

Betty lay quietly in bed next to her husband. She could not fall asleep. Thoughts of what she hoped to do swirled through her head. Today she had made little progress in gathering information concerning lonely seniors. This privacy thing was so heavy there didn't seem to be a way to get past it. Each assisted living and nursing home she called told her the same thing. They could not give her the information she was asking for. Betty felt discouraged. Maybe Brian was right; it may be impossible to do what she planned. Suddenly it hit her over the head. God instilled this dream in her heart and He would open doors which man could not.

She slipped quietly out of bed, trying not to disturb Brian, and made her way downstairs to the living room. There, she picked up her Bible from the side table and curled up on the sofa. Prayer was the key to opening closed doors. Betty turned the thin pages in her worn Bible and found the Scripture she would pray back to God. His Word will not return to Him without accomplishing what it was given out to do. She read, prayed, read and prayed. Her eyes grew heavy and she leaned back against the sofa, uttering thanks to God for hearing her prayers.

***

"Boys," Lillian began, "it's obvious we're dancing around the subject of what will happen to me."

"Mom," Ron interrupted, "you're going to be okay."

"No, son, I'm not. It's pretty clear my cancer has gotten to my liver, and the prognosis is not good. I want us to each understand I'm not afraid to die. Jesus is waiting for me and when He determines my last day, I'll be ready to go."

Both boys were stricken and unable to speak. Heads down, they choked back tears.

"It's time we make some decisions so when the day comes it won't be so hard. I already have my spot beside your dad; my funeral is planned and paid for. My will is with my attorney along with personal papers. The house will be sold and money divided between the two of you."

"Stop!" Jake said, standing abruptly. "I don't want to hear this! I won't listen to anymore!" He stomped out the door.

"I'm sorry, Mom," Ron said quietly as the door slammed behind his brother. "He's upset. I don't think he's ready to hear this stuff."

"And you are?"

"I have to be, I'm the oldest."

***

Rita spent a great deal of time this morning during church, praying for Ron's mother. Her surgery would be tomorrow and although it would buy her some time, the prognosis was bleak. It must

45

be devastating for both her sons, knowing they would lose their mother and not be able to do anything to prevent it. When Ron called last night, he sounded tired but determined to be at her side for as long as it takes.

He'd been gone a week and from the way Ron talked, it would stretch into at least another seven to ten days. She missed him. Rita thought about driving to Mesquite to be supportive, but their relationship was just beginning. It wasn't her place to intrude on a family situation as serious as this...or a family situation, period. Patience and prayer.

After church, Rita heated up the chili she made yesterday. She enjoyed cooking more now. A larger kitchen and shopping for groceries made it fun. Experimenting with seasonings was interesting and her chili turned out great, even if it took her over two hours. If Ron was here she would test it on him and see if he could guess her secret ingredient. Hopefully, cooler weather would stay for a while, so she'd have other opportunities to make it again. The problem is it wouldn't turn out the same. Just like in her sculpture, each piece was unique. No two alike. That's what makes it unique. She laughed, took a bowl from the cupboard, and ladled out a portion, inhaling the spicy fragrances. Rita found the square of leftover cornbread, and popped it in the microwave for fifteen seconds. She set everything on the bar, sat down and gave thanks to God. When she rinsed off the dishes Rita decided a short nap was in store. Later she'd phone Kat and ask how she was doing. Right now the bed called her name. She answered.

***

Rita abruptly sat up, trembling. She looked around and her studio apartment was quiet, undisturbed, and familiar. She was safe. It was a bad dream. Throwing her legs over the side of the bed, she went to the kitchen and prepared a cup of chai tea. Where did such a dream come from? She was a teenager again, coming home from school only to discover a note from her parents. They had moved their trailer, Rita's home. The bare concrete slab in her dream was a stark reminder of being discarded, left to fend for herself. Her few belongings under the note signified her parents no longer wanted her. Why would she dream this? Wasn't it painful enough when she lived it?

The kettle's whistle startled her out of the thoughts she never visited when awake. Rita poured hot water over the tea leaves, staring as they swirled, then settled to the bottom, her mind swirling as well. Maybe the chili caused her to dream such unsettling things. No, most likely it was because Ron may soon lose his mother. Rita grieved for him, but also for herself. Selfish. She wondered what her life might have been like if she had grown up in a loving home as Ron and his brother experienced; or like Kat, having parents watch out for her instead of leaving town while she was at school, deserting her. How would I be different or would I be?

She finished preparing her tea and took it outside where she could watch the neighborhood come alive. Evenings were filled with people, enjoying the eclectic atmosphere of the historical area. Rita scooted the refurbished cane seat chair close to the railing and placed her mug precariously. Her heart sat in similar circumstances, afraid to trust what was holding her up. Rita was disappointed as a child but not all parents were like hers. She honored them until they died, even taking care of her mom till the very end. The Bible says to honor your parents. She carried deep pain through the years and it wasn't until last Christmas at Kat's house, she finally let it go, knowing God could be trusted.

Rita heard a short blast of a Union Pacific train in the distance. It made her feel lonely. Tomorrow, Ron would call and update her after his mom's surgery. She took a sip of her tea and started praying favor for Mrs. Davis.

***

The Mesquite General Hospital, surgical waiting area, held a smattering of people trying to pass the time until a doctor came out to give them news. Ron observed a group of seven, seemingly related because of their resemblance to one another. They sprawled onto chairs, and a sofa. A child on the floor, outstretched on a blanket, was reading. Two teenagers occupied themselves with various devices. Ron heard beeps and crashes coming from one young man's game-loaded iPhone. A middle-aged woman spoke on her phone, occasionally dabbing her eyes with a tissue.

"The doctor said it would be three hours," Jake said, standing to stretch nervously.

"Yeah." Ron glanced at his watch. "Another thirty minutes maybe."

"How are we going to handle things once she comes home?" Jake said, shakily. "I mean, can you stay on and help care for her? 'Cause you know, I have to get back to work."

Ron stood so they were face to face. "Jake, I have a job too, but right now it'll have to wait. Those I work with know me well enough to cut me slack in emergencies. You've worked for the hotel how many years?"

"Five."

"Do you believe they would fire you because you took time off with your mother in a life and death situation?"

"You think she'll die?"

Jake looked like a quivering puppy. Ron softened. "Eventually...we all do. Right now? No. The doctor said she'd need chemo and care, but she will come home."

The expression on Jake's face smoothed a bit and he sat on the hard plastic chair. "This has been such an ordeal."

Ron took the seat next to his brother. "I know you carried the bulk of worry about Mom. I wish I'd known sooner." He placed his hand on Jake's arm, "I'll help however I can. I may have to drive back to San Antonio to take care of business, but it would only be a couple days. Then, I'll come back here and share the work we need to do."

"Thanks, Ron. I feel..."

Ron stood abruptly, cutting Jake off. "Doctor Gonzales, is Mom okay?"

Jake stood immediately, his hands in his pockets. "Were there any problems with the surgery?"

Doctor Gonzales, observing the now rowdy children across the room, guided the young men out of the waiting area. "Let's go across the hall to the consultation room for privacy," he said.

Closing the door, the doctor invited Ron and Jake to take a seat, as he pulled up a chair for himself close to them. "Your mother is fighting this cancer bravely. She's in recovery right now, so it'll be a while before you can see her."

"Please tell us what to expect," Ron spoke up.

"As I said before, the cancer spread to her liver, but other organs may be affected as well. I'm sending tissue to the pathologist and we'll know something later. Lillian has been very strong and although her body is in a battle, her spirit won't give up. Neither should either of you," he added, looking long at Jake, who seemed distraught.

"How long will she be in the hospital?" Jake asked.

"We'll keep her at least until Friday. The report should be back by then and Lillian will have time to gain a bit of strength."

"Thanks so much, doctor." Ron said, extending his hand as he stood up.

Jake followed suit.

"One more thing," Doctor Gonzales added. "I want both of you to leave as soon as you've seen her. Go home, take a shower, eat and get some rest. You can come back up this evening."

"We will," they said in unison.

"Good, and remember to pray," he said as he left the room.

Ron turned to Jake and smiled. "He's right. Let's do that now before we leave."

"Do what?" Jake asked.

"Pray."

They stood, two brothers, hearts aching for their mother's life; each in his own world of pain, unable to find his footing...until now. Ron put his left hand on his brother's shoulder, and clasped his right hand. Together they bowed their heads, lifting their mother up to God, The Great Physician.

***

Rita saw Ron's name on her caller ID and answered immediately. "Oh Ron, I've been waiting to hear. How is your mom?" Rita hung on every word concerning Mrs. Davis' surgery and how they were all holding up. He sounded tired. "I'm glad to hear she came through fine. I know waiting for the report must be nerve wracking, but I'll continue praying for a good outcome. You're welcome. I miss you too." She ended the call reluctantly, but he was leaving to go back to the hospital and spend time with Lillian. Lord, please cover them with Your wings.

It was almost time to get to the studio. Kids would be piling in the moment Rita opened the door. Today they would begin making self-sculptures; a piece which depicts how they see themselves. A 3-D selfie. She was as excited as they were; curious to discover what their self-image would turn out to be. She brought in a plenteous supply of flea market finds for them to choose from; materials most people would toss, such as leftover lamp parts, tins, chains, gazing balls, ornaments and a ton of other stuff. She promised them a self-sculpture of her own. At this moment, Rita didn't have a clue what hers would turn out to be. They would have one week to complete them and hopefully Ron would be back to host an exhibit inviting family and teachers. How might they react seeing how the children pictured themselves? The scary part is how would they react seeing Rita's? She would make it a fun event and hopefully, every child would leave feeling accepted.

***

The online search for a church in Kat's zip code area was driving Jared crazy. Over two hundred. Apparently churches are a booming business. It would take him years to visit all of them. With his luck, she would attend the last one on the list. There had to be a way to narrow it down. When they were in college at San Marcos, she mentioned she attended a church down the street. He remembered part of the name...something Christian. He did another search in the San Marcos area near the University and found a Central Christian Church and checked out their website. He didn't locate a similar one near her. This was becoming a full-time job. He made a list of eight in a five mile radius around Kat's house. This Sunday morning he'd visit one and attend another one at an evening service. In a few weeks he'd cover them and if he was lucky, she would show up at one. Sounds crazy even for me. He jotted down the name and address of the first one and put the folded paper in his shirt pocket. If he didn't leave now he'd be late for work. Jared grabbed his keys and pizza cap on his way out the door to the elevator. He was satisfied with his plan, at least for now.

"Hey, Jared," his boss called out as he walked in the door, "I've got three orders for you. Take off and make sure they arrive on time. After that you're off the clock."

"Sure, thanks." He shoved the hot boxes into insulated bags, taking note of the addresses first. One sounded familiar. He walked to his car, and looked again at the delivery location. Wow! This one's near a church on my list. What are the odds? Jared began whistling as he pulled the paper from his shirt pocket. In the same block. It's Wednesday and it has an evening service; a good time to scan the cars as they pull into the parking lot. If he parked near other black cars his wouldn't be so obvious. He wouldn't be able to hang around long, but maybe this church would be the one Kat attends.

***

"I talked to Lane Jennings today about selling the house," Betty said, loading the dishwasher.

"Great," Brian returned, only half listening.

Betty closed the appliance door, pushed the start button and took a seat next to her husband at the dining table. His face was semi-buried in paperwork as he made notes in the margins. She reached over, placed her hand over his, and asked, "Are you present?"

Brian looked up as he folded her hand into his palm. "I'm sorry, this contract is going to the boss tomorrow and I was making sure I crossed all my T's."

"I love you, Brian Hills." She kissed his hand before letting go. "I was telling you I called Lane Jennings today about listing my house. He was excited and would like to meet me there tomorrow."

"That's great, Honey. Wish I could tag along, but...."

"I know, this is a busy week for you."

"If I push this contract through it'll be a huge coup for me."

"I'll be praying." Betty gave him a hug as she stood to go upstairs. "I'm going to do some editing, then shower, and read for a while."

"Mmhmmm," Brian said, already focused on his work.

Betty smiled, shaking her head as she made her way upstairs.

***

Jared couldn't believe he made his three pizza deliveries and got back to the church just as people began arriving. He pulled his black charger next to another car similar in design for camouflage, turned off the engine and waited, hoping to catch a glimpse of her car. A glance at his watch said six-forty five. He leaned back against the smooth leather as people began showing up. Each found a parking space. He could hear the click, wonk, and horn blows as men and women locked their cars and made their way into the two-story building.

He wondered what he'd do if she pulled in. Several scenarios came to mind; get out and follow her in, wait until church was over and try to catch her before she leaves, or disappear and return on Sunday. He could just write a note explaining his actions and leave it under her windshield wiper. Jared sighed out loud and checked the time again. Seven-twenty. This must not be the church or she'd be here by now.

Jared started the motor and weaved around two cars parked haphazardly to his left and in front. He headed to the highway and pointed his Charger homeward. Good thing he called in after his deliveries and found out there weren't anymore. His shift was up anyway.

Gus's number appeared on his phone as it broke the quiet in the car. "Hey, Gus, what's up? Sure, I just finished my shift and don't have any plans. Mexican food sounds great. I'm tired of pizza," he said with a laugh. "Okay, I'll meet you at Tito's but we'll have to hurry, they close at nine. See you in a few." Jared pressed the end-call button and used his turn signal to move into the right lane to exit and make an U-ey. His dash clock flashed seven-forty-five. He maneuvered the car through the exit and took the turnaround, heading for South Alamo Street. Ten minutes tops. He loved Tito's place and could taste the grilled fajitas now.

A thought struck him suddenly. Why does Gus want to meet with me? Sure, they had gotten together a few times, but usually on a holiday or something regarding his car. Well, he'd know soon enough.

***

"Hi," Ron said to his Mom as cheerfully as he could muster. "Are you tired of this hospital room yet?" Today was the day Lillian was supposed to be released since her surgery on Monday. "Jake will be here in a bit, he stopped by the hotel to pick up his check."

Lillian received her son's gentle hug as he bent to kiss her. "I'm doing okay for the shape I'm in." She managed to jokingly produce a smile. "The doctor was in early and said he'd be back around lunch to give the final word on releasing me."

Ron looked at his watch. "Just an hour from now." He pulled a chair to the side of the bed and took his mother's hand. "Mom, Jake and I have finances worked out, so we don't want you worrying about the money. We also talked about your home care and between us you'll be taken care of."

"Honey, you boys have lives to live and jobs to go to. I don't want to be a burden to you. I actually feel pretty decent. After a few days I'll be a bit stronger."

"You'll need chemo and there will be doctor appointments. Jake and I will arrange things so you'll have transportation and help as needed. Now, don't think about it anymore."

Lillian looked at her son and tears welled. She felt him squeeze her hand and she returned it, although weakly. She suddenly felt tired and wanted to sleep. Her eyes closed and she felt herself drifting; with a vision of her husband's face in the distance.

Ron put his finger to his lips when he saw Jake come through the doorway bearing flowers. He quietly set the small, colorful vase on the bedside table, and then motioned for Ron to follow him out to the hallway.

"Has the doctor been in to release her?" he asked his brother.

"He was here early, but didn't sign discharge papers. He should be in shortly to check on her and give the final thumbs up. Jake, she looks really tired to me. He may not release her today."

Jake slumped and headed back into the room. He stood by the window looking down from his sixth-floor vantage point at the streets filled with vehicles and ant-size pedestrians traveling to their destinations.

"Good morning," Doctor Gonzales said, entering with a chart in his hands. "How's our patient doing?"

Lillian fluttered her eyes open at the sound of her doctor's voice. Seeing him and her sons staring at her, she smiled. "My, I doze off and my room is filled with handsome men."

Dr. Gonzales checked her over, asked some questions and then addressed Ron and Jake. "I've signed the forms to release her," he said sternly, "with the admonition that she is not to exert herself in any way. I'm having her set up to start chemo a week from Monday, twice a week." He turned to look at Lillian, his face softening. "You, my sweet, are to enjoy being pampered, and allow your sons to look after you. I want you back in my office in three weeks, or sooner if there are any problems."

Ron promised they would take excellent care of her and thanked the doctor as he excused himself to check on other patients.

"Jake, would you ask the nurse to come help Mom get ready? I'll take her things and the flowers down and bring the car around."

Jake was halfway out the door as he called back, "Sure, I'm on it."

Ron gathered personal items they had brought for Lillian and the flowers. "I'll get the car, Mom. The nurse and Jake will escort you down." He gave her his best smile as he left the room.

***

"You have a great house, Betty. I think I can get you top dollar for it. There are some things we need to take care of. I'll submit to have an appraisal done and we'll see what it shows."

"Thanks, Lane. I appreciate your coming so quickly. I love this house, but with the cottage in Wimberley and Brian's home, it seems excessive to hold on to it."

"When will you remove the furniture?"

"I've made plans for a big sale next weekend. Brian will round up some help to move some of it to our place this Saturday."

"That's great. I'll see if I can get this on the market before November. You don't have to worry about anything. I have people who will stage and handle the open house."

"How wonderful, you've taken a load off my mind. By the way, have you and Sheila heard anything from the adoption agency?"

Lane's face dimmed a little.

"No. I called last week, but they don't have a baby for us yet. Poor Sheila was heartbroken after the mother of the newborn changed her mind in February. I mean we were both glad baby and mother are together, but our hopes were knocked out from under us."

"I'm sorry, Lane. I'll be praying. You know, God has the perfect baby for you. She's just not available yet."

"That's what we've clung to. Thanks for praying."

"You're welcome; it's a privilege to intercede for others."

"I better get moving. Tell Brian I said hello."

"I will. Give Sheila a hug from me," Betty called out as Lane bounded down the steps to his car, waving in return.

Betty closed the door and sat in the recliner. She had spent many hours over the years, enjoying her teatime, praying and dreaming in this chair. She remembered asking God to bring the right man into her life. Daddy always said, "In God's timing." It turned out exactly that way. She closed her eyes and sent prayers up for God to escort the right baby to Sheila and Lane. Losing their twelve-year-old son to cancer was a heavy blow. Now they're ready to move forward and provide a home for a special bundle of joy. Lord, fulfill their dream just as you did mine by bringing Brian into my life.

***

"Mom," Ron said softly when he saw Lillian was awake. "While you slept, your deacon from the church called to check on you. He was glad to hear you are home and the surgery went well. His wife has a schedule set up for meals to be delivered starting tomorrow."

"They are a wonderful couple, Brother Tommy and his wife, Sue. Both of them would give you their last morsel if you needed food."

"Well, it sounds like they have quite a few morsels lined up for you. What a great thing for people to do."

"That's the way a church family is supposed to be. I just hope people aren't inconvenienced because of me."

Lillian remembered the many times she prepared meals for people who were in the same predicament she was in right now. Home from the hospital, unable to cook and do things they used to do. It gave her such joy to take a meal and have it received with grateful hands and hearts. She would accept the meals brought to her in the same manner.

"I think they're looking forward to providing them, Mom. He said whoever brings the meal will call first to make sure it's good timing."

"It'll be nice to see some of my church family. It's been a while since I was able to attend. I miss being there."

"Jake's gonna be off this weekend and will stay here with you. I need to drive to San Antonio and check on things at the studio. I'll be back Monday morning and drive you to your chemo treatment, okay?"

"Honey, it'll be hard on you, driving so far. Maybe Jake can take me."

"He has to work Monday. We've already talked and worked out a schedule, so don't worry. We have a plan. Now, how about a game of Scrabble?"

***

Gus found a booth easily. People were beginning to leave Tito's as it neared closing time. He knew Jared would arrive shortly so he ordered the fajitas and iced tea. At least the order was turned in so they wouldn't get rushed out at nine. He was glad the server brought the tea first.

It had been a long time since he and his half-brother sat down together just to talk. Gus knew he had to tell him about the detective's visit. He wasn't sure how he'd take the news, but meeting in a public place seemed the safest. Gus wondered if Jared would turn himself in or do something dumb. He hoped his idea would work, although it would put Gus at risk as well. He couldn't just abandon him, and who knows, maybe he would see the sense in voluntarily going to the police. I don't see that happening though.

"Hey there, Gus," Jared called out as he bounded to the booth and plopped down on the vinyl seat. "Told ya I'd make it in time. Have you ordered?"

"Sure did, fajitas as you like them."

As if on cue, the young woman working tonight brought out a large sizzling platter, warning unnecessarily about the plate being hot. Jared noticed her name tag. "Thanks, Elsa, this smells awesome."

She smiled, set the container of flour tortillas down and asked if they needed anything else.

"Nothing right now," Gus said, already piling some of the meat, peppers and onions onto his tortilla.

"Enjoy." She responded, laying extra napkins on the table.

"So what's up with the last minute call to meet and eat?" Jared asked, filling his own tortilla.

"I'm really concerned about you, Jared."

Jared's eyes shot upward directly at Gus. "Why?"

"You seem obsessed with the girl from the San Marcos University."

"Obsessed is pretty strong."

"Not when it involves slashing tires and vandalizing a car."

"Geez, Gus, I explained about that and paid for it."

"It wasn't what you did, it's why you did it. Thinking she had a boyfriend and slashing what you thought were his tires."

"It was a dumb, childish thing to do, I admit. The irony is the car belonged to her friend's boyfriend. She didn't even have a guy."

Elsa appeared at their table and refilled their glasses, leaving their ticket, then began cleaning nearby tables.

Jared looked at his watch. "Eight-forty, I guess she was subtly letting us know it was almost closing."

"I just wish you would focus on bettering your life. You can't deliver pizzas forever," Gus said, ignoring the time.

Jared finished the last of his fajita taco and stared at Gus. "I know, but I can't stop thinking about her. I got off on the wrong foot and messed up. Now I want to make it right but can't get near her."

"Why not check into a trade school?"

"Like what, Mechanic School?" he laughed

Gus didn't answer immediately. "Well, you could do worse."

"I hope you have another suggestion because that one stinks."

"Jared, are you even listening to what I'm telling you?"

"I hear ya. Maybe I should become your apprentice," Jared teased.

"Find something you're really passionate about and see what's available."

"I'll think about it," Jared said, rubbing his temple in a circular motion.

Chapter Four

Ron pulled up to the Blue Star Arts Center, parked his car and made his way to the office. He was tired from driving. Leaving his mom in Mesquite was difficult but he had to get back and check on things in the studio. They had several events coming up. He needed to get some feedback from the coordinators, and then check on the current displays. And Rita. He missed her terribly.

He grabbed the burger combo bag. *Not the healthiest food I've eaten. Oh well, tonight it'll have to do.* Slamming the car door, Ron headed to his office hoping there wasn't any urgent Post-it-Notes on his desk.

His office seemed lonely. Even the bright yellow walls didn't perk him up today. He wondered where the crew was; Lea, whom he affectionately named his advertising guru, Zeke, better known as Sparky, the lighting director for events, and Johnathan, the junk man, who brings in props and hauls out what doesn't work.

He woofed down his greasy spoon food, and then decided to hunt down the team. Ron only had the weekend, and they promised to be here all day today. Fridays were a productive time to get things done and it was only two o'clock. He tossed his crumpled food sack in the trash and carried his cola to sip on as he went to search for bodies. After that mission was complete, he'd settle in and call Rita; hoping she'd be free this evening...and tomorrow.

***

Rita had a blast at the Farmer's Market at The Pearl this morning. She found the freshest fruits and veggies, and enjoyed time with her friend, Cora. The Madhatters Tea Room filled her week, but Cora took today off so they could have some fun.

The beautiful salad Rita finished preparing was going to be perfect for tomorrow after church. She stretched the clear film over the bowl and placed it in the refrigerator. If Cora didn't have to work this evening, they could have eaten the salad and gone to a movie. Time spent with Cora was always a hoot. That girl knew how to have a good time. In any case, tonight Rita would stay in.

She gathered her sketch pad and pencils and settled at the table to put finishing touches on her self-sculpture for the Artsy Kids event. There would be many adults attending and she hoped everything would go off without a hitch. The ribbons came in to award each child for courage and creativity. Rita deliberately did away with competition. No first, second or any place ribbons. It wasn't even a contest, although a couple kids tried to turn it into one with a my-head-looks-more-real-than-yours, comment. But they were kids after all, and neither really cared whether it was or wasn't more real. The purpose in the project wasn't about realism, it concerned the image the child had of himself.

She'd asked herself that question a hundred times since giving the assignment. Finally she came up with an idea and worked on it until she came to the shoulders. How would her shoulders fit into the overall sculpture of herself?

The doorbell rang. Rita squinted through the peep hole and flung open the door. "Ron, I'm so glad to see you," she squealed almost like one of her Artsy Kids. "Come in. How's your mom? When did you get in?"

"Whoa, one question at a time," he said hugging her tightly and planting a kiss on her soft lips. "I've missed you."

Slipping her arm through his, she closed the door with her foot, all in one smooth motion. "I've missed you more," she teased. "Sit down, and I'll get us some tea. Then you can answer my interrogation."

Ron got comfortable on the sofa and suddenly felt exhaustion setting in. He leaned his head back, closed his eyes and listened to Rita's pouring tea, clinking ice cubes and stirring. He opened his eyes and found her staring into them with such compassion.

"You look worn out, Ron." She set the iced tea on coasters on the small trunk table, and sat next to Ron.

"I didn't realize how tired I was until I sat down. It's a wicked drive on a Friday. Traffic was bumper-to-bumper with miles of eighteen-wheelers. I was at full attention all the way. I got in about two hours ago, but was checking on things at work. The team has most everything handled, but there were a couple of hiccups we worked out."

"And instead of going home to rest you came here. Are you hungry? I made a salad I can bring out."

"No thanks. I stopped along the way and grabbed a bite. But, to answer your question, Mom is home and relatively pain-free thanks to the meds. Jake is staying with her over the weekend and I'll go back Monday to take her to chemo. Mom's church is going to provide meals for a while, so she's in a good place."

"Do you and Jake plan to keep up this pace long-term?"

Ron inhaled deeply. "That's the plan. We'll do whatever it takes, for as long as it takes, until we find another solution to provide her the best care."

"You're a good son, Ron. So is Jake."

Ron put his arm around Rita and pulled her closer to him on the sofa. "You're a good friend," he said softly. "Thanks for putting up with me. Now, tell me about the Artsy Kids event you've been working on."

"I thought you'd never ask. I was hoping you would emcee it, but with your mom's situation, I understand. The kids have been working, or maybe playing would be a better word, hard to finish their sculptures. Would you like to see what we have so far or are you too tired?"

"I'm fine, let's walk over. I think I can work it out to be here, unless something drastic happens."

"I'm praying nothing does." Rita got up and gathered her keys. "I think you'll love what the kids have done."

Ron stood and ran his hand through his sandy hair. He noticed a sketch pad on the table with abstract drawings of something resembling a torso. "What's this?" he asked.

Rita turned and flipped the pad upside down. "This is not for public viewing," she warned, shaking her finger at him. "Come on, let's go before you get into trouble snooping." She laughed.

He followed Rita out, waited for her to lock the studio apartment, and then clasped her hand in his as they walked the two blocks to Rita's Artsy Kids studio.

***

Kat started the car and left the church after her Thursday night small group meeting. She was excited and couldn't wait to get home and tell Betty about Clay. When she explained to him what Betty wanted to do for abandoned seniors, he was all ears. He had been looking for a film project and seniors were something Clay deeply cared about. He even knew a man in the church who would hook them up with several elderly saints. This whole project seemed to finally be making some progress. Poor Betty, she had several setbacks after being told by organizations she would be violating the privacy of their residents. Kat wanted to kick-start things and after talking to Clay, it looked promising.

She turned the corner on her block and for just an instant, had an uneasy feeling. A chill made her shudder. The street light was out, leaving her in darkness except for her headlights. She clicked the high beams and slowly made her way to the end of the street. Turning right and into her driveway, things seemed normal and the feeling left her. Would she ever get past the edginess of feeling stalked?

Kat turned off the motor, gathered her Bible and notebook, and pressed the lock button on her key fob. Just as she stepped on the porch, the front door opened and she was greeted by her dad's assuring smile.

"Hi, Honey, have any problems on the way home?"

"Not really," she said, remembering the darkened street and eerie feeling. "But someone needs to report a broken street lamp on Wilson. I had to use my high beams all the way to the end."

Brian gave his daughter the look. "Someone?"

"Okay," she laughed, putting her Bible on the table and opening the fridge. "This someone will call tomorrow," she said, taking out the tea pitcher. "Where's Betty?"

"She's upstairs working on the computer."

Kat poured a glass of tea and returned the pitcher to the fridge. "I need to talk to her, I have something exciting to share and I know she'll be thrilled. It's about her senior project."

"That will definitely thrill her."

"What will thrill me?" Betty asked, coming in from the hallway.

"Oh, Betty!" Kat squealed. "Remember my telling you about a guy from my church group who was into films?"

"I sure do, you were going to talk to him about our project. From the look on your face I'd say he's interested."

"He's very interested. I invited him over tomorrow evening to go through things we've decided and contacts we hope to make. Is tomorrow okay?"

"It's very okay. Your dad has a team organized to bring over some furniture from my old house. But we'll be done by mid-afternoon."

"Betty," Kat said, taking hold of both her stepmother's arms. "Clay knows someone who can introduce us to several seniors to get us started."

"Really? You've done a great job, Kat. Thank you for digging in to help get this project off the ground."

The two women hugged and Brian invited himself into it, wrapping his arms around them. "Can a guy get in on some of this?"

Laughing, the trio broke apart. "Okay," Kat laughed, "I'm gonna shower and then hit the books. I have a paper due next week." She put her tea glass in the sink and headed upstairs.

"I need to get back to my paperwork as well," Betty said.

"You gals go ahead and slave over your papers. I'm watching TV," Brian boasted. "It's a rare night when I don't have work to do."

Betty thought about his comment as she sauntered up the stairs. He's right, there are very few nights when Brian was home and work-free. A twinge of guilt hit her. Maybe she should tend to her paperwork another time and spend the evening with her husband. Turning to head back down, she smiled to herself. After all, we're still newlyweds.

***

Lillian sat in silence, welcoming the opportunity to be still without Jake's asking if she was okay, or trying to persuade her to take a nap. She loved her son, but he was taking his role of caregiver too serious. Today he received a call from the hotel and had to run over there and check on something only he could handle. Being the manager held certain responsibilities and his presence was required. He promised to be back in two hours. Lillian cherished this time alone.

A church member brought a meal over before lunch and Lillian ate the fruit, but put the rest in the refrigerator, planning to eat it tonight. Jake said he would grab something when he was finished at the hotel. Right now, Lillian wanted to sort her thoughts and figure out how to tell the boys her decision. It would be met with opposition, of that she was certain. Nonetheless, she would stand her ground.

Jake was a devoted son. After Ron moved away, he made sure she was looked after. He stepped into the role of his dad, maintaining the house, overseeing finances, and even providing some social activities to include her. Lillian felt guilty for pulling Jake into so much responsibility. He should have been dating, making a life for himself. He's only twenty-five and a very handsome young man. She was sure there were young women who were attracted to him. His job had odd hours, which made dating a bit difficult. The time he wasn't at the hotel, he was helping her. She wondered how he kept up his apartment.

Lillian pictured Ron, who looked more like his dad. The sandy hair and slender build attracted the ladies. He never found one he would bring home though. He'll turn twenty-seven in January and

67

should be thinking about settling down with someone, having babies and giving Lillian grandkids. She knew he loved his work. In all this time, she had never been to his studio and seen what he actually did. She overheard him on the phone Thursday night talking to someone named Rita. Lillian smiled to herself. She suspected they were dating and Rita was his reason for driving back to the studio. She hoped so.

Stretching out on the sofa, pulling the blue afghan over her legs, Lillian decided she was content with her decision and a nap was in order. She knew Jake would be back soon and would come close to make sure she was simply sleeping. One of these times when he did that, she would open her eyes wide and say BOO! She laughed out loud, thinking about his reaction. Turning on her side, she snuggled in with a bit of joy swimming in her heart.

***

Jake drove the short distance from the hotel to his apartment. He had to check on a guest problem, one the front desk could have handled if the head clerk had shown up for work. He figured he'd stop by the apartment to get his mail and grab the phone charger he forgot. Now, heading back to Lillian's place, Jake suddenly felt lonely. His life wasn't much different now than it was before her cancer diagnosis. Work, home and then to mom's, the same thing, day after day. She would try to get him to come by only on weekends, but somehow it didn't seem right. Once, she told him a friend was picking her up to go for coffee and shop for a birthday gift for a grandchild. He found out later she made it up so he wouldn't come. Maybe I have been a little overbearing. He only wanted to make her happy. She chastised him more than once, saying he needed his own life just like she needed hers. He sighed.

Jake walked into the living room, seeing his mom on the sofa, her blue afghan in a pile on the floor. He scurried over, picked it up and gently covered Lillian. He looked at his mother's face and leaned close, lightly kissing her forehead. She stirred but remained silent. He went to the kitchen and fixed a cup of coffee, plugged his phone charger in and set the smartphone for charging. That's when he noticed it. Jake walked toward his mother's bedroom and next to the dresser was a suitcase.

"Jake, is that you?" Lillian called out.

Bewildered at seeing her suitcase, he hesitated a moment, then answered, "Yeah, Mom, I'm back." He picked up his coffee mug and joined his mother in the living room. "How are you feeling?"

"I'm doing well. The short nap was just what the doctor ordered," she laughed.

Jake gave her a crooked grin, and then sobered his face. "Mom, why is your suitcase out?"

Lillian tried to lighten the mood after seeing his serious concern. "Son, you never know when a fast getaway might be needed. I thought I'd be ready in case the Lord calls me home." She smiled, hoping he realized she was joking.

"That's not funny and I'm not laughing. Now, what's going on?"

Lillian flipped the afghan from her legs and sat up slowly. She brushed off his attempt to help her. "I'm fine, Jake, really I am. I feel stronger and more like myself."

He sat on the edge of the coffee table and waited, watching her face.

"Okay, if you insist. I've been mulling over my choices, thinking about how I want my life to be lived. I don't wish to be hooked up to machines, doped into stupidity, or become so weak I can't take myself to the bathroom. I've made a decision."

"What decision? We discussed all this at the hospital and worked out everything so you'll be comfortable. Ron and I won't let any of your fears happen."

"No, neither of you get it. I'm not going to sit in this house every day, having others catering to me, especially you boys. The doctor explained what the chemo may do, and I have no desire to go through that. It's my life, my choice, period. I've decided not to have chemo."

"What? You're not serious. I need to call Ron and see if he can come back in the morning."

"No need for him to do such a thing. I have my suitcase ready and you can throw some things together. I want us to drive to San Antonio so I can see where Ron spends most of his time."

"You must be joking!"

"I'm as serious as sin. You and I are going to visit Ron, spend a couple days so I can see what San Antonio is like. Maybe I'll get to meet this Rita he seems to be taken with."

"I should call and warn him we're coming," Jake said, getting up to retrieve his phone.

"No, not tonight. We can call him when we're almost there tomorrow. It'll be a surprise."

"Oh, it'll be a surprise all right, you can count on it."

"Promise me you won't call him tonight after I'm asleep."

"Mom...."

"Promise me!"

"I promise," Jake reluctantly spoke the words. Ron was going to bite into him tomorrow, of that much he was sure.

"Thank you, Son. You'll see, we'll have a fun trip and maybe stop at a Dairy Queen along the way. Right now, I'd love a grilled cheese sandwich, how about you?"

Jake smiled and knew he was beaten. There was no talking her out of it. "Sure, why not. Do you want a slice of ham on it?"

"Not this time, just cheese and a small glass of milk to go with it."

"Coming right up," he said, bowing graciously, making her laugh.

***

Jake lay in bed, his phone in hand. He was very tempted to call his brother and fill him in about the plans their mother made for the weekend. He opted not to, partly because he promised, but also, he didn't want to listen to Ron rant at him. Maybe he should call Doctor Gonzales and make sure travel wouldn't hurt her. No, it's after eleven and besides, what could he do? If her mind was made up, no one, not even the doctor would stop her. As concerned as he was, he admired her spunk. She did the same thing with Dad and she always won out. Jake could still remember him saying, 'If Mama's happy, I'm happy,' and then he let her do it her way. Okay, Dad, we're doing this her way. He set his phone on the nightstand, turned off the lamp and left it all in God's hands.

***

Lillian sat in her rocking chair instead of going to bed. She wanted to think a while and knew if she succumbed to the inviting comfort of nestling amid the sheets and quilt, sleep would claim her immediately. Rocking always allowed her to think clearly and sort things out. Right now, sorting was what had to be done before leaving in the morning for San Antonio. Lillian was excited at the thought of going somewhere...anywhere, away from here. Being cooped up and facing chemo seemed unbearable. She felt it was the right decision to forego the treatments. Realistically though, she knew her health might very well diminish and she didn't want Jake blaming himself for letting her do this.

Her suitcase was packed and ready, but having a plan in case something went wrong was necessary. She placed her medications in her handbag, along with a written directive to be followed by those who may have to care for her while she's in San Antonio. Hopefully it won't be necessary, but just in case. She picked up the list from the nightstand and wrote out the places and things she wanted to see and do; The Riverwalk, Alamo, Ron's studio of course, and a couple museums. She quickly added several restaurants to the list. Sighing, she leaned back and closed her moistened eyes briefly. Lord, what are your plans for me? Will this cancer take me soon or do I have time to enjoy life? Suddenly, in a whisper, she heard, "I AM your life." Lillian's eyes shot open as she looked around. The glow from the small lamp assured her she was alone. The realization of God's speaking to her was humbling. She rose from her chair, knelt beside her bed, and prayed.

After turning out the light, she lay still, smiling. Jesus is her life. Every day with Him had been good. Even after losing her beloved Albert, joy filled her knowing he was with the Lord. Everything in her life had blessings of the Lord woven through it. Cancer could not, would not, steal her joy. Lillian would make the trip tomorrow with Jake, and they would create memories together with Ron. She pulled her quilt a bit closer, drifting off to sleep.

Chapter Five

Clay Young pressed the door bell and waited for Kat to answer. Ever since she mentioned to him about doing a documentary on senior citizens, he was excited to get started. He heard footsteps and then the door opened.

"Hi, Kat, hope I'm not too early. I know you said eleven, but I was so anxious to get started this morning, I thought I'd take a chance...."

"Its fine, Clay," Kat reassured him. "I'm actually glad."

He looked at his watch as he followed her into the hallway. Ten thirty. "I hope your mom doesn't mind if I'm half an hour early."

"Clay," she said firmly, "really, it's okay." She led him into the kitchen, inviting him to have a seat at the breakfast bar. "We can have some tea, coffee, soda, or just plain water."

He loved her smile. It was more of an upturned grin on one side of her face, kind of playful. He relaxed. "Iced tea, if you have it made."

"Coming right up," she said. Kat poured his tea, plopped in a few ice cubes and handed it to him. "Have a seat and I'll get Betty. She's my stepmother, just so you know."

"Oh, sorry, I didn't realize."

"It's okay, she's wonderful and I love her dearly," Kat said, heading up the stairs to find Betty. "We'll be right down."

Clay hadn't known Kat very long. When he met her in the small group at church, he found her attractive. Her love for the Lord was obvious and that appealed to him even more. He hoped they could work together on this film project and make it something great. Clay loved doing film work and wanted to make it a career, but also, have it be worthwhile. Helping seniors would fit right in with his plan. He turned at the sound of voices in the hall, and stood as Kat and Betty entered the kitchen.

"Betty, this is Clay Young, the man from my church group I told you about."

"I'm happy to meet you Mrs. Hills," he said, extending his hand.

Betty liked the strong handshake. It showed confidence. "I'm excited we finally get to meet."

"I'm still a student, but I'll do whatever it takes to launch your project."

"It'll be fun, all of us working together. Let's go into the study and we can brainstorm ideas," Betty suggested. "Clay, I want to hear about your study in film work. Kat said you're doing one at the church."

"Yes, Ma'am, and she's been a big part of it."

"Not a big part," Kat interrupted as they entered the study and took seats around the table. "Just poking my nose into different views." she laughed.

"Well, you can certainly poke your nose into this project," Betty said, hugging Kat. "We need all the direction we can get. I have ideas typed out and copies for each of us, so let's sit down and get busy."

Kat stared at her friend discreetly as he scanned the notes from Betty, hoping he didn't notice. He reminded her a bit of the actor, Nick Jonas, with the pointed jaw line and dark hair. Stop it, this is a business meeting. She turned to the papers Betty handed out, and smiled to herself.

"All right, here's my idea," Betty began. "I'll lay it out and then we can discuss how to begin."

***

The drive to Madhatter's Tea Room was alive with Clay's vision of the plans Betty shared just thirty minutes ago. He talked nonstop while Kat listened intently. Finally, as they pulled into the small parking lot, he became quiet and turned off the motor. Clenching the keys in his hand, he turned to Kat.

"Well?" he asked.

"Well what?"

"Comments? Do you think what I see for the filming agrees with your mom's...sorry, Betty's vision?"

"To a point. You have some great thoughts and I can see Betty going along with some of them. It's just...."

"Just what?"

"It's just that I know Betty's heart and perspective. She wants the filming to bring out the character of the senior. The people we'll be filming won't have family or close knit friends. They are alone, without children or siblings. Betty's hope is they will be acknowledged for who they are. Does that make sense?"

"I get what you're saying, but how are we going to do that if they have no one we can interview? I remember my mom talking about an old television show, 'This is Your Life', where people were honored and a parade of people from their past came on to talk about them and what kinds of persons they were."

"But we won't have that option."

Clay was quiet. "Okay, let's go in and have some tea. It's been said, tea solves everything."

Kat laughed, "I agree, let's give it a try."

***

Jake parked his silver Ford Escape at the Blue Star Art Center, and remained still. With Lillian dozing in the passenger seat, he kept the motor running so the air conditioning would provide comfort as he waited for her to wake up. She looked peaceful. He could always tell when her pain subsided because her face relaxed as it was right now. Maybe this trip was a good decision.

"You're staring at me again, aren't you?" Lillian teased, her eyes still closed.

Jake laughed. "You love doing that, don't you?"

She opened her eyes and sat up fully in the seat, rubbing her neck. "Sure do, I enjoy knowing you're thinking about me."

"We're here. This is where Ron spends his life," he said, pointing to the Blue Star logo on the building.

Lillian looked around and asked, "Where is everyone?"

"Maybe they're having an event today."

"Well, let's find Ron. You can call him now." She chuckled, glancing at Jake, waiting for him to rebound on her good-natured sarcasm.

"Will you shield me when he blows up because I brought you here and allowed you to refuse chemo?"

"Don't be silly, he'll be relieved he doesn't have to make the trip back to Mesquite Monday morning."

Jake didn't believe that for a minute. "We'll soon find out," he said softly under his breath. He took out his phone and punched in Ron's number. It rang four times before going to voice mail, so he left a message. He ended the call and looked at his mom. "What now?"

"We wait," she said matter-of-factly, reaching into her tote bag for the banana she didn't eat earlier. "Want half?"

"No, I'm good," he sighed.

Not knowing how long it would take before Ron called, Jake suggested they find a hotel, unpack and settle in so Lillian could at least lie down a bit.

"That's a great idea," she said, putting the other half of her banana in the zip lock bag. "I can pretty myself up a bit too."

He laughed like this was a normal trip and nothing was wrong. His mom wanted to look nice to visit her son and possibly his girlfriend, and she didn't have cancer. Just a simple run to San Antonio and then back home to a normal routine. Oh how he wished. He put the car in reverse, backed out, and headed toward the freeway. There was a Holiday Inn Express close by and it was easy to get to. "Holiday Inn Express okay with you?"

"Lovely and they have a free breakfast."

Just a simple trip and everything is normal. Jake focused on the road and Saturday afternoon traffic. His mom nibbled on the half banana, humming an unnamed tune.

***

Rita bent over the sculpture, hoping to finish what was supposed to reflect who she is. She glanced at the abstract clock over the sink and cajoled herself for not starting earlier this morning. Tonight was parent/family night at Rita's Artsy Kids, and Ron would be there to emcee the event. She was happy when he called last night to tell her he was in town for the weekend. He invited her to dinner after the art show and she couldn't wait. She missed his being here and seeing him almost daily.

She stood the sculpture piece upright and backed up to get the full effect. Her brows knit together as she pursed her lips in contemplation. It would have to do. She was out of time. The piece seemed right somehow. The kids wouldn't understand it of course,

77

especially the heart. To Rita, it made perfect sense.

The chime of the doorbell alerted her and she threw a cloth over the sculpture, shielding it from inquisitive eyes, before answering the door. A squint through the peep hole revealed her friend, Kat. Rita swung the door open.

"Kat, it's so good to see you, come in. What's going on that brings you out here?"

"Hi, Rita, I hope this isn't a bad time," she said, looking around to see if she interrupted anything.

"Seeing you is never a bad time. I've been trying to finish my self-image sculpture for the art show tonight. Have a seat. Can I get you some tea? I'm about due for a cup." Rita laughed.

"Only if you have time. I won't stay long, I know you're busy. I need to run a couple things by you and get some input."

Rita rattled some cups from the cabinet, found the tea bags, and put the kettle on. "Let's sit in the living room while the water heats."

Seated opposite Rita, Kat pulled her thoughts together, hoping she would make sense and not sound like a whining kid. "Remember I told you Betty wanted to do a senior project?"

"Yes, you said it would involve filming seniors who didn't have family or friends. How's that going?"

"Well, after a lot of red tape and being told it would invade their privacy, I think we found a way to pull it off. But, that's not the problem."

The whistle of the kettle startled both women and they jumped a bit at the sound, and then laughed at themselves.

Rita went to prepare their refreshments, adding cookies to the tray, and brought it to the coffee table, announcing in a faux British voice, "Tea is served, Mum."

Settled finally, Kat started. "I know what Betty wants to see happen with this project, and I've had a discussion with Clay, my friend from church. He's doing the filming."

"Has the filming started yet?"

"No, we are brainstorming how we will get background on each senior. We have only one person so far. Clay's dad suggested him. He lives in a facility near the University of Texas. We haven't been out there yet."

Rita took a sip of her Chai tea and said, "It seems to me, the best way to discover anything about a person is to become his or her friend. Building a friendship takes time of course, but I believe this man will share more if you have a relationship rather than consider him a project."

Kat stared at her friend and realized the profound truth of what she just said. "That is exactly what I needed to hear. I've been concerned about the distance between what Betty wants and how Clay was approaching it. She hopes to reveal the life of a person as meaningful and one to be remembered. Clay sees it as a one dimensional project."

"Where are you in all of this?"

"I think I'm the mediator," Kat said hesitantly. She had this light-bulb experience, where you suddenly realize what your purpose is. She sipped her drink and sat back. "Now I think I can help get things going in the right direction. I'll see if we can set a time to meet with the gentleman, Clarence. Thank you, Rita."

"You're welcome, although I didn't do anything except ask questions."

"You asked the right questions. So, did you finish your sculpture?"

Rita nodded in the direction of the table to the shrouded figure. "Yes, and I'm excited about tonight. I can't wait for Ron to get here. He's been busy doing something today, but when he called last night, he promised to be here at five o'clock."

"Can I see it?" Kat asked standing and moving slowly toward the table.

"Well," I wasn't planning to show it to anyone before the unveiling, but since you won't be there...."

They both stood next to the covered piece and Rita made a production out of removing the white cloth, inch by inch, slowly, until it was completely exposed. "Well????"

Kat stared in amazement. "I'm in the company of a burgeoning artist. I love the curves which suggests female and the open lock where the heart would be. Does that mean you learned to let people in?"

"Thank you. God unlocked it, but is there anything else eye-catching to you?"

Kat looked from top to bottom and shook her head. "No, what am I missing?"

"Look inside the lock."

"Oh Rita, a tiny key tucked inside."

Rita smiled at the puzzled look on Kat's face. "God unlocked my heart, Jesus lives there now. He is the keeper of the key."

Kat hugged Rita as tears wetted her cheeks. "What a beautiful way of looking at it. The sculpture is awesome."

"Thanks again, I'm glad I revealed it to you." Rita covered it up again as her friend prepared to leave. "I wish you could be there, but I know you have tons going on."

"Yeah, I hate missing your event, but I'll be praying for it to go well. I need to get some study time in, and then work with Betty on the film project."

"I'll fill you in on how it goes."

"Catch you later," Kat said waving as she walked to her car.

***

Ron finally found his phone. He must have dropped it in the trunk when he loaded props early this morning for Rita's event. No wonder there weren't any calls driving me crazy. It wasn't until he wanted to call Jake to check on Mom that he missed it. He figured he'd go ahead and get the props, run errands and grab something to eat at the coffee shop. If he hadn't heard a noise in the trunk...oh well, at least he had it now.

"Here you go, Ron," the owner said, setting the club sandwich down quickly.

"This is what happens when your help gets the flu; the owner has to wait tables," He added, as he headed to the next table.

Ron smiled, took a quick bite, checked his messages and saw one from Jake. "Rats, I hope Mom is okay." He muttered as he hit the key to return his brother's call. Ron glanced at his watch as the phone rang several times with no answer. Maybe she's sleeping and he turned off the ringer. He left a short message for Jake to call back, and ended the call. Leaning back in the booth, he saw another message, this one from Rita. He munched on the sandwich, and then returned her call. She answered on the first ring.

"Rita, it's Ron, did you call earlier? I lost my phone and just now am going through messages."

He assured her he didn't forget the props and would be there early to help arrange things. It's good to hear her voice. "No, I tried calling Jake, but no answer. I left a message." Ron looked forward to seeing Rita tonight, for the kids' event and also to spend some quality time together. It had been weeks since they had seen each other. "Okay, I'll see you about five o'clock." He laid his phone on the table while he finished his sandwich and Coke. *I wonder why Jake called?*

***

Kat pulled into the library parking space, shut off the motor, gathered her books and laptop, then headed in. As was her normal practice, she scanned the area, not wanting to find what she feared...a black Dodge Charger. Things seemed normal lately, no creepy feeling of being followed, but she couldn't shake the habit of scoping things out when she went somewhere. Would it always be this way? The library wasn't busy, very unusual for a Saturday, which pleased her. Maybe she would actually get some studying done and her paper finished. Kat found her regular study table empty and took a seat. This was too weird. She looked around, glancing between the rows of books, and saw only a few girls. She recognized one of them from her marketing class, although Kat didn't really know anything about her, not even her name.

Get to work girl. She opened her book and suddenly a flashback hit her. When she was in San Marcus, studying at that library, Jared joined her at the table. Shivers crawled down her arms and a sense of unrest settled in. *Why didn't she study at home as Betty suggested? Isolating herself wasn't the answer. She couldn't hide out in the house for the duration until the authorities find and arrest him. Again!* There was no assurance anything would be done even if they found him. No, she would have to put on her adult head and learn to live in freedom. *Christ has set me free.* No time for flashbacks, fear or foolishness. Kat opened her laptop, turned it on and found the file containing her paper. She turned to the chapter she needed for reference, and glanced at her screen. A reflection appeared behind her. Startled, she let her book slam shut, stood, and turned around.

"Professor Evans," she spilled out with a sigh of relief. "What are you doing here?"

The professor smiled, "Checking up on my student." He pulled out a chair next to Kat. "Mind if I join you for a few minutes?"

Kat was in shock. Relieved yes, but shocked because now she had two men to worry about. "For a few, I really need to work on my paper. It's due next week."

"I'm aware of the due date, I assigned it, remember?"

"Tell me again why you're here, the real reason. Have you been following me, Professor?"

"Following you? Of course not. I was driving by on my way to the gym when I saw you get out of your car. I only wanted to check on you and make sure you haven't had any more problems with that stalker. You haven't, have you?"

"No, there's been no sign of him at all. The police don't have a clue where he is and neither do I."

"I might be able to assist in tracking him down."

Kat's heart skipped a beat. She knew the look of fear must be on her face, and she didn't want Professor Evans seeing it. Quickly, she forced a laugh and avoided his eyes. "The last thing I want to do is track him down. My life has been good without upheaval from Jared Orlov. I'm working on a film project with my family and ..." There I go again, revealing too much information about myself. She stopped.

"And what?"

"Nothing, I'm just very busy and I really need to get back to my paper, so..."

The Professor stood, extended his hand and said, "Right, I'm sorry, I was just concerned about you."

She shook his hand but regretted it when he folded his other hand over the top of hers, much too intimately. Slipping her hand away, she bid him goodbye and turned to her laptop. She saw him out of the corner of her eye as he walked slowly toward the entrance; pausing to chat with the girl checking in books. He seemed quite friendly patting her arm before leaving. The girl didn't seem to mind.

Professor Evans was single, Kat knew, but she didn't know much beyond that. He was nice enough, but there was always this feeling of uneasiness in his company. In class he was always professional, straightforward, and sometimes strict. It was outside the classroom when she sensed something wasn't right. Now, with his hovering around her, he was another tug on her mind, keeping her from feeling the freedom promised to her. Why, Lord, can't I live freely instead of always having to be on guard?

***

Clarence Hartman sat in the TV room at his assisted living facility. He didn't watch many shows due to his failing eyesight, but his hearing was excellent for a man of 91. He enjoyed listening to sitcoms mostly because laughter was what kept him in a positive state of mind. He blocked out war memories, his hard scrabble life, loss of loved ones and friends. The only friends still around were those he'd made since moving to Mt. Laurel. The nurses always smiled and tried to help him get around better. His amputated left leg was the visible reminder of the war he couldn't forget. The government wanted to give him an artificial one, but he turned it down. At his age, why bother?

"Mr. Hartman, it's almost time to turn in, may I help you to your room?"

Clarence liked Josie a lot. She was short, squatty, almost square. But she made him laugh. Every day she had a funny story about her grandkids. Today, he had a story to tell her.

***

Brian was satisfied with how quickly he and his buddies from work, loaded, transported and unloaded the furniture Betty wanted brought to their home. The group managed it in only five hours. There were a few hiccups getting the last china cabinet upstairs, but in the end, it got done. He thanked his crew and sent them away with a gift card to a nearby steakhouse in appreciation for lending muscle to the task. Betty would be home from the store soon, so he hurriedly wrote his message on a card and stood it against her teapot, knowing she'd be making her favorite brew as soon as she came in. She was a creature of habit.

Time for a quick shower, then I'll tackle my manuscript and hopefully finish chapter twelve today. He bounded up the stairs wondering what his bride would think when she read the card he left on the counter. Chuckling to himself, he knew she'd cry. Brian wanted her to know this was her home now and she was free to decorate any way she desired. His love for Cassie did not diminish his love for Betty. Since Cassie's death five years ago, the hole in his heart mended. God stitched it together, enabling Brian to find love again by bringing him and Betty together at Mary Ludwig's estate sale last year. It was a turning point in his life. A gaudy hat caught his eye that day and she captured his heart. I love when she wears the blue hat with the rhinestone feather bobbing up and down over the top. Turning on the shower, he thought he heard Betty's car in the drive.

***

Betty placed the two grocery bags on the counter and was about to pick up her teapot, to fill with hot water when she saw an envelope with her name on it, written in Brian's handwriting. She held it for a moment before ripping the flap open. Her heart pounded. It wasn't her birthday, or any fun anniversary she could think of. The front of the card was beautiful. A huge bouquet of flowers spread out from a white vase with gold edging. She opened to the inside and read Brian's message.

"When I carried you over the threshold of the front door, this house became your home." She sucked in her breath, and then swallowed the lump in her throat before continuing. "Every square foot is yours. Our life together began when we said "I Do!", and continued as we entered this house. Today, as I brought the furniture you wanted from your home, and placed it where you specified, I realized things might be a bit difficult for you. My past is over. Yes, I loved once before I met you, and will never regret the years I had with Cassie. She's part of my past, but will live on through Kat."

Betty set the card down, dried her eyes and put water in the kettle. She found the tea and cup, anxious for the whistle so she could pour the boiling water over the tea leaves. Right now, tea is what she needed desperately. How did Brian know how I was feeling about living in Cassie's house? She put the groceries away and finally the kettle sang. Her tea was steeping and any moment now she'd be able to sip and ponder Brian's words.

The words on the card became smaller as he was running out of writing space. Poor guy. She smiled and when the tea was ready, she poured it into her china cup with hand-painted Peonies all around. Betty sat at the breakfast bar and continued reading even to the back side of the card. "You are my present and future and I would do anything to make you happy. Please feel the freedom to change anything in this house. I will enjoy seeing your signature on each room. I love you.

Hugs, Brian"

She was about to lay the card down when she felt Brian's arms around her shoulders and his breath on her neck.

"I do love you," he whispered, kissing her gently on the neck.

Betty sat quietly, unable to speak. Then, in a shaky voice, she uttered, "I love you more."

Turning to him, she laid her head against his chest. He smelled delicious right out of the shower. She looked into his eyes and silently thanked God for this adorable man. The card still in her hand, she pointed to it. "This is the most romantic thing you have ever done."

"There's more," he teased. He swooped her off the stool and carried her up the stairs.

"Brian Hills, just what do you have planned?"

***

"You're going to be a movie star?" Josie squealed, jumping up and down next to Clarence's hospital bed.

He laughed at her animated response to his news about the lady who wanted to do some kind of documentary about him. Even he laughed when Mrs. Hills, her daughter and some young man came out to talk to him earlier. He couldn't understand why anyone would be interested in an old man with one leg. But, he humored them and agreed to it.

"I signed a paper and we're going to start next week."

"Oh no, do you understand what you signed?" Josie looked concerned. "You have to be careful nowadays, people like to take advantage of the elderly."

He laughed again. "There's nothing they could get from me. In any case, yes, I know what I signed and it's just to assure everyone I'm okay with them talking to me about my life. I'll get a copy of the film, and any proceeds from it will go toward helping senior citizens. Can't beat that with a cane," he said, revealing a toothless grin. "Besides, I know the man who told them about me and he's a trustworthy guy."

"I hope I'm working when they come back. I want to watch."

"Sorry, they want it to be private, and I do too. When it's finished you'll get to see it."

Josie pouted a pretend sad face, lowering her head.

"I might even give you my autograph like them famous stars do."

She perked up at his comment and gave him a quick hug. "Good, it's something to look forward to. Do you need anything before I go? I get off work in twenty minutes."

"No, Darlin', I'll be fine. You have a nice evening with your family."

"Thank you I will." Josie turned to leave but not before Clarence added, "I can't wait to hear another funny story about your grandkids."

"There's definitely no shortage of those," she chuckled, closing the door softly behind her.

***

"Have you heard from your brother yet?" Lillian was anxious to surprise Ron by just showing up at his workplace, but it didn't happen. She sat on the wingback chair in the hotel room, examining her finger nails while contemplating how to reach Ron. She held her left hand up and scrutinized it carefully. "My nails look odd, don't you think?"

Jake looked up from his newspaper spread across his bed,

squinting to see his mother's nails. "They look the same as they did the last time you asked."

"That was a week ago. Today they look dark with maybe a hint of yellow." She rose from her chair and walked closer to Jake, holding her outstretched hand between him and the sports section. "Look closer," she urged, "see?"

"Mom, they look fine to me." He covered her hand with his and suggested she go wash them and apply some lotion.

"Do you think that will help?"

"Can't hurt."

Lillian relinquished his hand and headed to the bathroom.

Jake picked up his phone and discovered somehow it turned off. Great, I wonder how long it's been like this. He turned it on and checked his messages. Sure enough, he listened to the message and immediately returned the call. He glanced at the clock, three already. It rang twice before his brother answered.

"Hi Ron, sorry I missed you. Something happened and my phone got turned off accidentally. How are things going at the studio?"

"You didn't call to ask me about work. What's up? Is Mom okay?"

"Well, yes, but I need to tell you...."

"What?" Ron asked in an anxious tone.

"We're here...in San Antonio."

"You're where? How...why...?"

"It's a long story, but mom is fine and wants to visit with you and do some things together."

"You've got to be kidding me. Why didn't you call before you left? Actually, when did you leave? When did you decide to do this? She has her first chemo treatment on Monday."

Taking a deep breath, Jake tried to remain calm. "I know, like I said, it's a long story. We're staying at the Holiday Inn Express close to your studio. Can we meet you there?"

The line was silent for an uncomfortable length of time before Ron spoke. "Sure, come on over. I have to meet Rita at five though. Tonight she's having an art exhibit at seven for the kids in the sculpture class she teaches. I'm the emcee."

"Great, we'll be right there."

Lillian came out of the bathroom. "I think you were right, Jake." She slathered cream on her hands. "They do look better. Did I hear you on the phone?"

"Yeah, it was Ron. He said to come over. We can visit a bit, but he has an art exhibit to emcee tonight."

"I love art exhibits! Are we attending?"

"I'm not sure, I didn't ask and Ron didn't invite." Jake folded the scattered newspaper and placed it on the desk. "Where's your purse?"

"The proper term, my dear, is handbag and it's on my bed. I'll get it."

"Bring your sweater too; you may get chilly later if we do go."

Jake had no idea how Ron would react when he discovers Mom isn't doing chemo on Monday. It's bad enough we show up on his doorstep practically, and then have to dump all this news in his lap. "Come on, Mom, we need to go."

"I'm ready," she said a bit loudly, shuffling herself to the door.

Jake patted his shirt pocket, making sure he had the door key, before closing it. "Well, Mom, we're off and running on your wild weekend."

"Maybe not running," she teased, as they reached the car. He helped her in and jaunted around to the other side, plopping himself in the driver's seat.

"Thank you," Lillian said softly.

Jake looked at his Mother and his heart swelled. She looked content, as if her Make-A-Wish just came true. He reached over to check her seatbelt, then gave her a kiss on the cheek. "You're welcome, whatever makes you happy."

"That's exactly what your Dad used to tell me after he gave in to something I truly wanted."

They both laughed as he started the motor and headed over to the Blue Star Art Studio.

***

Rita busied herself with last minute details of the art exhibit. Ron should be here within the hour. She had a gift for the students and knew they would enjoy it. Having their own personalized sculpture kit was something they could call their own and use to work through difficulties in the years to come.

She was grateful to Mr. Roddis for soliciting the items for the kit, as well as providing the aluminum container on wheels. What an exciting evening it would be. Her phone vibrated in her pocket. She glanced at the number. "Hi, Ron, things going well? Are we still on track for five o'clock?"

"I won't be able to come by your apartment. Something came up."

"What's wrong, you sound a bit frustrated?"

"You wouldn't believe me if I told you."

"Try me."

"My brother brought my mom, who is in stage four cancer and has a chemo treatment scheduled for Monday, to San Antonio so she could see me and play tourist."

"You're right, I don't believe it. Why would he do such a thing?

Shouldn't she be resting?"

"That's why I can't come over. They're on their way to my office. I'm about to have a one-on-one with Jake."

"Don't do or say things which might upset your Mom."

"Can't promise, but I'll pray when I see them drive up."

"And I'll be praying for all of you. I'm so sorry, Ron. I wish there was something I could do."

"Praying will be the best thing. I will be there tonight to emcee the event."

"Ron, your priority right now is family. I can wing it if I have to."

"No, I'll be there, even if I have to bring them along."

"That's a great idea!"

"Well, we'll see how great. At least I can keep an eye on her. Gotta go, they'll be here any minute."

"Okay..." was all Rita could say before he hung up. Poor Ron, how will he handle this situation?

***

Ron spotted the car as it pulled into the parking space by his office. He watched as his brother got out, went to the passenger side and helped his mom from the vehicle. She balanced her handbag on one arm and a sweater draped over the other. The smile on her face camouflaged any pain or discomfort she might be in. Happy. She looked happy. Guilt crept in as it had a way of doing when Ron was not directly involved in his mother's care. If he had stayed in Mesquite, there wouldn't be a situation like this. Then again, he would miss being at Rita's event tonight. A headache threatened across his temples. Stress. He headed to the hallway and main entrance, but they were already coming down the hall.

"Hey Mom, Jake, how was the drive down here? Hope you didn't run across any construction like I did yesterday."

"No," his brother said lightheartedly. "Signs were on the side of the highway, so I guess they quit for the weekend."

"Ron," Lillian squealed, "it's only been a day since I've seen you, but it seems like a week," she teased, hugging him close.

"It's good to have you both," he said, looking over her head at Jake with a big question on his face. "Come in to my office and I'll fix us a cup of tea, or get you a cold soda. I want to know about this surprise trip and how it came to be."

Ron plugged in the electric pot to heat the water, found cups and teabags, and then took a seat behind his desk.

"Sooo, Jake," he said, keeping eye contact with his brother, "what inspired you to bring Mom from her comfortable home and drive almost five hours to see me?" He kept a smile on his face so Lillian wouldn't think he was mad.

Before Jake could answer, Lillian jumped to his rescue. "Don't blame him. It was all my doing and I made him promise he wouldn't call you."

Ron turned his attention to her and became serious. "Do you know how this could affect your recovery? You have chemo Monday and you should be resting, not carousing down the highway."

Lillian and Jake looked at each other nervously.

"What aren't you two telling me?"

She lowered her head. "I've cancelled my chemo treatments," she mumbled.

"You did WHAT?"

Lillian's head shot up when Ron's voice raised. "I said I cancelled my chemo. I'm tired of being prisoner in my home. I'm tired of being treated like an invalid. If the good Lord wants to take me, I'm ready, but I want to enjoy the days I have left." She matched his stare eye-to-eye and didn't flinch.

The room was silent as the brothers looked at each other, grinned, and said in unison, "If Mom's happy, we're happy."

***

Rita brought her own self-image sculpture into the studio and set it on the last empty space in the display section. Like all the sculptures it was covered with a white cloth. It was six-fifteen, which meant kids would soon be arriving with parents, teachers and friends. Mr. Roddis came early, set up folding chairs and arranged the sculpture kits behind black draping near the back. Butterflies flitted in Rita's stomach. She had never done anything like this before and hoped it would be well received. Several of the youngest had made some adorable sculptures, while a few older ones got serious about theirs.

She remembered suddenly, Ron was supposed to pick up a few props and the blue ribbons. I hope he didn't forget. Voices from the front entrance caught her attention. "Kids already? They must be excited," she mumbled heading to the door. Instead of students Ron, his mom and brother strolled in.

"Hi, Rita, sorry I'm a bit late. We have special guests for our exhibit tonight. This is my Mom, Lillian, and brother, Jake."

"I'm so glad to meet you, Mrs. Davis; Ron has mentioned you quite often." Rita gave Lillian a little hug before shaking hands with Jake. "It's great meeting you too, Jake, I'm glad to have you both here. Come have a seat."

Lillian returned the greeting to Rita and beamed proudly, having her two sons beside her. They helped her find a chair and Ron promised to be right back. He and Jake went to get the props and ribbons from the car.

"You boys go do whatever you have to do. I'll be fine. This is so exciting!"

As they left, several parents, teachers, and kids arrived. Rita welcomed them and escorted the children to their seats up front, and directed the adults to the back. The room started buzzing with voices of nervous children, chatty adults, and occasional clanging of folding chairs being scooted around.

Ron and Jake returned, positioned the props, and gave the ribbons to Rita. She thanked them profusely for their help.

The room filled fast. All the participants were there, except one. Tanesha Cole. The clock said six-fifty. She still had ten minutes. Rita squatted beside Brenda, Tanesha's friend, and asked if she knew where the girl might be.

"Don't know, Miss Rita. She was planning to be here and seemed excited about it."

This news concerned Rita, but the show must go on. By now, everyone was seated and Ron was at the podium, ready to welcome the group and begin the exhibit.

"Good evening, folks. I'm Ron Davis and I'd like to welcome all of you to our first art exhibit by Rita's Artsy Kids." Pointing to the row of children in the front, Ron asked for a round of applause for them. He turned toward Rita, who was standing stage left. "Also, the teacher who devotes her time and energy into helping your children develop a positive view of themselves through the art of sculpture." He applauded and was joined by the others, including the children.

Rita gave a quick bow and came to the podium to stand with Ron. "I'd like to tell you a story about a girl. She was about fifteen and came from a dysfunctional home. The father drank a lot and the mother wanted to please her husband. The girl had a sister who the father adored and favored. He had no use for the young girl. They lived in a mobile home and the girl walked to and from school. One day, she left home and went to school. Afterward, she walked the three miles home, only to find out her home was gone and a bag containing her clothes and things, sat on the concrete where the home used to be. A note, saying the parents had moved and didn't want her, was pinned to it. The parents had discarded the girl." Rita held her tears, determined to tell the story not for pity, but for praise to God. The room was silent except for a few sniffles. Her next words were, "I was that young girl."

Ron moved close and put his arm around Rita's waist, drawing her to him. She continued, fully aware of his support. "I know beyond doubt, God watched over me in the ensuing years, and He helped me get past the feeling of being discarded by the two people who should have cared the most about me. The important thing is God will never discard or reject me, or you." She looked at the front row of young faces watching her intently. "I believe God enabled me to start this class, and He provided everything we needed, including the building and supplies."

Applause broke out, people stood, many of them exclaiming, "Amen. Praise the Lord."

Rita was choked up but asked everyone to be seated so they could begin the exhibit.

Ron asked Frankie, the first boy seated, to come up to the stage and stand behind his sculpture which bore a number one. He took his place and Rita asked, "Frankie, would you please tell us how the sculpture reflects who you are?" She removed the cloth and the audience oohed and awed.

"I created a bird. Sometimes when I feel bad I want to fly away." His sculpture was not like a common bird, but more of a fantasy species. He used bits of different color tin for feathers, a few plumbing sections for bird parts, and trinkets of unknown sources to create the fantasy effect. The two feet were made with bent forks.

"How do you feel now since creating your bird sculpture, Frankie?"

He broke out in a wide smile, revealing a missing front tooth. "I feel great!" He raised his right arm high with his hand in a fist. A camera flashed as hands went together applauding and he beamed. Rita presented him with his blue ribbon and sculpture kit, along with a handshake. "Thank you, Frankie. You may take your seat."

"Rose, you're next. Would you come forward please?" The ten-year-old walked slowly to where Ron stood. "Mine's not very good," she whispered. He shot a quick look at Rita, who took Rose's hand and stood by the sculpture. "Rose worked long and hard on her self-image piece. She came up with something I wish I had thought of."

The girl looked at Rita with wide eyes as though she couldn't believe what she heard Rita say.

"This young lady built a flower," Rita continued. "Rose, would you remove the cloth please?"

A bit reluctantly, the girl pulled the white shroud away, revealing a single metal rose with big thorns the length of the stem.

"Tell us why you chose the flower with so many thorns to represent how you see yourself."

She was quiet, but soon found her voice. "Since my name is Rose, I wanted it to be me. The thorns are there because I was bullied a lot. Thorns hurt and bullying hurts."

"Do you feel better since making your flower?" Rita asked.

JUNE CHAPKO

"Yes, now I want to help stop bullying in my school."

The audience was quiet. Rita hugged Rose, thanking her for being so brave. "I feel sure you will have some help in doing just that." Rose's mom was up front with her phone to take a photo. She mouthed the words, "I love you."

Ron called the next student forward, "Okay, Anthony, let's see what you put together."

"Everyone calls me Tony," the boy said, looking at Ron.

"I'm sorry. Tony it is. Show us your sculpture."

He removed the cover, letting it fall to the floor. "I made a chess piece, a knight."

"Tony, it's awesome. Can you share why you chose it to represent you?"

"Well, I don't have a dad and my mom works hard, but she doesn't get treated good at work. She needs someone to take care of her. Sometimes at the library I see kids playing chess and noticed the knight. I always liked King Arthur because he protected people. I'd like to be one...a knight, and protect my mom."

The shiny aluminum piece stood proudly as Tony stared into the crowd directly at his mom, who was crying. People began clapping and the woman next to his mom gave her a hug.

Ribbon in one hand and the sculpture kit in the other, Tony returned to his seat. Rita asked Ron to announce a short intermission before moving on to the others.

"What's up?" he asked.

"I'm hoping Tanesha will show up. I'm really concerned."

Ron scratched his head. "Do you want me to drive over and check on her?"

"Oh, would you?"

"Of course, give me her address."

She jotted it down and he hurried out the door. *Shouldn't take long, I can stall a bit.*

Rita encouraged everyone to get some punch and cookies and mingle a bit, then went to visit briefly with Jake and Lillian. "How do you like the show so far, Mrs. Davis?'

"Please call me Lillian, my dear. I'm enjoying everything. Where did my son go?"

"Ron went to check on one of the students. He should be back in a few minutes. Would either of you like something to drink or nibble on?"

Jake spoke for both of them saying, "No, we're fine right now. Thanks."

Making the rounds to say hi to some of the teachers and parents, Rita kept an eye on the door, hoping to see Tanesha show up. Fifteen minutes went by and she couldn't stall anymore. Rita went to the front and called everyone to their seats.

"We'll resume the awards, and I'm sure Ron will be back with Tanesha before we finish. Sandy, you're next. Come up and share about the sculpture you put together."

Sandy jumped up excited, wearing a huge smile. "I had so much fun making mine. I see myself as a butterfly." She almost sang the words as she unveiled her work. She spread her arms out as though she really was a monarch with sweeping wings.

"Tell us why you feel you are like the butterfly."

"I learned in school about how butterflies come out of a cocoon. They really struggle and it makes their wings strong so they can fly. The teacher said it's a transformmma...."

"Transformation?" Rita suggested.

"Yes, they get transformed into a butterfly. This class makes me feel that way. I'm different now from when I first started. I feel strong."

Tears formed in Rita's eyes. "You are strong, Sandy." She hugged the girl, presenting the blue ribbon and sculpture kit, escorting her to her seat.

The door burst open and all eyes turned to the back. Ron, Tanesha, and her mom rushed in. "We're here," Ron called out. "Sorry to interrupt, but car trouble was the problem." He seated Mrs. Cole and brought Tanesha to the front. Her eyes were puffy and she looked a bit distraught.

Rita winked at the girl and smiled. Soon a grin emerged on Tanesha's face and she relaxed.

Ron announced the next young man and then two more girls, before it was time for Tanesha to come up. She was nervous and reluctant, but managed to make her way to stand next to Rita.

"Let's see what Tanesha saw in herself as she put her sculpture together. Would you like to show us?"

The twelve-year old carefully folded back the cloth and stood silently. Her eyes darted around the room as if waiting for comments. Rita whispered to her, "Tell us what you've made and how it relates to you."

"I made a book because I can go anywhere I want when I read. Books make me happy, they teach me things and someday I will write one of my own."

There was a lot of affirmation coming from the crowd. "You will, Tanesha, and it will be a best seller." Rita assured her. She gave out the blue ribbon and the kit as Ron took her back to her place.

"These kids all deserve a hand, don't you think?" Ron shouted, clapping while the others followed suit. "Now, a special moment as Rita shares her own self-image sculpture with us."

She stood next to her art piece and removed the covering. "Mine is focused on the heart because it's where God did a lot of work on me. The head is a see-through wire ball. God sees my thoughts. I used a lock for the heart, but it's open and there's a tiny key inside. It was God who unlocked it with His love and Jesus lives there. He's the keeper of the key."

Everyone clapped loudly, especially the kids. They all came forward, surrounding her with a group hug. Rita was in tears by now. She looked at Ron who winked at her and smiled.

The evening had been a success, even with Tanesha's arriving late. Lillian enjoyed the show, the kids and social time. She seemed tired though, so Jake took her back to the hotel to rest. Ron and Rita drove Tanesha and her mom back to their apartment, promising to get help in fixing their old car. He had seen a mechanic fairly close by, who advertised himself as "Gus Mancheck, Master Mechanic". Ron told Mrs. Cole he would contact the guy Monday morning.

***

The restaurant was crowded when Ron and Rita arrived. Neither cared, they both just wanted to sit and enjoy a light meal and spend time together, something they hadn't been able to do in a long while. With Lillian's being ill and Ron's staying in Mesquite for several weeks, she missed him terribly. They were seated in the back, away from the flow of incoming guests. Rita was glad. The server brought their drinks, took their order, and disappeared.

"Finally!" Ron said, exhaling loudly. "I didn't think I'd ever get to be alone with you."

She gave him a wink. "I know, but at least we have a booth in a quiet section. I've missed you so much."

Ron stretched across the table as she met him halfway, sharing a kiss that lingered. Parting, their eyes held a gaze which spoke more than words. As Rita leaned back, she bumped her water glass, sending it rolling, saturating the tablecloth. They both grabbed napkins to soak up the wetness. Rita moved over to avoid getting her royal blue dress slacks wet. A server passing by came to their rescue and moved them to another booth. Embarrassed, Rita kept apologizing. "It's okay," Ron assured her. "A little water never hurt anyone."

Their server found them and brought Rita's soup and salad along with Ron's hamburger. The couple thanked him and after blessing the food, they dug in.

"I didn't realize I was so hungry," Ron said, dabbing his mouth with his napkin.

"Me, too. I guess I worked up an appetite tonight. The show went well, don't you think?"

"It was perfect. You did a great job with helping the kids create the sculptures."

"I only asked questions and tried to pull out their thoughts about how they feel."

"You must have had the right questions because their sculptures were great. Yours, too, by the way."

Rita looked a little sheepish. "Really? Do you think it was okay?"

"I see the outside of you and it reflects the goodness on the inside."

Rita smiled, finishing her soup. "So what will happen with your mom since she's not going to have chemo treatments?"

Furrows appeared on Ron's forehead, and she regretted asking the question immediately. "I'm sorry; I shouldn't have brought it up tonight."

He reached and patted her hand. "It's okay, I can't ignore the situation. Tomorrow I'm going to the hotel and have a talk with her and Jake. Maybe I can convince her to go ahead with the treatments. The thing is, if it were happening to me, I can't help but think I'd do exactly what she's doing...living life her way."

"We each have to make those decisions on our own. I'll be praying for all of you. Does it mean you'll drive back to Mesquite on Monday?"

"Possibly, but first I want to get Mrs. Cole's car looked at. I'll call a guy, Gus, is his name, I think. Maybe he can go out there early and see if it's an easy fix or not worth fixing. She's a single parent and needs transportation."

"I know and I appreciate your taking time to help her. Tanesha is a good student and has had a rough childhood. Her mom used to be on drugs. The dad is nowhere around. Mrs. Cole went through treatment and finally got Tanesha back. I'm praying they make it."

"Sounds like they've struggled. Where was Tanesha during her mom's treatment?"

"She stayed with an aunt for a year and a half. Mrs. Cole finally found a job and has been clean for two years. I want them to succeed so badly."

"I'll do what I can," Ron promised.

The server came by trying to entice them to indulge in a molten brownie for dessert, but Rita held her hands up, determined to not be tempted. Ron thanked the girl and asked for the check so they could leave.

***

Once back at her studio, she invited Ron in for a cup of tea. He accepted quickly, glad they could really be alone. She busied herself preparing the Chai while he made himself at home on the sofa. Rita felt happy, content, and yes, in love.

Ron blocked out thoughts of his Mom, Jake, Tanesha, and everything else. He was where he wanted to be right now. He was with the person he needed in his life.

Chapter Six

Jared woke this morning feeling rotten. His body ached, and he couldn't get warm. He spent most of the night running back and forth to the bathroom. "I knew I should have gotten a flu shot," he chided himself. Reaching for the thermometer on the bedside table, he saw his phone blinking. No way am I calling anyone right now. He slid the thermometer under his tongue and lay back on the pillow. He checked the numbers, 101.2. At least it came down a little. Jared pulled the covers up to his neck, hoping the chills would wane and he'd fall asleep. He was so cold and his skin felt clammy. Just when he thought he'd doze off, it was bathroom time again. Flinging the blankets back, he made a dash down the hall as fast as his aching body would carry him. Ugh! I'm gonna die.

Finally, Jared managed to recover enough strength to grab his phone and call Gus. Maybe he can pick up some meds for me to take. He pressed the numbers, moaning as he lay back down, waiting for his half-brother to answer.

"Yeah, Jared, what's going on?"

"I'm sick as a dog, man."

"Did you eat in some dive to save a penny?" Gus joked.

"Seriously, I've got the flu and I need something to help me stop the up-chucks and bathroom runs."

"Whoa. Too much information there little brother. I can't un-see that!"

"Gus, I'm dying over here. Can you run by the store and get me something?"

"Sure, not a problem. It'll take me about half an hour though. Charles had to go get a part for the Chevy, but should be back any minute."

"Hurry, please."

"I gotcha covered."

Jared pushed the end button on his phone and buried his head in the pillow. Why me? Why now? Just when I had a plan to set things straight. I have to be better by Monday.

***

Kat finished dressing and was excited thinking about her date tonight. She glanced at her reflection in the full-length mirror. The blue sweater with jeans was comfortable. She hoped he liked it. Clay was taking her to the Roxie Theater to see Rockin' the Planet. She heard good things about it. Most importantly, the production is based on the Bible. He told her it was the greatest story ever sung. Its message was to bring peace, love, healing and hope.

She enjoyed spending time with Clay and discovering so many unique things about him. He plays the Mandolin and offered to teach her. His work in films fascinated Kat the most. The documentary he put together about the homeless situation in San Antonio was very moving, yet provided possible solutions to the problem. She couldn't wait to get started on Betty's senior citizen film. The working title, "Remember Me", sounded great to Kat, and Clay liked it too.

The doorbell rang. She heard her dad welcome Clay, took one last glance in the mirror, gave a quick brush of her rogue bangs across her forehead, and headed downstairs.

***

Kat relaxed during the drive to the theater, listening to Clay detail a conversation he had with his mom. They must be very close...like I was to mine.

"She wants to meet you," Clay said softly.

"I'm sorry, you caught me thinking," she said, embarrassed.

"No problem. I just said my mom wants to meet you. Were they good thoughts?"

"Oh, are you good with that...my meeting her?"

"I am. I think you'll like her and I know she'll take to you."

"I was thinking about my mom while you were talking about yours. I still miss her so much."

Clay came to a stop at the light. He looked into Kat's eyes and saw the pain. He patted her hand. "Losing a parent is never easy and the ache doesn't go away. I know others who have lost one or both parents, and it's a difficult journey." The light turned green and he continued on toward the theater. "How are you with your dad re-marrying?"

"I'm happy he found someone to love. Betty is a very sweet woman and has so much compassion. I'm actually responsible for their having met each other."

"How's that?"

"I made him go with me to the estate sale last year. He really didn't want to go, but I insisted. Betty was there and that's how they met."

"Wow, maybe it was a divine appointment."

Kat looked at Clay's profile as he drove. "I believe you're right. They are good for each other."

He kept his eyes straight ahead. "I think we're good for each other, too."

Kat wondered to herself. I hope so. "Oh, look, there's the theater. I'm really excited about seeing the show."

"I'm glad. Afterward, we can grab a bite to eat somewhere if you want." He pulled into the parking lot and found a spot. Clay turned off the motor, went around and opened her door.

"You're such a gentleman," she said, as she slipped out of the seat.

He took her hand as they headed toward the entrance. Clay decided then and there he would make the evening last as long as possible.

***

Lillian rested on the sofa at the hotel. It had been a full day. She attended church with her sons, and after lunch said goodbye to Jake. He had to be at work in the morning so Ron offered to take her home on Monday. He knew she wanted to do some sightseeing, so along with Rita, the three of them made an afternoon of it. The Riverwalk sights and sounds were beautiful, and a visit to the Alamo was very interesting. Ron suggested getting a wheelchair when they visited two other missions, and she quietly agreed. Even with wheels, Lillian was tired. Being back at the hotel after dropping Rita off was a relief. But it was worth the discomfort to spend time with him and his girlfriend, seeing a bit of San Antonio.

"Are you hungry, Mom?" Ron inquired, feeling his stomach growl.

"Maybe just a bit. I think we worked up an appetite."

"If you want to nap first, I can order something."

Lillian agreed to his suggestion. It was almost five. Maybe a short nap would make me feel better. She got up slowly, as he came to her aid and helped her to the bed.

"I should've brought you back sooner."

"No, I wanted to continue and had a wonderful time."

He kissed her on the forehead and covered her with the blanket. "I'm going to read a while. If you need me, just call out."

"Thanks, Son," she whispered as she closed her eyes and drifted off.

Ron grabbed a pillow from the other bed, the Bible from the nightstand and made himself comfortable on the sofa. He wished hotels had better lighting. *Too bad I don't have my headlamp to wear. The lamp on the desk would be enough.* He didn't want to have the other lights disturbing his mom. He read through many verses he always prayed for his mom, and settled on Jeremiah 17:14. *Heal me (her), Lord, and I (she) will be healed.*

Closing the Bible, Ron leaned his head back and allowed memories of childhood to run through his thoughts. Both parents brought the boys up according to their faith, the Bible, and going to church. When Jake had complications from measles and nearly died, Ron watched them kneel before his hospital bed, asking God to spare their son. Time and again, their faith never wavered as they trusted the Lord during the hard times, and praised Him in the good ones. *I wish my faith was as strong as Mom's. God, increase my faith and heal her.* No matter how hard he tried he wasn't able to convince her to go ahead with the treatments. She was ready for whatever God had according to His plan. Ron only wished he knew what the plan was. *Or do I?*

Lillian stirred, stretched and yawned. "What time is it?"

Ron checked his watch. "Almost six-thirty, are you hungry now?"

"I could eat some chicken and dumplings," she laughed. "But I doubt we'd get it delivered."

"Let me see what I can do," he said, examining the hotel menu for room service. "Sorry, but they do have chicken noodle soup, will that work?"

"It's good enough. What will you eat?"

Scanning the list, he responded, "A cheeseburger should quiet my stomach."

They laughed as he picked up the phone and placed the order. Lillian went to find her medicine and a glass of water. "Ron?"

"Yeah, Mom?"

"Thank you."

He looked up and his heart was full. She looked vulnerable and yet determinedly strong. "For what?"

"Understanding."

Tears threatened, but he choked them back. He rose and went to his mom, hugging her close. "You're the best, Mom. I should be thanking you for all you've done for me and Jake through the years. I couldn't have asked for better parents than you and Dad."

Lillian smiled and at that moment both her and Ron's stomachs growled in unison. They both laughed. "Like mother, like son," she said.

Ron turned the other lights on and the television. "Let's see if we can find a decent show to watch."

"Maybe they have the Hallmark channel."

Ron sighed, hoping they didn't.

***

Jake arrived home, showered, and then heated up a frozen dinner. The drive from San Antonio drained him. Not having his mom to talk to made the drive seem much longer. He hoped she didn't wear herself out today, trying to do and see too much. For some reason she was bent on experiencing the tourist thing, even in her condition. He was hopeful Ron could convince her to go ahead with treatments after he brings her home tomorrow. Jake knew how headstrong she could be. He wasn't holding out much in the way of odds. In any case, his brother promised to try. Maybe I should call Ron and see how she's doing? The microwave beeped so he retrieved his dinner instead. He was hungry, regretful of not stopping on the way home to eat. He looked at the skimpy portion of meatloaf, pale green beans and runny mashed potatoes. Oh well, it is what it is. I'm going to bed early anyway. He carried the dinner into the living room, set it on the TV tray and found the remote. The news was on but he was so tired of the politics and commentary, he surfed through and landed on the Hallmark channel. Ha, mom would love this. He left it there and wolfed down his meal. Christmas romance and happily ever after. Too bad life isn't that way, I'd be married and Mom would have grandkids to spoil. Jake stretched out on the sofa, punched up the pillow and drifted off.

***

"Rita," Ron said into his phone as he sat in the hotel parking lot, ready to head to Mesquite with his mom, "I almost forgot, would you have time to call the mechanic, Gus Mancheck, about looking at Mrs. Cole's car? I promised her I'd have someone out there today."

"You know I will. Thanks for caring about them. I'll call as soon as we hang up. Drive safe and tell Lillian I said hello."

"Thanks. Rita said hello," he relayed to his mom. "She says hi back."

"Okay, call me after you get there."

"Will do," Ron said, ending the call and turning to Lillian. "Well, we're off to Mesquite and we'll stop at the Dairy Queen on the way."

"Good," she smiled, settling back in her seat. "Looks like it will be a pretty day."

He put the car in drive and headed to the expressway. Surprisingly, traffic wasn't too bad for a Monday morning. Of course, rush hour was over so maybe they would get out of town without any hassle.

"Mom?"

"Hmm?" she asked.

"Tell me about our trip to the coast when Jake and I wandered down the beach out of sight."

Lillian thought for a bit, and then laughed. "It's funny now, but it scared us half to death at the time." She began the childhood story as Ron drove, his mind picturing the scene from so long ago. He loved hearing her relay all the tiny details of what they had to eat, the color of their swim suits, and description of the lifeguards. Her memory was intact and she relished the retelling. This story would last through Austin.

***

"Master Mechanic, Gus speaking."

"Hi, my name is Rita Crawford and I'm hoping you can help a friend of mine."

"I'll try, what's the problem?"

"A parent of one of my students has car trouble, and I'm trying to get someone to look at it. She's not far from your shop, so if you could go by there and take a look, I'd appreciate it. She's a single parent and could use some help. If it's fixable, we'll make sure you get paid...if it's reasonable."

"I don't mind checking it out, but I'd have to tow it to the shop.

Give me the address and I'll make my way over."

Rita told him where it was and asked him to call her back when he knew what the situation was regarding cost and time for repairs. After hanging up, she decided to walk over to the studio and get things in order. After the art exhibit Saturday night, nothing was put away. She needed to move the sculptures to the the Blue Arts Center, so people visiting during the week could view the work of the children. It was Ron's idea, actually, and she heartily agreed. The kids would be thrilled to know their sculptures were on display.

She called Mr. Roddis and asked if he would have time to meet at her studio and discuss the process of moving them. Rita changed into her jeans and tee with the Blue Star logo on it, remembering, too, she had to finish another project for the arts center. Then, there was a presentation they wanted her to do for a community fair. She couldn't complain; it was part of her agreement when she moved into the accommodations here. Rita already knew the topic she would present, Art in a Child's Life. She would have photos of the children's sculptures blown up poster size and their story mounted next to each one. She smiled broadly, knowing it would make news in the community. The mayor would be there as well as several city council members. A representative from the San Antonio Public Library had promised Ron she would come. This might turn out to be a big deal.

***

Gus pulled his truck up behind a grey Ford in front of the brown house on Hickory. He checked the address, making sure he was at the right place before approaching the door. As he stepped out of the truck, a thin woman with black, shorn hair appeared on the rickety porch. Gus introduced himself and mentioned Rita Crawford's name as the person requesting him to stop by. The woman smiled and after thanking him profusely, handed him the keys.

"I hope it's something simple," she said wistfully.

"Sometimes it is," Gus said, feeling sorry for her immediately. "I'll take a quick look, but may have to haul it to my shop."

She nodded as he headed toward the car. Mrs. Cole sat down on the porch step, watching as the mechanic got in and tried starting her car. Nothing. She saw him get out and raise the hood, tinker with something, and then try again. Still nothing. Her hopes of it being an easy fix faded quickly. He slammed the hood and closed the door. She stood as he walked toward her.

"Ma'am," Gus said in a sad tone, "I'm sorry, I'll have to tow it. Ms. Crawford told me to call her when I knew more."

"That's good. I don't have my phone anymore. She'll let me know later."

He gave the woman his card and began the process of hooking up her car. He hoped repairs weren't major, for her sake. She didn't look like she could deal with car repairs of any size. Maybe Ms. Crawford plans to foot the bill. In any case, Gus would be fair and only charge what was necessary. He did have to pay his help.

He planned to stop by Jared's apartment and check on him. After picking up some Imodium, Pepto-Bismol, Campbell's Chicken Noodle soup, and saltine crackers yesterday, Gus wanted to be sure he was making a comeback to the land of the living. Once Mrs. Cole's car was in the shop and Charles began running diagnostics, he'd make a quick trip to Jared's, being careful to keep his distance though. The last thing Gus needed was to catch the flu. Even with getting the shot, he could still come down with it.

***

Brian volunteered to drive Betty and Kat to Mt. Laurel Assisted

Living and meet up with Clay to begin the first segment of the film involving Mr. Hartman. He wanted to meet this WWII Veteran and thank him for his service.

As the three of them approached his room, a nurse, with, "Hi I'm Josie" on her name tag, came out carrying a food tray. Betty introduced everyone, explaining why they were there.

"Oh, go right in, Mr. Hartman is expecting you. Matter of fact, he's asked me several times if it was two o'clock yet," she half whispered, then chuckled. "This is all so exciting."

"Thank you," they each said, opening the door.

"Good afternoon, Mr. Hartman," Betty greeted him with a handshake.

"It will be," he responded gruffly, "if you call me Clarence."

Smiling, she agreed. "Let's start over. Good afternoon, Clarence."

His broad grin revealed missing teeth. "I'm just messin' witcha. I'm glad you're here. Where's that young fella, the one with the camera?"

Kat spoke quickly. "He should be here any time."

As if on cue, a slight knock on the open door and in walked Clay. "Sorry I'm late, I had a tough time finding a parking spot. "How are you, Mr. Hartman?" he said, setting down his equipment.

Both Kat and Betty corrected him in unison, "It's Clarence!" They all laughed as they explained why.

Brian introduced himself. "I'm Brian Hills, Betty's husband, and Kat's father. I'm thrilled to meet you. I want to thank you for your service to our country."

"Glad to meet you, too," he said, shaking hands as he shifted in his chair. "Can't stand up for the ladies," motioning to his missing limb. "No need to thank me, I was just doing my duty like the other young men back then."

Clay suggested they find chairs while he set up his equipment. "Just pretend I'm not here."

"Mr. Hart..., I mean, Clarence," began Betty. "I would like to get to know you better. Would you be willing to tell us a little about your parents, your childhood, and well, about your youth?"

Brian found a seat and scooted it back near the door so he wouldn't be in the way, while Betty pulled up a cushioned one next to the wheelchair.

"Do you mind if I turn on my small tape recorder so I don't forget anything?"

"I don't care if you record me. I may not say anything worth remembering," he joked. "My childhood was a long time ago, so I hope I can give you what you need."

Kat stood behind Clay, in case he needed her to do anything. She didn't want to distract Clarence from his memories.

"One thing I'd like to say before I walk down memory lane."

"What's that?" asked Betty, turning on the recorder.

"All my life I've struggled. I never had it easy, even as a child. I've walked a rocky road and had a lot of hills to climb. No one really took notice of me, not that I cared. All my family is long-gone, friends too. They done died and the man upstairs still keeps me here. I don't know why, but maybe it's so you folks can tell my story."

"Clarence," Betty said softly, "you matter to us, and to the many people who will see your story. The important thing though, is you matter to God."

A slow smile came over his face. He relaxed back in his chair, and began. "My parents, rest their souls, were God-fearing people who raised ten young-uns to be the same. There weren't no cussin' in our home, and the good book was read every day. The place we grew up in was so small, there weren't no room for a field mouse to bed down." He laughed and saw the interest in the eyes of his visitors.

"You had nine siblings?" Kat asked, moving from behind Clay.

"Yep, sure did." His face dimmed a little. "Two of 'em died young. One drowned and Ma nearly died after the accident. She blamed herself, but the preacher helped her get over it some. The other one, my sister, Pearl, fell off a horse and died two days later."

"How sad," Kat moaned.

Clarence grew quiet, collecting his thoughts, while memories began appearing in his mind. Things he hadn't thought about in many years. "My Pa was a hard-working farmer and he never seemed to get ahead. We almost lost our farm one year."

Betty listened intently even though she had the recorder going and Clay was filming. She was drawn into Clarence's story. Into his memories. This man had so much to share and until today, no one to share it with. She felt tears behind her eyes as he struggled at times to convey the pain he and his family experienced through the years. She knew they must not overtax his energy though, so as he began to falter for words, she turned off the recorder.

"Clarence, this has been a wonderful visit and we have enjoyed hearing your story. We must end our session today, but we'll be back next week."

"I am a bit tired. Memories can wear you out."

"Indeed they can," she agreed. "You get some rest and we'll be back before you know it."

"I can do that real good...rest."

As Clay gathered his equipment and Betty prepared to leave, Clarence reached for her hand.

"There's something you might like to see," he said, indicating the drawer in his desk.

Betty looked at the drawer, then at Clarence. He nodded for her to open it. She pulled it out and saw photos in a small pile.

"Take them and maybe you can find some use for 'em."

She stared at the faded, well-worn pictures. An old shack, a man in a WWII uniform, a couple surrounded by a bunch of little kids, and a few others she couldn't figure out.

"Next time you come, we can talk about those."

"I'm looking forward to it, Clarence," she managed to choke out the words.

"They're not in too good a shape, and it's all I have left of my life."

Betty bent down and hugged the old man, whispering in his ear. "You're at the top of all the hills, Clarence. The rest of us are still climbing."

He hugged her back and as she released him, there were tears in his eyes.

***

Gus used the key Jared loaned him yesterday. It was better than making him get out of bed to let him in. Sure enough, the apartment was quiet and when he soft-stepped to the bedroom, he heard sporadic snoring on the other side of the door. He creaked it open just a bit and Jared stirred, squinting at his brother.

"Are you alive?" Gus asked.

"Not sure, what time is it?"

"Seven."

"Why are you here so early? Shouldn't you be tearing some car apart?"

"It's seven in the evening. How long have you been asleep?"

Jared shoved the covers back and sat up, feeling his forehead. "Evening? I'm not sure. I took some meds and think it was about midnight when I faded to black." He tried standing but his knees threatened to buckle, so he resumed his spot on the bed.

"You better stay put," Gus ordered. "Can I get you something to eat? Your tank is empty."

"Nah, I think I'll just lie here a while."

"Look, I'll bring you some of the apple juice and some crackers I bought. You can eat them when you feel up to it. I think you need to see the doctor, though."

"No way I feel like getting dressed and sitting in a doctor's office with a bunch of other sick people. I'll make do here. Thanks for checking on me, Gus."

"Okay. I'm heading home. If you need anything, call me."

Jared glanced at the nightstand and spotted his phone. "I will," he said, lying back down, wrapping himself with the blanket as he assumed a fetal position.

Gus felt sorry for him and wished he could drag Jared to get a shot or something, but he was stubborn. Slipping out, he locked the front door as he headed down to his car. Rain drops! That's all I need now. Gus disliked rain. It always made his work more difficult, not to mention dangerous. Driving and towing cars in weather like this made him nervous. The pelts of rain began coming stronger. He ducked his head and jumped up into his truck quickly. None too soon. The sky opened up, unleashing buckets. Jared's lucky he's in bed, warm and dry. He started the motor, checked the rear view mirror and backed out onto the street. At least now I'm going home and don't have anything hooked to the back.

***

Ron carried in the two suitcases and put them in Lillian's bedroom. She was already in the kitchen making coffee. He wished she would just sit down and rest.

"Do you want me to help you unpack?" he offered.

"No, Son, I'll do it tomorrow." Lillian set out two cups and some cream, along with cookies she found stashed in the cabinet. "Come, let's sit in here and talk a bit." She remembered the enjoyment they shared when the boys were younger and would sit in the kitchen while she baked cookies. Of course, they wanted to sample them hot out of the oven, but she loved when they would share their day with her.

Ron came into the kitchen and took a seat at the chrome table. He watched his mom pour coffee into the cups, knowing better than to suggest she let him do it. There were some things she needed to feel in control of.

"Mom," he began.

"It's nice to be home," she interrupted. "I love going places, but then coming home feels good, don't you think?"

He smiled, allowing her the pleasure of being in the moment. "Yes, it is, Mom. Just like the old days." Maybe he needed to give her this piece of time when she doesn't need to think about cancer, tomorrow or the future. Why drag her mind through the muddy waters of worry? What good would it serve? She knows the consequences of cancer untreated. Sure, he promised Jake he would try to convince her to have the chemo infusions, and he did mention it on the drive home. Her response was, "I've already made my decision. Oh, look at the horses in the field. One has a baby." End of subject.

"Remember the time when I was about six, and we went to the mall and I wandered off?"

Lillian thought back to that frightening day, recalling the helplessness she felt, not being able to find her son. "Sure do and I vowed then to never lose track of you again. I don't know why it was so appealing to you boys...running off where I couldn't see you."

"We were adventurous, I guess."

"You were. Then you enticed Jake to go along." She laughed.

"I love you," Ron said, suddenly feeling an enormous amount of admiration, devotion and concern for the woman sitting across from him. "You are the strongest woman I know." He felt tears well up and didn't know if he could push them back.

"I love you more," she responded, displaying a huge smile which covered her face.

Lillian placed her hand over his. "Ron, please don't be anxious about my health. I know it's taking up a lot of space in your head. Put it out of your mind and trust the Lord. He will take very good care of me. He always has, don't you think?"

Thinking it over, Ron agreed. "Yes, He has."

"Drink your coffee, it's gonna get cold," she reminded him as she sipped hers. "These are your favorite cookies and you haven't eaten one bite."

"Chocolate Chip, ummmm, thanks," he said, biting into the thick, round chunk. "You always did make the best cookies in town."

She beamed proudly, refusing to acknowledge the sick feeling pulsating through her body right then. "Thank you, Son."

***

Jared couldn't believe his good fortune. There she sat, smiling at him as he walked toward her. Kat looked like a movie star clad in a

121

heavily beaded jacket over designer jeans and zebra boots. She leaned in, the closer he came, lifting her hand to wave and catch his eye. Her smile dazzled him, making his heart pound uncontrollably as his feet broke into a run. The harder he tried to shorten the distance between them, the further away she seemed to be. He could hear his heartbeat grow louder and louder. He was now sweating profusely, salty drops stung his eyes. He stopped running and she faded from sight, still waving.

Jared sat upright in bed, feeling the dampness on his face. The sheet felt wet where he had lain. Kat had smiled at him. She smiled. He moved his hand across his forehead and realized his fever was gone. Why would he dream her there only to have the girl he obsessed over disappear? Must have been the fever.

In the bathroom mirror, his reflection told him how sick he'd been. Pale, sallow skin, and dull eyes stared back. He would shower and then try to get something decent in his stomach. He felt hungry for the first time in days, or had it been weeks? Jared didn't know what day it was or how long he had slept. He vaguely remembered Gus stopping by, but when, he had no idea. He turned on the shower. She smiled at me. He smiled back. Too bad she wasn't there to see the sincerity in his face. I have to make things right with her. If not, I'll keep running and she'll always disappear. Jared knew what he must do and it would take courage.

***

Rita hung up the phone, glad Kat was available to drive her to the mechanic's place so she could bring Mrs. Cole's car back. Mr. Mancheck finished repairs on it and even put on a current inspection sticker. He explained what was wrong, but Rita didn't know much about cars, so it went over her head. The important thing, she told him, was that it was fixed. Rita couldn't wait to see Mrs. Cole's face when the car was returned to her. Now, Tanesha and her mom would have reliable transportation. Rita decided she'd stop and fill the gas tank before taking it to her.

Kat would be here shortly so Rita finished her paperwork on the presentation she planned to give next week. Later, she'd pick up the posters of the kids' sculptures and get the rest of the display materials. Excitement was building as she thought about the possibilities from this. Perhaps even some attention from City Hall would evolve. She could dream anyway. The kids in her program, along with many more to come as her class grew, deserved attention. Rita thought about training someone to help her with future classes.

She heard a car honk and knew Kat arrived. Grabbing her keys, checkbook and wallet, she bounded out the door, filled with hope and bubbling over with ideas to share with Kat.

Opening the passenger door, she scooted in. "Thank you so much for doing this. Ron won't be back until the weekend, and I want Tanesha's mom to have her car as soon as possible."

"I'm happy to help," Kat said, smiling. "I had an early class. It's wonderful, what you're doing. You don't even have a car and you're making sure someone else does."

Rita laughed. "Ironic I guess. But living here, I don't really need one. Besides, this was actually Ron's idea."

"I'd say it's a team effort. You really like him, don't you?" Kat asked with a hint of knowing.

"He's very special to me."

"Come on, Rita," Kat teased, "he's more than just special."

"Well, of course, but we're taking things slow. Right now his mom needs all his attention."

"Sure, but I've seen the looks you give each other. I think love is around the corner."

Rita's head swung slightly at the mention of love. She looked at Kat and the word hung in the air. "Love," she said softly. "I'm not sure if what we have is love or just a very special friendship."

"Time will tell," Kat said, pulling onto the highway. "I'm still waiting for my chance at love."

"What about the young man who's doing the film y'all are working on? You're dating him aren't you? Any chance it might go anywhere?"

Kat took a right turn and headed south. "I don't know, he's fun and interesting...."

"Not to mention, very good looking?" Rita interrupted.

"Yeah, that too. But I've thought of him more like a big brother. He teaches me things and we mainly talked about the film, church and regular things."

"Has he kissed you?"

Kat laughed. "Not a real kiss."

"Explain what your idea of a real kiss is," Rita teased.

"I remember a conversation I had with my mom about kissing when I was in junior high."

"Junior high? Wow, was it one of 'those talks'?"

Kat started to giggle, almost as if she were back in eighth grade. "No, I had told her about a friend who said a boy tried to kiss her and she slapped him. Then my mom said not to let it happen to me either. In my naivety, I asked her what a boy/girl kiss was like."

"What did she say?"

Her answer was, "It's a sweet touch of the lips that makes you think you're so totally special, nothing else matters."

"Aww, what a great answer."

"The best thing was when I saw my dad standing in front of her when I came in from school. He leaned close, gave her a light kiss, and then just stared at her as she looked directly into his eyes. I think that moment was one of the real kisses she told me about."

Rita was quiet, pondering her friend's story.

"We're here," Kat announced, breaking into Rita's reverie. She drove to the left and parked her VW next to the grey Ford. "Look, he even washed it."

"What a nice guy," Rita said, smiling as she exited the car.

Gus had seen them pull into the yard. He stuffed his grease rag in his back pocket, wiped his hands on his twill work pants, and walked over to the vehicle.

"Hello, I'm Rita Crosby," she offered, getting out of the car. We spoke on the phone. I'm here to pick up Mrs. Cole's vehicle."

"Gus Mancheck," he said. "Excuse my hands, they're greasy," he mumbled, not wanting to get her hand dirty. "The car is ready to go. I had my helper give it a quick wash when I knew you were on your way. I have the paperwork in the office if you'll follow me."

Rita motioned for Kat to get out and walk with them. As her friend approached, she introduced them. "This is my friend, Kat Hills. She drove me over to pick up the car."

"Happy to meet you, Miss Hills." He nodded as they headed toward the office.

While Rita and Gus were inside, Kat hung out by the door and surveyed the yard filled with car parts scattered around. It looked organized though. Next to one wall she spotted a couple hub caps containing an assortment of nuts, bolts, and springs. It reminded her of an odd wind-chime she'd seen at a craft show she went to when living in San Marcos.

Rita finished talking with Gus after handing him a check. He gave her the keys as they came outside. Kat nudged Rita. "Those would make an awesome project for your students," she said excitedly.

Gus looked to what Kat pointed to. "That rusty stuff? If you want it, I can load it in your car."

The women bent down, looking at the contents while Kat described the wind-chime she had seen near the college when she was there. Gus caught a little of the conversation.

"Excuse me, did I hear you say you lived in San Marcos?"

Kat turned toward him. "Yes, I went to college there for a while. Why?"

Gus thought quickly, not wanting to reveal anything about Jared. This has to be the girl he has been obsessing over.

"Oh, I used to know some people there years back. It's a nice place to live and go to school. Did you get your degree from there?"

"No, I moved back home last year."

Gus knew. The name, Hills, clicked.

Rita broke into their exchange, thanking him for all he did to help. "Mr. Mancheck, we appreciate all you've done to provide a safe vehicle for Mrs. Cole." She started to offer her handshake, but remembered he was still greasy.

He held up his hands and smiled at both of them. "Let me get those bolts and stuff into your car so you can be on your way and I can get back to work," he said in a friendly tone. He picked up the two hubcaps overflowing with car parts and followed them to Kat's car. Yep, he said she drove a VW. I know that's her.

Kat closed the hood, thinking the loose junk would probably rattle all the way to Mrs. Cole's and back to Rita's. She watched as her friend got into the Ford and started it up before turning on her engine to head for the gate. She glanced in the rear view mirror and saw Gus staring after them, wiping his hands on his grease rag. Suddenly an eerie feeling come over her.

***

Gus sat in his office arguing with himself. Should he should call Jared and tell him about the college girl he'd been chasing after, showing up in his shop today? Gus knew the problems Jared went through concerning her but without heeding their warnings. The scary thing is, if he knew she was here, what would he do with the information? Camp out in Gus's shop in case she came back? It's not likely she would, she was only the driver for her friend. Besides, Gus didn't want to encourage Jared to hang on to his obsession with her, or possibly renew his passion for contacting her. No, I'll keep this to myself.

***

Kat arrived home but sat quietly in her car. She never mentioned to Rita the qualms she had after leaving the mechanic shop. What would she say? I have a weird feeling from being there? Kat chastised herself for the things she said to the guy. Once again, I shared too much information with a stranger. I told him where I went to college and about moving back home. And, Rita told him my name! The last time she let her mouth run on about private information, she ended up being stalked. This was different though. The image of Mr. Mancheck standing there, wiping his hands on a greasy rag, reminded her of some horror film from years back. She shuddered. Not that he looked menacing. He actually was a good-looking guy. Maybe I'm just acting paranoid.

Glancing up, Kat saw Betty at the front door. She picked up her handbag from the seat and got out, waving to her step-mom. The smile on Betty's face as she approached the door relaxed Kat. She was home. She was safe. There's no place like home, there's no place like home, she thought, mentally clicking her heels together. Smiling back, she greeted Betty with a hug as soon as she opened the door. The hug lasted a bit longer than usual.

"Is everything okay?" Betty quizzed, after Kat released her from the embrace.

"Yes, I'm just happy to be home."

Chapter Seven

The computer screen glared at Brian Hills. He kept his eyes focused on the blank page. It seemed to demand he type something. When he first started writing, "Miracles in Flight", his first book, the thoughts came easily, covering many of the miracles God had brought about in his life. Now, the hour spent in a stare-down with the screen, nothing happened. No words, thoughts, or typing took place.

Brian loved being here in the Wimberley Cottage his wife received from the estate sale last year. It was quiet, comfortable and ideal for writing his book. He had taken a couple days off from work at Boeing, thinking he'd make some progress. Getting up, Brian went to the kitchen and put on a pot of Southern Pecan Coffee. He loved the aroma as it brewed. No Keurig cup would do, he needed the whole pot. His muse must have left for the week, because nothing was brewing in his brain right now. Roaming around the cottage, Brian tried to refocus his thoughts about what direction the book had started in and where he was with it currently. Stuck, that's where he was! Just plain stuck. Am I on the wrong track, God? Show me if I am. I need some direction here.

Waiting for the coffee to brew, he ambled to the breakfast nook and sat, staring out the bay window. Betty loved this area of the house. She said it was her inspirational corner. Maybe if I sit here and work, I'll get inspired.

He thought about their visit to the assisted living home the other day where he met Clarence. Brian liked the old man and for some reason was deeply moved by the humility he saw. That guy has been through toughest of times and it just rolled right off of him. He'd lost a leg, yet didn't see the need to get a prosthetic even when it was available to him. It seemed he didn't think he was of any importance, and the thought disturbed Brian. It was a miracle Clarence survived the war when many of his buddies didn't. The memories he shared with Betty, which were filmed by Clay, touched Brian's soul in a way he couldn't fathom. Clarence experienced so much loss in his life and yet even now, he refused to look at himself as having any significance. This man had a poignant story. Possibly the one Brian needed to write.

The aroma of pecan floated through the room. He returned to the kitchen, poured a cup of the roasted blend, and found himself back in front of the computer.

"I'm ready for you now," Brian declared. "I have direction, so stop glaring at me," he reprimanded the empty screen. He realized it wasn't the story of his own miracle experiences which should be written, but those in Clarence's life.

His fingers touched the keys but not before he praised God, thanking Him for the inspiration needed to bring significance to a man no one remembers. He looked at the empty document on the computer and typed, His Life Matters. Brian already knew what the final three words of his book would be. "Yours does, too." This book would be a testament of a life lived, unobserved by man, but overseen by God, Who gives meaning to a person's life not measured by what he accomplishes, but by who he is in God's sight.

Brian smiled, took a sip of coffee, and began telling the story of one man and a big God.

***

Betty felt there was something going on with Kat, but hesitated questioning her. Both of them settled in the living room with tea and chicken croissant sandwiches. They made small talk and caught the evening news.

"I think your dad made some progress on his book. He called this morning and sounded excited about a new direction."

"I'm glad. He seemed frustrated over it last week."

"Writer's block, perhaps," Betty said, putting down her sandwich and taking a sip of her Earl Gray. "He's back up and running though, so we probably won't hear much out of him until Sunday when he comes home."

"I miss him," Kat remarked.

Betty looked at Kat's eyes and the thought struck her again of something's being amiss.

"You are struggling over some issue; I see it in your eyes."

Kat finished chewing her bite of croissant, set it on the snack plate and leaned back. "It's probably nothing," she said, choosing her words carefully so as not to alarm her step-mom. "I drove Rita to pick up Mrs. Cole's car this afternoon and after we left I had an uneasy feeling."

"What do you mean? What happened?"

"That's just it. Nothing happened. Well, except for my pouring out my life story to a perfect stranger again."

"Life story? What did you say?"

"I was telling Rita about a wind-chime I saw at a craft show in San Marcos. The mechanic, Gus, picked up on my comment abruptly, asking questions about my being there. So, dumb me, I tell him I went to college there but returned home last year." Kat's hands shook a bit as she reached for her teacup. Also, Rita told him my name when she introduced us.

Betty was quiet for a moment. "Do you think this Gus has any connection to the young man the police are searching for?"

"I have no idea. It would be a one-in-a-million shot if he were. It's just...."

"I can talk to your dad and see if he thinks the detectives should be notified."

"Please don't bother him. He's writing and I wouldn't want to get him off track. It can wait. I don't plan to go back there anyway."

Betty wasn't so sure about waiting, but promised Kat she wouldn't call Brian. He'd be home Sunday. They could discuss it then.

"Okay, I won't," she agreed. "Let's finish our sandwiches and go for a short walk, unless you're too tired."

"I think I'd rather take a hot bath and maybe read for a while, if you don't mind." Kat smiled.

"I don't mind a bit. I can go over some of the recordings I have of Clarence. You relax and enjoy your bath."

Kat gathered her plate and cup and headed to the kitchen. "Thanks, Betty," she said as she disappeared into the hall.

Betty finished her tea, hoping she wouldn't regret the promise she just made. *I can't get in the middle of father and daughter conversations. Why do things happen when Brian isn't here?*

***

Kat ran water into the tub and dumped in her lavender bath salts. While it filled she looked at her reflection in the mirror. She saw a glimpse of her mother in her eyes and the rounded nose. *Mom, I wish you were here to hold me and tell me things will be fine.* Tears snuck up on her, but she shoved them away, and hurriedly slipped into the

132

welcoming heat of the lavender-scented water. She leaned her head against the tub pillow, closed her eyes. She allowed the steam to soothe her mind and the heat of the water to soak away the day's stress.

Tomorrow she had a three o'clock class with Professor Evans. Kat slid further down in the water, until she was in up to her neck. Seems I always end up in hot water somewhere, she sighed.

***

Kat listened intently as her professor explained an aspect contained in her Business Ethics class. "Your ethics are formed and influenced by the people and the environment around you," he finished. I wonder who influenced him to think he could hover over me so intimidatingly?

Students were filing out and not wanting to be left alone with Professor Evans, Kat hurriedly grabbed her books and assimilated into the throng. She admitted he was a good teacher and the course was beneficial to her. The ironic part of his teaching though, showed up as he covered building business principles, when he lacked personal skills in this area. At least she thought so from the lack of any evidence in him personally. Although females in his class steered clear of him not liking his physical pushiness, she never heard any evidence of wrong doing on his part.

Kat unlocked the car and tossed her books onto the back seat. She wanted to get home and talk to her dad about the incident at the mechanic shop last week. He didn't get in from Wimberley until late last night, so there wasn't a chance to discuss it with him.

She glanced at her gas gauge and gulped. Empty. Kat knew she could make it to the station though. The VW almost never ran out of gas, but she had been so distracted the other day after the episode with Gus, filling the tank didn't enter her mind. She turned on the ignition and headed to the corner convenience store. She would pick up a coffee to sip on and fill the tank at the same time.

***

Jared was happy to be back at work after a horrible week of being down with the flu. If it hadn't been for Gus's checking in and bringing him stuff, he'd probably be dead by now. He owed his half-brother big time. At least now Jared could follow through on his plan to make things right over the so-called stalking issue. He was tired of always looking over his shoulder, thinking any minute he'd be arrested. The plan had been to go to the police station, turn himself in and try to explain his actions. He had paid for the incident in San Marcos and kicked himself for his behavior. The only reason he continued searching for Kat was to apologize and let her know he wasn't trying to harm her. Granted, the situation on the freeway over the holidays wasn't exactly apologetic and could have ended much differently. He shouldn't have tailed her from the mall. My bad.

"Hey boss," Jared addressed Mike after getting back from his last delivery. "I need my schedule for next week so I can work in some business I need to take care of."

Mike looked up from the pizza oven. "I'll have it posted by five. Right now, I need to see what's going on with this oven. I don't know if the temp is off or user error is to blame, but the crusts are coming out under baked."

"Okay, thanks. Did you call someone to come out and look at it?" Jared removed his apron and cap and prepared to leave for the day.

"Not yet, thought I'd check it first. Are you busy around noon on Saturday?"

"Depends on your new schedule I guess."

Mike laughed, shut the oven door and helped himself to a fountain drink. "There's a kid's birthday party from eleven-thirty to one. Terry is working it, but she might need some help. Doesn't hurt to have an extra set of hands."

"Sure, I'll help out, though she's good with kid parties."

"This one is more of a school celebration I think. Some kids did some art sculpture and it caught the attention of our City Council. Anyway, they want to celebrate it with pizza. Can't beat that."

"Sounds like Terry might need extra help." Jared's thoughts roamed to it's involving city council people and who knows, maybe police.

"Thanks, I appreciate your being flexible." Mike searched for the number to the repair guy and picked up the phone, waving Jared off as he left.

***

Brian put in a call to Detective Winters. Since Kat told him about her uneasiness of being at Gus Mancheck's mechanic shop last week, he fought the urge to just drive over and confront the guy. Betty gave him plenty of reasons why that would be a bad idea and in the end he agreed. Unfortunately, the detective wasn't in when he called. If this man was connected in some way to Jared Orlov, the police need to pick him up for questioning. Of course, Jared was never charged with the highway incident, and he hasn't bothered Kat in a long time, but still. Knowing where he is and what he's up to would put his and Kat's minds at ease.

Betty caught her husband's attention as he put down the phone and prepared to work on some contracts.

"No luck?" she asked, knowing the answer to her question by the furrow on his brow.

"He wasn't in, but the woman who took my call said she'd give him my message as soon as he was available."

Betty slipped both arms around Brian's neck, laying a kiss on his cheek. "You did the right thing in calling Detective Winters instead of charging over to the shop. Besides, maybe the man isn't connected. You'd be accusing him falsely."

Brian swiveled around in his chair and smiled, releasing the wrinkles in his forehead. "You're right, as always," he said, kissing her back as he placed his hands on her slender waist. "Thanks for keeping me from doing something I'd probably regret."

She released him from her embrace. "Let's go for a walk," she suggested.

"Okay, sounds good. Let me shuffle my paperwork, and I'll meet you at the door."

"I'll leave a note for Kat," Betty said. "She'll be back shortly."

***

Detective Winters hung up the phone after trying to reach Brian Hills. The daughter said he was out but would be back soon. Wonder what's up? It had something to do with the Jared Orlov case, but Mr. Hills didn't elaborate in the message. He only said to call. Ray Winters had grown weary of this so-called case. The guy paid for the vandalizing crime in San Marcos and although there were accusations about his stalking Kat Hills, nothing was ever proven. As far as he was concerned, Mr. Orlov should be left alone. Just to be sure nothing new was going on, Ray decided he would check records and see if any evidence had been submitted or new charges were brought. If not, then he would tell Mr. Hills to put it all behind him and move forward. There are more serious crimes and dangerous people out there than a guy who might have a thing for a girl.

***

"Thanks, Kat, I'll see you Saturday," Rita said before ending the call. She was pumped up thinking about the pizza party for her Artsy Kids celebration. Rita considered having pizza delivered to the studio, but didn't want to deal with the cleanup. Besides, the kids would love all the play options at Dominique's. Ron would be back and was planning to attend. He said his mom was doing okay, had lots of help lined up, and ordered him to return to San Antonio. He planned to take her to the doctor on Thursday so he would know what was going on. His brother would also be there, so they could discuss any issues necessary with Doctor Gonzales. Rita knew how relieved Ron would feel getting back to the studio. He loved Blue Star and she was sure everyone there missed him terribly. I sure do!

Right now, Rita needed to sketch out an idea for a project using all the nuts, bolts and junk she brought home from the mechanic shop. Kat suggested making wind chimes from the various parts. It would be something fun for the kids, so she started drawing out ideas and would present them in class next week. She needed only a good title. Time to Chime. Rhyme and Chime. Free to Chime. She could go on like this forever. She laughed at herself as she sat down at her dining table, staring at a hubcap filled with old parts. Maybe she would sort them out first and get an idea of what all she had to work with. Rita slid her sketch pad to the side and unfolded the morning paper. She dumped both hubcap contents in a heap, separating pieces into different piles until the entire table was filled. Her studio was beginning to resemble a mechanic shop. She smiled at the small levers which reminded her of birds, and the springs brought back memories of slinky toys. I think Kat was right, this stuff will be perfect for making wind chimes. The kids will have so much fun. She retrieved her sketchbook and settled on the sofa to jot down some abstract lines. She would fill in details later, but right now didn't want to lose the thought processes going on with her creative muse. She was so happy about Gus's generosity in giving her all the car parts. She might go back and see if he has any other small stuff he'd be willing to donate.

***

Betty couldn't believe the phone call she just received. Emily Gardley called and they had a lengthy chat. Since the wedding in June, they'd spoken only twice, so it was great to catch up. They were coming to visit for Thanksgiving. Last year, their holiday meals were different because neither couple was married. Matter of fact, Brian surprised her by proposing at the Thanksgiving meal the estate sale group enjoyed. She also remembered the night they went to Emily's apartment for an intimate Christmas Eve dinner. Emily and Seth invited them to have a double wedding in England in the home Mary Ludwig left to her. She couldn't wait for Brian to get home so she could share the wonderful news with him. And Kat. She will be thrilled to see Emily again. Betty went upstairs to her desk, sat down and began a timeline for the upcoming event. Thanksgiving, six weeks away! Wow, not much time to plan. Emily did say they would arrive two weeks early though. At least, between her and Emily, they'll be able to work out the menu and details. She heard the downstairs door open.

"Anybody home?" Kat shouted.

"I'm up here in my office," Betty called down. "Come on up, I have some fantastic news to share."

Kat bounded up the stairs. "What's up?" she quizzed excitedly.

"You'll never guess who's coming to dinner. Thanksgiving

dinner."

"I give up, who?"

"Try to guess," Betty teased.

Kat put her finger to her chin, looked around for an answer, and then snapped her fingers. "I know, Clarence Hartman!"

Betty stared at her step-daughter for a moment. "That's not who's coming, but you just gave me a wonderful idea. I'm going to see if we can arrange for Clarence to be here. It would be great to celebrate him."

"It would. I hope he'll agree. Maybe Mt. Laurel provides transportation."

"It doesn't matter," Betty said thoughtfully, "if they don't, our guys can be his escort."

Kat loved the idea of Clarence's joining them for Thanksgiving. He would certainly make their celebration a major event. She wondered how long it had been since he enjoyed a holiday meal anywhere except the assisted living home.

"So, if he wasn't the person you had in mind, who is?"

"Emily and Seth Gardley are planning a trip back here. They'll arrive two weeks before Thanksgiving."

Kat jumped up and down like a high school girl from the fifties, pulling Betty up from her chair to bounce around with her. "Yay, it'll be so good to see them again. Woo Hoo!" she almost sang. In their noisy silliness, they never heard Brian come in.

He stood, leaning against the door frame gawking at the two women in his life, wondering if they put too much sugar in their tea. "Ahem," he spoke a bit loudly to make his presence known.

Both women froze in place turning just their heads and burst out laughing.

"Brian, you're home," Betty managed to tumble out.

"Yep, but the better question is, what's up with you two?"

Kat pulled her dad into the room, hugging him in the process. "Betty has guests coming for Thanksgiving. You'll never guess who."

***

Lillian put down the phone and turned onto her left side. She couldn't seem to get comfortable no matter how she positioned herself. Today had been a rough day for pain and feeling nauseous. Hopefully, her doctor would call back soon and possibly send out a different medication. The one she was taking didn't seem effective anymore. Lillian didn't want to bother Jake yet. If the doctor must see her, she'd call him to pick her up. Truthfully, the thought of getting dressed and into a vehicle was overwhelming at the moment. She felt tired but sleep was out of the question right now. She shifted again in her bed, this time to her right side. A surge of pain took over, bringing her body to an upright position. She screamed in anguish. Lillian was glad Ron left for San Antonio, unable to hear her outcry of pain. When it subsided, she tried once again to get relief and rest. She drew one leg up a bit, and then leaned into it. Aah, now if I can stay this way and fall asleep. Just as she felt herself drifting, the phone rang. The caller ID displayed Dr. Gonzales's name, so she answered quickly.

"Hello, Dr. Gonzales. Thank you for returning my call."

"My nurse notified me immediately after hearing your message. Your voice sounded frantic to her. What's going on?"

She explained the increased nausea and bouts of severe pain. "I don't want to worry my boys unless there is something really serious for them to be aware of."

"Lillian, you have an aggressive cancer. You made the decision to not have chemo...."

"Because I didn't want to end up sick and going through pain," she interrupted her oncologist. "Yet, here I am having to deal with it anyway. Is there a different medication you can give me for both issues?"

"Not over the phone, my dear. Tell the guys to bring you in and we'll see what's going on. I may admit you so we can run a couple of tests."

Lillian fought off another sharp pain and felt light-headed. Her voice weakened and her words faded from the doctor's ear.

"Lillian? Are you there?" No response. He quickly hung up and phoned for an ambulance, advising them the side door would be unlocked, and to get there STAT. He notified Jake Davis to meet him at the ER. He knew Lillian was in trouble.

"EMS is bringing Lillian Davis in shortly. Please notify me as soon as they arrive," he told the ER staff, "I'll be in my office."

"Will do, Doctor," responded the matronly nurse.

***

Ron approached the San Antonio city limits when he received the call that his mom had been taken to the hospital. He pulled into a gas station, filled the tank, and headed back to Mesquite. His mind was racing. What was I thinking? I should have stayed. Jake wasn't with her at the time either. Poor Mom, alone and to have this happen. Actually, neither Ron nor Jake knew what really took place. Jake mentioned something about the doctor being on the phone with her and then she passed out or hung up or who knows what. Dr. Gonzales ordered an ambulance to pick her up. Thankfully they had all agreed to let medical teams know about the unlocked side door. At least Jake will be there to know what's going on. He promised to call. Ron pressed his foot harder on the gas pedal as he hit the highway. We shouldn't have allowed her to be home alone.

***

Jake rushed like mad and pulled into the ER parking area. He jumped out, clicked the alarm on the car and plowed through the double doors to the desk.

"I'm Jake Davis, where's my mom?" he growled at the nurse, fear overtaking his mouth.

"What's her name?" she asked calmly.

"Lillian Davis. The ambulance brought her in."

"Let me check and see if they've arrived yet."

Jake tapped a nervous cadence on the counter with his fingers, not knowing what condition she was in or if, God forbid, she was dead. No, he wasn't allowing his mind to go down that road.

"They just pulled in," the nurse said, disrupting his train of thought. "If you'll have a seat, I'll call you as soon as they get her settled and are able to tell you something."

"Can't I go back now? I need to see her." His voice almost broke.

The nurse assured him it would be best to allow them to triage her first, but if need be, she herself would come out and get him. She disappeared into the ER examining rooms.

Jake hung his head and reluctantly walked over to the window. He pulled out his phone and called his brother.

When Ron answered, Jake updated him, promising to call immediately when he knew anything.

"It'll take me at least another three hours to get there," Ron grumbled. "Heavy traffic heading in your direction."

"Just drive carefully, I don't want you ending up in the hospital too."

"I will, I only wish I hadn't left. I should have insisted on staying."

"You know how she is, Ron. I feel guilty because I wasn't with her."

"Hey, you have a job and Fridays are hectic."

"Well, you have one too, and driving back and forth does a number on you. Anyway, it is what it is. As soon as I see her, or talk to the doctor, I'll call you."

"Thanks. See you in a few hours," Ron said, pressing the end-call button on the steering wheel.

***

Rita was heartbroken for Ron. He'd called while on the road, to let her know he wouldn't be at the kid's party tomorrow because of his mom's being in the hospital. She couldn't believe he was almost back and had to turn around. He must be exhausted. Ron asked her to pray for all of them. She wished she knew the extent of Lillian's condition, but even Ron didn't know.

Rita called Kat and left a message asking if she could pick her up for the party tomorrow. Without Ron here, and still not having a car, getting to Dominique's would be cumbersome on the bus. I need to think about buying a car – and soon. Rita prepared a cup of Chai tea, cleaned up her lunch dishes and decided to spend some time in prayer. Actually, she needed to do it more often. After the sermon last Sunday, she felt the Lord moving her into doing just that. She gathered her Bible and notepad and found a cozy spot in the corner of her bedroom. First and foremost was praying for Lillian, her doctors, and her sons. She lifted up Ron especially, knowing he was driving as she prayed.

***

Kat checked her messages before going into the library and noticed Rita called. After listening to the voice mail, she immediately phoned and told her she'd be glad to pick her up. Kat knew Rita must be disappointed at Ron's not being able to attend, but maybe the party would take her mind off things. Right now, Kat needed to get her paper finished so she could turn it in on Monday. Hope Professor Evans is satisfied and gives me a decent grade.

She locked her car and walked slowly toward the entrance. It was such a gorgeous day, one like she used to spend with her mom. They would go shopping, visit the Japanese Tea Garden, or just walk in the park. It would be a beautiful day to visit with her and not think about school or anything. Kat stopped in her tracks. She looked at the sky, and turned back toward her car. Her paper could wait.

As she fastened her seatbelt, her phone buzzed. Dad. She pressed the talk button. "Hi, Dad, what's going on?"

"Nothing big-I thought since I got away from work early and Betty is busy, I'd see if my favorite daughter would like a DQ date."

She hesitated.

"Of course, if you're tied up...."

"No, it's not that. It's just, well-I'm headed to the cemetery."

"Oh. Any special reason?"

"No, I suddenly felt I wanted to talk to Mom."

"Want me to join you?"

"I'd love it. But, could you give me some time alone with her first?"

"Sure, Baby Girl. I'll see you in about an hour?"

"That'll work."

"I'll be there," he assured her.

"Dad?"

"Yes?"

"Can you pick up some Laughadills."

Brian was quiet. "Of course."

She ended the call and smiled. Her mom changed the flower name, Daffodils, when Kat's high school sweetheart broke her heart. Cassie gave her the flowers and told her to laugh because there would be other boys who would break her heart before the right one found her. "Better to laugh rather than cry," her mom would say. She started the car, backed out and headed north.

***

Brian stared at his phone, wondering what prompted his daughter to feel the need to go to the cemetery today. Not that she needed a reason to visit her mother's grave, but it seemed unusual for her to just up and go without it's being a holiday or birthday. He hoped it didn't have anything to do with Jared Orlov.

Brian left a note for Betty before locking up. He could stop at David's Flowers and pick up some fall-blooming Daffodils. David was used to the Hills' household ordering them at different times of the year, so Brian knew he'd have some. Whatever was bothering Kat must be deep or she wouldn't feel the need for Laughadills.

***

Kat eased herself to the ground, brushed leaves from the area in front of the headstone, and sat cross-legged, quietly, not knowing where to begin, what to say, or how to explain her visit. "Hi Mom." She paused, knowing there would be no "Hi, Sweetie" in return.

Why was she here?

It seemed as though her life was in chaos and all around her there was turmoil. First, this thing with Jared, and then her professor's weirdness. Both men caused her so much anxiety. She didn't want to tell her dad what was churning inside her. Then Rita's friend, Ron, and his brother are facing the loss of their mother. She knew first-

145

hand what that felt like, and had so much empathy for them. Kat thought about Clarence. He was old, alone and yet so humble. When he dies, who will attend his funeral? He has no one but us.

She poured her thoughts and feelings out to the silent grave, willing her mother to hear her heart and provide some comfort. She wanted to feel Cassie's presence and experience the embrace which was always available. Tears flowed.

***

Brian found his daughter crumpled against the granite headstone, sobbing. He held himself together so he'd be able to help Kat with whatever was going on. He laid the Laughadills on the grave and wrapped his arms around her as she cried her eyes empty. Brian gently released her and patted her cheeks with the corner of his shirt. He reached for the flowers, pressing them into her hands.

Kat looked up at her dad and down at the flowers. They both laughed, breaking the tension.

"It's better to laugh than cry," he reminded her.

She laughed again. "Thanks, Dad, they're beautiful," she said, hugging the flowers carefully, before placing them in the vase next to the stone.

"Thanks, Mom, for listening," she whispered, placing a two finger kiss against her mom's name on the cold granite.

"Want to talk?" Brian spoke softly.

"Yes, let's go to Dairy Queen and maybe you can help me figure out my life."

"That's what dads do, you know." He grinned at his daughter's tear stained face.

They stood and each blew a kiss toward Cassie's grave before heading to their cars.

"Drive carefully," he admonished, "I'll meet you there in ten minutes."

"I will, Dad. Save me a seat."

***

Ron arrived at the hospital in record time – two hours and fifteen minutes from when he turned around on the outskirts of San Antonio. He approached the ER information desk, identifying himself, tumbling out questions as to his mother's whereabouts.

"Follow me," the male nurse instructed matter-of-factly.

Ron stayed directly behind the young man, moving briskly down a hallway, into the elevator, up to the ICU. The nurse walked him to the entrance, and then pulled open the curtain where Lillian lay quietly except for the beeping of machines. Jake stood immediately and embraced his brother. They stood stalwart, each in his own thoughts, afraid to speak. Finally, Ron found his voice.

"What's the prognosis? What did the doctor say?"

"It's not good," Jake managed to choke out his words. "The cancer has invaded her liver and bones." He backed against his chair and fell into it, unable to continue.

Ron moved to the side of the bed and placed his hand gently on Lillian's discolored arm. It was bruised from the IV and her skin was mottled.

"I'm sorry I left this morning, Mom." He couldn't think of anything else to say. His eyes burned. He turned to his brother. "Will she wake up or did they give her something?"

"The doctor said he wanted to keep her sedated. She regained consciousness in the ambulance, but after they arrived and ran tests, he ordered an injection. She should come around sometime tonight."

"I want to talk to the doctor. I'll be back. Text me if she wakes up."

Jake nodded as his brother left the room.

***

Betty Hills worked in her office most of Friday morning, until she received a call from the same assisted living home where Clarence lived. The Director, Mr. Cavanaugh, heard about the film she was doing with Clarence, and wanted to talk to her about another resident who might be a prospective subject for her work.

While waiting, she ambled around the director's office, reading the framed credentials. There were numerous honorary degrees and several awards from city leaders, applauding his work on behalf of the city's homeless.

"Good Afternoon, Mrs. Hills," the distinguished-looking gentleman greeted her. "I'm Kenneth Cavanaugh, the director here at Mt. Laurel. Thank you for coming in."

"I'm happy to meet you," she said, as they shook hands. "I was surprised to get your phone call, and very curious about the woman you mentioned."

"Please, have a seat," he said warmly, indicating a soft, tan leather chair opposite his desk.

She sat down, making herself comfortable, as he slipped into his chair behind the oak desk. His coffee mug sat on a warmer near the phone. Glancing at it, he asked, "Would you care for coffee?"

"I'm really a tea drinker, but if that's not convenient, it's okay."

He picked up the phone and called his secretary, Dottie. "Do you have any of your wonderful tea bags left? Great, would you mind bringing Mrs. Hills a cup? Thanks."

Turning his attention back to Betty, he continued. "The woman's name is Greta Garson. I'm not sure if you'll be able to work with her though, that's why I wanted to talk with you."

"Why wouldn't I?"

"Ms. Garson doesn't like anyone. She is outrageously rude to the staff, complains loudly about the food, and refuses to bathe regularly."

"Oh," Betty uttered in amazement. "I can see why you would think this would be troublesome. Why did you call me then?"

"She's a lonely woman needing attention. Greta needs an ear but she thinks we're not listening."

"And you think doing a film about her would change things?"

"There's a slim chance. If you can get through the rudeness and explore the woman inside, it might. Her father committed suicide during the depression. Her mother died of a lung disease when Greta was in her twenties." Mr. Cavanaugh shook his head sadly. "There's a lot of pent up anger in that woman."

Dottie knocked on the door frame gently. "Tea time," she announced with a smile. "Nice to have another tea drinker in the house." She set the cup on the side table.

"Thank you, it smells fantastic."

"You're quite welcome," Dottie said before exiting the office.

Taking a slow sip, then setting down the cup, she asked Mr. Cavanaugh, "How do you know all this if she has no one?"

"She shouts to anyone nearby about her misery in life. Which is why I think there's a possibility she might dump it all out for you. Of course, you may not want that kind of content for your film, I don't know if she'll keep it a PG rating."

"I'd like to meet with her before I make any decisions."

"I can take you to her room when we finish talking. If you have time."

"I do and I appreciate how you're trying to help her. You seem genuine and that means a lot."

"By the way, how is the film going with Clarence?"

"Fantastic. We hope to wrap it up by the end of the month. Then we'll do the editing and see how it looks."

"That's great! Would you like to meet Ms. Garson now?" He smiled.

"I would indeed," she said quickly. "Does she drink tea or coffee?"

He laughed. "You'll have to ask her," he said as they proceeded down the hall to find Greta.

They arrived at her room, knocked gently on the door and waited. No answer. The director knocked again. "Ms. Garson, its Mr. Cavanaugh. I've brought someone to meet you." He looked at Betty with a knowing sigh and whispered, "She's there. I can hear movement." Finally the door was opened just a crack and two penetrating eyes peeked around the edge.

"Who wants to meet me?" she quizzed in a gravelly tone.

"If you'll open the door properly and allow me to introduce this lady, you'll find out," he said, with a wink of an eye.

The door opened slowly, revealing an eclectic-dressed woman. She kept one hand on the door knob, as if she might need to slam it shut at any moment.

Betty gave an encouraging smile and held out her hand. "Good afternoon, Ms. Garson. My name is Betty Hills, and I am quite happy to meet you."

"Harrumph. What's to be happy about?" she returned, ignoring Betty's hand. "I'm no one famous and I don't have no money. Friends neither for that matter!"

Betty exchanged glances with the director, but refused to be put off by Greta's hostile attitude. "Who knows, we might become friends if you'll give us a chance. Do you drink tea?"

"Why do you want to be friends? And no, I drink black coffee."

"If we could sit awhile and talk, I'll explain why I'm here and the reason I'd like for us to get to know each other better. Would that be okay?"

Greta eyed Betty suspiciously, looking her up and down, and then glancing at Mr. Cavanaugh. She saw him nod his approval and while she didn't consider him her friend, she knew he was in charge. "Fine, you can come in for a minute, but I'll warn you right now, the coffee here is terrible."

Betty smiled. "Mr. Cavanaugh, would you be able to locate some good-tasting coffee for Ms. Garson?"

"I think I know just the place. Maybe you both would like to use the sitting room down the hall. It's quiet and has comfortable chairs."

"Thank you."

"My pleasure," he responded.

Betty looked at Greta, who squinted at them, causing her eyes to fade further into their sockets. She detected an odor of poor hygiene coming from Greta but purposely ignored it, determined to get through the outer layer of hostility, and find the soul in need of love.

"If you'll follow me, I'll show you where the sitting room is," he instructed.

Betty carefully put one hand on Greta's shoulder to encourage her to come along. She didn't want to seem pushy, just friendly. She felt the woman stiffen at her touch, so immediately removed her hand. She guessed making friends with Greta would not happen easily. First, she needed to gain her trust.

"I don't need no help. I might not be young and spry like you, but I can still get around this place. Besides, I know where the sittin' room is. That's the room the counselors use. If you think you're gonna counsel me, you can forget it right now."

In the hallway, Mr. Cavanaugh turned around and corrected Greta. "Ms. Garson," he said a bit sternly, "It's not a counseling room. When guests visit the residents here, it provides a place to relax and talk in private if desired."

"Oh, excuusse me, Mr. Director. I guess I'm an ignorant old woman. I've only lived here for fifteen years and don't know the difference between counselors and guests?" she rattled in a loud voice.

Both Mr. Cavanaugh and Betty turned a deaf ear to her rant.

They entered the room, and Betty admired the softness of the furniture, muted paint on the walls, and fresh flowers by a window. "This is nice and it does seem relaxing."

"If you ladies will excuse me, I'll get the good coffee and return shortly."

"Thank you," Betty called as he disappeared into the hallway.

"He likes to impress visitors," Greta informed.

Betty ignored the sarcasm in her voice. "Why don't we sit down and I'll tell you a little about myself while we wait for your coffee?"

"Suit yourself," she answered, plopping her generous hips onto the cushioned chair.

Betty heard the whoosh of air leave the padded seat as Greta immersed herself, albeit not so graciously. This is not going to be easy. She placed herself strategically on the other side of Greta's chair, but angled hers so they could talk face-to-face.

"Like I said," she began when they were both settled, "my name is Betty Hills. I'm forty-nine years old and just married for the first time last year to a wonderful man, Brian."

Greta gave her a look of disbelief. "You mean no man ever took you to the altar in all them years?"

Betty gave a small laugh. "Well, one almost did, but he wasn't the one God had in mind I guess."

"God? What's he got to do with it? Did the guy jilt you or did you jilt him?"

What was I thinking when I agreed to do this? "Neither, Ms. Garson, we mutually agreed to go our separate ways. But God does have a say about whom we marry...if we'll listen."

"Harrumph. Nonsense. I never married and it didn't have nothin' to do with God."

Mr. Cavanaugh cleared his throat as he entered the sitting room. "Here you go, Ms. Garson, a special mug of coffee. I'm sure you'll enjoy this one." He set it on the table next to her chair and discreetly winked at Betty. "My secretary, Dottie, had it prepared just for you." He placed a cup of tea down for Betty.

"It's probably cold. Took you long enough." Greta retorted.

Betty picked up her teacup. "Thank you, Mr. Cavanaugh for the tea and the coffee."

"You're welcome. Now I'll leave you two alone so you can enjoy your drinks and get to know each other."

Greta watched him leave the room and took a sip of coffee. She almost burned her lips but there was no way she would let on to Ms. Spring Chicken.

Betty resumed their previous conversation. "Would you like to tell me a little about yourself?"

"Not much to tell."

Betty felt stuck. She tried to think of questions requiring more than four words to answer. "Were you ever engaged?"

There was a haunted look in Greta's eyes. She seemed suspended in a dark tunnel, but quickly returned to their conversation.

"I had a beau, but there wasn't no time for such nonsense, my ma needed takin' care of. After a while he found some gal and married her."

"May I ask about your father?"

"NO!" Greta said sharply. She held her coffee mug, sipping the now-cooled liquid. She wouldn't admit it, but this was a good cup of coffee.

Betty knew she was on shaky ground, but decided to ask anyway. All Greta could do is refuse, again. "I don't know if you're acquainted with a gentleman resident here named Clarence Hartman. But...."

"That one-legged old coot? Sure, but he doesn't mingle much. Probably cause he can't get around too good."

"Mr. Hartman is a veteran from WWII, where he lost his leg."

"Oh," she mumbled.

"I'm doing a documentary film about his life. I hope to show the world the man he was and is."

"Why would you want to do that?"

"Because every person has a story and when people outlive their family and friends, sometimes they get forgotten. I don't want elderly people to disappear without their story being told."

"Maybe no one wants to hear it," she threw back at Betty, with a twist of her mouth.

"I believe they do. That's why I'd like to ask you to participate in the film project."

"Me? You're kiddin'."

"No, I'm not. We'd just talk to you about your life. My daughter, Kat, and her friend, Clay, will do the filming.

"Harrumph. I don't want a bunch of people gawkin' at me."

"There would only be three of us. You'd be able to express yourself about things which happened to you and how you reacted to those situations."

Greta was quiet. She set her mug down harshly. "I'll do it! There are a few things I'd like to set straight about how my life turned out. People will see what a rough life really is."

"Thank you, Ms. Garson. Now are we friends?"

"Well, I guess you could call me Greta."

***

"Ron, like I told your brother earlier, Lillian is in a precarious state. The cancer metastasized into her liver and bones. The prognosis is bleak. Medications I've had her on are not reigning in the pain."

Ron's eyes held steady with the doctor's, but his voice quivered as he spoke. "How much time does she have?"

"Only God knows for sure, but using the knowledge He gave me as a physician, I'd say a month? Maybe more, perhaps less."

Ron sucked in his breath loudly before letting out a sob. He stood and moved toward the window overlooking the wing where his mother lay. "Will she need to stay in the hospital?"

"I'll keep her another week. We'll be giving pain injections so I need to monitor her closely. At the end of the week I'll re-evaluate and decide what's next."

"We need to tell her," Ron said solemnly.

"I suspect she's aware and probably wondering how to tell you boys. Come, let's walk over there together." He stood, putting his hand on Ron's shoulder briefly before turning to leave the office. Ron followed, stifling his emotions.

***

Kat snuggled under the quilt thinking about the conversation with her dad after their visit to the cemetery. She tried to explain to him the turmoil going on inside of her, but even as she spoke her words seemed crazy. *I wanted to carry out the legacy Mary left.* She was a woman determined to leave part of herself to others. Qualities like generosity, compassion, and love. Kat liked to think she'd developed some of those growing up. Her parents taught her to think of others more than herself and to help those in need.

"Legacies have a path but we must choose to follow. Live your own legacy, the one God designed for you," Dad had told her as they lingered at DQ. "That's what Mary was trying to leave with us." *You're right, Dad.*

Her heart no longer wanted to work in advertising, marketing, or event-planning. She thought about Betty's film project and Clay. How did she feel about him? Then, of course, there's Jared, a disturbance threatening her quality of life. She knew her fear must go. *Fear and faith can't exist together in my heart.*

"Help me, Lord. I give You my fear, my future, and faith. Walk with me down the path you've chosen for me. Amen." Kat turned on the bedside lamp, took her journal and pen from the nightstand drawer and sat up. Journaling her jumbled thoughts always seemed to put things in perspective. This was a good time to sort out the words which felt confusing earlier. Somehow, just writing caused her to feel calm and at peace.

Chapter Eight

"It's a good thing I drive a bug," Kat told Rita as they pulled into Dominique's parking lot.

"You're not kidding. There's barely room for a bicycle to park. I appreciate you so much, Kat, for picking me up."

"No problem, I planned to show up anyway."

Rita looked at her watch. "Wow, the kids and their families must have arrived as soon as the doors opened. I'm excited, but hope we don't overrun the place." She laughed nervously.

"At least it's only a party and you don't have to do a presentation. Do you?"

"I just plan to say a few words of appreciation and brag on the kids to all the adults who came. Since we won't start classes again until January, it seems like a good time to wrap things up."

Kat unbuckled her seatbelt and opened the door. "Shall we make a grand entrance?"

"Let's get this show on the road," Rita agreed, as she slipped off her seatbelt and exited the car.

Inside, they located their group. "Why don't you go on in while I check with the manager," she told Kat. "Would you count heads while you're there?"

"Sure, just the kids, or adults too?"

"Just the kids."

"Consider it done," Kat agreed, making her way toward the

clamor of chatty juveniles.

Rita found Mike, the manager, and went over the variety of pizza she wanted. "I'll have a kid's count in just a minute and be paying for those. The adults will take care of their own."

"That works for me. I have two people scheduled to work your party. Terry's here and I expect her helper any time."

"Thanks Mike, I'll try my best to keep the kids in check."

"No problem. That's why we have a party room." He laughed.

Kat approached her friend. "We have nineteen kids to feed," she said, emphasizing the number.

Mike grinned, "Is that all?"

We should have two more, but five pizzas should cover them all with two slices each."

"Great. I think Terry's helper arrived. He'll work with her to get drink orders for now. He's probably already back there."

Rita turned to Kat. "Would you mind holding down the fort a minute? I want to call Ron and get an update on his mom."

"I'll take care of them. I sure hope everything turns out okay for Ron and his family. I've been praying."

"Thanks, I've been too. I'll be right in."

Kat made her way to the back room again; her thoughts on Lillian Davis. She really prayed Ron's mom would make it. As she walked into party central looking for a landing place, she spotted Terry at the front table asking the kids for their drink order. As she moved toward the back, she caught sight of a server talking to a student. Kat approached and the man turned around. She sucked in her breath. Jared!

Kat couldn't believe her eyes. Here she stood an arm's length away from the man who had stalked her since she attended college in San Marcos last year. Her legs threatened to buckle for what seemed an eternity. All these months she lived with the fear of his finding her.

She reached down for the back of a chair at the table occupied by several kids who had stopped talking and stared. Her body wanted to lower itself onto the seat, but Kat refused to budge. Should I say something? Should I run? I can't, my legs won't carry me. Suddenly from deep within she recalled the words, "The Lord is my helper; I will not fear; what can man do to me?" Strength rose up, her legs felt strong, and she released her hold on the chair. Kat watched Jared shift from one foot to the other, an order book clenched tightly in one hand. He didn't seem menacing now. At that moment she realized her stalker hadn't been Jared at all. It was fear.

"I'm not hiding from you anymore." She put one hand firmly on her hip and glared.

It was his turn to take hold of a chair. "I'm sorry, Kat. I never meant...."

"Yes, you did mean to. From the day you slashed my tires at the university, you meant to intimidate me. I don't know why, it really isn't important anymore. Whatever was in your mind about me or us, forget it. I have a life to live and I refuse to cower in fear. I'll pray for you, but I have no desire to have a relationship with you." She turned to face the stunned students and parents; their mouths gaping and eyes bulging.

"Okay, kiddos, let's get this party started. She clapped her hands and chanted over and over, "We want pizza!" as they all joined in.

Jared felt a knot tighten in his stomach. The aroma of hot pizza from the ovens sent him running toward the back. He had to get away from here. His life was in shambles and this job was pointless.

Rita entered the room and joined in the chant with Terry close behind carrying the first round of pizza.

"Good going, you have the kids in the party mood. I should hire you."

She laughed with relief. "I have a great reason to party. You have no idea."

A puzzled look appeared on Rita's face.

"I'll tell you about it on the way home. Did you talk to Ron?"

"Yes, we'll talk about his mom's condition later, too."

***

Brian listened to his wife relate her previous day's encounter with their newest film star, Greta Garson. He was alternately dumbfounded and hysterical with laughter as Betty repeated some of their conversation. He couldn't believe she was actually going to take on this obviously discontented woman and make her the focus of a film.

"Are you convinced she'll allow you to explore her life in front of a camera?"

"Thoroughly. I believe she needs a platform to express her lot in life. She's hostile even where God is concerned and that makes me more determined than ever to work with her."

"She's become your mission?"

"No, she's a woman who needs Jesus and I feel God is going to use me to lead her there."

The look in Betty's eyes convinced Brian of one thing. Ms. Garson didn't have a clue who she was dealing with. He knew the passion his wife had when it came to sharing Jesus with people, and he believed Greta would have her eyes opened before the filming was finished.

"When do you start?"

"Thursday morning. I think Clay and Kat are both free and Greta agreed only if we can be there at eleven sharp. She pointedly told me she would need time to bathe and fix her hair." Betty chuckled, remembering.

"Why is that funny?"

"It's one of those things which might fall under the right-to-privacy acts."

Brian scratched the back of his neck. "Okay, if you say so."

Betty looked at her watch. "When is Kat supposed to be home from the pizza party? It's almost three."

"I think she was going to drop Rita off first. Why?"

Betty removed her favorite red cookbook from the shelf on the kitchen island, and sat on the stool. "I'm just excited about Thursday and wanted to go over things with her. If it's all right with Kat, would you mind if Clay joins us for lunch after church tomorrow?"

"It's fine with me and I don't think she'll mind. He seems to be fond of her."

Betty wondered silently if the feeling was mutual between them. They were friends and dated a few times, but it didn't appear to go any further.

"I'm sure she'll be home soon, or call if they have other plans."

Brian suddenly had an unsettled feeling hit him. I wonder if I should call her. Nah, just an overprotective dad's imagination.

***

Ron and Jake were quiet as they observed Dr. Gonzales go over their mother's chart. They exchanged glances as he hmmm'd and cleared his throat.

"Jake, has she been asleep all the while I've been gone?" the doctor asked.

"Yes, Sir, although she was moving a little."

"Hmmm."

A nurse came into the room and initiated an update with Dr. Gonzales. He authorized new medication and asked for periodic reports throughout the afternoon. As she left, he turned to the boys. "You may as well get something to eat. Your mom will remain asleep for a while. I have your numbers and will text you if anything changes. The new meds will be started and we'll see how it goes. It'll take time before we know if they help. I'm going to reduce the sedation but the main thing is to keep her out of pain and comfortable. Once we have her stable, you'll be able to talk with her."

"Thanks, Doc," the brothers said in tandem.

"You boys have been through a lot. Go eat, get some rest, and trust God."

"She will come around, won't she?" Jake asked with a fearful look on his face.

"Yes, we'll just move slowly." He squeezed Jake's arm in reassurance. "She should be holding a conversation with you later tonight or tomorrow morning." He gave them a small grin before leaving the room.

Neither of the brothers seemed in a rush to eat so they stood, one on either side of her bed and held their mother's hands. Ron began with a prayer and Jake joined in when he finished. Neither was aware of the nurse standing just outside the door, listening and praying along with them.

***

Nurse Heartie, as coworkers lovingly addressed Annie, because of her obsession with Hallmark movies, waited until everyone left

Lillian Davis' room. She approached the bed where moments before, the two sons of this precious lady had stood. Her heart broke listening to the desperate prayers of the young men, pleading for God to intervene and restore their mother.

Why, God? Annie gazed first at Lillian's face, then upward, wondering if God was looking too. She was on duty when Mrs. Davis was brought in by ambulance. Overwhelming commitment by the triage team saved this woman's life. Now, after all the tests and evaluations, the prognosis was bleak. "Why, God?" This time her question echoed in the room. She looked at her patient, cradled her hand and spoke softly.

"Mrs. Davis, I'm sorry you've endured so much pain and discomfort. Your sons were in and prayed over you. When you wake up, they'll be here waiting. Even though I don't understand why this is happening, I think God may have something planned. I'm going to pray He will reveal whatever it is. Maybe it's simply to cause a woman like me to realize real life stories don't always end like a Hallmark movie."

Annie said a silent prayer, and then slipped out to look in on her other patients.

***

Brian shouted, "He was there at Dominique's?" His hands shook holding the mug and sent coffee splashing over the rim. He slammed it on the table.

Betty stood quietly; ready to intervene if her husband became too upset.

"What did he do? Did you call the police?" He followed Kat into the kitchen and watched as she pulled a bottle of water from the fridge and turned to face him. "Well?"

Taking a quick drink of water, she recapped the bottle and leaned against the counter. "Dad, I'm fine. Jared works at the pizza place. I didn't have a clue. I'll admit I was pretty shaken when he turned around and I recognized him."

"Did he do anything? Say anything?"

Kat recounted the scene, assuring her dad she was able to handle it. "I admit I was afraid at first, but then I sensed strength filling me. A Scripture you mentioned yesterday came to mind reminding me not to fear."

Recollection crossed her dad's face so she continued.

"I looked at him and realized he was a mixed-up guy whom Jesus loves as much as me. I promised to pray for him, but communicated there never was and never would be any relationship between us. He left and I joined the party."

Brian hugged his daughter. "I'm so proud of you, and I know God is too. Thankfully, you listened to the inner voice telling you to do the right thing."

She finished her water, placing the bottle in the recycle bin. "I think I'll go upstairs and journal for a while."

"Are you hungry?" Betty interjected, "I have sandwich fixings I can pull together quickly."

"Thanks, but I think I ate a little too much pizza."

Betty winced a little at the pizza overload thought. "But was the party a success? After the drama?"

Kat burst into laughter. "I suppose it was drama. Some of the expressions on the faces of kids and parents supported it. In the end we all enjoyed it and Rita was so gracious, bragging on her students."

Betty hugged her neck. "Then the day turned out well. Oh, would you be open to asking Clay to join us for lunch after church tomorrow?"

"Sure, anything I should know when I ask?"

"We have a new subject for our film. Her name is Greta Garson."

Kat's eyes widened at the name. "Sounds like she's an interesting person."

"You have no idea, my dear, which is why I'd like Clay to come over. I need to prepare both of you for our first meeting."

"That interesting, huh?"

Betty wore a secretive grin as she hummed her way out back to water the plants.

***

A beautiful rendition of "How Great Thou Art" stirred Kat during the morning worship. Wetted eyes reminded her it was her mom's favorite hymn. Pulling a tissue from her bag, she dabbed her eyes. I wonder if Dad remembers. She glanced at him. He sat still, seemingly without emotion as Allen held the final notes, causing many to stand in applause, her family as well.

"Amen," Brian called out before resuming his seat. "Allen did outstanding, don't you think?" he whispered to Kat as the congregation settled down for the sermon.

"It was awesome."

Brian stilled himself, but not without a fleeting memory of his late wife's being there with him. Cassie always cried during this song.

Betty listened attentively to the sermon. The title was "Listen and Observe". Pastor Greg was talking about the ability to understand the needs of others, especially the elderly. There it was, exactly what she searched for in dealing with Greta. The director mentioned Ms. Garson wanted to be heard but thought no one was listening. Betty was happy she took notes and decided to share some of her insight with Kat and Clay this afternoon. While she knew Greta needed a listening ear, there was the observe part which needed to be done. Pastor Greg suggested, when speaking with others, using the phrase, "tell me more", to encourage people to express themselves and open up their lives to others.

Would Greta respond to it...to me? She wouldn't know unless she tried.

***

Home felt good to Rita. When Kat dropped her off yesterday, the first thing she did was kick off her boots, make a cup of Chai tea, and curl up in the overstuffed-chair which welcomed her like an old friend. She rehashed the conversation with Kat about the stalker encounter at Dominique's and was still in shock. Shocked, but highly impressed to realize her friend handled such a volatile situation so well, diffusing what might have ended in a dangerous outcome. Kat seemed at ease all the way home and freer than she'd ever seen her.

Rita busied herself with prepping part of her star sculpture so she could add the blue stones later. Her thoughts were with Ron. I wish I could be with him right now. She knew he was going through a valley, right along with his brother, Jake. She prayed a long time last night, asking God to send comfort and strength to both the guys. Rita hoped Lillian would regain consciousness today and be able to communicate with them. They needed to hear her voice and feel her love surround them. Part of Rita wanted to rent a car and take off for Mesquite. The rational part of her knew they were in God's hands and the Holy Spirit would do the comforting.

Rita couldn't make her mind focus on work. A short walk might clear my head. Stepping outside, the crisp air reminded her it was fall and the holidays would appear in a heartbeat. A flash of orange leaped down from a mesquite tree and landed on all fours in front of her. Startled, she jumped back, only to be followed by an adorable orange-striped cat in a playful mood.

"My, aren't you full of zest. That was some leap of faith you took. It's good you have nine lives." Rita squatted and the bundle of feisty fur wasted no time in making contact. She rubbed and purred, then backed off.

"What? You don't like me now?"

The cat rolled onto its back, then over again before running off.

"Well, that was short. Are you abandoning me?" she called after the feline. Rita decided against the walk and opted instead to sit on her small porch. For some crazy reason, the cat's running away saddened her. She sat on the wicker chair and again, her mother came to mind. She never discovered why her parents drove their mobile home from the property while she was in school, and left her to fend for herself. She closed her eyes and leaned back, feeling a slight breeze, and...what was that foul smell? She opened her eyes and leaned forward abruptly. There at her feet was the spirited cat...with a dead field mouse which she dropped at Rita's feet.

Not wanting to chase this newfound friend away, she rubbed her head between the ears. "No one has ever gifted me a dead mouse before. Thank you." Rita noticed the absence of a collar. "Have you been abandoned, little one?" The four-footed feline stared and tilted her head.

"Would you like to spend the night? It includes supper and breakfast."

The cat looked at Rita, jumped eagerly onto her lap and nuzzled against her arm.

I think I'll name you Pekoe, after the tea. "Let's go inside. I'll make tea and find you a bite to eat. No mice though. I'll take care of your gift later."

***

Nurse Annie sat in the hospital café during her break. Lillian Davis's sons were with her and were anticipating their mother's awakening. It didn't happen Sunday, but Dr. Gonzales assured them she was okay and would soon come out of her sedated state. Those are two dedicated young men. She hoped one day to find a man who had the faith and strength of either of them. Besides being a nurse, all Annie ever wanted was to marry and have babies, lots of them. When she worked in the nursery a few years back, she loved seeing parents cuddling their newborns. It cut her heart out though, when occasionally things didn't go right and a baby didn't make it. She asked to leave the nursery because it hurt to see it end so painfully for parents. Annie wanted a home, strong husband, and healthy children.

She heard voices and turned to see the Davis boys come in. They ordered coffee and looked around for a table. When they saw her, she smiled and motioned for them to come over.

"You're welcome to sit here," Annie said in a warm tone. "I'll be going back on duty in five minutes."

"If you're sure we aren't intruding," Jake spoke up.

"Not at all. Any change with your mom?"

Ron shook his head. "Not so far. They're checking everything and ran us out, but promised to text if she woke up." He laid his phone on the table as he took a seat on Annie's right, while Jake pulled a chair out on her left.

Jake sipped his Pecan-flavored coffee, then carefully set it on the table. He turned to Annie and smiled. "We wanted to thank you for

168

being so kind to our mother. It's helped a lot knowing she has a good nurse watching out for her."

Ron raised his cup in agreement. "Yes, we appreciate you so much."

Annie blushed. "I love what I do, most of the time."

"I don't want to lose my mother." Jake lowered his voice, fearing it would break. "I've lived near her for years and I'm not sure I can handle losing her." There it was, his words ended in a sob.

Ron's eyes closed but not enough to dam up the tears.

Annie tenderly took hold of each boy's hand. "Please allow me to pray for you and your mom."

They nodded silently.

Annie's mature but gentle voice carried her plea for strength upward. "Father in heaven, I ask You to surround these two young men with comfort as they stand by their mom in her time of need. Support them where they are weak and fill them with Your power. Help Lillian's medical team to do their part in her situation. Help them to use the knowledge You've gifted them. Be with sweet Lillian, relieve any pain she may encounter as she wakens. Thank You for what You will do in this family. Amen." When she said, "Amen," both boys found handkerchiefs and tried to compose themselves.

"Thank you," Jake managed to say.

"It was my privilege." She looked at her watch. "I need to get back. Take your time and enjoy your coffee. I'll make sure we contact you if there's news before you return." They both stood as she rose from the table. How polite, their mother taught them well. She waved through the window as she turned into the hallway and headed to the elevator.

***

169

Dr. Gonzales was checking Lillian's vitals when he noticed her eyes fluttering, yet still closed. As he leaned in and whispered her name, she gave a kitten's whimper. He repeated her name and stroked her arm, encouraging his patient to open her eyes..

"Lillian, it's time to wake up. Your sons will be in to see you."

She uttered a few light, grunting noises, moved her head ever so slightly, and with a barely audible voice, called, "Jake." At least Dr. Gonzales thought she said Jake. He patted her hand softly. "Jake will be here very soon. Ron too." He took out his phone and sent a text to Jake.

"Ron," she mouthed.

Annie came into the room and put her hand to her mouth when she saw Lillian's eyes open. She tried to control her excitement and casually moved toward the bedside. "I'll get a wet rag to freshen her face." She went to the restroom and brought back a damp cloth which she used to gently glide over Lillian's face and eyes. "How does that feel?"

Lillian blinked and managed to focus her gaze on the one she knew as Nurse Heartie. "Thank you," she creaked out, "very nice."

Dr. Gonzales checked her over and gave her slender arm a friendly tap, just as her sons spilled into the room.

"She's awake!" they declared, scurrying to one side of the bed, opposite the doctor.

Annie watched from the foot of the bed. Her heart beat loudly as her thank you praise went up silently.

"Mom," Jake spoke first, "we've been waiting and praying. God gave you back to us."

Dr. Gonzales motioned for Annie to follow him and whispered, "Let them have some alone time."

She nodded as they left the men with their mother.

Lillian scanned her sons' faces. Her vision was a bit blurry, but she'd know them anywhere. "I need to tell you both a few things. Can you lean in a little closer?"

Ron carefully repositioned the tubes hanging from the trolley, and stretched down nearer to his mom's face. Jake bent over her legs gingerly and supported himself with his arms.

"I'm sorry I can't talk louder, so listen fast." She smiled, remembering how she used to tell them to sleep fast, when time was short. "I want both of you to move on and enjoy your lives. The Good Lord will soon take me home and I don't want either of you claiming blame." She stopped to get enough strength for another sentence. "I love you." Tears slipped out of the corners of her eyes.

"Mom, no," Ron managed to utter. "We need time. Hang in there. The doctor said he could give you different meds and they might help. Please don't give up. We need you."

Jake could barely stand watching his mother like this. He pulled himself up and went around to the other side of her bed and took her hand. "Our lives won't be the same without you, Mom."

Lillian turned toward him and relaxed her hand in his. "No, it won't be the same. I want you boys to find someone to love. Get married. Have children. Honor me with how you live your life. Create a path of love." She spoke slowly in small spurts between labored breaths.

"We will, Mom, we promise." Ron nodded his head. "We love you so much. You're the best mom a guy could have." His voice broke uncontrollably.

Hearing his brother's words being sobbed out was more than Jake could stand. He removed his hand from his mother's and found the doorway before breaking down. Thankfully he was close to the waiting area and it was empty. Taking a seat, he buried his head in his hands. He sat for what seemed a long time before feeling someone's presence in the chair next to him. He looked up. "Nurse Annie, I'm sorry, I didn't hear you come in."

"Good, I hoped I wouldn't intrude. I saw you rush from your mom's room and felt you needed to be alone. I only wanted to be here in case you needed someone to talk to."

Jake removed his handkerchief from his pocket. He stood to dry his eyes and blow his nose before stuffing it back in his pocket and resuming his seat. "I appreciate your concern. You're such an understanding person."

"Your mom is a sweet lady and I really care about her."

"Thank you, yes, she is. I probably need to get back in there."

"Certainly, but please take this." She handed Jake her card. "If you ever need someone to open up to, please call me."

He looked at her gentle eyes and knew she was sincere. "I appreciate your thoughtfulness." Jake tucked her card into his shirt pocket before moving slowly toward the doorway. He turned. "Annie?"

"Yes?"

He didn't know what he wanted to say. "Thanks," and watched as a soft smile formed on her face. There's something about her....

Jake made his way down the hall, back to his mom's room and was relieved Ron and she were still communicating. Mostly Ron, but her eyes were open and she seemed alert. "Sorry," he said, approaching the bed. "I had to step out for a bit."

"Mom just reminded me of something you should know," Ron said, catching Jake's gaze.

"What?" his voice quivered.

"Tomorrow is their wedding anniversary."

Both sons immediately cast their eyes on Lillian. It seemed she was reliving memories of decades past. They stood quietly watching her eyelids close as she fell asleep.

Ron motioned for Jake to follow him out and when they reached the hallway, he told his brother about a plan for tomorrow. Jake nodded his approval and they left the hospital to gather what was needed before going back to their mom's house for the night.

After arriving, they immediately went to the bedroom closet where his mom kept a box of mementos. He pulled it out and took it to the dining table. Searching through the cards in the cardboard box, he found it. "Ron, here it is, the card I told you about."

Ron took it from his brother's hand and gently opened to the inside. No date. He read the sentiment out loud. "When I found you, I found my soul mate. God knew our love was meant to last into eternity. We're bound in this life and the next. Happy Anniversary. Love, us."

He looked at Jake. "You mean they gave this card back and forth each year?"

"Exactly. She would stand it on the shelf every year. Neither of them signed it."

"Wow, I never knew." Ron stared at the card until Jake provided an envelope to slip it into.

Ron stood there in disbelief. "I can't believe I wasn't aware of this tradition between them."

"Well, you were in San Antonio," Jake said. "It's easy to not notice some things." He hoped Ron didn't get upset with him for saying so, but it was true. He wasn't there very much. Jake picked up his phone,

"I'm gonna order something to eat. What sounds good to you?"

"I mean when we were kids, did they do this then?"

"I'm not sure. But I do remember seeing the card pretty often. Do you want Chinese or Mexican?"

Ron sat down at the table and rubbed his temples. "I don't care, whichever. You know, thinking back, it seems I do remember seeing it next to their wedding picture."

Jake did an online order for tacos, set down his phone and joined his brother at the table. "That's right; we need to take the photo too." He disappeared into Lillian's bedroom and removed the silver framed picture from her dresser, then brought it to Ron.

"Yep, now I can visualize it from childhood." Ron couldn't take his eyes off the images in the frame. They were young, about his age now, and the expressions they wore revealed so much hope for their life ahead. His dad had an arm around Lillian's slender waist, pulling her just a bit toward him. She was beautiful, no wonder Dad fell for her.

"I'll be back in a minute." Ron told his brother. He set the photograph on the table and headed toward the door.

The need to be alone for a bit overtook Ron, so he retreated out back and sat in the glider on the porch. It just hit him. He suddenly realized the depth of love his parents felt for each other. He thought about the pain his mother must have dealt with through the years after losing the only man she ever loved. Ron had assumed she gradually got over his dad's death and was able to move forward. Now he felt sure she carried the pain like the bottom of an iceberg, unseen. He finally understood what she meant when she asked them to create a path of love. It was her legacy to them. I will, Mom, I promise.

***

Nurse Annie had received a call last night from Lillian's son, Jake, explaining what he and his brother wanted to do. She agreed to help, so on her way to work she picked up a few balloons, then stashed them in the closet. After arriving, she gathered markers and poster board to make a sign. Annie was so excited; you'd have thought the party was for her. It would be an unusual day to say the least. She informed the other nurses and, of course, Dr. Gonzales. Everyone was giving Lillian extra attention to make sure she was up to the surprise.

"How are you feeling this morning, Mrs. Davis?" Annie inquired when she checked her vitals.

Lillian mumbled something indistinguishable so Annie leaned closer. "Are you in pain?"

"No. It's my anniversary," she managed to say.

"How many years?"

"Fifty. We're going to celebrate tonight," she said.

Annie changed out the saline bag. I wonder if Lillian heard about their plans.

"Well in that case, you better rest. Your sons will be here in a little while." Her words went unheard. Annie glanced at Lillian and noticed she was asleep, wearing a little smile. The nurse in her automatically checked for a pulse. It was there. Weak, but there. She tucked the blanket around her patient, then went to enter her information into the computer. It was almost noon, so Jake and his brother should arrive shortly.

***

In the waiting area down the hall from Lillian's room, Ron and Jake welcomed their mom's pastor, her deacon and his wife, Sue.

"It's good of you to come," Ron expressed, giving them each a slight hug.

175

Pastor Bill pressed his palms to his heart. "We care deeply for your mother and remember well the love she and Al had before he passed. This is a wonderful day to celebrate their fiftieth wedding anniversary. Thank you, boys," he continued, looking at both sons, "for inviting us to be here."

Jake busied himself with his camera, not wanting to deal with emotional greetings at the moment. He simply nodded in the pastor's direction.

Sue took a seat in the corner and reminded her husband, Tommy, to turn off his phone. They both looked up as several church members filed into the room, exchanging hugs and expressions of their friendship. Just like Sue, the women came bearing cards which a nurse placed in a basket on a table near the door.

"If I might have your attention for a minute," Ron addressed the group, "I'm going to check on our mother and prepare her for this somewhat impromptu party. She has no idea friends have come to help her celebrate their golden anniversary. I don't want it to shock her." He gave a small smile.

Dr. Gonzales entered the room and was surprised at the large group. He took Ron and Jake aside and briefly explained it would be better to only take in only two people at a time. "She'll tire very quickly."

The boys agreed. Jake suddenly had an idea. "Would all of you gather toward the back of the room where Sue is sitting, please? I'd like to take a group picture so Mom can see how many friends came."

They followed instructions quickly. Nurse Annie, who had been at the doorway, took the overflowing basket of cards and set it in front of the group. Jake took several photos.

***

Annie arranged the mementos the guys brought – the anniversary card and wedding photo – as Lillian slept, then slipped out to the waiting area to find Jake. Catching his eye, she whispered, "I'll go back and see if she's awake. Give me few minutes."

"Okay. I'll have Ron bring her pastor in first," Jake agreed. He cornered his brother to go over the plan. "I'll wait a few minutes before bringing in Tommy and Sue."

Ron, Bill and the doctor found Lillian in good spirits. She blinked at seeing her beloved pastor there. "Pastor, you certainly know what this day is," she smiled. "You married us."

"I did indeed, Mrs. Davis. Happy Anniversary," he congratulated as he leaned down for a tender hug.

Jake hovered at the door with Tommy and Sue close by, so Pastor Bill said his goodbyes to allow time for the deacon and his wife.

"Hi, Lillian," Sue spoke in a soft voice. She reached into her handbag and brought out a tiny bottle of perfume. "Here's the perfume you once mentioned Al bought for you." She held it up so Lillian could see the White Shoulders label.

"Be a dear and dab a bit on my temple."

Sue looked at Jake for approval and seeing him nod, she accommodated Lillian's request.

"Just as I remember," Lillian whimpered a little. A path of tears rolled down her cheeks. "Thank you, Sue. It was very thoughtful. You know this is our fiftieth anniversary?"

"Yes, and I'm happy we were able to come celebrate with you. Get some rest now." She blew pretend kisses toward Lillian and they followed Jake to the waiting area.

Two by two, friends came and left, each sharing a memory of the couple and expressed thanks for being invited. Jake had taken many candid photos in the process of people coming and going until no one was left but him and Ron.

Lillian looked at the two of them standing at the foot of her bed, blocking the table from her view. "Mom," Ron began, "we wanted to make this day special for you...."

"And your dad," she added.

"For you and Dad," he continued. The boys parted to reveal the display Nurse Annie had arranged and rolled in to surprise her. A small vase containing two roses, one red and one white, sat on one side. Two gold balloons, one on each side of the table, framed Lillian's personal items. Lillian saw her wedding photo and the card. She inhaled too quickly and began to cough. The boys quickly assisted her, but she waved them off. She managed to control her breathing, but her hands were shaking. The smell of White Shoulders swept her back in time.

"Hand me the card, please."

Jake grabbed it and placed the white paper between her fingers. She held the memory up and moved it slowly across her lips. "Happy Anniversary, Us," she whispered. "May I have the wedding picture?"

Ron reached and brought it closer. "You look radiant here," he commented as she stared. "Dad was quite the man in that tux."

"He was quite the man, period!" she corrected.

Nurse Annie quietly entered. Hearing Lillian cough, she wanted to make sure she was okay. "You must be tired," she spoke soothingly. "How about resting a little and you can visit more later?"

"I'd like that. We're going to celebrate later. I'll rest now." She hugged the photo and card, closed her eyes and drifted.

The guys returned to the waiting area. "Did everyone get some cake and coffee?"

"Sure did," Tommy spoke up. "It's the best I've had in a while."

Sue rolled her eyes. "That's what you said at potluck Wednesday night."

Everyone laughed and then inquired about Lillian.

"She's taking a nap. I know seeing y'all here today pleased her. She thinks there'll be another celebration tonight so she wanted to rest up. Obviously there won't be, but thanks for coming. Your presence has meant so much to her, Jake and me."

Hugs and goodbyes taken care of, they left and the room was quiet. The boys plopped down on the sofa, neither of them saying much.

"I think it turned out good," Jake pondered. "So why do I feel as though something's off?"

Ron turned and stared at his brother. "I have that same feeling."

***

"Al, can you believe we made it to our fiftieth anniversary?"

"Yes, my love, our golden one. But they've all been golden to me."

"Did you enjoy the party earlier?"

"It was great seeing the boys and all our friends."

"Good. Now it's our turn to really celebrate. Being with Jesus is the very best celebration we could ever have. I've missed you, Al."

"I've missed you, too. You sure smell nice."

She smiled. "White Shoulders, remember?"

"How could I forget?"

She felt him slip his arm around her pencil waist, and kiss her lightly on the cheek, as together they explored their new home. Together forever.

***

Ron and Jake had drifted off in the waiting room. Annie whispered just enough to wake them. "You should come," she encouraged.

They followed her to Lillian's room where she slept peacefully with her wedding photo and card held to her chest. On her face was the biggest smile. Not a grin, but a full smile. The boys looked at each other, realization settling in.

"She's gone, isn't she?" Ron asked in a crackling voice.

Annie could barely say the words. "She went to a bigger celebration."

Jake stepped closer removing the photo and card from his mother's grasp. "She doesn't need this now, she has the real thing." He brushed his fingers across her cheek, then kissed her.

Ron pressed his face lightly against Lillian's. "I'm making a path, Mom. A legacy of love."

Chapter Nine

Betty pulled into the parking lot at Mt. Laurel Assisted Living. She scanned the area to see if Kat's VW was anywhere in sight. She'll be here soon, I'm sure. Betty was excited and nervous at the same time. Waiting for Thursday to arrive seemed to take forever, but here she was, ready to greet Ms. Greta Garson and begin her story. The phrase her pastor suggested in last week's sermon, tell me more, drummed in her head. She hoped to get inside Greta's heart and help the truth come out. What truth? The truth she covers up with hostile words and actions perhaps.

Kat's silly VW horn startled Betty. Turning to look, she watched Kat give her a goofy grin, hop out of her car and tap on Betty's window. "Come on, Movie Producer, we have a show to do."

Betty undid her seatbelt, gathered her tote bag and notes, and left her car. Together they laughed at Kat's Hollywood mood. "You're certainly in a different frame of mind," Betty commented. "By the way, where's Clay? I thought you two would ride together."

Settling back into her own persona, Kat hooked one arm around her step-mom's. "He'll be along shortly. He had something to do first, but promised to be here by eleven."

They reached the door and entered the facility.

"Be sweet," she said, giving Kat a friendly warning, then added, "even if she's not."

Kat's eyes widened a bit. "I promise to be on good

behavior...especially if she's not."

They headed down the hall to the other section where Greta's room was located. Betty looked at her watch. "It's just 10:45," she whispered. "We need to wait. She told me eleven sharp."

Kat glanced around. "I'll walk back to the lobby and see if Clay is here."

"Good idea," Betty agreed, as her step-daughter scurried away. *She's such a sweet young woman. I wish she were really my daughter.* Betty always felt a bit of sadness in knowing at this stage in her life she would never have a biological child. *Brian was blessed with a wonderful marriage and lovely daughter before his wife was killed in the car wreck. Although Kat was like a daughter to Betty, there was always the knowledge she wasn't really hers. I understand how Lane and Sheila feel since their only son died, and she not being able to conceive anymore.*

Betty stared out the window overlooking the garden. A few residents sat on a bench or in a wheelchair, talking with their visitors. *At least they have someone who cares enough to spend time with them.* She sighed, thoughts going back to Greta. *Mr. Cavanaugh said she hasn't had any visitors except professionals trying to help her.* Voices from the hallway broke her reverie.

Kat and Clay approached quietly, camera in tow. Betty looked at the time. She chuckled, "Just under the wire. It's 10:58. Let's see if our star is ready."

They walked the short distance, knocked gently, then waited for a response. The door opened and the trio stood in shock. Standing elegantly, one hand resting on the door edge, was Greta, reinvented, dressed as if she'd stepped out of a silent film. Three mouths collectively dropped open. Betty had a sudden vision of Gloria

Swanson waiting for her Sunset Boulevard close-up and let out a gasp. "Ms. Garson, you look..." she paused for the right word, "amazing."

Greta lowered her eyes just a smidgen. "Thank you, dahling, I'm ready to be seen."

Betty was certain she had seen the movie. "Let's get started then," she agreed, and they entered Greta's room. Surprise greeted her again as she noticed things cleaned up, and the absence of the smell she had encountered the first time she visited.

She introduced Greta to Clay and Kat, and watched the expression on their faces as Greta looked them up and down, especially Clay, as he extended his hand.

"I'm very pleased to meet you, Ma'am."

Greta slowly lifted her hand allowing him to grasp it. A nod of her head was all she offered.

Kat's gaze took in the old-fashioned pearls adorning her neck. "I love your necklace."

Greta dropped her hand from Clay's and looked at Kat while caressing the antique beads. "They belonged to my mother." She turned back to Clay. "Where would you like me to perform?" Greta inquired, quite seriously.

Clay pulled out a chair for her. "Let's have you sit by the desk. The lighting will be better."

She seated herself, feigning royalty. "Thank you, young man."

Betty exhaled and tried to move things along. She found a chair and positioned it near Greta. "Let's do some preliminary work first, before the camera starts rolling. I'd like to just cover some brief guidelines for our discussion. This way you'll know what we want to portray in the film. Clay will start filming and I'd like you to relax and be yourself."

"I guess you don't want me to cuss."

Betty grinned. "If you should slip, we can edit it out. I'd like to get to know the Greta deep down inside. Would you like to tell us more about your mother?"

Greta was quiet, touching her necklace, pondering her thoughts. "My mother lost everything and I inherited her bad luck. She lost her husband, children, all except me of course, and her life." Her voice raised an octave. "I lost a husband prospect, was denied children, and now I wonder if I'm dead and just don't know it."

Deafening silence. Betty had, it seemed, opened a Pandora's box and watched Greta's elegance fade. She remembered her pastor's sermon and the next words she spoke echoed his. "I hear what you're saying, Greta. Tell me more about your mother, special things you remember about her."

***

A waitress shuffled quickly around her section, taking orders, bringing plates of fajitas, sizzling loud enough to be heard in the parking lot.

"She must be exhausted," Kat commented.

Clay looked up from checking his phone. "Who?"

"The woman working this section, she looks wiped out."

He glanced at the booth across from where he and Kat were sitting. "Probably, but she smiles at everyone."

Kat ignored his comment, scanned her menu, then set it aside.

"Good evening, my name is Delores," the matronly woman said cheerfully as she approached their table, "but everyone calls me Dori. What can I bring you?"

Kat noticed the genuine smile she wore. "Hi, Dori, I'd like two puffy tacos, no onions please."

"You'll love 'em, they're Hank's specialty." Turning to Clay, she inquired, "Have you decided on something?"

"Yes Ma'am, I'd like the La Fiesta plate."

"Another great choice. Onions?" She gave a slight wink toward Kat.

Clay stifled a laugh. "Yes, and lots of them."

Dori eyed him first, then looked again at Kat. "Whatever the man wants," she said in her sweet-tea voice. She circled around checking on customers, and finally made her way toward the kitchen.

Kat tried not to laugh, but it came out sounding somewhat like a snort.

"Stop it," Clay whispered, "you'll have me doing it too."

"I can't help it," she said. By now she was holding her rib cage. "Shame on you for eating onions with your date, or so she thinks."

Clay grew serious. "Isn't this a date?"

"Kinda, but not a date, date." She stopped laughing. "I'm sorry; it was just the look she gave you."

"Kat, I love working on this film project with you and your mom, uh, step-mom, but I enjoy just being with you."

The look on his face touched Kat deeply. A lump in her throat kept her from speaking right then. She took a sip of water. "I always look forward to time spent with you, Clay. We've both been busy with school, church, and the film...."

"Maybe too busy?" he broke in.

What do I say? Kat hesitated. "I've been through a lot recently, Clay. My head is still spinning from last weekend's drama. I do enjoy being with you, but..."

Dori appeared seemingly out of nowhere with their dinners. "Here you go," she said, placing Kat's puffy tacos in front of her. "No onions, my dear." She set Clay's platter down, reminding him it was mucho hot. "I brought your onions in a separate dish in case you decide you'd rather pass." She set the raw onions over to the side and winked at Kat. "Can I get you anything else?"

"No, we're fine, Dori." Clay assured her. "And thanks for the onions on the side. That was thoughtful."

Dori left before the couple once again burst out in laughter.

***

Gus left his mother's house with a twinge of uneasiness and walked to his truck. Did I do the right thing? Will Jared go along with it? "It's too late now," he confided to a young squirrel near the pecan tree. The rodent flicked his tail, defending his right to the pecans scattered about. Gus paused, stared at the nut gatherer and smiled. "Guess I need to let you know, I'm the new owner here and I have plans for those nuts." The squirrel stuffed a nearby pecan in his mouth, and looked at Gus daringly before scurrying up the tree.

Back in the truck, he glanced at the house for which he had just signed the papers of ownership for. His mother and step-dad bought a home in the King William Area, and didn't want to let this one go to strangers. They asked – he bought. Stole would be a better term. Of course, there was one small catch. They insisted Jared share the home. Now, the real sale would have to happen; getting Jared on board with moving. In his situation right now, having quit his job, and distraught about that girl, Kat, it seemed the best time to approach him. Gus placed a call.

"Hey, little brother, can you come by the shop? I want to discuss something with you."

"I guess, when?"

"I'm heading there now; see you in about fifteen minutes?"

"Okay," Jared agreed, "What's going on? It's a work day. Business slow?"

"No, Charles is handling it for the moment. I won't keep you long."

"Oh?"

"I'll explain when I see you."

Jared disconnected from the call and pulled a muscle shirt over his head. Nothing better to do, might as well go see Gus. He locked his apartment and checked his mail downstairs. Just one piece of mail and he didn't want it right now, his lease payment. I wonder how long I'll be able to even pay rent. He stuffed the envelope in his back pocket, head down, and scraped along to his car.

***

Gus sat in his cluttered office when he spotted the familiar Dodge Charger bump through the yard. The chug holes left after a recent rain made it hard to maneuver around out there. His brother parked and sluggishly pulled himself from the vehicle. He looks pathetic. That mess with the college gal did a number on him.

"Hi," Jared mumbled coming in the door.

"Glad you could make it. I've got some news to share and a proposition for you."

Jared's eyes narrowed suspiciously at his half-brother. "This sounds like some kind of intervention thing."

Gus laughed. "Sit down. No intervention going on. This is something great which should appeal to you, but it'll only work if you're in all the way."

"You've got my attention," Jared said, slowly sitting on the edge of the stained oak chair.

***

Rita busied herself with packing her spinner suitcase. She held an ache in her heart for Ron and his brother, knowing they faced a painful task of putting their mother's funeral together. She told Ron she'd be there in the morning and wouldn't take no for an answer. He needed her. At least in Rita's mind he did. More than anything, she wanted to be by his side and help if necessary, but really for moral support. The lump in her throat refused to leave and a shaky feeling came over her. Pekoe brushed against Rita, doing a figure eight around her legs. She sat on the sofa and took her new friend into her arms. Stroking the striped orange fur, she remembered her dream last night. Crazy memories of her own mother who abandoned her when she was in her teens. Ron's mom never did anything like that. She had a mental picture of her mother lying in a hospital bed, dying, and Rita saying, "I love you. I forgive you."

Rita was relieved Kat was willing to stay at her place and look after Pekoe while she was in Mesquite.

"Girlfriend," Kat called from the kitchen, "did you pack some Chai?"

"Yeah, a whole box."

Kat poked her head around the corner. "You sound sad."

"I miss my mom." What am I saying? Why would I miss the woman who abandoned me?

Kat came into the living-room and saw the downcast look on Rita's face. "I totally understand."

"No, I don't even understand it. Ron's mother passed away last night, and I'm missing mine? It doesn't make sense. You know the trauma I went through in my childhood."

"First of all, Rita, I'm sorry to hear Ron lost his mother. I'll be praying for him and Jake. Second, your mom is still your mom, so of course you miss her. The past doesn't and will never change that."

Rita managed a tiny smile as Pekoe purred in her lap. She was grateful for this kitten from heaven and Kat's friendship. "Thanks," she uttered when she found her shaky voice. "You're a good friend."

"It's what friends do. They listen with their heart and mine hears your pain."

"I think furball and I will turn in. It's been a long day. I hope you're comfy on the pull-out."

Kat reached out and scratched Pekoe's ears. "I'll be fine. We'll be fine, won't we? Kat will take good care of the cat." She chuckled at her own joke.

Pekoe gave Rita's house-guest a meow before laying her head back down. Kat laughed. "You both get some sleep. I'll have tea ready in the morning."

"Thanks," Rita said as she stood cradling her new family feline. "I'll probably be out in a wink once my head hits the pillow."

"I'll say a pillow prayer as soon as my head hits one."

Rita smiled at the vision of Kat praying as she drifted off. "Goodnight."

***

Seth Gardley hung up the phone and couldn't wait to find his bride and share the good news. The house Mary Ludwig left to him after the estate sale last year, finally sold. The realtor, Lane Jennings, lived next door to Mary and knew the house well. He was able to find the perfect buyer, a Mr. and Mrs. Orlov. The King William District in San Antonio was highly sought after, and Mary's home was in great condition. Lane said there'd been many viewings and offers, but this was the best.

Emily walked into the study. "Who was on the phone?"

"You'll never guess," he teased. "Go ahead, guess!"

She looked up, placed her finger under her chin and rolled her eyes. "Hmmm, your secretary in San Antonio, telling you to leave England and return there immediately?"

Seth laughed. "No. Guess again."

She sighed heavily, pretending impatience. "Was it Brian saying they want us to come earlier for Thanksgiving?"

He chuckled and put his hands on her shoulders. "No, silly girl. It was Lane."

Emily stared at him. "And?"

"He found a buyer for Mary's house, and they're paying the asking price."

She threw her arms around him. "Oh, Seth, that's wonderful. Now we can make changes to this place like we planned. When do we leave to take care of the paperwork?"

Seth loved seeing her excitement and knew she was a bit homesick for Texas. They both loved living in the English cottage Mary left to Emily here in Essex, but she was a Texas girl, after all.

"Calm down." He patted her on the back, then gave her a squeeze. "Lane said there were a few things the buyer would like done, so he's working on it. Once he gets everything on paper, he'll contact me and then we can make the trip. I'm guessing two weeks."

"Oh my goodness, I need to get busy." She released her husband and scurried out to make her list. At the door to the study, she paused, then turned around. "It'll be so wonderful seeing all our friends again."

"It will for sure. Plus, I can check in at the office and make sure no one has deserted," he joked.

Seth loved living in Essex. He had the best of both worlds. His law practice in Texas ran smoothly via teleconferences, internet service, and great staff. It enabled Seth to devote himself to his bride of just four months. She deserved his undivided attention. But, he also realized his career needed attention as well. Going back to San Antonio for the holidays was planned, but if they go early, he could get in work time while Emily caught up with friends. Yes, the best of both worlds. He decided to call Brian and give him a heads up on their early arrival. Besides, he wanted to see how married life was treating him.

***

Brian pulled into the driveway and pressed the remote for the garage door just as his phone rang. "Hello," he answered, looking at the caller ID. "Seth, how are you? How's Emily?"

"We're fantastic. I just got word my house in the King William District finally sold. Lane called to see if we might be able to come back earlier."

"I hope you told him yes."

"I knew if I didn't, my Bubble and Squeak breakfast would burst and scream," Seth quipped.

Brian laughed. "When will y'all get here?"

"Emily's making flight plans as we speak, but probably two weeks."

"I'll let Betty know; she'll be bubbling and squeaking. Congratulations on the sale. Do you know who the buyer is?"

"Some couple by the name of Orlov. Victor Orlov, I believe."

Brian was quiet.

"You there, Brian?"

"I'm here. Did you say their name was Orlov?"

"Yeah, why? Do you know them?"

"No, I don't think so. It's just an unusual name."

"It is," Seth agreed, "I don't recall hearing it before. Anyway, I'm sure Emily will let Betty know as soon as she has our flight scheduled."

"Okay, my friend. See ya soon."

As Brian ended the call he shook his head in disbelief. No way could they be related. He wouldn't say anything about it to Kat until he knew more. Maybe he'd give Lane a call. He needed to talk to him and Sheila anyway to fill them in on Thanksgiving Dinner plans. It would be great to see everyone from the estate sale group. Brian liked getting together with them on Thanksgiving as they did last year. It was a perfect time to share what's been happening and see how Mary's legacy is being carried forward.

He pulled the car into the garage, exited his vehicle and pressed the remote to close the overhead door. He smelled pot roast. On cue, his stomach growled. Betty must be home.

***

Betty heard the garage door close, and turned to see her husband come through the connecting door. "Brian, you're home." She set the spoon down and greeted him with a kiss. "I hope your day was stress-less," she said happily.

He plopped his briefcase on the breakfast bar and gave Betty a warm hug.

"It wasn't so bad. I finished the contract we've been fighting over all week, and it's ready to turn in Monday. How did things go with Ms. Garson?"

"It was great and mysterious at the same time."

"It must have gone well, you're smiling."

"Better than well," she said, handing him a glass of tea.

Brian inhaled the robust aroma coming from the crockpot and was about to lift the lid. "I'm starving, how long before we can dive into this?"

Betty put a warning hand on his arm. "Get your hand off the lid. It's not quite ready. Go take your shower and I'll finish getting dinner on the table. I'm dying to tell you about our meeting with Greta, so hurry."

"Okay, okay," he said, heeding her advice. "I've got some news to share with you too."

"Oh? What about?"

He kissed the tip of her nose. "I'm not spilling the beans until I get a bite of pot roast."

Betty gave him a playful pinch before he headed upstairs. "Go," she said, moving quickly before he returned pinches.

***

Rita turned off the Interstate and after a few twists and a u-ey, she found Anchor Street. Half-way down she spotted Ron's Jeep, pulled to the curb and shut the car off. She inhaled, and then breathed out slowly, allowing her body to relax. Rita wasn't sure how this trip would go, but the Lord rode with her and together they made it safely. She looked at the frame house, small and inviting. She wondered if the guys would sell it. This was going to be a difficult time in their lives, having to go through their mom's things and make decisions no child wants to make. They loved their mother dearly.

Rita never had much to deal with when her mother passed away. There wasn't anything of value. The old mobile home had long since disappeared, of that she was glad, even though she never knew the details. Her mother lived in an apartment until she became ill. Rita could still remember the grotesque way her mouth curled up after the stroke. She seemed to be taunting Rita, although she knew it couldn't be helped. The image stayed in her mind for years. The ache she had for her mother did too.

Rita looked up to see Ron approaching the car and the look on his face endeared him to her. She opened the door and was gathered into his arms almost before she could remove her seatbelt.

"I've missed you so much," he said with a husky voice.

"Oh, Ron," was all she could say.

His face buried in her neck, they stood in silence, half leaning against the car. He finally stood back a bit and looked into her eyes. "I'm glad you're here but I'm sorry you had so far to drive."

"It wasn't bad. No problems until I exited, but my GPS sorted me out."

"Let's go in. Jake fixed spaghetti. Are you hungry?"

"A little, I didn't stop except to stretch my legs and grab a Coke."

They walked side by side into the house and immediately Rita felt like she was intruding on Lillian's space, or her memories here. She did a quick intake of breath and took hold of Ron's arm. Lillian's lap robe lay at the end of the sofa, her wedding photo was on the coffee table, and a Bible sat next to it.

Rita looked quickly at Ron. His eyes were rimmed red, and his face withdrawn. Her heart broke.

Jake came in from the kitchen and welcomed Rita. She shook his hand, then hugged, not quite sure which to do.

"I'm so sorry, Jake. I know things are difficult right now. I'd like to help in any way I can. If either of you need me to make calls, arrange details, or cook, I'm available."

The brothers thanked her in unison.

"Spaghetti's hot and I'm sure the bread is too. Let's eat and then we can talk."

***

Betty curled up next to Brian on the sofa. He was the perfect husband, at least from her perspective. A man who worked hard all day, possessed a wonderful sense of humor, and was so romantic. All this and helped clean the kitchen after dinner. She lifted her head and gave him a warm kiss.

"Mmm, what did I do to deserve such treatment?"

"You married me." She sat up and poked him gently in the ribs. "Now, what's the news you have to share?"

"Oh no, you're gonna tell me about Greta first."

Betty began her replay of the filming, starting with yesterday. "Remember I said she told me to come back alone today?"

"Yeah, that was odd."

"Not for Greta." She laughed.

"True. Why did she want you to see her alone without Kat and Clay?"

Betty became serious. "Wait here." She slid off the sofa and retrieved an item from her handbag. Returning to the living room, she sat on a chair across from Brian. Betty held a small notebook tenderly in her hands.

"This, dear husband, is why."

He still didn't get it. He held both hands out as if waiting for her to throw it to him.

Shaking her head, she spoke two words. "Her journal."

"What? She kept a journal? How far back?"

"Brian, she poured out the pain of losing her father onto the pages I'm holding."

"What possessed her to allow you to have it?"

Betty had asked herself the same question all the way home. "I don't know. I think in a way, she's been waiting all these years for someone, anyone, to come along who would listen to her. Someone who expressed an interest in who she really is."

"And God sent you," Brian said softly.

Betty hugged the book to her chest, feeling her own heartbeat underneath. "I'm going to be her friend. I am her friend."

"Can you share any of it with me?"

"Not yet. I promised I'd read it before we meet next Tuesday. She wants me to visit her then and we'll decide what, if any, she'll allow me to use in the film."

Brian nodded his head. "That's best."

"Okay, I told you about Greta so it's your turn. What news are you sitting on?"

"Seth called as I pulled into the driveway."

Betty brightened up. "When are they coming?"

"In about two weeks. He said Lane called to tell him the house in King William District sold, and Seth would need to sign papers and stuff."

"Two weeks?" Betty made mental notes of things to do before their friends arrived. "That is exciting news. You could have told me that in the beginning."

Brian hugged his wife. "I enjoy watching you try to fish things out of me."

"You're so bad," she said, giving him a playful pout.

"Guilty as charged," he confessed, raising both arms above his head.

She smiled meekly. "If you don't mind, I'm going upstairs to read a little."

He stood, moved close, and lightly brushed his hand against her hair. "You go ahead, I'll be up later." He bent and left a kiss on the top of her head.

***

Settling into the wing-back chair in the corner of her bedroom, Betty opened the fragile cover of Greta's journal. The curled edges and time-stained pages pulled her into details of the story Greta shared the previous day. She gave up memories about her mother's illness and passing. When mention of her father came around, Greta couldn't continue. Instead, she reluctantly removed the journal from its hiding place and handed it to Betty.

"My memories of him are here," she indicated, patting the tattered bundle.

Betty was dumbfounded at being trusted with such private information, so she questioned Greta about allowing her to read it. She responded firmly.

"If you wanna know who I am on the inside, readin' this is the only way to find out."

Betty wanted to hug the feisty woman, but sensed it would be rejected. Instead, she simply thanked her before leaving. Once in her car, it was all she could do to not sit and read before exiting the parking lot. The pages seemed to call her name during the drive home.

Now, here she sat with nothing to stop her perusal of the person Greta couldn't speak about. The first page was titled generically: sickness. It played out how she viewed her parents going through her mother's illness. Several pages in, Betty found insightful entries which illuminated Greta's disillusionment because of the indifference her dad displayed concerning his wife's health. One sentence read,

"Mother's coughing always drives him to leave for a spell. Why? How does love abandon during such time?" Another similar entry expressed her doubt about God. "Will God allow father to abandon me if I get sick?"

Betty stopped reading and sighed. She tried to picture Greta as a young lady, being witness to her father's lack of compassion for his dying wife. Was it truly lack of compassion? Could fear have caused her father's separation from the woman he loved? Greta's view of it grew seeds of doubt and animosity in her. She loved her father, but couldn't understand his actions. In time, those seeds matured and became her view of God as her heavenly Father. Would He abandon her? No, Greta, no. His love and watchful care is forever.

Betty closed the journal for the time being and shut her eyes. "Lord, Your daughter, Greta, needs You desperately. She's not a young woman anymore and her time here may not be long. Speak love and compassion into her spirit. Help her understand the difference between the love of her earthly father and You. Allow her to feel Your presence as You draw her near. Amen."

Voices drifted upstairs, letting her know Kat was home. Betty placed the journal in a drawer and glanced at the couple in a picture frame on top of the dresser. "Thank you, God, for my parents and the way they lived their lives as an example of Your love."

**

Sheila Jennings finished cleaning the kitchen, started the dishwasher, and took her cup of tea into the living room to join her husband. She guessed Lane had been waiting to talk, but he knew her obsession about not leaving a dirty kitchen. She set the cup on the antique table in front of the sofa and tucked herself easily next to him.

"The kitchen has been put to bed for the night," she said

lightheartedly.

He patted her thigh without looking at her. "Mmm, that's good," he said, continuing to read the papers he held.

"Did anyone call you today?"

"Hmm?"

"Lane," she said, taking hold of his chin with her hand, and turning his face toward hers. "Are you present?"

He grinned, taking hold of her hand. "Sorry, I was reading some of this stuff the Orlov's want included in the sale of Mary's house. I explained about the historical restrictions of the King William District, and I don't think they get it."

"Please, put the paperwork down so we can talk."

He placed the sheets on the side table, retrieved his lukewarm coffee, and peered at her over the edge of the mug. "No, I haven't heard anything from the adoption agency." Immediately he saw the smile on his wife's face disappear. He squeezed her hand gently. "We could get a call any day. We have to keep trusting."

"I know, it's just, well, I've had this feeling, and we've put so much work into converting David's room into a nursery."

"Shush," he whispered, putting two fingers to her lips. "We've done our part and now it's up to God. His timing is always right."

"Yes, but...."

"No buts. We wait with hope." Lane set his coffee mug down and pulled her close. "We'll have our baby when the time is perfect, and not until." Please, Lord, let it be soon.

"I've been thinking about something," Sheila confided.

"Oh? What's going on in that lovely head of yours?"

Sheila hesitated a moment. "This is just an idea I've been mulling around in my lovely head. Tell me what you think."

Lane tapped his wife's head softly. "Tell me."

"What would you think about our becoming foster parents?" There, she said it. Holding the thought back had been gnawing at her. She'd been afraid to give up on her dream of adopting a baby, but then after spending time with the Lord, she realized she and Lane had so much to offer children, not the least of which was an enormous amount of love.

Lane looked at his wife in amazement. "Honey, that's an outstanding idea. It would bring a child and us so much happiness. We're in a perfect position to make a safe and loving life for a child. Why don't we visit with the adoption agency and get some direction on how to go about it?"

Sheila's heart filled with joy at Lane's response. She'd been afraid he had his heart set on adoption. She smiled and nodded, holding back tears. "I'll call tomorrow and make an appointment. By the way, Betty Hills called me today."

"I bet she filled you in on Emily and Seth," Lane said, switching gears mentally from babies to England.

Sheila cradled her china cup and sipped the hot brew. "We talked about Thanksgiving dinner and she said there'd be at least one guest, maybe two, from outside our estate sale group."

"Did she say who?"

"A gentleman at an assisted living place will come, and possibly an elderly woman from the same home."

"That's a surprise."

"I thought so, too, but all she said is it was a long story, then laughed. I asked if she had heard from the Moreno's yet, but there hasn't been any communication since last month."

"Are Blanca and Bree still on the mission trip in Mexico?"

"I suppose. I hope they're able to come for the holiday. I'd love to see them and catch up with what they've been doing."

Lane remembered the tragic accident which took Carlos, Blanca's husband, last year. She and her daughter had mountains to deal with. Bree was never able to know her father and then he was killed. Everyone was surprised when Blanca took a leave of absence to go with Bree on a mission trip. Maybe it was therapy for both of them.

"I just had an idea," Lane said suddenly.

"What?"

"Let's go on a short mission trip."

"What? When?"

"After we talk to the adoption agency and figure out our next steps."

"Where would you want to go?"

"We can check with the pastor and find out when and where the next mission trip will be."

"Well, maybe, it might be interesting. I'd like it to have something to do with children."

"I'm sure there'll be options in that area." Lane clicked the remote. "Want to watch that Alaska show on television?"

Sheila giggled, "You want a mission trip there?"

"Might be fun," he teased, sitting back. He slipped his arm around his wife's shoulders. "We could snuggle close in an igloo."

"You're a realtor, see if there's one on the market," she laughed.

"I'll do my best," he boasted.

"David would have loved the thought of being in Alaska," she said.

They sat quietly, each holding private thoughts of their deceased son, as they watched a grizzly move through the cover of snow-laden trees.

***

"So," Jared said slowly, "let me get this straight. If I'm hearing you right, my parents just signed over their house to you, my half-brother, on the condition that I move in with you?"

Gus thought for a moment. "When you put it like that, I guess so. But, they aren't giving it to me. I'm paying for it. They want to move but don't like the idea of total strangers moving in."

"Why wasn't I involved in the decision-making from the start? I mean, since I seem to be the weak link here." Jared flopped back in the chair, balancing it precariously on the two rear legs.

"They approached me first to see if I was interested. If I said no, it wouldn't have gone any further."

"I suppose our mother figured I couldn't afford to buy it," Jared said sarcastically.

Gus ignored the tone. "She knew you wouldn't be able to get financing, that's all. They both want you to live there. That's why Mom made it a condition. She'd like us to take care of the place together. How about it, are you in?"

"I don't have a job, remember? I can't pay rent."

"Did I ask you to?"

"Then what's the purpose of my moving in with you?"

"Here's the deal I want to propose. Once we're settled, probably after Thanksgiving, we see about your getting into either college or a trade school...."

"Stop! This is an intervention. There are strings attached."

"Hear me out," Gus said, holding a hand up, school-guard style. "I'm only suggesting it because I know you're interested in and excel at cyber security stuff. I'm thinking you might push toward getting some certification in that field. You'd probably land a job where you could work from home." Gus could almost see the wheels turning in his brother's head, so he kept going, hoping to get him excited.

"Who knows, at some point, you might be able to form your own company. The guest room could be converted easily into a home office."

Jared sat silent. The measured tapping of his fingers on the windowsill reflected his contemplation of Gus's offer. He let the chair hit on all fours with a thud. "How soon could we move in? When are they moving out?"

"Mom said right before Thanksgiving, so we could move in any time afterward."

"I just got my lease payment notice, but I don't have enough to pay it."

"Tell you what, why don't you pack up and come stay with me until we can move in. You can help me out around here if you want."

Jared looked at Gus and realized his brother was sincere. They'd always gotten along, but were never real buddies. Now he felt their relationship was changing.

"Thanks, I think I'll take you up on it. I don't know how much help I'd be, but I'll do what I can."

"You can drive and I always need parts to be picked up."

Jared stood and reached to shake on it.

Gus grasped his brother's hand tightly. "Great! This is the start of something good."

"We'll see if you still think so after a couple months."

Gus came around from his desk and jabbed Jared on the shoulder. "I will."

***

Pastor Bill provided a wonderful memorial to honor Lillian, and shared her favorite verses, including John 3:16. There were tears flowing, sweet memories, a myriad of flowers, and an ache in many hearts. Lillian's church family provided a wonderful meal after the funeral, and encouraged Jake to call if he needed anything after his brother returned to San Antonio. He promised.

The ride back to their mother's house was quiet. Jake drove in silence and Ron stared at the houses as they zipped by. It had been an emotional day and both sons were drained. Rita made a few comments from the back seat, about how compassionate the people were during the meal. She looked at Jake, who would soon be alone once she and Ron headed home.

"Jake, I'll package up some of the food they sent with us, and freeze what I can. You won't have to cook for at least a week."

Suddenly both guys laughed. Rita followed suit.

"I don't want to look at another casserole, chicken drumstick, or bowl of chili," Jake blurted out.

"They do have great cooks in that church," Ron pointed out.

The two glanced at each other and began laughing again.

"Am I missing something here?" Rita asked

Ron turned to Rita. "Every church lady who brought food insisted we try her dish because it was one of mom's favorites. We couldn't refuse of course. Did you see me take my plate to the kitchen once?"

"Yes, I figured you needed space or something."

"No, I found a baggie and put some of the food in it, then stashed it in the fridge." He held his stomach. "I was stuffed."

"But I saw you eating brownies, cookies and cake."

"Rita," Jake chimed in, "they forced it on us. Besides, you were munching away as well."

It was her turn to laugh. She stretched her neck to peer into the back of the Ford Escape to size up the hoard of food. "Looks like a cafeteria back there. Don't worry, most of it will keep well in the freezer. Ron, do you want to take some back?"

He grunted. "No thanks, Hon. I'll be good for a month at least."

Jake pulled into the driveway and cut the motor. "We made it."

They each waited a few moments before exiting the car. Jake went first. "We can't sit here all night. Might as well go in."

Ron got out and opened the door for Rita. Together, they unloaded some of the dishes from the back. "We'll have to make three trips," he moaned.

"Pull Jake out here and we each can make one instead."

"I like your way of thinking," Ron said, pausing a second to kiss her cheek. "Thanks for being here."

"I wouldn't want to be anyplace else."

Jake appeared suddenly. "Load me up," he said, holding out both arms. "Let's get this food in the house. We have work to do."

"Work?" Ron asked.

"Mom's papers, remember? I don't want to go through all that stuff alone."

They walked carefully toward the house, so as not to drop any delicacies.

"Sure, but can't it wait until morning? I'm beat."

"We're supposed to meet the attorney at ten."

"You're right, and we may run across papers we'll need to go over with him," Ron agreed. "Rita, you want to come along? We can stop on the way back and grab a bite to eat."

Rita stopped in her tracks, causing the guys to do the same.

"You're joking, right?" She asked, looking at the containers of food they each held.

They all laughed and entered the house.

"I'll stay here and make sense of all the concoctions the church ladies created, and when you two get back, I'll have a nice meal ready. You won't even recognize it as leftovers," she said, giving a confident smile as they set things down on every flat surface available.

***

Jake combed his hands through his hair. "I'm stunned! Is your letter the same as mine?"

Ron sat across from him at the kitchen table. He set his coffee mug down, shaking his head back and forth. "I think so. I can't believe it."

They found the box Lillian had described to them before she died. She made them promise to open it only after her death. Neither wanted to talk about it then, but now it was time. The box had Miscellanies scrawled on top in black marker.

An envelope for each son was carefully labeled and placed inside, along with identical leather bags with their names inscribed. The letters they held had been written by their dad, years before he passed away. Each bag contained a key and instructions on what to do with it. A manila envelope was included in the box, easily identifiable as coming from their mother. Hearts adorned the flap. She always added them when she mailed cards or letters. Sometimes it was a sticker, but often, lacking them, she'd hand draw one in red ink. It was her signature.

Jake opened it and removed a legal looking document. "It's the deed to this house." He looked at his brother inquisitively. "I never knew it was paid off. Did you?"

"You were the one helping with her finances. How could you not know?"

A short note fell onto the table. "It's from mom." He scanned it quickly. "Listen to this," he told Ron.

"My dear boys, I can almost see your jaws drop at discovering you now own this house. After your father died, I used the majority of my money to pay off the mortgage quickly. That's why my savings went down and I was always in a bind. We had taken out a second mortgage some years ago and it just never seemed to get paid off. I didn't want either of you dealing with this, so I prayed God would show me a way. The life insurance wasn't much and didn't last long, but I was determined to pour every dime I could scrape together into it. Last year, I made the final payment, so it's free and clear.

If you want to lease it out, feel free to do so. Or, you may decide to sell it, and split the proceeds. Either way, you will each have something from it. The attorney will cover things with you, and my will is specific about personal items I want you to keep. I love you both. Mom"

Jake set the note down, then rose and put a k-cup in the brewer. He set his coffee cup on the plate, pushed the button and waited.

"You know, Ron, she's full of surprises. No wonder she was always saying she needed extra money for things."

"I am sitting here, looking at her note and still don't believe she pulled it off." He laughed as he shoved the chair back and stood to stare out at the darkened street. "Mom was able to accomplish in a few determined years, what they couldn't do in many."

"She was on a mission and knew there was only one way to do it...with God's help," Jake said as he brought his coffee back to the table and sat down.

Ron returned to his seat and picked up the other envelope. Removing it, he saw his dad's familiar handwriting. He began.

"Dear Ron,

If you're reading this, you are mourning the loss of your precious mother. I'm sorry and wish I could give you a strong shoulder. The best I can do is provide for you, now that Lillian and I are both gone. I've always tried to take care of my family, but my life's pursuit was to make sure you boys would be okay without us. To that end, the key you have is to a safety deposit box, one for each of you. We lived frugally through the years for a reason. I wanted you to have resources to pursue your dreams, whatever they might be. I did tell your mother that if hardship came to her, she was welcome to use what she needed, but there was no way she would touch it. I have full confidence everything is there.

We loved you boys more than life. Lillian is with the Lord and me now. You and Jake have each other. Remember love works both ways. Find it and give it. God loves you, we loved you, and you must be there for your brother, just as he must be there for you.

Remember, the legacy you live today will mark the path you leave behind. We each leave our own unique mark for those coming after us.

Love, Dad"

Ron rested his head on his arms and sobbed.

***

As Rita approached the kitchen, she paused as she overheard Ron's heart-wrenching cry. She wasn't about to intrude. Backing away quietly, she retreated to the patio, and sat quietly on the glider to pray for Ron and Jake, and express thankfulness for a loving Father. Rita was glad she came and was able to be some kind of support to

Ron and his brother. But, even beyond that, Rita gained a deeper love for God. She had watched Him weave a legacy further down the path of this family. It reminded her of what Mary did through her passing and the estate sale last year.

Chapter Ten

Kat rushed downstairs carrying her phone. She found him in the garage digging through some boxes. "Dad," she said, breathlessly, "look at the text I just got!"

Brian quickly straightened from his bent-over position, shoving the box to the side. "Who's it from?" he asked, flashes of Jared going off in his head.

"Bree, it's from Bree Moreno. She and her mom will be here before the end of the month. Isn't that great?"

He hugged his daughter, relieved the text was friendly and happy to hear from the Moreno's. "So they'll be here for her birthday and our Thanksgiving dinner. Betty will be overjoyed. We're gonna have a houseful."

"If the weather is good, we might be able to have it outside."

He kissed his daughter on the cheek. "I doubt Betty will want an outdoor meal. We'll make room. Besides, it's one advantage to having a large house."

"When will she be home?"

"Within the hour I think. She met with an author who needed some work done."

"Good. I can't wait to tell her about Bree."

"By the way, was Pekoe happy to have her owner back?"

"Yes, she purred constantly. I was sad to say goodbye, but I'm very glad to be back in my own bed."

"It was nice of you to cat-sit for Rita."

"I actually enjoyed the little fur ball. You should see how much she loves the laser beam. It hyped her up until she was acting crazy. Maybe I should think about getting one."

"A laser?"

"Dad," she said, giving him an exasperated look. "No, a cat. Or maybe a kitten."

"If you're serious, we could check the Humane Society."

A car pulled in the driveway. "She's home," Brian said. "Now you can get her hyped-up with your news."

Brian watched as Kat sprinted to Betty's car. He smiled to himself as he observed the intimacy his wife and daughter shared over such a simple thing as a phone message. Together, they walked shoulder-to-shoulder toward him. He greeted Betty with a kiss, asking how her meeting went, as the three of them ambled inside.

"I'm happy to know Bree and her mom will be joining us for Thanksgiving meal this year. I bet they'll have amazing stories to tell us about their mission trip," Betty said, as she put the kettle on. "Anyone want to join me for tea?"

"No thanks," Brian called from the recliner, "I'm snacking on popcorn from earlier."

"Do we have any chai? Rita got me hooked on it. I can smell it now," Kat said, inhaling the imaginary fragrant leaves.

Betty laughed. "You're so funny. I think we might have some tea bags, but no loose tea."

Kat feigned disappointment with a pout. "It'll have to do, I suppose." Recovering quickly, she helped Betty with the cups, sweetener, and milk. They both stood at the stove waiting for the whistle.

"Have you talked to Clay?" Betty asked. "I wonder how he's doing with Clarence's final film edits."

"I know he's working on them. He seemed more excited to get to Ms. Garson's, though. But seriously, he should be done this week. When do you finish up with Greta?"

"I'm still reading her journal, but I'll see her Tuesday so I'll know more then. She'll require a little more work than Clarence. Greta has some unresolved issues, which is why I need to have one-on-one time with her."

The shrill of the kettle startled both women back to the task of preparing their teatime. Betty poured boiling water over the bags while Kat found a blueberry muffin and sliced it in half. Each carried her cup to the table and waited for their brew to steep.

"I love this," Kat said. "Remember when we were in England for the wedding and we gals all went to tea?"

"Yes, it was a lovely experience. I'm glad you were part of it."

Kat squeezed her teabag, taking in the fragrant spices of the chai. She added sweetener and milk, then stirred thoughtfully. "When we were at the tearoom in Essex, I recall one young lady refer to another as 'Mum'. I think that's a sweet term. Don't you, Betty?"

"Yes, I do," she agreed, busying herself with making her cup of tea ready to sip.

"Why do you suppose they say Mum?"

"An author I worked with said there were different opinions. Some Americans think it's really, 'Ma'am' but with the accent sounds like 'Mum'." Others believe it's used to refer to a superior, and many accept it as a reference to their Mom."

Kat sipped her tea, looking at her step-mom over the edge of the chintz cup. Slowly, she set her cup down. "Would you mind if I called you 'Mum'?"

Betty nearly dropped the muffin she held to her lips. She set it down gently while she recovered from Kat's surprise question. "Honey, I'd be honored." Betty felt tears cover her cheeks. She reached over, grasping Kat's hand and smiled. Betty noticed a tear streak down Kat's face as well.

The two were wiping their eyes with napkins when Brian strolled into the kitchen.

"What's up in here? I dozed off a bit, did I miss something?"

***

The afternoon crowd at Bill Miller BAR-B-Q had thinned out by the time Jared and Gus pulled into the parking lot. Since Jared spent the day moving from his apartment into Gus's place, his appetite was overtaking his tiredness. In addition to packing, moving, unloading and then running to the parts store for Gus, he was worn out and hadn't eaten all day.

"I appreciate your driving us," Jared said as they climbed out of the truck. "I'm almost out of gas and too tired to turn the steering wheel. Maybe some brisket will revive me."

Gus laughed. "No problem. I'm glad they're not busy, though."

"Me, too."

They went through the sparse line, Jared choosing the Rancher Plate with extra meat, and his brother getting the Poor-Boy Plus with fries.

Gus picked a table by the wall and they settled down to enjoy their meal. Surprisingly, they both remembered to bring their tea mugs and had them refilled on the cheap.

"Thanks for treating," Jared said as he took a swig of his drink.

"The way I live and work, it's cheaper to eat out than buy

groceries. Besides, I'm not much of a cook."

Jared had taken a healthy-sized bite of brisket, so he mumbled in agreement. "Question," he said, still chewing a bit. "Why don't Mom and Dad want to talk with me directly about moving into their house?" By now, he had swallowed, and his urgent appetite was satiated. He sat still, waiting for Gus to respond.

"Well, the way I see it, after the fiasco you caused in San Marcos over that student and got yourself kicked out of college; they threw their hands up after trying to steer you in the right direction."

"Fair enough. I can deal with that. So if that's true, why all of a sudden do they want me moving in with you to their house? Why not just kick me to the side of the road and be done?"

"For the same reason they provided some money for you to live on after it happened."

Jared finished off his coleslaw and washed it down with the remaining tea. "And the reason is?"

"You're an idiot if you can't figure it out. Because they love you. You're their son," Gus said a little too loud. One of the servers glanced their way. Gus winked at her and smiled.

"But they don't want to be around me so they get you to make the deal?"

Gus was becoming frustrated with his half-brother. "Don't you get it? Mom wants to see you make something of yourself. She knows you need space to sort your life out and thought I might be able to help. That's all. I think in time, things between you will heal to the point where you can reunite. I hope so, anyway."

Jared sat quietly, nibbling on the rye bread. He took his mug and went to the beverage counter.

Gus watched him amble over for his refill. He hoped this issue with Jared and his parents didn't become a bone spur in his life. Being a go-between wasn't the position he asked for, but he wanted to help Jared get squared away and become independent.

Seated again, Jared thanked Gus for being there for him. "I know this isn't easy for you, having me underfoot and all. Just want you to realize it's hard on me right now with no income and feeling dependent on you."

Gus chuckled. "You'll get to work for your room and board, trust me."

Jared relaxed a little. "Can you afford to treat us to a couple of those brownies I spotted?"

***

Pekoe's rough tongue stroked Rita's arm until she opened her eyes and greeted her street cat. She looked at the green eyes staring at her. "Good morning, Precious," she cooed. "What's this?" Rita looked at a grey object next to her pillow and jerked back. "Not another mouse gift," she squealed. But looking closer she realized it was a toy rodent and heaved a sigh of relief. Apparently, Kat bought it last week.

"Thank you," she said, giving her pet a gentle squeeze. "I guess you're hungry. Let's have breakfast." She watched Pekoe jump with ease to the floor. Rita stretched full length, yawned, and thought of Ron. She drove home early so Kat wouldn't be tied up with Pekoe too long, but Ron said he'd be along after they talked to the attorney.

Ron explained to her later that he and Jake inherited more than they imagined. At first both guys were a little taken back, thinking all this time Lillian was near broke. Essentially, she was, because she didn't intend to touch any assets earmarked for the two boys. But, after it sank in, they became humbled at what their mother had done for them.

Rita mentally compared Lillian with her own mother, and the ache grew stronger than it had been during Lillian's funeral. She was happy for Ron and his brother, but inside, the angst she felt concerning what her own mother did, nagged at her.

"Meow."

Rita raised her head from the pillow and saw Pekoe's nose nudged against the bedroom door. "Poor Pekoe, I'm sorry," she said, throwing back the comforter. Rita padded to the doorway and scooped up her orange-striped bundle of fur.

A second meow sounded.

"Okay, Okay, let's go check out the pantry."

***

Betty handed the journal to Greta, took a deep breath and sat down. She saw something different in this puzzling woman. Not just her appearance, which was greatly improved. The silent film persona was gone and in its place was a woman with a troubled heart.

"I read it all."

Greta twisted the handkerchief around her fingers as she rocked gently.

For the first time since meeting her, Betty witnessed tears leave a path down Greta's cheeks. She stood and took the creased hankie from the elderly woman's hands, and dabbed the wetness from her face. Without speaking, Betty placed the lace-edged linen in Greta's lap and returned to her seat.

"Now you know."

"I know only that people express pain and love in different ways, and we shouldn't judge them," Betty said softly. "Your father had a mountain to climb and you couldn't help him."

"But he took his life. He abandoned my mother. He left me alone to deal with it all."

"In his pain, watching your mother suffer, and then losing everything when the market crashed, he took the only way out, that to him, seemed reasonable. I'm not saying it was right, but we cannot judge him. Only God can do that."

"How can I trust God after all I've been through? I've lost everything. I'm lonely and no one cares. Not God. Not me."

Greta's head bent down and she allowed her feelings to pour out. Betty went to her and knelt, taking her hands. They were ice cold. She rubbed them until some warmth was restored.

"God does care and so do I. When I read your journal I cried for you, and my prayers have been that you will come to know God as I do, as a loving Father."

Greta lifted her face and looked into Betty's watery eyes.

"I can see your concern for me. Your eyes show it. I can't see God's."

"I'm His eyes. Let's pray together and I'll ask Him to reveal His love to you. Will you open your heart a little and allow God to come in?"

Greta hesitated.

Betty refused to lose eye contact. This was the moment she had asked God for and she wasn't going to let it pass.

Greta nodded.

A huge smile formed on Betty's face. She still held Greta's hands, which were now warm. "Father in heaven, Greta is waiting with an open heart to receive assurance of Your love. Help her to feel Your presence right now. Pour out Your Holy Spirit on her and let my friend know You will never abandon or forsake her. Give her confidence that You are with her always and she can call on You anytime. Amen."

The two women lifted their heads. Betty released Greta's hands and hugged her tightly. She felt the hug returned.

"Thank you, Betty," she said, sitting back in the rocker. "I haven't felt this peaceful in many years."

"That means God has moved in. You'll never be alone anymore."

Greta smiled. "This should have been filmed," she said lightheartedly.

"No, this was between you and God. But, the change in you will show during our last session this week."

Greta's smile faded. "Already? I was hoping you would stick around longer."

"I'm not disappearing. We would like to bring the film up here Saturday afternoon so you and Clarence can view it before we show it to the rest of the residents Thanksgiving week."

"What? Are you trying to play matchmaker?"

Betty laughed. "No, I just want you to approve it before we go public."

Greta's eyes lit up. "I'd like that. Make it one o'clock."

"Good, it's a date."

"This is exciting. Thank you for being here for me." Greta's voice quivered a little.

Betty stood and her knees creaked. "Oh dear, my age is catching up with me. My joints don't like squatting too long."

"Honey, you don't have a clue what's comin' later." Greta laughed.

Betty looked at her watch. "I need to go, but we will be back Thursday and finish up. I'll check with the director and let him know about our Thanksgiving plans."

Greta remarked as Betty neared the door, "That whippersnapper, he better agree."

Betty turned before closing the door. "Now Greta, you know you love him." She hurried and shut the door before a rebuttal ensued. Laughing to herself, she made her way down the hall, to the director's office, singing under her breath.

***

Greta sat quietly, rocking, holding her journal. She looked up. "Are you really there, God?" Silence. Suddenly, she remembered her father's arms holding her after she had a nightmare as a small child. His arms held her tightly until her fear went away and peace returned. She felt that peace now.

***

Clay was on top of the world. He finished editing the Garson video, and put it together with Mr. Hartman's. He still needed the wrap-up and credits, but this film pleased him. Tonight he'd take what he had and show Kat and her step-mother. Clay felt sure they would be pleased with the human element and how he did some of the close-ups. Ms. Garson was actually photogenic and that surprised him. In the beginning, he figured the editing would be enormous.

The phone rang. It was Kat. "Hey, Girl," he said, loving the sound of her voice.

"How's the film coming along?"

"I just finished what I needed to get done and only lack a few parts. But, our stars turned out fantastic. I can't wait to show it to you."

"That's why I called. Well, part of why I called. Betty wondered if we could arrange to let our leading lady and man preview it on

Saturday. We could take it to their residence and allow them to see and approve it."

"Sure, I'll touch up what I'm lacking and be ready to go. What time?"

"In the afternoon, one o'clock promptly. You know Ms. Garson."

Clay laughed. "Sure do. Not one minute early or one minute late. What was the other reason you called?"

"I need to talk to one of my professors and I'd rather not go alone. Would you have time tomorrow at eleven, to just be there with me?"

Clay was a little puzzled, but it was a chance to see Kat and he wouldn't pass it up. "Sure, then maybe we could grab something to eat after you're done."

"Thanks, Clay. I really appreciate this. I've been a wreck thinking about going."

"What's the problem? Which professor?

"It's a personal issue I'd rather not go into details about. I just prefer not to be alone when I see Professor Evans. He's a bit quirky."

"I understand and I'm happy to help."

"Okay, I'll see you tomorrow then."

"I'll meet you at the arch."

Clay agreed and hung up, wondering what personal issue she was having with this professor. He hoped it wasn't too personal. If she wants me to know, she'll tell me.

He decided now was a good time to run by his parents' house and invite himself to dinner. He was starving and his mom was a great cook. She always had a meal stashed away for her hungry, working son. Clay locked up the apartment and headed to the parking lot, feeling content. Tonight I'll put the film to bed. Tomorrow I'll be Kat's knight in shining armor, ready to save the damsel in distress. He laughed out loud at the mental image of himself in a suit of armor.

***

Ron's office looked the same as before he left. Time stood still here while his world zoomed chaotic in Mesquite over the past several weeks. He still couldn't believe his mother was gone. The memorial and funeral went well, thanks to Rita helping with much of the detail work. He was blessed to have her in his life.

He switched on the Keurig and waited for the water to heat. Looking around at the bright yellow walls and artistic touches, he remembered reading what to do if you felt an anxiety attack coming on. Not that he did, but it seemed important to do them anyway, to make sure it didn't sneak up on him. The article said to look around and find five things you can see. Bright yellow walls, coffee mug, Keurig machine, picture of Rita, windows. Next find four things you can touch. Desk, chair, phone, computer. Three things you can hear. Traffic, a woman singing, coffee machine gurgling. Two things you can smell. Coffee, leather. One thing you can taste. coffee. AAH.

Ron took a sip of the hot liquid, then set it on the desk. "Okay, now I'm grounded," he said out loud to no one. He sat down and rifled through folders with red sticky notes attached. Ron was grateful for a dedicated staff. They all pitched in while he was gone. Now, he needed to pick up and begin a new normal. He was still in shock with what his parents had done. Both he and Jake could now do whatever they wanted without worrying about money. Ron was happy for Jake. Maybe now he'll make a life for himself, settle down and find a good woman. Like Rita.

He picked up the phone to call her. Hesitation. He put it back down. Right now he needed to focus on at least seeing what events were coming up, where he was needed most, and tackle the phone messages. Rita would be his last call, his reward for accomplishing things on his first day back on the job.

***

Jake faced his coworkers at the hotel and thanked them for doing such an outstanding job while he was gone. It was difficult holding back tears as they each expressed their sympathy and either shook his hand or hugged him. He wanted to escape to the privacy of his office and allow his emotions to subside so he could fold back into the daily work.

"Mr. Davis," the administrative assistant said, pulling him aside, "a Miss Donovan is on the line and would like to speak with you."

"I don't know a Miss Donovan...oh wait, yes I do. I'll take it in my office." He excused himself from the group and once settled at his desk, the phone rang.

"Annie," he answered cheerfully, "how are you?"

"I'm fine. I called to ask you the same question. You mentioned you'd be back at work today, so I thought I'd take a chance and call."

He leaned back, feeling the wood press against his spine. He hated this chair.

"Truthfully, I'd rather be anywhere else right now, but I know I have to face reality eventually. Might as well be today."

"I've been praying for you, Jake. I wanted to let you know I have a book you might benefit from. It has to do with grief. Would you like to borrow it? You could stop by the hospital and pick it up tomorrow."

Jake's cheerfulness faded. She called to give me grief counseling, not because she wants to talk. "Thanks, but I'm not much of a reader and besides, I know pretty much how to grieve."

"I'm sorry, I didn't mean anything by it. I just thought...."

"Not a problem, thanks for offering. I really need to get busy here."

"Sure, take care. I'm praying for you."

Jake hung up the phone and guilt set in. He kicked his foot against the leg of the desk, immediately wishing he hadn't. His toe screamed at him. I shouldn't have been rude. She was only trying to help. He looked at the phone and toyed with the idea of calling Annie back, but decided now wasn't the time. He needed to straighten out his head and figure out how he would function without the routine of being at his mother's house so much. There were decisions to be made. Ron said if he wanted to move in it was fine with him. I can't live there. Too many memories. The thought of selling the home he grew up in made him nauseous. Jake got up and decided to do a walk-through of the hotel and see how everything was going. It would take his focus to where it was needed.

***

Annie sat in the hospital coffee shop, sipping her tea. She was upset and wished with every fiber of her being she hadn't called Jake. It was too soon. He was still raw from the funeral and his brother's leaving. I need to apologize to him. He didn't need her interference in his life. She barely knew him, but felt some kind of connection. Annie hoped to get better acquainted, but didn't want to force herself into his life when he just lost his mother. What was I thinking?

Her break was over so she headed back to her floor. There were two other patients nearing the end unless God intervened. Annie didn't know where their hearts were regarding their relationship with the Lord. She tried not to judge, only show compassion, but sometimes it was difficult. She loved taking care of Lillian Davis because Annie knew where her heart was. It was a joy to even be around Jake's mom.

The elevator pinged. She entered with two others, one was near tears. Annie asked which floor. "Oh, that's my floor too," she said softly. The doors closed as they rode up together, in silence.

***

Brian raked up another pile of oak leaves. He wouldn't have minded near as much if they were from his tree instead of the neighbors'. It was always the same; the wind blew the leaves into his yard, he'd rake them, and a couple days later the job would start again. The part of it he found contentment in was it gave him time to think. The process of pulling the leaves toward him and scooping them up to dump into the bag was therapeutic. Lately, the mention of the couple named Orlov moving into Mary's old house had his mind fluttering around like leaves in the wind. He wanted desperately to scoop them into a bag and get rid of what caused him concern about his daughter. Brian couldn't wait for Seth and Emily to arrive next week so he could get more information. If, in fact, they were related to Jared, he didn't know how to deal with it. It's not like they're moving next door to me. I won't be raking their leaves. So why was he disturbed by this news?

"Brian," his wife called from the back door, "would you be a sweetheart and run an errand for me?"

He turned, momentarily forgetting previous thoughts, and smiled at Betty. "Sure, anything to get out of finishing this job." He laughed and carried the rake to the patio, leaning it against the post. "What do you need, my love?"

"I have three things going at once and would like to get this in the mail before they close. Would you do the honors?"

"I'm at your service," he said, taking hold of the manila envelope. He bent from the waist in an exaggerated bow.

"Thanks, and by the time you get home, the cabbage rolls will be ready."

"Bribery," he answered, making his way to the garage.

Brian backed the car out of the driveway and headed to the corner. Thoughts about Mary's house and the Orlov's buying it returned. He could call Lane. After all, he was handling the sale of Betty's old place, too. Tomorrow he would contact the realtor, just to find out a little information. Of course, it would depend on whether Lane would give any of it up. But since he lived next door, he might be a little freer about discussing his new neighbors.

***

The Director, Kenneth Cavanaugh, knocked on Greta's door. He waited, then knocked again. "Ms. Garson, it's Mr. Cavanaugh, are you in? I'd like to talk with you." No answer. He used his phone to call the nursing director to see if she'd had contact with Greta this afternoon. It was unusual for her to not be in her room at this time of day.

"Okay, thanks. I'll check outside," he told Denise. He knew it would be a long shot for Greta to be out in the garden, but the nurse thought she saw her there earlier. He headed to the solarium to see if he might catch a glimpse of her.

Kenneth stood by the window and stared in disbelief. She was in the garden sitting on a bench talking to Clarence Hartman. Shaking his head, he grinned. I think I'll wait and talk to her later. He watched for a moment longer, noticing Clarence's animated response to whatever she was sharing with him. He slapped the arm of the wheelchair and whipped his head back, laughing. Whatever she was saying must be hilarious. I think doing the film brought Greta out of her shell. Maybe he'd speak with Mrs. Hills instead of Greta. He left the room and decided to give Mrs. Hills a call.

***

Clarence Hartman watched Greta leave the garden to return to her room. She said she needed her beauty sleep and it was past time for her afternoon nap. He finally settled himself after hearing his new friend's story. He laughed so hard he had difficulty catching his breath. He had to admit; he was intrigued how this woman had changed so much. She used to scowl at him in the dining room and never gave him so much as a grunt when they passed in the hall. He thought she despised him or looked down on him because he had only one leg.

The other day when her filming wrapped up and Mrs. Hills brought them together over coffee, Greta treated him with respect and kindness. He chuckled again, at her recalling about squirreling away every dime she could find, and the day she added it up, she had two dollars to her name. She told him, "Two stinking dollars. That wouldn't buy me a change of underwear!" She had a way of telling a story which would crack you up and make you cry at the same time.

The nurse approached Clarence and asked if he'd like her to wheel him back to his room. "It's getting a bit windy out, Mr. Hartman. Maybe it's time we go in."

"Thank you, Josie. I can get myself there but I am a bit tired. That woman wore me out laughing, so today you can push me to my room."

"Good. I don't get to see you as much now that you and Ms. Garson have become friends. She's stealing you away from me."

"Ha, no chance of that. You're my best gal. Besides, you bring me snacks in the evening."

Josie took hold of the handles on the back of his chair and pushed him to the solarium door. Another nurse was coming out and held it open as they bumped their way over the threshold. "Oops, sorry. I'm not such a good driver."

"That'll cost you a chocolate snack later," He cautioned with a laugh.

She bent to whisper. "Shush, we don't want the others to know. I'll get in major trouble," she giggled.

Clarence zipped his lips closed and pointed toward his room.

***

Kat helped Betty clean up the kitchen and load the dishwasher. "The cabbage rolls were fantastic. Is it a family recipe?"

"Yes, my mother used to make them every Friday night. Dad loved cabbage and it became his favorite dish. I'm glad you and your dad enjoyed it." Betty looked at Kat. "Did your mother have a favorite recipe?"

Kat paused, thinking. "She made a stuffed manicotti recipe we loved. I never learned to make it the way she did."

"Do you have the recipe?"

Kat put the towel down and went to her bedroom. She found the red box in the small chest where she kept a few mementos of her mother. She carried it tenderly to the kitchen and set it on the breakfast bar. Kat took a seat on the stool. "This was her box of recipes. When we saw her bring it out, we always got excited. These were her specialty dishes."

Betty watched Kat run her hand over the lid gently, almost lovingly. Do I dare suggest it? "I might be able to help you make the manicotti dish if the recipe is in there. Only if you want me to," she added.

Kat looked up at Betty, and then opened the lid. "I'd like that," she said softly.

"Thanks, Mum."

Betty walked over and stood behind Kat, hugging her. "You will master it and make it your own recipe to carry on to your daughter one day."

Kat sighed. "If I ever marry and have a daughter."

"How are things with you and Clay? Do you have feelings for him?"

"It's kinda strange. Mostly I look to him as a brother, but then there are times when he looks at me in a certain way and...."

"Don't worry, if he's in God's plan for you, the time will come when you'll know."

"Thanks, you always seem to know the right thing to say."

Brian popped his head in the doorway. "Are y'all done in here? The movie's coming on."

"We're on our way," Betty said.

Kat got up and put the red box back in the pantry. She stood there in the darkened room for a second. You'd like her, Mom.

***

Halfway into the movie, the phone rang. Betty slipped out of the room to take the call. She looked at the caller ID and saw it was Mr. Cavanaugh, the Mt. Laurel director.

"Good afternoon, Mr. Cavanaugh, or should I say evening?"

"I suppose it is getting to be that time of day. I hope I'm not interrupting your dinner or anything."

"Not at all, how can I help you?"

"I observed something today I thought you'd be interested in knowing about. It concerns our Greta."

"She's okay, isn't she?"

"More than okay. I saw her and Clarence Hartman out in the

garden area, having a great discussion and laughing together."

"You're kidding me."

"Glad to say I'm not. She seemed to be sharing something extremely funny, because he was letting the laughter out loud."

Betty was astounded. Greta and Clarence willingly getting together and having fun? "How wonderful. I'm still in shock, but it's fantastic they are opening up with one another."

"You had a lot to do with it. This film project has been a godsend and I'm hoping you'll be open to a suggestion."

"What do you have in mind?"

"I know you wanted them both to view it to preview before moving on with the documentary, but I have an idea. What would you think if we showed it in our rec room and invited our other residents and staff to attend?"

"I think it would be wonderful. We could do it like a theater. Greta would love that. She has the perfect outfit to wear."

"We might be able to find a uniform for Clarence as well."

Betty's hand flew over her mouth in excitement. "I might cry any minute. Thank you so much. I'm seeing Greta soon, and I'll talk to Clarence too, and get their reaction. This is fabulous, thanks for thinking of it."

Kenneth was pleased his idea went over big. "I have other ideas for the event popping into his head. I'll transform the rec room into a movie theater and find a red carpet to roll down the center between chairs. This will be thrilling for all concerned."

"You started it all." He laughed and bid her good evening.

Betty returned to the living room and joined Brian and Kat for the remainder of the movie.

"Who called?" Brian asked without turning away from the

screen.

***

Lane sat at his desk, going through paperwork, when his secretary buzzed him that he had a visitor. "Who is it?"

"A Mr. Hills," she announced.

"Send him in, please," he said, getting up and greeting Brian at the door.

"Come in, Brian, how've you been? I'm still hoping to seal the deal on your wife's house this month. I've had several inquiries."

Brian shook hands, thanking Lane. "That would be great. She's been hoping it would have sold before now."

"The market has been a bit slow. Have a seat. Can I get you coffee or something?"

"I'm fine, thanks. I was in the area and thought I'd drop by for a few minutes just to see how things were going."

"Believe me; I'd like to get it sold too. Between yours and Seth's places, it's kept me hopping."

Lane sat back at his desk and pointed to the papers spread out. "I've been here more than home. I'm thinking about going on a short mission trip with the church and I'd love to finish up the two houses before then."

"That's great, about the mission trip. Sounds worthy. No word on the baby yet?"

Lane's facial expression seemed troubled. "I'm sorry, it's none of my business, I shouldn't have asked."

"No, no, it's okay. We've waited so long and been disappointed twice. Sheila took it hard. We started talking about the possibility of becoming foster parents."

"Really? That's a great idea."

230

I made an appointment to talk to the adoption agency. We'll see if they can steer us in the right direction. At least Sheila is open to the idea. I thought doing a mission trip would get her mind off things for a bit."

"I'll keep you both in my prayers, Lane."

"Thanks."

"I hear you'll be getting new neighbors."

"You must have talked to Seth. Yeah, they want to move in by Thanksgiving, so I've been working nonstop. I had to meet with the Historical Society on a couple issues. The Orlov's want to change some things, so I had to get approval first."

"Are they nice people?"

"Seem to be, as far as I can tell. I checked references and all that."

"Do they have kids?"

Lane stared at Brian. "Okay, what's with the third degree about this couple?"

Brian leaned forward and rubbed his temples. "Sorry. I'm a little shaken by the name Orlov. I'm not sure if you were aware of the guy who stalked my daughter last year and has been a thorn in our flesh this year. His name is Jared Orlov."

"You're kidding me." Lane dropped his pen and fell back in his chair. "I never knew his name. You think this couple may be related?"

"It's a possibility. Not that they're to blame or anything, but I'm just thinking if they are his parents, wouldn't it make sense he'd be visiting from time to time?"

"Certainly would."

"It's just that I feel him inching his way closer and closer. He seems to pop up more and more."

"Where else have you seen him?"

"My daughter attended a pizza party some weeks back and it turned out he worked there. She confronted him."

"Wow, did they arrest him?"

"No, he didn't do anything, he was just there. No sign of him since, but now this," Brian said, pointing to Lane's paperwork.

"Truthfully, there's nothing I can do to prevent them from moving in if everything is approved. Seth and Emily will be here in a couple weeks to sign papers. I'm really sorry, but if the cops have no reason to arrest him and he isn't bothering Kat now, I'd suggest you try to put it out of your mind."

"That's what Betty tells me too. I guess I'm just an overprotective father making something out of nothing."

"I'd be the same way if it were my daughter," Lane assured him. "Besides, there is a chance they aren't related. Let's not jump to conclusions."

"You're right. I should be going. I have contracts to pour over. Thanks again, Lane."

Lane stood and the two shook hands before Brian left.

"Cheryl," he turned to his secretary, can you do a little research on that Orlov couple?"

"Anything in particular?"

"See if they have any grown kids."

"Yes sir, I'll get right on it," she said.

Chapter Eleven

Kat was beginning to think her ethics class with Professor Evans would never end. He seemed to be covering the same hypothetical issues over and over. "What would you do in this situation?" his raspy voice droned each time he illustrated a new scenario. A few meager answers were offered. It wasn't until he posed the same question about intervening with good intentions, if it involved a relationship that she sat up straight and took notice. Where's he going with this?

Her mind flipped back to the times Professor Evans tried to intervene when she was being stalked. The problem was, he didn't seem to have the right motive. His hovering around her became disturbing. His visit to the library when she was there studying, was overbearing. She shuddered a little and the dismissal buzzer sounded.

She looked at the clock. Ten till one. Clay is probably on the steps outside, waiting. Class members disappeared out the door, so she approached the professor.

"Professor Evans," she said with minimal confidence, "may we talk for a few minutes?"

He was surprised, she could tell by his raised eyebrows.

"By all means," he replied, as he walked toward the door, preparing to close it.

"Can we go outside where the fresh air is?"

"If you like, although it's more private in here."

She didn't care for the smirky smile he wore. "It's not anything needing privacy; I just want to discuss ethics with you."

"Of course," he said, suddenly changing his demeanor back to professor mode.

Kat led the way out the door and through the front entrance. She spotted Clay on a nearby bench, looking half at a book, and glancing about for her. When their eyes met, he looked down at his reading material inconspicuously. He's here.

Feeling more confident now, she sat down at a small table under a mesquite tree. Professor Evans did the same.

"What did you need to discuss with me? This is all so mysterious."

"I know you're aware of my dilemma surrounding the guy who stalked me since I left San Marcos. My dad came up here and talked to those who would have some control over security."

"Yes, I do remember the difficulty you experienced, which is why I've tried to keep you clear from any potential danger. Have they caught him?"

"Let's just say the situation has been addressed and he is no longer a threat. The point I want to bring out in this conversation is this. I don't need your protection. Your hovering around me is disturbing..."

"Disturbing?" he interrupted Kat. "I take offense at that. Define disturbing."

He seemed ruffled and his face had a pink flush. She glanced over to where Clay was positioned before continuing.

"I feel uncomfortable when you get in my personal space, and it doesn't seem appropriate for a professor to be seeking out a student in the manner you've been doing. The library scene was out of line."

"Are you accusing me of trying to hit on you? If so, you're way out of line. You're the one today who wanted a private meeting with me. How would you like it if I said you were infringing on my personal space?"

Kat stood abruptly, eyes blazing through him.

The professor rose from his seat and shook his finger at her. "As your professor, I'd advise you to tread lightly in the area of accusations. Others have tried it and failed in more ways than one."

Kat was about to respond when she saw Clay walk up behind Professor Evans. She closed her mouth.

"Is there a problem here?" Clay asked, looking at the threatening teacher while slipping his arm around Kat's shoulders.

The professor gave Clay the once over, sizing him up. Ignoring the question, he looked at Kat. "Looks like you did address your old problem."

"What...is that...supposed to mean?"

"It means either your stalker reeled you in or this is big brother trying to butt in where he doesn't belong."

"Listen," Clay stated very firmly, "I don't know what's going on, but people in a university leadership position have no right to be imposing fear, anxiety or intimidation on their students. What I've observed in the last fifteen minutes would qualify for an HR investigation. I suggest you get back to your classroom and do whatever it is you do there."

Kat's silence and glare caused him to see he was not winning this round. She watched as he huffed across the lawn, up the steps and into the building. Kat sat down, shaking from head to toe.

Clay took a bottle of water from his backpack and offered it.

"Thanks." She took a long drink and set the plastic container down. "I'm sorry, Clay. I never dreamed it would end like this."

"Do you want to tell me now, what's going on? Stalker?"

She looked him in the eye. "My life just never gets to be normal." Kat burst into tears.

"Okay, this probably isn't the best time to talk about it. Let's go grab some food and do something fun. We can talk when you feel better."

"I just want to go home, Clay. I'm sorry."

"Stop apologizing. You have every right to be upset. I am going to follow you home though. In the state you're in, I want to make sure you get home safe."

She nodded her head as she got up.

Clay walked Kat to her car and returned to his. While he waited for her to get moving, the professor's words nagged at him. "It means either your stalker reeled you in or this is big brother trying to butt in." He was concerned someone was stalking Kat, and why he would think it was Clay. But the words, this is big brother, rang in his head. He remembered the time she said she looked at him more as an older brother than a boyfriend. Maybe his standing there as her protector looked like her brother ready to take up for his sister.

He saw her tail lights come on and she pulled forward. He started his car and followed. We will need to talk, and soon.

***

Kat drove carefully, aware she was still shaking from the encounter with her professor. She tried taking deep breaths, speaking scripture, and praying for calmness. "Please, Lord, I need help from the sanctuary." She took a quick peek in her rearview mirror and saw Clay behind her. Her hands became steady on the steering wheel and her breathing returned to normal. "Thank You, Jesus. Thank you for Clay's friendship and protection today."

***

Brian was livid after hearing Kat's encounter with her professor. "You need to write out everything and contact the office of student affairs. That professor needs to be held accountable for his actions."

"I know, Dad, but finals are around the corner and I don't want to fail his course because I report him."

"He can't fail you, even if he threatened too. As long as you pass your exam he can't do anything."

"I know and I will document what happened when Clay was there."

"Not just that. You need to write out what's taken place up to that point, especially at the library."

Kat looked so dejected, Brian softened. "Honey, I'm sorry you're having to deal with this." He wrapped his arms around his daughter, patting her on the back. "It'll be okay, I promise."

"I just want to live a normal life without always having to look over my shoulder." Kat moved from her dad's embrace and headed upstairs. "I'm tired. I think I'll journal a while, and catch a nap."

Brian watched her ascend the stairs. Her stooped shoulders reflected the heaviness she carried inside, and it saddened him. As a father, he felt crippled, unable to protect his child. First, Jared, now this. He remembered a verse from his morning devotions: An anxious heart weighs a man down, but a kind word cheers him up. Brian quickly called his daughter's name. "Kat."

She stopped mid-way up the stairs and turned to look at her dad without speaking.

"God and I love you, we've got this," Brian said with a smile as big as he could make. He watched as her face changed from anxiousness to peace in the wake of his words.

"Thank you, Daddy. I needed that," she said, and continued upstairs.

"Please deliver my daughter from the troubles surrounding her right now. Give her a space of grace. Amen."

***

Blanca Moreno and her daughter, Bree, finished unpacking in between munching their tacos. They had stopped on the way home from their church and picked up half a dozen, intending to have a few for later. They each wolfed down two before arriving at their home in San Antonio. Once inside, after opening windows and airing things out, they tackled their suitcases after grabbing just one more bean and cheese deliciousness.

"Momma, I'm stopping to make iced tea," Bree called out as she zipped one suitcase shut and emerged from her room. "Do you want some?"

When Blanca didn't answer, Bree looked in her mother's bedroom. She lay, sound asleep, fully clothed on her bed. The foil-wrapped taco sat on the nightstand, untouched. She must be exhausted after the long drive. The checkered suitcase sat open on the floor, clothes still inside.

Bree removed the coverlet from the chest at the foot of the bed and spread it gently over her mother. She switched off the lamp and padded her way out of the room, closing the door behind her.

In the kitchen, she made the tea, prepared herself a glass and meandered to the sofa in the living room. It felt good to be home. The mission trip was exciting and fulfilling, but home was calling her back. Home grounded her, providing a launch pad to her future. Bree propped a pillow behind her head and stretched her legs on the cushions. Closing her eyes, she drifted, thinking of the brown, tear-stained faces of rag tag kids clustered around her and the rest of the team. A vision of a tiny girl with matted curls, and cow-brown eyes, haunted her as she dozed off. Will you be my mama? Will you be my mama?

***

Blanca woke up in darkness. It took her a few moments to realize she was home in her bed and not on a mat in a small Mexican village. She lay still, listening to the silence, half expecting squalls of hunger cries to start any time. The experience of trying to meet the needs of so many hungry children was life-changing. Blanca knew poverty existed everywhere, but felt helpless to fill the stomachs of the multitudes. Jesus fed five thousand with a loaf of bread and fish. I'm not Jesus. What can one soul do, Lord?

She rose, noticing she was still in yesterday's clothing. A shower is definitely in order. Blanca looked at the clock. It was early evening, barely eight. She went to the kitchen and passed Bree, sound asleep on the sofa. Poor baby, I know she's exhausted. She returned to her room, retrieved the coverlet and put it carefully on her daughter, then crept quietly back to her room. The shower could wait till morning. Tiredness wins tonight.

***

Rita sat in Ron's office, happy to see him back in familiar surroundings. Back at work and seemingly falling into a normal routine. She waited, knowing he had to sign off on an event coming up next month. She was glad she completed the last of the stars he commissioned her to make last year. Her sculptures seem to please him and board members. Rita wondered what her next project for the art center would be.

Ron sauntered in with a cup of chai tea for her and roasted pecan coffee for himself. He handed Rita her tea and set his mug on the desk. He bent to kiss Rita, lingering. She enjoyed his playfulness and loved feeling his lips on hers. "Okay, my sweet," she said, pulling away, "your coffee's getting cold."

He laughed and pulled a side chair close to her, grabbed his mug and sipped carefully. "It'll take all day for this to cool. How's your tea?"

"Perfect," she answered, cradling her cup with both hands. "Do you like the stars?"

"Perfect," he said, staring into her eyes.

"Ron, what is up with you? You're acting odd. Silly and odd."

He reached for his mug, blew on the creamy liquid and took a drink. "Sorry, I just haven't worked out my emotions yet." He set his mug down, shaking his head. "It's been a wild ride but I think the coaster is slowing down. Now I need to get my balance so I can work and function again."

Rita placed her cup on the desk and took Ron's hand. "It'll take time and prayer. I'll be right here to help. Sometimes, work can be good therapy."

"I know. My brother needs to decide what to do about the house. I have a feeling he may move in. I'm looking at everything my parents did and I want to honor their sacrifice."

"God will show you what to do. I think about Mary's legacy and how she wanted to leave something of herself behind for others to carry on. Maybe you need to see how to carry out your parents' legacy."

"Their letters said pretty much the same thing. I've had several ideas floating around in my head. Why don't we run over to the Madhatter's and get some lunch and I'll share one of the things I've been mulling over."

"I'd love to. I haven't been there in almost forever." She looked at the clock. "Let me sprint over to my apartment and feed Pekoe first. I'll meet you back here in half an hour."

"I'll pick you up; you're too pretty to be jaunting down the street." He leaned over and kissed her again.

"Deal! See you soon." Rita tipped her cup for the last drop of chai, then handed it to Ron, before heading out.

***

Madhatter's wasn't crowded, much to Rita's surprise. The normal lunch-goers had come and gone obviously, but there were usually tourists and Southtown residents in and out. The lull was nice though, they were able to order and be served quickly.

Rita enjoyed her Panini and hot tea. "I love this place," she said, after taking a sip of the sweet chai. "It's nice having fewer people for a change."

"Yeah, especially today."

"Today?" she asked. "Why today?"

Ron reached into his shirt pocket and retrieved the item he stored there. He stretched his hand across the table to grasp Rita's open palm and deposited the surprise. Removing his hand, he watched as she gazed upon the halo infinity, black gold diamond engagement ring she now held. Her eyes widened and mouth gaped as she slowly lifted her head to meet his questioning smile.

"Will you marry me?" he asked, to be sure she understood the ring's meaning.

"Ron."

He waited. She began to cry.

Ron took the ring from her palm and slipped it on her left ring finger. "Will you?" he repeated slowly, "marry me?"

"She gazed once more at the circular set diamonds and intertwining rows of sparkling stones on the black gold band.

"Yes," she nodded, "yes, yes, yes."

Ron stood and came around to her side of the table. No one was nearby so he gathered her close in his arms and kissed her tenderly. "I love you, Rita," he whispered after releasing her from his embrace. "I want you in my life. Together we will create a legacy, just like my parents had."

"That's where I want to be," she managed to choke out the words. "In your life, forever."

Ron stayed next to her and retrieved his tea and sandwich from where he had been sitting, and took a bite.. "So, when would you like to become Mrs. Ron Davis?"

"Wow, you really know how to knock a girl's balance off." She held her arm out and stretched her fingers to watch the diamonds sparkle in the light. "I would love a spring wedding, but let me think about it. I'll need time to plan, and we will decide when and where to announce our engagement, and..."

"How about April 15, next year?" he interrupted.

She looked at him and smiled. "Tax day?"

"My mom's birthday."

Rita loved the idea of marrying on Lillian's birthday. "And the beginning of our creating a legacy," she added.

They raised their cups and toasted the date.

Chapter Twelve

Emily watched as Seth retrieved their baggage from the carousel and placed it on the trolley. She offered to help but he lovingly resisted, encouraging her instead to check with the car rental clerk for their vehicle. Having done that, keys in hand, she waited as Seth rolled the trolley toward her.

"Think we over-packed?" his baritone voice resounded above the airport din as he approached.

Laughing, she helped him steer the cart, laden with suitcases. "The good news is that we won't have as many on our return flight. We couldn't arrive from England without gifts for our friends."

"I think we brought more gifts than clothes," he teased. "Got the rental car?"

Emily dangled the keys and directed him to the agency's rental area through the side entrance. "I can't wait to get home, shower and make a pot of tea."

"Me too, at least the shower part," he agreed. "That flight seems longer each time we make it."

They stepped outside, into the sunlight. "I don't think San Antonio got the memo," Seth reported, looking at the sky. Beads of sweat broke out on his brow. "It's fall, not mid-summer. I bet the temp is at least eighty-five."

"We're definitely not in England, Toto," Emily said, clicking the remote as they found their rental car. "Air conditioning will be flowing soon. I'll start it up while you get the luggage loaded."

"Didn't I mention I would let you take care of it?" he joked. Too late, she was already in the car.

Emily seated herself in the driver's seat, started the motor, and turned on the air. A sudden rush of coolness hit her face immediately. She felt a bump each time Seth dumped a suitcase into the back, then finally a thud as he closed the hatch. He tapped on the window and gave her one of his poor Seth looks.

She laughed, opened the door and asked if he needed assistance. Their playfulness was one of the most endearing things she enjoyed in their marriage. Seth could be funny and romantic, at the same time.

"Ma'am," he inquired politely, "would you be so kind as to allow this overheated gentleman a chance to sit in your cool vehicle for a short time, just long enough to prevent heatstroke?"

She got out and stood close. "Only if you would do me the favor of driving me home."

He pulled her to him, wrapping both arms tightly around her. "You'd be doing me the favor," he said huskily before kissing his bride.

Seth escorted her around to the passenger side, clicked the seatbelt snugly and returned to the driver's side. He buckled up and headed for the highway.

***

Lane and Sheila sat nervously in the office of the Foster Care & Adoption Services. The middle-aged woman behind the desk perused the paperwork they had filled out and never lifted her eyes. Her name, Rose Menke, on the desk nameplate, seemed to fit her. She wore a black blouse with small roses covering the front.

Finally, she clasped her hands like paperweights on top of the application forms.

"So, you would like to foster to adopt?"

"Yes, Ma'am," Lane offered, clearing his throat. "We are in a position to provide a stable, comfortable and loving home. We hope a girl would be available."

"You attended the orientation. Do you have any questions about anything you heard?"

"None except how soon can we begin the process?"

"We don't get in a rush. Placing children in foster homes is something we take very seriously. Your application has been approved, but there will be training sessions you'll both need to attend."

"How long does that last?" Sheila asked.

Rose smiled. "Anywhere from four to ten weeks. But, it will give you a chance to learn about children in care, meet other families, and prepare to actually bring a child into your home."

"When can we start training?" Lane said quickly.

"Right away if you like. I can set you up the first of next week. Would you prefer Saturday morning or an evening class?"

"Evening," Sheila said.

Rose looked at her, then Lane. "I think you'll make wonderful foster parents. Once you complete the training, then there will be a home study done."

She saw a visible concern cross Sheila's face.

"I know the process seems daunting, but, let's not jump too far ahead. You'll enjoy the training and getting to meet other foster parents."

Lane stood and accepted the papers Rose held out for him.

"This is what you'll need when you show up for the first session. I included my card in case either of you have any questions before then."

"Thanks so much for all your hard work in helping us," Sheila said as she moved to stand beside her husband.

"I love seeing families come together. It's the best part of my job."

Lane and Sheila left the office and walked, arm-in-arm to their car.

"How about some lunch to celebrate the completion of the first step to foster parenting?" Lane suggested. "Italian, Mexican, or Chinese?"

"How about Olive Garden?"

They settled themselves into the car. "Olive Garden it is," Lane said, easing out of the parking space to feed into the line of traffic.

"You know, it sounds odd, at our age, becoming parents again."

Lane nodded. "Loving a child doesn't stop with age."

Sheila smiled. "It'll be wonderful having a child in the house again."

He watched the traffic carefully as thoughts of David swirled through his mind.

"I know. I've missed that."

Sheila leaned against the headrest, closed her eyes and tried to envision having a little girl in their home. A girl to love, guide and raise. There would be tea parties, sleepovers, and picnics. She smiled to herself as she played a mental movie of all the plans she and Lane talked about. Even now, Sheila knew in her heart, God was preparing the very girl He wanted them to have; a girl who needed them as much as they needed her.

***

Emily was thrilled to be back in San Antonio, even with the unseasonal temperatures. It would be sweet getting together with old friends and enjoying their hidden haunts and favorite restaurants. She and Seth had gotten in yesterday and dumped suitcases willy-nilly. Now she had to face the task of unpacking. She chose the two suitcases containing gifts for the Hills and the other estate sale friends. Seth bought Cadbury chocolate for everyone, and she prayed it hadn't melted. They put it in their carry-on, but you never know. She unzipped the bag and found the boxes. After inspecting them, she was relieved to know the chocolate survived. Emily emptied the small suitcase and set it aside. The turquoise bag was next. She spread it open and began the process of removing each gift and making a note as to its intended recipient. Kat will love this Waltz of the Flowers music box. Emily looked at it fondly, especially at its stunning figurine of a New Forest Gelding, with a sleek, tan physique and flowing, cream-colored mane and tail. She couldn't wait to see Kat's face light up with memories of her time in Essex. Horseback rides were the main event for her.

Seth lumbered through the door with steaks for the grill. "I'm back," he called out.

"Great," Emily greeted him as they met in the kitchen. "You can help unpack."

"Hey, I sacrificed myself at the crowded store so we would have food to feed our guests tomorrow night."

Emily put the steaks and other cold items in the fridge, then began pushing him toward the living room. "You're still in one piece, so come help."

"Slave-driver," he said, laughing.

"Let's at least get the gifts out and labeled."

"What's the hurry, aren't we giving them out at the Thanksgiving meal in a couple weeks?"

"I know, but it'll be one less thing we have to do later. Please?"

As they worked together, unpacking, Emily asked, "Do you plan to discuss your thoughts on the house in the King William District with Brian tomorrow?"

"I was, but wouldn't it be better to do it another day? I wanted dinner to be fun, easy-going."

"You're probably right. There's time enough for business later. We could haul out the Scrabble board."

"AWWW, please, no," Seth moaned, remembering how she and Betty whooped the guys last time.

"Then you pick a game."

"How about darts?"

Emily moaned this time. "If we do, you and Brian better not turn your backsides to us," she warned.

"Maybe we'll just talk," he tossed out.

Emily zipped the last suitcase shut. "That would be fun too. Now, would you do the honors and carry the bags to the garage?" She gave him her best indulge-me smile.

"I repeat, slave-driver." Seth picked up several bags and headed for the garage.

"Thank you, sweetie. I'll make your favorite dessert while you're doing such hard labor."

"Now you're talking," he said as he let the door slam behind him.

She strode into the kitchen and began gathering ingredients for a Texas Sheet Cake. He never could resist a slice and rarely stopped at one. He loved a cold glass of milk with it. She guessed it was the young boy inside of him.

***

"Seth, the steaks were perfect," Brian said, patting his midsection, "and the avocado salad was as great as I remember from last time you fixed it, Emily."

"I guess I need to copy down your recipe," Betty said. "I meant to get it from you after our holiday meal last Christmas."

"I'll make sure I give it to you," Emily promised.

"Why don't we go into the living room and scare up a game of Scrabble," Seth suggested, winking at Emily.

"While the gals set things up," Brian began, looking at Seth, "may we talk about something?"

"Sure, we can clean off the table at the same time," Seth agreed, standing and gathering some of the dishes.

Brian followed suit, and they went into the kitchen.

"What's up?" Seth quizzed.

"I know you have a buyer for the house, but I'm wondering if you know anything about them."

Seth paused at the sink and turned to Brian. "Yes, I've spoken to Lane about the situation. I planned to bring this up later, and that's probably still a better idea. I want tonight to be enjoyable for all of us, especially for our brides. To set your mind at ease for now, I have a plan B regarding the deal, one I think you'll be interested in."

Brian's eyebrows raised a bit. "Oh?"

"Let's not talk about it anymore tonight, but just know I think the world of you, Betty and Kat. There's no way I would bring more stress or concern into your family if I can possibly avoid it."

Brian felt relief flood his body. Seth was an attorney, but more than that, he was a good friend. "Thanks, buddy, I appreciate you a lot."

Seth threw his arm around Brian's shoulder. "Now, we need to finish clearing the table so those two women can beat us again. I hate Scrabble."

"Then why did you suggest it?"

"Because Emily loves it," he whispered.

***

Gus wondered what was taking Jared so long to get back with the parts for the truck Charles was working on. It shouldn't have taken him more than thirty minutes, and here it's been almost two hours. Hope he's not into some kind of trouble. The two weeks since his half-brother moved in with Gus have gone surprisingly well. Except for his moodiness at times, and complaints about not having enough money, they had gotten along surprisingly good. Gus tried to encourage him to save ten percent of his pay each week, but Jared persistently spent every dime. He didn't want to lecture him, but there has to be some cooperation if their living together was going to work long-term.

Jared's car pulled hastily onto the lot, he slammed the door and sauntered in to the office.

"Here are the ignition parts," he said, slamming the boxes down on the desk. "The guy had to search for them, then gave me the wrong ones, so he went to the warehouse and searched for another half hour. Talk about dumb."

Gus picked the boxes up and examined the part numbers. "I'm glad you checked them before you left there. Good work. Can you run these out to Charles real quick so he can get busy replacing them?"

Jared rolled his eyes and sighed. Picking up the boxes, he headed out the door.

"Come back in when you're done. I'd like us to discuss something."

Gus heard Jared mumble something under his breath but thankfully couldn't make out what it was. This time it was Gus's turn to sigh. He retrieved a couple cans of Pepsi from the office cooler and returned to his desk to wait for Jared.

When his half-brother/employee came in they settled in their chairs. Gus looked Jared in the eye. "What is going on with you today? It has to be more than the parts episode."

Jared pulled the tab on his cola and stared out the window. "It's everything. It's nothing. I don't even know. I'm just tired of always being broke, living off you, and not having any privacy. I can't even date anyone. I'm frustrated." He took a long swig and set the Pepsi can on the desk before slumping in the chair.

Gus took his time sipping his drink; more to stall and to choose his words carefully. "Well," he began, "you know this is temporary, right? I mean once we move into mom's house and you get some type of job training, you won't be dependent on me."

Jared's attention turned on to the last part of what Gus said. "What do you mean I won't be dependent on you? I won't be earning any money in job training, and my hours here will be cut."

"Mom agreed to provide a monthly allowance for you once we move in. Provided you obtain an education or training of some kind."

Jared's jaw dropped. He picked up his can and took another gulp, finishing it off. "What? You didn't say anything about that before."

"I didn't know about it until I finished reading the paperwork she sent with the house papers. I think she guessed how you'd feel and added it later. In any case, this is a temporary situation until we get moved in. That's why I've encouraged you to start saving a portion of your pay. Get used to doing it now so when you begin getting the other money, you won't be broke all the time."

Jared wasn't sure he liked the idea of his mother setting conditions about the money she'd provide. But then, it was her money. "I need time to think about all this. I still won't be independent."

"Not right away, but down the road you will. Open a savings account and put ten percent of all the money you get into it. Before long, you'll have money enough for a start-up business, and then you will be independent."

The phone rang. Gus answered and discussed some repair job with a customer. Jared wandered around the office a minute before going out to his car. He needed to think. Gus made sense, although Jared didn't want to admit it to him. If I can hang on till next year, I can get a business going. The idea of being involved with cyber security appealed to him. Next year, yeah.

Chapter Thirteen

Bree woke up shaking. The dream felt real. "Daddy," she uttered, "please come back." She stretched out, realizing her bed was the sofa. For a moment it seemed she was with her daddy on a mission trip. She blinked her eyes, hoping it wasn't a dream after all. Bree pulled her legs in and hugged her knees, wishing she could have changed the past while she slept. The image of his lying helpless, unconscious, in the hospital, would never leave her. What were your last thoughts when your truck flipped? Bree hoped they were of her. She remembered the memorial held and the testimonies from people he shared Christ with. Lives were changed because her daddy lived and told others about Jesus. Lord, help me carry on the legacy my daddy left behind. Show me where to go and guide my words for the lost to hear.

Bree got up, folded the coverlet, and went to the kitchen to put coffee on. She knew it wouldn't be long and Blanca would be padding in, ready for caffeine. Time with her momma the past month had been wonderful. Serving together, with the mission team from church was so rewarding. For once, Bree had a better grip on what she felt was God's plan for her future. With her teaching degree framed and on her wall, she looked forward to using it as a pathway to reaching the lost with the Gospel.

"Good morning," Blanca surprised her daughter.

Bree jumped a bit at her mother's greeting, letting the spoon fall to the counter. "Momma, you startled me. I was a hundred miles from here in my head."

"Sorry, baby, I smelled coffee. How ya doing this morning?"

"I'm good. Had an odd dream though."

Blanca took a cup from the hook under the cabinet, poured the black richness and added sweet and creamy concoctions before sitting at the table. "Want to tell me about it?"

Bree placed leftover coffee cake in front of Blanca, and joined her, coffee in hand. "Daddy was with me and we were telling children about Jesus," she answered, taking a seat.

Blanca smiled. "He's always with you." I wish I had told her about him sooner.

Bree took a slice of blueberry coffee cake and broke off a small corner, nibbling absentmindedly. "I will never forget how he touched lives for Jesus. I want to do that too."

"You're in the perfect place, honey. Ask God to show you how."

"I have been. The work we did all month was great and I know we made a difference the short time we were in Mission, Texas. I've been asking God to show me where my mission field is."

Blanca was quiet for a moment, wanting to help her daughter and yet —

"Your mission field is wherever you are," Blanca said.

Bree looked at her mother and grinned. "You're so wise, Momma. Thanks, that really helps. I'm going to make an appointment and talk with the pastor as soon as he has some free time."

Blanca picked up a piece of coffee cake and devoured a third of it before finishing her coffee. "That sounds like a plan to me. My plan is to unpack, do laundry, and start preparing my brain to go back to driving the bus next week."

"You know," Bree offered, "you really should think about retiring."

"Retiring? Now why on earth would I want to do that?" she laughed.

The phone rang and Bree scooted her chair back to go grab it. Blanca watched her disappear into the other room. *I need to think about my own mission field. Maybe even take my own advice about asking God to show me how.*

***

Kenneth Cavanaugh loved the suggestions Betty Hills offered for the showing of the documentary starring Greta and Clarence. Her idea of making it a Thanksgiving event would bring excitement into the assisted living place. *Many residents don't have relatives close by, or aren't able to travel for the occasion.* He promised to provide the turkey and dressing if she would arrange for the side dishes and desserts.

"Let's have the event on the Tuesday before Thanksgiving," Betty suggested. "Maybe show the film at one and then have the meal at three?"

"Sounds perfect and I'll make sure we bring in extra staff to help out. I'm sure they'll be happy to as long as we feed them."

"I'm glad you decided against the popcorn," Betty said, "sometimes older folks have difficulty swallowing it and we wouldn't want any mishaps."

"You're right," he agreed, "I caught myself on that one. I have this obsession with movies and popcorn, so I carried it here." He laughed.

Betty rose from her chair and prepared to leave the director's office. "Thanks again for all your help in getting this set up."

Kenneth came around from his desk and clasped her hand. "No, thank you. This project gave our place a breath of fresh air and pumped excitement into the staff, residents and me. I've never seen Greta in such an agreeable...no, such a friendly, state of mind. She is pleasant and nice to encounter now."

"She only needed someone to listen to her. Soon she'll have many people leaning in to hear what she has to say on the screen."

"Let's not forget Clarence," Kenneth added. "He's come out of his little corner of the room. He even mentioned to me about possibly getting an artificial leg."

"Really?" Betty asked in surprise, "I'm so happy about that."

Kenneth laughed. "Those two have been spending a lot of time together out in the garden area and dining room. I hear them chuckling out loud."

"I would never have paired them up, so it must be God."

Kenneth walked Betty to the door and watched as she made her way to the car. She's a special lady.

***

"Kat, I really need to see you and talk," Rita spoke into her phone with urgency. "Can you come by for a bit?"

"What's going on? Are you okay?"

Rita didn't want to tell her over the phone about Ron's proposal. She held out her left hand and smiled at the black gold engagement ring sitting proudly on her finger. "I'm fine. I'm more than fine. I just need you to stop by for a few minutes."

"Okay, calm down. I need to finish my class paper. Is this afternoon doable?"

"Bring your laptop, books, paper, whatever you need, and you can work on it here. Can't you come right now? Please?"

"You're lucky you're a dear friend. I wouldn't drop all this exciting school work for just anyone. I'll be there in about twenty minutes."

"Thank you, thank you. I promise, you won't be sorry."

Rita sat out on the porch, watching for Kat to pull up. She stroked Pekoe's orange stripes and was rewarded with soft purrs. "Are you content, my little bundle of joy?" More purring. "Guess so. Your favorite cat-sitter is coming over any minute," she whispered into her fur.

The VW pulled in and barely had time to stop before Kat hopped out and joined Rita on the porch. "Okay, I'm here in record time," Kat said a little breathless. "What's the urgent secrecy?"

"Let's go inside," Rita giggled, rousting Pekoe from her lap to her shoulder.

"Yeah, cause me to almost get a speeding ticket rushing over here and now you take your sweet time to tell me what's going on," Kat poked at her friend and gathered the furball to her chest. "Pekoe, what is this woman up to anyway?"

Inside, Rita sat on the sofa and patted the cushion next to her, being careful not to reveal her left hand. "Come sit. Let that silly kitty go play. I need to tell you something."

Kat released the kitten and plopped herself down. "WHAT?" she quizzed in an exasperated voice, and holding her hands out, palms up.

A smile, which reminded Kat of smiley face stickers, appeared on Rita's face, as she placed her left hand, palm down, on top of Kat's. Kat looked down, her jaw dropped and she squealed. Their eyes met. "Oh Rita," she said, hugging her friend, "I'm so happy for you. Thanks for not telling me over the phone."

Rita was crying, Kat was crying, and Pekoe jumped on the back of the sofa.

Kat took Rita's hand and examined the black gold infinity ring up close. "It's stunning. Ron knows you so well. It's the perfect ring for a sculptor. You're going to be a beautiful bride. When did he propose? How did he do it? When's the wedding?"

"Wow, that's a lot of questions. We decided on April 15th, Lillian's birthday."

"Awww, that is so special. So tell me everything and don't leave out one single detail."

Rita laughed. "I guess you're not working on your paper?"

"I actually didn't bring anything with me. I'll do it tonight." Kat winked.

"Let me put the kettle on and I'll tell you the story. I was just as surprised as you."

***

Betty began making calls to the estate sale group, inviting them to the Thanksgiving Event planned at Mt. Laurel to show the documentary film, "A Legacy Within". She had already talked with Emily and Seth, and they seemed very excited. The phone call to Sheila and Lane was done. Kat promised to contact Rita and Bree. Of course, Clay was in the know and would arrive early to get set up.

The excitement was beginning to build and in just a few weeks, her labor of love would be introduced for the first time in its entirety. Clay did an over-the-top job of adding Betty's introduction and Kenneth's story of how he came into the lives of these people. The crowning pieces though, were Clay's inserts of WWII clips, the photos Clarence provided, as well as Greta's few pictures of her mom, a couple clips about the stock market crash and several flashes of silver screen actresses. The ending will bring down the house.

Betty wondered if Brian would be working late today. She wanted to drive out to Wimberley tomorrow and spend some quiet time with him. It seemed to her they had been preoccupied with work and projects, so it would be nice to spend a weekend away. It's only midafternoon, maybe he'll call before leaving the office.

***

Ron hung up the phone. He sat back in the recliner and recalled his brother's words after hearing that Ron and Rita were engaged. "I'm happy for you and I know Mom would be pleased. Of course I'll be your best man." He didn't seem surprised although the date took him back a bit. Getting married on their mom's birthday jarred Jake a little, but in the end he was okay.

Right now, Ron felt content. After so many months of sadness, worry, and grief, happiness came down from heaven. Thank You, Lord.

The phone rang. Rita's face appeared on his screen and he hit talk. "Hey, sweetie, what's going on in your world right now?"

Her voice was quick with excitement. "I just talked to Kat and they are showing the documentary the Tuesday before Thanksgiving and we're invited."

"Sounds like fun, I'll schedule it at work so I can take off."

"I told Kat about our engagement and asked her to be my maid of honor."

"Was she surprised?"

"Completely. Tearfully. Joyously."

"I just talked to Jake and shared the news with him. He was happy for us and said he felt honored to be my best man."

"Well, we have that taken care of, now all we need to do is plan the wedding."

Ron smiled. "You plan the wedding, I'll take care of the honeymoon."

Rita laughed through the phone. "Why doesn't that surprise me?"

"I have a feeling you'll have plenty of volunteers to help. Whatever you come up with will be all right by me. Except for one thing."

"What's that?"

"I'd like my mom's pastor involved. Maybe we could take a run up to Mesquite and talk to him?"

Rita hesitated a moment. "Do you want us to be married there?"

"Not necessarily, unless you'd like it. I think he'd be happy to come here."

"It would be nice to have him perform the ceremony here so our friends could all attend. Why don't you make an appointment with him for after Thanksgiving."

"I'll put that on my wedding to-do list, right under find-a-romantic honeymoon location."

Rita laughed again. "I love you."

"I'm so madly in love with you, Rita. I've never loved a sculptress before," he teased.

"I wish I could see your face so I'd know if you're serious or joking."

"Honey, I'm as serious as you are about your work."

"I can't wait to become Mrs. Ron Davis."

"Ditto for me."

Rita smacked a couple kisses over the phone line before saying goodbye.

Ron hung up and decided to hunt down one of those meals Rita put in the freezer. Chili sounded good.

***

Brian looked at his watch and realized he had worked on the contract way past quitting time…if there was such a time. When he takes a day or two off, it ends up giving him crunch time when he returns. He really was trying to tie this one up so he could have a free weekend. He needed to get away and also wanted to make some progress on his book, "Miracles in Flight". He hadn't been to the Wimberley cottage in weeks. Maybe Betty would like to hide out there with him for a couple days. Since she and the film crew finished, she probably needs down time too.

He picked up the phone and pressed 2 on his speed dial. He listed her as Gaudy, the name he gave the hat she wore at the estate sale. It was the hat that caught his eye, but she who won his heart.

"Hi honey, I was thinking about you earlier, wondering if you'd be late," Betty said softly. "Are you still at work or on your way?"

"I'm about to leave. I worked on the contract so I could have a stress-free weekend with my favorite lady."

"Who would she be?" Betty teased.

"She's Miss Gaudy. Do you think she might enjoy a drive to Wimberley for the weekend?"

"I've already packed our bags. I was going to suggest it tonight."

"Soulmates stay connected even when apart. Do you want me to pick something up for dinner?"

"No, I have it waiting for you. Put yourself in that car and head home."

"Great, I'll be there before you have it on the table."

"Drive safely, bye."

Brian hung up the phone and put the contract in the folder. It was staying here. No homework this weekend. He couldn't wait to lock up and hit the road.

***

Seth felt his decision to take the house in the King William District off the market was the right thing to do. After hearing back from Lane that the Orlov couple did indeed have a son named Jared, Seth knew he couldn't allow the sale to happen. He felt sure they would be unhappy, but he made it clear he had other plans for the house. After talking it over with Emily and finding her in agreement, they would move forward with the required paperwork to gain approval of their plan from the King William Historical District. It would take a while, but there was a lot to do before it became a realization anyway. Now he only needed to call Brian and set his mind at ease. He placed the call.

"Hi, Seth, glad you called. Anything new going on with the house?"

"Glad I caught you, is this a good time?"

"I'm on my way home and talking hands free, so yeah."

"I took the house off the market today. Lane told me Jared is their son. Even though he doesn't live with them, I felt it right to dissolve the deal."

"I don't know what to say, Seth. Thanks seems insufficient considering you've lost a chance at making a good sum of money."

"I'm not worried about the money. I do have plans for the house and it will bring much more satisfaction than making the sale. Lane is helping me with details and when I have it lined out, Emily and I will share our endeavor."

"Mysterious, but I am appreciative of what you've done. You're a good friend."

"Are y'all doing anything this weekend?"

"Betty and I are sneaking away to Wimberley. We need some time to just put each other first and not think about work or projects for a couple days. Now, thanks to you, I'll cross that house situation off my mind too."

"Have fun and say hi to Betty for me, we'll see you at the film event in a couple weeks."

"I will, and yeah, we're all looking forward to that. Bye." Brian pressed the end-call button and smiled. "Thank You, Lord. You bless me in so many ways, but this call was a gift from you." He couldn't wait to give Betty the good news. He was happy he never told Kat about Jared's connection to the buyers.

***

Gus couldn't believe what he was hearing. He stared at his mother and shook his head. "What do you mean you're not moving? What happened to the house in the King William District?"

Ruby Orlov sat on the divan, holding the letter from the realtor. She shook it in the air toward Gus. "You tell me! All I know is the house was taken off the market. The owner decided not to sell because he has other plans for it."

"Can he do that?"

"I guess so. He's an attorney so he knows the laws."

Gus took a seat and rubbed his hand through his hair. "This is just great. Now where does that leave me? I've got Jared living at my place expecting to move here in a few weeks."

"Thanks for thinking about how I feel," Ruby threw back at him. "Vic and I had plans for that house too. It was the perfect spot for what we wanted to do."

"I'm sorry," Gus offered with little sympathy. "Now I have to take my place off the market."

"Well, you didn't have any offers anyway, did you?" She countered.

Gus sighed heavily and stood to leave. "I don't know what to do. Jared won't be able to stay with me where I'm at, it's too compacted. Besides, getting him to look at education and career ideas was dependent on our moving here. I doubt he'll do that now either. He's out of a job and an apartment."

"I'm sorry, it's not my fault. You saw the letter. Vic is upset too."

Opening the door, Gus turned. "But you don't have Jared here. He's your son and I think you need to take some steps to help him. I've provided temporary work but can't keep him on full-time. He needs a place to live and a way to afford it."

Gus walked out and shut the door a little too hard behind him. Now comes the difficult part, explaining this to his half-brother. Jared wouldn't take it nicely either, so it wasn't a scene Gus was looking forward to. He got in his truck and headed to the shop, not knowing if he'd tell him there or wait until they were at home. Home! For the first time in years Gus was dreading being there.

***

Annie Donovan finished her shift at Mesquite General Hospital and exited the elevator. Standing in front of her was Jake Davis. His presence immediately made her smile. "Jake, what brings you here this afternoon? Are you okay?"

"I'm fine, well, physically anyway. I wanted to talk to you though. Would you like to get something to eat?"

"I'd love to," she said, walking so close to him she could almost hear his heart pounding. "It's been a long day and I skipped my break earlier."

"How about IHOP? There's one close by. I feel like having breakfast for dinner."

"Sounds good to me," she laughed.

Jake took her hand as they left the hospital and stepped out into the crisp fall air. "A hearty meal will make you feel better. Is it okay if we go in my car and then I'll bring you back?"

"I'd like that." Annie cast a quick glance at his face when they approached his car. He seemed troubled. She had wondered why he cut off communication between them last month after her offer to loan him a book on grief. Annie figured it best to give him space and allow him time without her in the picture. After all, she hadn't known him long.

Jake unlocked the car and opened the passenger door. He helped her in and paused before closing the door. "Annie?"

She glanced up at his tender face. "Yes?"

"I've missed you...a lot."

She smiled. "I've missed you, too."

***

IHOP wasn't busy for a change, so because Jake and Annie had their pick of seating, they chose a booth in the back. After ordering and receiving breakfast for dinner, they settled in, made small talk, sipped on hot coffee and enjoyed their meal.

"I owe you an apology," Jake said suddenly, looking straight into Annie's green eyes.

She raised her eyebrow a bit. "For what?"

"The last time we talked, I was rude when you offered to loan me a book about grief. But, it's not just because I was rude. I'm apologizing because I pushed you away when your heart was reaching out to me after my mother died. I didn't realize it at the time, but you were exactly what I needed then."

Annie reached out and took his hand, hooking one finger around his. "Apology not necessary, but accepted. I knew you were grieving and the book was the only connection I had to that place deep inside of you. After we hung up that day, I cried...for you. I've never stopped praying that God would help you through those difficult days."

The smile on Annie's face almost crushed his soul. It was tender, warm and filled with something he couldn't identify. It wasn't pity or even compassion. She seems connected to my soul.

"Thank you. I needed your forgiveness."

"How are things moving in your life now? Is work going well? How's your brother doing?"

"Work is good, I've thrown myself into it and even hired an assistant to help implement a couple new services. Ron is doing great."

The server stopped by the booth and removed dirty dishes. "More coffee?" he asked.

"Yes, that would be wonderful," Jake responded.

"I got some news from Ron the other day. He and Rita are engaged."

"Wow, that's exciting. When's the wedding?"

Jake grew quiet for a moment. "Next year. April fifteenth, our mother's birthday," he finally said.

"Oh, what a sweet tribute. I think Lillian would be thrilled."

Jake nodded. "And, she'd be right in the middle of things helping with the wedding plans," he laughed.

The young man returned with a fresh pot of coffee. "Anything else I can get for you?"

"No, just our ticket. Thanks."

"I have it right here," he said, placing it next to Jake's cup. "Thanks for coming in."

"You're welcome." Jake grinned as the server left. After refilling both their coffee cups, he reached for his wallet pulling out bills for their meal and tip.

"Jake, I have enjoyed our being together today."

"That makes two of us, and I'm hoping we can do it again soon. Maybe take in a movie or something?"

"I'd like that."

"Right now though, I want to hear about you and what's been going on in your world. How's the job?"

"My work, unfortunately isn't always fun, but I do get satisfaction from spending time with my patients."

Jake remembered how Annie took such wonderful care of his mother. "You're a good nurse and very special. I'm hoping we can spend more time together."

Annie sipped her coffee and coyly said, "I have Thanksgiving week off."

Jake set down his cup and smiled. "I have an idea. Would you like to go with me to San Antonio?"

"Is there something special going on there?"

"My brother's friends have some kind of documentary film which is being shown on Tuesday and they have a Thanksgiving meal planned afterward. I'd love to have you as my guest. I think my future sister-in-law, Rita, would let you stay with her. You met her at the funeral, remember?"

"Sounds interesting, and I'd enjoy being there, but only if you check with her first. I do recall how friendly she was, and so helpful to both you and Ron."

"I'll call him later and get it all settled."

Annie stood and excused herself. "I'll be right back. Too much coffee I think."

Jake watched as she disappeared past tables and around the corner. Thank You, Lord, for humbling me, and allowing Annie back into my life.

Annie walked toward the other side of the restaurant, knowing Jake's eyes followed her. She loved how it made her feel special, wanted, and cared for. She enjoyed her job but it was consuming her. Being a nurse was rewarding, but also draining. She remembered reading somewhere that happiness was having something to do, someone to love, and something to hope for. Annie felt like Jake was somehow mixed up in all three areas. She smiled and felt truly happy right at that moment.

***

Blanca sat straight and stretched. She had been going over her finances and working on her plans for retiring in the coming year; if nothing changed her mind. She still had a large resource to fund her later years, thanks to Mary's generosity. The valuable jewelry collection she received in the estate sale last year was there when she needed it. She had enlisted a financial planner and worked out a few investments, something which was foreign to Blanca. Having Seth recommend a reputable person gave her confidence and she was in a good place. Her retirement from the city and social security would take care of most things. Bree is becoming independent and will soon be out creating her own legacy. I need to work on mine.

The phone rang. Blanca answered and was happy to hear Betty's voice.

"How are you? Have you and Bree settled into a routine since getting back?"

Blanca smiled into the phone. "Ha Ha, I don't have one yet, but it's nice to know I'll start back to work soon. That'll help speed up the process."

"I know Kat mentioned our film event to Bree, but I wanted to give you a call and personally invite you."

"Yes, Bree told me, but it's nice having you call. It sounds interesting. What's it about?"

"The elderly stars have no one. They've outlived family and friends. I wanted to make sure they aren't forgotten. Both are unbelievable people and I know you'll enjoy meeting them."

"We'll be there. Thanks for remembering us."

"Listen, Blanca, our estate sale group is special. We've bonded because of Mary, and her legacy continues to work its way in and through each one of us. That's one thing I love about our commitment to meeting annually. We can catch up on where her legacy has taken us, but more importantly, share where it's headed."

"You're right. We're looking forward to it." Blanca hung up, excited about the event.

Chapter Fourteen

Jared wondered what was up with his brother. Gus called and told him to head to the house, there was something they needed to discuss. What now? Jared's thoughts ran rampant. Maybe Gus was kicking him out. Where would I go? The drive to his half-brother's house didn't take long and Gus had beaten him home. He parked his Charger facing out, his usual direction in case he needed to leave quickly. It had become a habit from way back.

"What's up?" Jared asked, entering the small frame house. Gus was in the kitchen seated at the square table by the window. Jared guessed he'd been watching for him. The look on Gus's face was somber. Bad news.

"I need to talk to you about a situation and I'll tell you right now, it's not something you're gonna be happy to hear."

Jared sat opposite Gus and stared at him. "What? The business going under and you have to fire me?"

"The business is fine." Gus mumbled, unsure of how to break the news that they wouldn't be moving into their mother's home.

"Then what? Stop beating around the bush and spit it out."

Looking his brother in the eye, he spoke quickly before he lost his nerve. "Mom is not moving. The seller took the house off the market." He watched Jared's face wash white.

"And that means?"

"Don't you get it?" Gus shouted, flinging his arm in the air. "They aren't moving, we aren't moving."

Jared swallowed the lump in his throat, unable to speak. He really had no words anyway. Standing, he shoved his hands into his jeans' pockets and walked to the door, then looked back at Gus. Jared turned and headed to his room.

"Jared, I'm sorry," Gus called, following after him. "Mom was upset too, they had plans." He stood in the doorway and watched as Jared pulled a small suitcase from under the bed and began tossing stuff into it.

"What are you doing?"

Jared remained silent and worked to fill the suitcase before zipping it shut. He pulled keys from his pocket, removing the house and shop key Gus had made for him, and tossed them on the bed. "You're better off without me here," he said matter-of-factly. "I need to be on my own anyway. I can carry my own weight and don't need a nanny."

"Jared — "

Gus moved from the doorway as his brother pushed past him and went outside. Gus jumped when the door slammed behind him. The car started and gravel flew as Jared sped away.

That didn't go well. Gus wondered if he should call his mom, but then decided now was not the time. He walked back to Jared's room and wondered what he was supposed to do with the rest of his things. Maybe he'll cool off and be back in a couple days. He closed the bedroom door and decided to go to the shop for a while. Work had a way of getting his mind off things.

***

Jared drove without knowing where he was going. Maybe the house deal's falling through was a sign he wasn't supposed to move there anyway. It sounded too good to be true, and everyone knows the outcome of that way of thinking. Right now it didn't matter. His parents didn't care. They preferred to work through Gus rather than talk to Jared. *I'm a loser; homeless, jobless and hopeless.*

***

Lane and Sheila pulled out of their downtown parking space and headed home. The training class went well and they learned some things which would help them raise their future foster child.

"What do you think she'll be like?" Sheila asked. "I mean, after the facilitator emphasized how most foster children come from seriously broken home environments, it's a little scary."

"That's why we're taking the classes, to prepare us." Lane kept his eyes on the road, even as similar thoughts were tumbling around his mind. "We just need to keep praying God will provide the kind of child we can learn to love."

"Lane, Mr. Gray also mentioned there were many handicapped children needing foster parents. Do you think we would be up to taking a child with extensive physical challenges?"

"We did it with David after he developed cancer," he said, taking a quick glance at his wife.

Sheila was quiet. "What about a child with emotional problems? Are we positioned well enough emotionally ourselves to handle a fragile young mind?"

"Honey, let's not second guess our decision to do this. You know how long we've prayed over it and we agreed to trust God to bring us the right child. He knows our heart, our emotional capability, and physical stamina." He stopped at the red light, turned and gave Sheila a quick kiss. "We have lots of love to give and that's what children need most."

"You're right. I'm just a little nervous after hearing so much tonight. It was almost as if Mr. Gray were trying to discourage everyone in the class."

Lane saw a traffic backup ahead, so he turned to avoid it by taking the back roads. "It was intentional. I believe it was done to weed out any who might not be fully committed to fostering a child. If they don't come back, he'll know. But, he was telling it like it is and not sugarcoating the job."

"I know," Sheila agreed, and I'm glad we have the Lord working things out."

Lane nodded without speaking, trying to maneuver around the closed-off street and take the detour. "On a different note, I'm glad Seth took his house off the market. Did I tell you the prospective buyer called me and was crying?"

"No, what did you say?"

"I let her cry a while, then explained it was out of my hands and her deposit would be returned to her."

"That should have pleased her."

Lane laughed. "Ha, are you kidding? It made her more upset. She said she didn't care about the money and something about it has torn her whole family apart."

"Wow! It sounds like some backstory is happening with them. Maybe it's a blessing Seth took it off the market."

"Yeah, and Seth even wanted to give me a prorated commission because I lost the sale. I told him I wouldn't accept it."

"Good. I hope the couple finds a place though. They must be very disappointed."

"They will, the buyers' market is good right now. I'm more curious about what Seth wants to do with the house. He has some remodeling planned once approval comes through. It's all secrecy right now though."

"Maybe they will reveal something at the Thanksgiving event on Tuesday. I'm looking forward to the film and the dinner," Sheila said excitedly.

"I doubt he'll say anything until the paperwork is signed and ready. But, from the way he talked when he first told me, Mary's legacy will be involved."

"Hmmm," Sheila said, "that's intriguing. Maybe Emily will give me some hints."

"You're too curious, my dear," Lane chuckled as he finally entered the King William District residences. "How about some popcorn and a movie when we get home?"

"Sounds great, how about a Poirot mystery since we have the whole season on CD?"

"Ah, the little mustached Belgium, one of my favorite TV characters. Hercule Poirot it is."

***

Clay finished the edits on the film and was extremely proud of the piece. He put so much energy into this project and it was enjoyable working with Kat, and her step-mother, Betty. Of course, Clay anticipated having more of a relationship with Kat throughout the project, but it didn't seem to materialize. He cared a lot for her and although she seemed to like him a great deal, there were times when she treated him like a brother. He stayed confused and had no idea how to deal with it.

Tuesday the film would debut at Mt. Laurel, and Clay had to admit, he was excited about showing it. He knew both the stars, Clarence and Greta, would get tons of attention afterward, and that made him feel good. He really grew to like Clarence, and hoped to stay in touch. Greta, well, she was feisty in the beginning, but doing the film seemed to mellow her. Now of all things, those two seemed to be attracted to each other. At least she doesn't treat Clarence like he's her brother. Clay laughed at the thought. Maybe if Kat and I get to that age, she'll be more attracted to me. He laughed again, trying to visualize them at ninety-seven.

He settled himself on the bed, picked up his Bible and prepared to study for the small group he would lead at the end of the month. It was an honor when the pastor asked if he'd be willing to bring a lesson. Lord, give me a topic so I can start preparing. The phone rang. Maybe God's calling with what He wants me to teach. Clay smiled when he saw Kat's number on the ID.

"Hey there, Kat," he said with enthusiasm, "What's happening in your world?"

"We have so much going on here, with Betty sewing up last minute things for the film. We're baking pies and taking them to Mt. Laurel to store in the freezer until Tuesday, and Dad wants to eat them faster than they come out of the oven," she laughed.

"Maybe I should come help him."

"He'll fight you for them."

"So, how can I help then?"

"Well, I hoped we could meet and go over a few details concerning Clarence."

Clay became serious. "He's okay, isn't he?"

"Oh, he's more than okay. There's been a couple things happen though and I thought we might need to adjust the program a little."

"No problem on this end. How about Starbucks in thirty minutes?"

"Perfect, the one on the corner by my house?"

"Works for me. See you in a few."

Clay hung up the phone and was almost prone to dance a few steps of joy. *Thank You, Lord, for bringing that phone call and opportunity to spend a little time with Kat.* He turned off the light, grabbed his Film Project notebook, and headed out. *I wonder what Clarence is up to?*

***

Ron loaded the star sculptures into the car, then joined Rita in the studio. "Okay, they're ready to travel."

"Good, so that means you're pleased with how they turned out?"

He planted a kiss on her cheek. "More than pleased, my dear, they're outstanding. I can't wait to get them installed."

"What a relief. The largest one had me a nervous wreck."

Ron sat on the stool by one of the work stations. "You always do unique pieces of art. We need to enter some of your other creations in an art show."

Rita sat on the opposite stool. "Do you think they're good enough, really?"

"I wouldn't suggest it if I didn't. I'll check around and see what's out there and you go through your sculptures and decide which you would like to submit."

Rita was thoughtful. "I think I know already."

"Good." Ron stood to leave then sat down again. "By the way, would you mind having a house guest next week?"

"Who?"

"My brother invited Nurse Heartie...I mean Annie, to come down for the film project and Thanksgiving. He asked if it would be too much of an imposition for her to stay with you."

"I'd love to have her as my houseguest. She's not allergic to cats is she?" Rita laughed.

"I don't have a clue, but I'll let Jake know you have one so he can warn her ahead of time. They'll be here Monday. My brother's staying with me."

"It'll be fun having a roomie. Tell Jake I'm looking forward to it."

Ron stood once again and took her hand. "Come walk me out and I'll get those stars transported."

"Be careful with them," she teased, "they're valuable and would be very expensive to replace."

He slipped his hands around her waist and kissed her softly before leaving.

She blew him a kiss as he drove off. *I surely do love that man.*

***

Blanca busied herself cleaning the house, preparing enchiladas, and getting the guest room ready. Rosie accepted the invitation to spend time with her and Bree over Thanksgiving, and assured her she would have fun at the film debut. Rosie had been on her mind all week and the thought of her spending the holiday alone, since her son was stationed overseas, was unthinkable to Blanca. Bree was excited about having her come too. It would be good for all of them since Rosie knew Carlos and they were all connected by a special bond.

"Momma, I'm home," Bree called out bouncing through the door. "You'll never guess what our pastor said at our missions meeting today."

Blanca wrapped her arms around her daughter, brushing a kiss across her cheek before letting her loose. "No, I'm not a good guesser. What?"

"He asked ME to lead the next Missions group when we go back to Mexico."

She looked at Bree, noticing her shoulders back and head held high. "I'm not surprised. I saw how you took hold of things during the last one and the whole group accomplished so much. I'm very proud of you."

"Thanks, Momma, I'm excited and praying I do well. Pastor said it would be advantageous to have the leadership skills when I apply for the Missionary Board."

"He's right. The experience will be important."

"Did I see you putting enchiladas together?" Bree mentioned as she rubbed her stomach.

Blanca laughed. "If that's a hint, you'll have to wait. Rosie is coming, remember?"

"What time will she be here?"

"About six this evening. I'm sure she'll be hungry so I thought I'd have it all ready."

Bree pouted in fun. "I need food now," she pleaded with a sad face.

"I have a nice salad in the fridge. Thought we'd enjoy that for lunch."

"I'll go set the dishes out," Bree offered with a smile as she blew a kiss to Blanca.

"Wow, food moves you fast."

"I heard that."

***

Rosie drove her old car down the highway, hoping it would make it to San Antonio. She was apprehensive about visiting Mrs. Moreno and her daughter, fearing she would break down on the road and be stranded. So far, so good. She had taken time off work because

Thanksgiving week was always slow. Alfredo, her boss, closed during that week. It was always nice when Rosie's son was home, but with his being in the military, she would be spending the holiday alone. When Mrs. Moreno called and invited her to come, she agreed. I hope I made the right decision. I really don't know her well, but she's been so kind to me, I couldn't refuse.

Traffic was light and she was careful to do the speed limit. If she calculated right, she'd arrive about six. Her only stops were for gas and potty breaks. It'll be nice to visit San Antonio, and be able to do something different. Her life was lonely without her son. All she did was go to work at the restaurant, attend church, volunteer at the animal shelter, and tend to her little garden. Rosie was thankful for Carlos's having shared Jesus with her. When he was alive, she talked to him often about the Bible and he even helped her memorize some verses. She missed him a lot. This was the highway which claimed his life.

Rosie pulled into the convenience store lot next to the pump. She decided to gas up and then go inside for a cup of coffee to settle her down a little. The pump clicked the gallons away and when finished she replaced the gas cap, retrieved her receipt, and pulled the car around to the Circle-K entrance and went inside. Very few people were there so getting her coffee took only seconds. She found a seat by the window and settled herself, wondering if Carlos might have ever stopped here and maybe even sat in this very spot.

Outside the window, people stopped for gas, and zipped back onto the highway in just minutes. Travelers, families, business people, and most likely many lost souls. Her heart skipped a beat. She remembered Carlos's telling her about a time when he shared Jesus with a man getting gas. She smiled. He would do that. Rosie wondered if Mrs. Moreno knew the real heart of her husband.

Sipping her coffee slowly, she knew time was slipping away and she needed to get on the road. Rosie found the restroom and then headed back to her car. Somehow, the realization of what she wanted to do managed to sink in. She smiled again. Thank you, Carlos. Rosie started the car and entered the highway humming "At the fountain weary traveler...."

***

Kat stuffed the newspaper section into her back pocket before heading out to meet Clay at Starbucks. Earlier, she had scanned the articles when one caught her eye. "University professor resigns after complaints against him were reported." After reading it she discovered her professor...Professor Evans was the one resigning. She had called her friend from school to see if she had been the one who reported him, but she wasn't.

It was unbelievable. Kat took a deep breath. Thank You, Lord. Now I don't have to worry about him sabotaging my grade. Kat mentioned it to her dad in a note, promising to discuss it when she returned. She locked the house and jumped into her car. Her call to Clay to discuss Clarence was half true. The other half was to ask him if he had reported the professor. Surely he wouldn't have registered a complaint on her behalf. He did witness the scene between them. No, he wouldn't do that without asking or telling me. Would he?

***

Betty tidied up the cottage while Brian gathered their things to load in the car. It had been a wonderful couple days together in Wimberley. She loved reading, relaxing, and their taking time to shop the stores.

Brian gave her his manuscript, His Story, to do final edits on and although it wasn't a working weekend, she took time to look at it quickly before they would leave. It was certainly a tribute to Clarence, bringing out the humility by which he lived his life. This book was genuine and she believed it would touch many hearts.

The plan in the beginning was to write only about Clarence, but since watching God transform Greta, Brian decided to write a sequel about her. It was exciting to see how Brian's writing took a turn in a completely different direction. The focus changed from Brian to Clarence and God was in the midst.

"Honey, you about ready?" Brian called from the kitchen.

"Yes, I've put clean sheets back on the bed, took out the trash and turned off the computer. I'm ready to roll," she teased.

He met her half-way in the breakfast room and hugged her close. "I'm glad we came," he murmured.

"Yes," she said, hugging him back. "It was a nice pause for us."

He released her, but took her hand. "Let's go tackle the traffic. Maybe we can stop at DQ before hitting the city limits."

Betty laughed. "Sometimes I think you love Dairy Queen more than you love me."

"It depends," he chuckled, "do you have strawberries and hot fudge?"

They laughed, locked the door, and got in the car.

***

"These enchiladas are very good, Mrs. Moreno."

"Please, call me Blanca, and thank you. I'm glad you enjoyed them."

Rosie smiled and sat back in her chair. She was delighted in being here with Blanca and her daughter. The car made the trip with no problems, but she did get turned around trying to find the house.

"You're so nice to invite me and I'm looking forward to the event and seeing your friends. It wasn't a happy time when we were together last year."

Blanca rose from her chair. "No, it wasn't, but I'm happy you were able to come and I know everyone will be glad to see you. Why don't we go to the living room and relax. I know you must be tired from all that driving."

Rosie stood, and started to pick up her dish.

"No, no, Mrs. Trevino," Bree said, getting up from her chair. "You and Momma go sit down and enjoy your time together. I'll clean up in here."

"I don't mind, really," Rosie offered, "I do it at the restaurant all the time."

"Exactly," Blanca said, "and here you're our guest."

Rosie set the plate down and followed her hostess to the other room. "Thank you for your kindness."

"I'll bring tea in shortly," Bree called out. "Unless Mrs. Trevino would rather have coffee."

"Tea will be fine," Rosie answered. "Thank you."

The two women settled on the sofa while Bree busied herself in the kitchen. Rosie leaned back and rested her eyes a bit.

"I have some cookies we can have with our tea, if you like," Blanca said. She looked at her guest and realized she had dozed off. Blanca quietly stepped away to the kitchen and told Bree to hold off on the tea. "She's exhausted. I hate to leave her sleeping on the sofa, but don't want to wake her either."

"Give her a few minutes and see if she wakes up on her own," Bree whispered.

Blanca decided to help Bree with the dishes and give Rosie some moments to cat nap. "Bless her heart, she looks very tired."

"A nap will be good. Driving wears you out."

"Yes, I remember when you and I made that long drive.

"I do too, Momma, and it was a sad time for us." She put her arm around Blanca and squeezed. "I love you."

Blanca put down the dish towel and embraced her daughter tightly. "I love you more."

***

Clay and Kat were both quiet as they sat in Starbucks. He reassured Kat he had no part in reporting the man. She felt confident he was telling the truth and was relieved. Part of her felt a little guilty though. Maybe she should have done something at the time. Her thoughts had only been about her grades. Now it seemed selfish. If she had said something then, maybe he wouldn't have made another girl's life miserable. God, please forgive me.

Clay reached for her hand. "Are you okay?"

"I'm good," she said, nodding. "Thanks for coming and talking to me about this."

He squeezed her hand, then stood, assisting her from the chair. He escorted Kat to her car, making sure she was tucked inside. "I'll see you Saturday when we go to Mt. Laurel."

"Yeah, I'm looking forward to it. Thanks again, Clay. Goodnight."

He went back to his car, but turned as he slid onto the seat. She was still watching him. Clay felt at times as if she cared for him. This was one of those times. He smiled, waved, and drove off.

***

Kat opened the front door and smelled brownies. She followed the aroma to the living room and saw her Mum and Dad snuggled close on the sofa, watching Sherlock and Watson solve some crime.

"Hi," they said in unison. "Come join us, it just started," Betty added.

Kat stepped into the room, planted a kiss on top of each of their heads. "You made brownies while I was out?"

"The mood struck and we couldn't resist," Betty said, laughing.

"Well, I need a tall glass of milk with mine. I'll be right back."

"We'll talk about the news article later," Brian called after her.

"Later is good, but it's no big deal," she sang out.

As promised, she returned quickly, milk in one hand and brownie in the other, then made herself comfortable in the recliner.

Brian had paused the movie briefly to give her time. He couldn't resist asking about the professor incident. "So you weren't the one who reported him?"

"No, Dad. I have no idea who was responsible. I talked to Clay and it wasn't his doing either."

Brian exhaled. "God will bring justice in that whole situation."

"Amen," Betty agreed.

"Can you restart the movie?" Kat asked, savoring the melted goo.

Brian hit play on the remote and smiled. "Here we go."

***

Clay drove home slowly, wondering about Kat's professor. Here she was so concerned he might crash her grade because of the encounter they had on campus, and then he resigns because he was harassing other female students. Clay hoped his departure didn't mean he'd be free to go to a different university and repeat his offenses. Surely he would be charged and made to pay for his actions. At least now, Kat didn't have to worry about him and would be able to ace graduation. *I need to get my own career moving forward. This project with Kat has been fun but there's no pay with it. Of course, it* will be part of my portfolio and help me show people what I can do. My part-time work helps pay the rent and a few extras, but that's about it.

He pulled his car into his parking slot, locked and went upstairs. He wanted to watch the film again and be sure it was ready to show Greta and Clarence on Saturday. Then sleep!

Chapter Fifteen

Kenneth Cavanaugh closed the door to the sitting room and stepped softly down the hall back to his office. Mrs. Hills and her film crew were settled in and preparing to allow Clarence Hartman and Greta Garson to preview the documentary featuring them. He smiled to himself, pleased at the change he had observed in both his residents since the filming began.

In his office, he picked up where he left off before the crew arrived. With the Thanksgiving event for them and the residents of Mt. Laurel just three days away, his checklist was far from being completed. He managed to order the turkeys. ham, and dressing. Well, his secretary took care of that. She also pooled the staff to supply all the side dishes except desserts. Since Mrs. Hills promised to cover dessert, most of which was already in either the cooler or freezer, the meal was taken care of.

Kenneth decided to ask some friends to help transform the social room into a theater of sorts. They would arrive Tuesday morning. All Kenneth had to do was order the decorations and props to make it happen.

The ringing phone drew him away from his list. "Good afternoon, this is Director Cavanaugh, how may I help you?"

"Ken," responded Rich, his long-time friend, "hope your day is going well."

"It couldn't get much better. What's up? Are you still on tap for

Tuesday morning to work your magic in the social room?"

"We had a little hiccup with one of the guys. His wife is in the hospital so we're a man down. That's why I'm calling. We might need your help with a couple things."

"No problem, I'm happy to pinch hit for your guy. I hope his wife doesn't have any serious issues."

"They think it's her gallbladder, so they're running tests. It may turn out to be nothing, but Jerry felt he couldn't commit to helping."

"Of course not. I'll be praying for her."

"Thanks. We'll get there at eight Tuesday morning if that's okay with you."

"Eight is fine. I plan to come in at six, so if you want to show up earlier, just show up. I have the decorations and props ordered for delivery on Monday."

"Well, we're all set then. Have a great weekend and we'll see you in a few."

"You too, Rich. See you soon."

Kenneth hung up, made some notes, and looked at his watch. It was after 1:30, so he decided to grab a bite to eat while the film was being previewed. He was hoping they would invite him to sit in, but Mrs. Hills explained it would be best if Greta and Clarence saw it privately. She said emotions may be unpredictable and wanted to allow them both to process it without an audience. He certainly understood and respected that.

His stomach growled. He should have eaten before they arrived.

***

Greta and Clarence had front row seats in the sitting room usually set aside for visitors of the residents at Mt. Laurel. Today it was turned into a private viewing room. Clay had set up the large screen earlier and, upon Greta's arrival at 1:00 sharp, escorted her to her seat. Clarence had rolled his own wheel chair in prior to Greta's punctual timing for her arrival.

Betty offered drinks, but both preferred none.

"Would you cut the lights please?" Clay asked Kat, who was pausing near the switch.

The room darkened and the film began with an introduction by Betty. She shared how the film was born from her own discovery of a woman's photo in a silver frame at an auction years ago. Clay did an excellent job of panning the background: Betty's desk with various picture frames, with the one she talked about front and center.

The room was quiet except for the faint music in the background. The title page came on the screen and bold black letters proclaimed, "His Story" followed by a photo of Clarence in his WWII uniform. It was one he had given Betty last month. Yellowed and a bit tattered, but a photo of a handsome young man ready to serve his country.

Greta leaned over and whispered to him, "My, I bet you were a real ladies' man."

Clarence laughed out loud, but sat a little taller in his wheelchair.

***

Jared realized he'd been driving a long time when his leg began cramping. He looked around, searching for a rest stop, gas station or any place he could pull over. He needed to stretch his legs fast. Glancing at the gas gauge, he knew it wouldn't take him much further without a refill. He spotted an old service station in the next block and pulled in just as the cramp overtook him. He slammed on the brake, threw the car in park and jumped out. Limping around, stomping his foot in the ground and massaging his leg must have looked ridiculous, but it was working. The cramped leg started to relax and then pins and needles began tingling his whole leg.

"You okay, fella?" an ancient looking guy asked, approaching Jared from behind.

Jared did an about-face quickly, somewhat startled. "Sure, I had a leg cramp from driving too long. It's gone now."

"Better drink some water or you'll be a hoppin' around in another few miles. My name's George Banks," he said, extending his right hand.

"Good to meet you, Mr. Banks. Jared Orlov," he replied, returning the handshake. He couldn't help but notice the old man's left arm from the elbow down was missing.

"Aw, just call me George." He noticed Jared staring at his missing limb. "Lost it in a machine accident 'bout ten years back. Glad I ain't left-handed," he chuckled.

Jared grimaced. "Ouch, that had to hurt. Glad you're doing well now."

"Yep, I pretty much hang out with the other geezers and swap stories. Not much else to do when you hit eighty."

They both laughed.

"I used to be a pastor in my younger days."

"Oh?" Jared said, surprised. The old guy didn't look like a pastor. But then, what does a pastor look like when he's eighty.

"Yes sir, I preached in a tent for many years, trying to set them young folk on the right path, you know, the straight and narrow one."

Jared began to feel a sermon coming on, so he tried finding a way out. "I need to gas up. By the way, where am I? What town is this?"

"Young man, you're in Blanco, Texas. Where ya from?"

"Blanco?" Jared asked. I left Gus, headed south and now I'm going north?

"I live in San Antonio and struck out on a whim. Guess I got turned around. Must not have been paying much attention."

"You're not in trouble with the law are you?"

"No, Sir. Just needed to put some space between me and family."

"I can understand about family troubles. Had my share. But, I'll give you a bit of friendly advice young man. Keep family ties strong. When you're in trouble, sometimes they all ya got. Besides the good Lord, of course." George smiled a toothless grin. "When I had this here accident," he continued, tapping his left elbow, "my relatives surrounded me and came to help. They all prayed for me too. Wore their knees plumb out"

Jared didn't feel like airing his problems with this stranger, although by now he knew quite a bit about him. "That's great, George, I'm happy for you. I really need to gas up and go."

"Sure 'nuff," said the old man. "If yer hungry, there's a diner couple a blocks down main. Tim owns the joint. Tell him I said to fix you George's special and give you the same price."

"Thanks, I'll do that." Jared watched him shuffle off to who knows where.

He filled the tank, grabbed a cold bottle of water, paid the little gal inside, and slid back in his car. He wasn't hungry but didn't know where to go or what to do. Family. Ha. George doesn't know my family. He crossed his arms on the steering wheel and rested his head in the middle. Maybe he should disappear. Drive to some little town where no one would bother him and he could start a new life. His head began to throb across his temples. He sat up and rubbed the cold water bottle on his forehead. After several minutes he opened the bottle and took a long drink. It helped. His stomach growled. Maybe he'd stop at the diner and eat a bite before taking off. I don't have to be anywhere, so why not? Jared started the car, pulled out onto Main Street and drove a bit before spotting the diner. He pulled his Charger around the side, and backed into the parking space. Backing in was a habit he had developed which had served him well on several occasions.

Inside the diner Jared noticed a table in the corner where some working guys in uniforms sat. They laughed loudly. Western music played, also a bit loud. A booth near the door was empty so he slid in quickly. A young gal, probably nineteen or twenty, came around with a plastic menu and tall glass of water. She placed a straw on the table and smiled.

"Hi there, I'm Sarah. What can I get you today?"

"Well, a guy named George told me to tell Tim to give me George's special and his price." He smiled back. He loved her rusty hair that bobbed up and down when she walked.

She called out in a rather loud voice, "Tim, George sent another one in for his special."

"It'll be out in just a few," she said in a softer tone.

"Thanks. By the way, what is George's special?"

She laughed. "You'll see soon enough."

Jared watched as she moved quickly from his booth to check on the uniforms at the corner table." Maybe I should have asked George what the special was before I came in.

***

Gus finally found the courage to call his mother and relate the outburst with Jared. Now she was mad at him, even though it was because of her, his brother took off in a huff. Gus came back to the shop if for no other reason but to kill time, hoping Jared would show up. Maybe after he cools down he'll realize he doesn't have anywhere to go.

His helper, Charles, had left hours ago, leaving Gus by himself in the building. It always seemed lonely when he was the only one there. You can shuffle invoices, prepare part orders, and inventory stock only just so long until you find yourself shooting baskets with wadded up paper. He wasn't ready to go home, so the only other choice was stop somewhere and eat. He certainly wasn't going by his mother's. One confrontation with her was enough for today.

***

"That's it!" Ruby yelled at her husband, Victor. "I've had it with Jared. We've tried to help him and what does he do? He disappears and leaves his family to worry over him."

"Now, now," Victor tried calming his wife. "He'll come to his senses and show up at Gus's place soon. This was a shock to all of us."

"Yes," she continued her high-pitched rant, "and he doesn't care about how we feel, not getting the house. He's not interested in how upset I am. That's what I get for trying to provide for him. He's a grown man and here we are, putting money in his checking account so he won't become destitute."

"Ruby, we haven't given him money in a long time, remember?"

A light came on in Ruby's eyes. She cleared her throat. "Well, that's beside the point. He should still have consideration for his mother."

Victor Orlov put his arm around his wife and patted her arm affectionately. "Let's go grab a bite to eat and talk about our next step regarding our home."

She seemed calmer as she spoke. "What next step? We're stuck here. I am hungry though. Maybe just something simple."

Victor laughed. "Okay, I'll surprise you." He closed the blinds and picked up his keys. Why can't she just be happy here?

***

Seth thought about his earlier conversation with Lane. He had notified the Orlov couple that the house had been taken off the market, so now Seth would move forward with his plans to do something entirely different. He sent the ideas and plans to the King William Historical Society for approval and hoped to hear something soon. Ideas were bursting in his head about how to continue Mary's legacy, one which would change more lives for generations to come. Having Emily on board made the plan all the better.

"Hey, Sweetie," Emily said, coming up behind him in the living room, "You're lost in deep thought again."

Seth turned and smiled as his wife came around and sat next to him on the sofa. "I'm contemplating our new adventure and wondering about our time frame."

"Much depends on the historical society board and how fast they approve the paperwork, but it's really our self-imposed time frame."

Seth laughed. "If they approve it, and yes, I'd like to get started as soon as possible. Maybe even get the remodel completed by early spring."

"We need to trust God in this. Remember, it's His timing, not ours."

"You're right. I get nervous a little though, thinking about what we want to do and the possibility of it's all falling through."

"If that happens then it wasn't meant to be."

"I love how you approach everything. You're so organized, so straightforward, and yet your faith accepts the unknown as God's plan."

Emily snuggled close to Seth. "God's plan for our lives can be much different than our own plans. We need only to wait on His providence. Now, speaking of plans, how about taking a drive to the mall?"

"You wanting something special?"

"In a way, although I'm not sure of what. I'd like to get a small gift for Betty. She's been working so hard on preparing for the film event this Tuesday. I just thought it would be fun to surprise her with something."

Seth stood, pulling Emily up, and kissing the tip of her nose. "You have a generous heart and you really care about others. I'm so blessed to be married to you."

She cupped his face with her hands. "I love you more than my heart could ever express." She kissed him gently, then suddenly grabbed his hand. "We better go before the mall closes or I change my mind."

***

Rita tidied up her studio apartment. Small as it is, there wasn't much to do, but she wanted to make it nice for Jake's friend, Annie, for her arrival on Monday. Rita rearranged the living area so the couch was on the other wall, and placed a privacy screen on the side of it. It wasn't much but it helped. Clean towels were in the bathroom, and she even bought fresh flowers. Rita liked the look, and hoped Annie would enjoy it too. I should keep fresh flowers here all the time.

Monday morning Rita would make a quick run to the store and pick up fresh crescents, fruit and popcorn. Maybe the four of them would enjoy a movie night in. You must have popcorn on movie night.

The knock on the door drew her attention. Pekoe meowed. Rita looked through the peephole, then threw the door open. "Ron," she said excitedly, "this is a surprise." She hugged him thoroughly before realizing he had another welcome.

Pekoe rubbed Ron's leg, purring softly. He reached down and scooped the furry, orange bundle into his arms.

"I should arrive unannounced more often if I get this kind of welcome."

Rita shut the door as Ron set the kitten on the floor.

"Would you like some coffee?"

"Not unless it's made and you join me; with tea of course."

She laughed. "It'll only take a minute. Let's use the breakfast bar. I rearranged things for when Annie gets here and want to keep it looking nice."

Ron hoisted himself onto the bar stool. "Are you saying I'm messy?" he teased.

Rita busied herself making the coffee and tea, pulling down the mug for him and setting out the china cup for herself. "Of course not my love, but since my apartment is small there's not a lot of leg room."

"I've been thinking about that. We should begin discussing where we'll live once we're married."

Rita turned and looked at Ron. "You're right," she said, surprised she never thought about where they would settle. "I love my studio apartment, and Pekoe does too, but it is a bit small."

"Do we want to stay in this area, live in an apartment, or buy a house? These are things we need to talk about, don't you think?"

She poured the finished coffee into his mug, bringing it and her steeping chai tea to the counter, taking a stool opposite Ron.

"How do you feel about apartments? This area is convenient to my class studio."

"I'll be happy anywhere with you," Ron said. "You know, my

apartment isn't much larger than this one. I don't mind apartment living, but a house would be an investment."

"And a lot of upkeep."

Ron sipped his coffee, contemplating their conversation. "It's not a decision we need to make immediately, but we will have to give notice ahead of time. Yours isn't a real lease, but mine is. It's up at the end of March."

"Okay, then we should find a place by March 31st and you could move in there. I'll give my notice six weeks ahead and once we're married you can carry me across the threshold to our new place."

They smiled at each other, pleased at reaching at least one decision.

"So," Rita changed the subject, "did you have another reason for this surprise visit?"

Ron took her left hand and ran his finger over her engagement ring. "As a wedding present, I would like to set you up with your own studio for Rita's Artsy Kids. Harry Roddis has a fantastic building he wants to sell at a great price. It's central to this area, so current kids will still be able to get there."

Rita put her free hand over her eyes and shed tears of joy.

Ron looked at her and squeezed her hand. "Hey, if you'd rather not, I can always get you something else."

She smudged the tears onto her arm, sniffled and smiled. "I would love to have my own building. You are wonderful to think of doing something so amazing. Thank you."

Ron rose from his stool and went around the counter. He pulled her close, encircling her with both arms. "You're amazing. I want to make you the happiest woman in the world." He kissed the top of her head, then tilted her face toward him. "So it's a go? I can tell Harry we'll go take a look at it for your official approval before I give him a check?"

Rita nodded her head, stood and hugged him until he feigned pain.

"You're gonna squeeze the life out of me."

"When can we go see the building?" she squealed. "Today? This afternoon?"

"Hold on." Ron pulled out his phone. He located Harry's number and pressed talk.

"Harry," Ron said, "she likes the idea. Can we run by today? Great, one hour. Thanks."

Rita did a little happy dance. "Oh, this is so exciting. Hurry, drink your coffee."

"It's hot now, you just heated it."

She removed his cup to the kitchen. "I'll make another when we get back."

***

Jake and Annie pulled into a parking space at Rita's apartment. The drive from Mesquite had been pleasant, mainly because Annie was a great conversationalist. She managed to get him sharing things about himself and his childhood, which he hadn't thought about in years. Time flew and now here they were.

"Do you think you should call her before we show up on the doorstep?" Annie asked.

"We're expected, so I think we can just knock." Jake looked at his travel companion. "It's okay, really." He smiled and she relaxed.

Jake got out and went to the passenger side to open the door. "We can leave your suitcase in the car for now. I'll come back out and get it later."

"Okay," she agreed as she stepped out and adjusted her jacket.

As they approached the steps, the door swung open. "Hi, Jake, Annie." Rita stepped onto the porch and hugged each lightly, then invited them in.

"Thanks for having me as a house guest," Annie offered.

"I'm glad to have some company. I hope you don't mind the small space."

Annie looked around and was touched at the homey feeling in the place. "It's perfect."

"Is Ron anywhere close by?" Jake asked.

"He's at the office, but wants you to come on over. Do you remember where it is?"

"Yeah, but I have my GPS in case I get in trouble." Jake turned to Annie. "I'll run out and get your bag before I head off to see Ron."

Rita couldn't help but notice the tenderness between them when Jake placed his hand on her arm.

"Thanks, Jake, I almost forgot about it."

"Let's enjoy a cup of tea while he takes care of that. Do you have a favorite?" Rita asked.

"I love orange spice if you have it."

As if on cue, Pekoe, who had been sleeping in her basket, stretched and languidly made her way into the kitchen.

"Oh she's beautiful. Jake told me you had a cat. What's her name?"

"Pekoe, and she loves to have her head scratched."

"Her orange color is gorgeous. Orange Pekoe tea?"

Rita smiled. "It just seemed right."

Jake came in with Rita's suitcase and placed it near the door. "I'll let you gals get reacquainted." He gave Annie a lingering hug, nodded to Rita, and headed out, closing the door gently behind him.

Rita had the teapot steeping, and brought out two china cups. One had a single yellow rose on the side, while the other was decorated with blue forget-me-nots. Both sat atop mismatched saucers. She took a seat at the breakfast bar next to Annie, who had made herself comfortable.

"Hope you don't mind the odd cups and saucers. I'm not one for formal things. I've managed to pick up a few things from sales and auctions. Besides, I figure we are all a little mixed up in some way."

They both laughed and fell into conversation easily. Almost as though they had known each other many years.

"Tell me more about the film event tomorrow. Jake didn't really have a clue."

"Truthfully, I don't either. My friend's mom, Betty Hills, who I met at an estate sale last year, has put together a documentary about two lonely, elderly people and we're sort of guinea pigs to preview it. Afterward, the assisted living place is having a Thanksgiving meal for all of us."

"It sounds interesting. I'm thrilled to be part of this."

"I think it'll be fun. Okay, tea should be ready." Rita poured Annie's cup, as the spicy orange fragrance twirled into the room, enticing oohs and aahs from both. After filling her own cup, Rita wrapped her hand around the china's warmth.

"Your ring is beautiful."

Rita's eyes shot a loving glance at her left hand. "Ron is so generous. I'm so in love with him."

"It shows when you say his name."

Rita allowed a tender smile to curve the corners of her mouth upward.

"Let's hear a little about you, Annie. We met only briefly at the hospital and memorial for Lillian. Tell me about you and Jake."

Annie lowered her head a bit. "There's not a lot to tell, yet." She grinned.

Rita chuckled. "Okay, now we're getting down to the good conversation."

They laughed out loud together and sipped their tea.

"Where do I begin?"

"At the beginning, where every good story starts."

Chapter Sixteen

Betty stood speechless as she approached the social room of Mt. Laurel. The foyer walls were decorated with large photos made to look like vintage movie posters. Greta, dressed in her lovely gown, smiled down from one, while Clarence, in his WWII uniform, stood proudly on another. Other photos, depicting old movie actors, plastered the walls, while giant cardboard gold stars glimmered in the lights. The burgundy, velvet drapes prevented a view of the room.

Kenneth Cavanaugh stood next to her gauging her response to the hired decorators' work. He guessed it had her approval. "Do you like it?"

Her mouth hung open. "What an entrance," she finally managed to say. "I can't imagine what the rest looks like."

"I wanted you to see this before we actually bring the residents in. I thought we'd get them all seated first, and then have Greta and Clarence make a grand entrance. What do you think?"

Betty inched closer to the drapes. "It would be perfect." She looked at the director. "Can we go in now?"

"Certainly. Let me escort our producer inside the Mt. Laurel Theater." He placed his hand under her elbow and pulled one side of the drapes enough to give them entrance.

"Close your eyes while I turn on the lights."

She followed his instructions.

"Okay, have a look."

Betty let out a delightful squeal, and clasped her hands together with joy. "How on earth did you get this done in one day?"

"I know people." Kenneth laughed. He watched her walk down the center isle covered with a red carpet.

"Oh Mr. Cavanaugh, you know the right people. Look at the stage...the enormous screen...theater chairs. This is absolutely amazing."

"Thank you, I'm glad you like it. We reserved places for our two stars, plus your family, up front on both sides."

"Like it? Oh no, I love it. Everyone else will too. This is so much more than I ever thought possible."

"I have another surprise."

Betty turned, wide-eyed. "What?"

"I have a friend who is involved with public television. I was telling him about the film project and he was quite interested. I invited him to attend. I hope that's okay."

"Okay? It's more than okay." She lowered her voice an octave. "This is almost overwhelming. You've done so much to help us tell the story of two beautiful people. Thank you."

"I've had a blast seeing all this come together. You and your film crew were responsible for the real transformation. Seeing Greta and Clarence now is so rewarding. That's the only thanks I want."

Betty looked at her watch. "Guess we should check out the dining area. I think all my bakers brought the desserts. I know the food is being taken care of, I smelled it when I arrived."

"Oh yes, my wife has been overseeing that part. She has the best cooks in the area in charge of the roasting, steaming, throwing together, or whatever else happens in the kitchen."

They both laughed and headed to the dining area.

"Brian is helping Clarence get ready, and my daughter and her friend, Rita, will be assisting Greta," Betty explained. "So the stars will shine."

"Did Brian mention the surprise concerning Clarence?"

Puzzled, Betty pursed her lips. "Another surprise? No, he didn't. What is it?"

"Oops, foot in mouth. You'll find out soon enough."

Betty walked on ahead to the dining area, unaware that Kenneth slipped off toward Clarence's room.

***

"Do you think Betty will like our gift?" Emily quizzed her husband.

"I think she'll treasure it forever."

"She won't know what's in the flat box," Emily giggled. "I can't wait to see her eyes when she pulls it out."

"We couldn't have found anything more fitting," Seth said, focusing on the road as they made their way to Mt. Laurel. "When do you want to give it to her?"

"I thought about after the film, but I think we should wait until everyone is served at the meal."

"You're probably right. Brian mentioned that the film is a little bit solemn. Since the gift is fun, it's more appropriate to wait."

Emily chuckled. "I can picture her now, a smile first, then an outburst of laughter."

"I still think its sweet of you to even think of presenting Betty with a gift. You're so thoughtful. No wonder I snatched you up and put a ring on your finger before someone else found you."

"Seth," she said, giving his arm a little poke, "you just wanted a caregiver for when you're old."

He laughed. "I hadn't thought about it, but I have the best one around."

"Well, we both have a lot of future before we get to caregiver days. Let's live each day as if it's our last."

"I vote for that, my dear."

"There it is, Mt. Laurel," Emily said, pointing to the white sign in front of a Texas Mountain Laurel tree.

"It's a beautiful place," Seth commented as he pulled into the drive and found a parking space. "There's a lot of cars here, I hope we're not late."

"No," Emily said, looking at her watch, "It's just now ten-thirty."

Seth put the car in park, exited, and went around to help Emily out of the car. After they retrieved the large box which contained the surprise for Betty, they headed to the front entrance.

***

Kenneth Cavanaugh had begun seating residents and provided them with a program. He enjoyed mingling and listening to their chatter. He noticed the women had taken care to dress up a bit for the occasion, while the men were a bit more casual.

"Good evening, Mrs. Tobin," he said with earnest friendliness. "You look lovely this evening."

The elderly woman offered a warm smile. "Thank you, Director Cavanaugh, this is a special event and I wanted to look my best."

He pressed his hand to her elbow, walking her to the special seating at the front. "You always look your best," he complimented as he helped her to her seat.

"You're so kind," she returned.

Kenneth spotted Betty's husband at the curtained doorway, motioning his attention.

"Excuse me, Mrs. Tobin, duty calls."

She waved him off as he walked briskly down the red carpet to where Brian waited.

"What's up?" he asked.

"Clarence is having a bit of difficulty and I think he could use your help."

"Okay, I'll run down to his room. Can you help seat people?"

"Sure, happy to help."

Seth and Emily appeared as Kenneth left.

"Hey Brian, they put you to work I see." Seth laughed.

The two shook hands and Brian gave Emily a quick hug.

"Can you seat yourselves while I escort some residents to their seating section?"

"Let me get my bride settled and I'll lend you a hand if you like?"

"A true friend. Thanks."

***

Betty finished going over the program with Clay and Kat.

"We're about ready," she announced. "Clay, you know the cue for our stars to make their entrance, right?"

"Yes ma'am, I'm heading to my place right now," he assured her as he left.

Betty turned to Kat. "Ready or not — "

"Here we come." Kat finished. "I'll go get Ms. Garson and wait for the signal. This is so exciting."

They hugged and went in different directions.

Betty reached the entrance to the transformed theater and bumped into Brian. "Why aren't you with Clarence?" she asked in a worried tone.

Brian grasped her shoulders. "Don't worry, it's under control."

Now she was really worried. "What's under control? Did something happen to Clarence?

He shook his head. "No, he's fine. He had a little technical issue which required Kenneth's intervention, so he'll be bringing Clarence in."

She didn't look convinced.

"Really," he said, giving her a hug, "everything is under control. Go take your place and get this show started."

Betty relaxed a bit, and headed to the stage to welcome everyone. She spotted Ron and Rita, along with Jake and Annie. A hand waving from the back caught her eye. It was Blanca and her daughter, Bree. They also had Rosie with them. Betty blew a kiss in their direction. Near the front on the left, Sheila called her name. Lane had his arm around his wife and gave Betty a wave. The gang's all here. She smiled and walked confidently to the stage and turned to face the room filled with family, friends, and strangers. After today, none of us will be strangers.

"Welcome, everyone," she said into the microphone, "I'm excited you could all join us on this special occasion." Betty motioned her hand toward the two unoccupied places on her right. "Our special guests will be arriving any moment, and as they come down the red carpet to take their place of honor at the front, please stand and applaud."

Betty nodded toward Clay, who then started the Hollywood music, and watched for Kat to present Greta to the audience.

"Ladies and Gentlemen, please welcome Ms. Greta Garson."

The heavy drapes were pushed aside. All those capable of standing, did so, applauding and echoing a few appreciative whistles. They watched as Greta, aided slightly by Kat's arm, walked regally and slowly, nodding to her adoring fans. She played the glamorous part quite well, smiling all the way. Her name appeared on the giant screen and didn't go unnoticed by Greta.

With Greta and the audience seated, Kat moved quietly to Clay's place at the back of the room.

As The Caisson Song began playing. Betty stood and announced, "Ladies and Gentlemen, let's honor our male star, Mr. Clarence Hartman.

The drapes once again opened. There stood Kenneth and standing by his side was Clarence, dressed in his army uniform.

Betty felt tears rolling down her face. Clarence was standing! On two legs! Her mouth dropped open and applause overtook the music.

Slowly, step-by-step, Kenneth kept his hand on Clarence's arm, and paced himself according to this war hero's ability. The new prosthetic leg was not an exact fit, but Kenneth had worked with him to make it do for at least long enough to take him down the red carpet.

They reached the front and Clarence moved from Kenneth's grasp, turning to face the crowd. He stood at attention as the music faded, and seeing the American flag at the side of the room, stood at attention and saluted.

Betty's throat threatened to close with unshed tears. She heard sniffles and sobs among the people. Watching this humble man, Betty was so moved with love and compassion.

Kenneth took Clarence lightly by the arm and helped him to his special chair. The two men shook hands. As Kenneth walked away, he took out a handkerchief and wiped his eyes.

Everyone resumed sitting while Betty composed herself. Once again she welcomed them, along with Greta and Clarence. She introduced herself and the film crew and acknowledged the people who worked to transform the room into a theater, as well as those who provided the food.

"I can smell the turkey already," called out an elderly man in the back. Laughter broke out.

"Let's begin our film then." She announced. "Clay, roll-em!"

The lights were dimmed and Betty took a seat in the back next to Brian. He took her hand, squeezing it as he whispered, "You're wonderful."

She squeezed back. "Thank you."

***

Jared decided to stay the night in Blanco. After his meal at the diner he felt sleepy and didn't want to chance driving until he slept a bit. He laughed to himself about George's special. That old man was hilarious. Made it out to be a real winner and it turned out to be just liver and onions with all the sides. The thing about George's special was the price was right. Sarah, the waitress, told him whenever George sends someone to the diner to ask for his special, he foots the bill. Jared didn't know what to think about that.

It seemed a little chilly out so Jared pulled a jacket from the back seat of his Charger and slipped it on. He would sleep in his car and get an early start in the morning. To where? He had parked his car near the outskirts of town on the side of a closed gas station. Hopefully no cops would light him up, thinking he was doing something he shouldn't. He got in the driver's seat and stretched his legs, trying to get comfortable. Jared locked the doors and settled in, closing his eyes.

***

As the screen faded to black, Betty made her way to the front of the room. Applause broke out once again and to her amazement, everyone stood. When finally the room grew quiet and the guests took their seats, Brian and Kat came forward, ready to escort the stars to the dining room.

"Mr. Cavanaugh," Betty said, "would you say the blessing as we prepare to receive our food, and thank God for our blessings?"

Kenneth moved toward the front and stopped midway. In his strong voice he began. "Lord, we stop and offer our thanks to You for all our many blessings. It's only by Your grace and love we stand here today. Bless those who prepared the meal, those who will be serving it, and everyone present today. Amen"

Betty thanked Kenneth, then gave the nod for Brian and Kat to escort Greta and Clarence to the dining room. "If everyone will pause until our stars have left the room, each of you will be helped to the table as well."

Suddenly, Clarence said in a firm voice, "Wait! I have something I want to say."

All eyes were on him. Betty was surprised. This wasn't on the program.

Clarence turned to Greta. "Ms. Garson, I'm unable to get down on one knee, but would you do me the honor of becoming my bride?"

The whole room gasped at the same time. Betty looked frantically at Brian, and then Kenneth. They both shook their heads and hunched their shoulders. No one spoke. People waited for Greta's response.

She looked only at Clarence, nodded her head. "Yes, I will marry you Mr. Hartman. We should do it soon though. Neither of us is getting any younger."

The room seemed to shake with laughter as Clarence embraced his bride-to-be. He turned to Brian. "I'd like to escort this lovely woman to the table."

Brian gave a little bow in agreement. As the couple slowly made their way down the red carpet, Brian and Kat walked behind them as a precaution. People applauded the entire time, some calling out congratulations and one shouted, "Way to go, Clarence."

Greta held on to Clarence's arm and beamed as she walked beside him.

Betty started toward the door as the guests finally emptied the room, and Kenneth stood with his wife, Jewel.

"Wow," Kenneth said, "sure didn't see that coming."

"I didn't either," Betty responded. "I guess Clarence stole the show completely."

***

Kenneth's wife, Jewel, had enlisted help from her church by bringing some of the youth to serve the meal. Since they were out of school for Thanksgiving, it was fitting they volunteered to help. Kenneth was up to his elbows in the kitchen alongside his wife, making sure food was plated and ready to be delivered to the table.

The sound of voices joined in laughter, well-wishes for the newly engaged seniors, and conversations around the room, filled Kenneth with goodness. He couldn't wait to introduce Betty to a visitor he'd invited. She would be thrilled by the news waiting for her.

Everyone busied themselves with their meal, and table companions. Before dessert was to be served, Kenneth stood and tapped the table with his knuckles. "Ahem," he announced to get their attention.

All eyes turned toward him.

"At this time, I would like to introduce a guest of mine." He motioned for a gentleman seated at the corner table, to come forward. "I invited Mr. Hopewell—Hal," he said, smiling as he placed his arm across his friend's shoulders, to attend our event and view the film. He is involved in programming at our Public Television Station."

Applause broke out spontaneously and many uttered a hearty welcome.

"Mrs. Hills, would you please come up here?"

Betty rose from her seat and joined the two men.

"Hal, this is the creative woman I told you about—Betty Hills."

"I'm pleased to know you. After seeing the film and talking to Kenneth, I would like to discuss with you, the possibility of airing your documentary on our channel."

Betty stood speechless, looking from one to the other. "I can't believe it, thank you, yes." She shook his hand vigorously. "Thank you, so much." She held back tears before gathering her senses. "Clay," she called out, panning the room, "would you please stand?"

From the left side, Clay stood. "Over here, Mrs. Hills."

Betty turned and acknowledged the young man. "Clay is the film maker and creative backbone in this venture."

"Great job, Mr. Young. We'll be talking soon. Talent like yours shouldn't be wasted."

Clay beamed. "Thank you, sir. I look forward to meeting with you as well."

Hal returned to his seat, while Betty remained standing.

"Are there any other surprises begging to be shared?" she asked.

Lane Jennings raised his hand.

"Stand up and tell us what's on your mind, Lane."

He pulled Sheila to stand with him. "We received a call about a foster child," he said, smiling from ear to ear.

"Oh Lane, Sheila, what wonderful news. You've waited and prayed and God heard and answered."

"There are mixed feelings," Sheila said with hesitation, "but we're so happy. The girl has been recently orphaned. Her parents died in an automobile accident." She paused to collect her emotions. "She's two years old."

"As some of you know," Lane picked up where his wife stopped, "we asked for a baby girl and we planned to name her Mary, after Mary Ludwig. Also, our son's name was David. Well, this precious girl's parents were David and Maryanne Wiggins."

All those from the estate sale understood the significance in the names, and were touched by it.

"God had a plan all along," Emily said, sitting at the same table with Sheila and Lane.

Others joined in agreement with "Amens".

Betty thanked them for sharing. "Does someone else have anything he or she can't keep quiet about?"

Ron Davis stood. "Some of you know, but for the rest, I've asked Rita to marry me. We're making it an April wedding."

Applause went crazy.

"If we were younger, we'd make it a double wedding," Clarence joked.

Laughter broke out, along with congratulations. Ron sat down and Rita was showing her ring to their tablemates.

Jewel and her crew of youth scurried about clearing plates and returning with trays filled with an assortment of desserts.

"That's great news. Any others who would like to speak?"

Seth rose from his chair, walked to the front and stood by Betty. "I recently took the house Mary Ludwig gave me, off the market. After discussing it with my bride, we have decided to carry on Mary's legacy. The house will be transformed into a bed and breakfast, but will have a uniqueness which will honor what Mary started."

Emily spoke up. "Yes, but we aren't revealing the details just yet. Actually, we're still working on them."

"And," Seth continued, "everything was approved by the King William Historical Society, so we'll begin the transformation full-force after the holidays. We're naming the house, "Texas Tribute B & B".

Brian began a loud applause. "Way to go, Seth. I am really happy about that and can't wait to hear all about it."

Betty followed with her question. "What will you do about the house in England?"

"We have plans for it," Emily remarked from where she was sitting, "but we've decided not to live there full-time."

Seth rejoined his wife at their table. "We'd miss our friends and besides," Seth commented, looking over at Lane and Sheila, "with a new youngster moving next door, we want to watch her respond to a loving set of parents."

Lane and Sheila, smiled happily.

Blanca stood up. "May I share a decision my daughter and I have made?"

"Certainly," Betty replied

"We invited Rosie, a dear friend of my late husband, Carlos, to come and spend Thanksgiving week with us."

Rosie nodded her head in response to several welcoming comments.

"Bree will soon be leaving for the mission field. Our church is sponsoring her to teach in a Mexican village. I'm proud of her and I know her daddy would be too."

"We are too," Kat shouted.

"Thank you, Kat," Bree returned.

"Bree and I talked about how I would be without her around and although I know I'd manage, it would be lonely. Since Rosie has been with us, we've talked a lot and we have invited her to move in with me."

Seth stood briefly and clapped. "Wow, that's great, and we'll look forward to getting to know you better, Rosie."

Blanca smiled and placed her hand on Rosie's shoulder. "We're excited too. I've decided to retire at the end of the year, so the two of us may do some traveling."

Betty walked over and hugged the ladies. "Congratulations to all three of you. Lots of changes are taking place. Speaking of changes, Brian and I also have a few to mention."

Brian strolled up to the front and took his wife's hand. "Since my wife had fallen in love with producing documentaries, I've decided to join her. I'm going to retire in January and begin working with Betty. I also plan to write the stories as companions to each film."

Seth gave thumbs up to Brian and motioned to Hal. "There you go, Hal, I told you this was a winning team."

Kat had been quiet concerning her own plans, but felt it was time she shared something about her future. She stood and looked straight at her dad and Betty.

"I suppose I'm the odd ball here because I haven't quite figured out where my life is headed. I will graduate in the spring, but beyond that, I don't know."

"There's no rush," Brian said.

"I know, Dad, but I hear about all the exciting things everyone has planned and I feel inadequate."

"God will give you direction in His time. Meanwhile, your mum and I will be here for you."

Clay walked up behind Kat, and whispered in her ear. She smiled broadly.

"Clay wants me to come into the film business with him."

Betty clapped. "I wouldn't mind that a bit."

Jewel announced there was still an overabundance of dessert, although the sweet potato pie was gone. She busied the youth once again to carry trays to the tables.

Jake decided at the last moment to speak. "Although I haven't made any concrete plans to change anything in my life at this point, I did decide to move into my mom's house after all."

Ron knew of his decision beforehand, but flashed his brother a broad smile and did an air high-five.

"Also," Jake continued, "I'm pleased to have Annie visiting this week. She was the nurse taking such great care of my mother during her final days." Jake put an arm around her and she snuggled a little closer to him.

Kenneth stole Jewel from the serving counter and brought her to the front. "I want to thank my fantastic wife for organizing the kitchen and getting our great group of youth in here to serve today."

The entire room of guests gave her a round of applause.

Jewel accepted the thanks and went back to serving.

Emily and Seth came forward with a large box. "Betty," Emily began, "Seth and I wanted to present you with something special for the wonderful event you put on today. The film was fantastic and has inspired so many of us to live out our legacies and pass them on to others. The documentary is the first of what Seth and I feel will explode onto the screen as you explore the lives of those who feel alone or abandoned."

Seth handed her the box, but helped her as she untied the ribbon and took out the contents.

She looked puzzled until Seth helped her unfold the object. The wood chair was finally assembled. She put both hands over her gaping mouth, finally uttering, "A director's chair!"

The red canvas back sported the title, Director, and Betty on the front. It was bar height to give her the most advantageous view of what was going on. "I adore it," she said, thank you both." Betty hugged the couple before trying out the chair.

"A perfect fit," Kenneth called out.

"This is the end to a perfect day," Betty said. She thanked all the guests for attending and urged them to mingle and chat while the youth cleaned up. Several residents announced they were tired and planned to go take a nap.

The estate sale group clustered together after the residents returned to their rooms, and Betty remained in her chair. Kat approached her quietly.

"Mum, I think I'd like to help you more in future films, if you really want me to."

Betty flung her arms around Kat. "Oh yes, I would love it. But school first my dear."

"I know, but my schedule is flexible. We need to start looking for new stars."

They both laughed and hugged as Brian approached.

"Can a guy get into this hug?"

They each put an arm out and pulled him in. "Group hug," they said in unison.

***

Seth spotted Lane and Sheila at a table near the window, and made his way over.

"Congratulations to you both on becoming parents. I know the little one will have a loving home."

Lane stood to shake hands. "Thanks, Seth, we're pretty excited. We were just talking about how our lives will be changing. I have to admit, now that it's becoming a reality, I'm a little nervous."

"Every parent gets nervous when a new arrival comes into their lives. I'm sure when Emily and I reach that point, we'll be calling you and Sheila."

"I know you're right, Seth. It's more our age. It's been a long time since we've had a toddler in our home. Even so, we're still excited and can't wait."

"Didn't you mention she lost her family in a car accident? Was she injured?"

"Both her parents and older brother were killed. There are no other living relatives. She was with a babysitter when it happened."

Seth's heart melted and he pulled out a chair to sit down. "God knew what was ahead and spared this girl. He also knew where to place her," he said softly.

Lane nodded his head.

***

Brian and Kenneth approached the coffee station at the same time.

Kenneth found cups and filled them. "Your wife did a fantastic job, Brian. I know you're more than proud of her."

Brian took a sip of his steaming brew. "She never stops amazing me with the things she does."

"Now it looks like she'll be off and running with a new project. Be sure to let me know when it's ready to be viewed."

"You can count on it."

"Our plan to help Clarence sure went off well. I didn't think he would accept the prosthetic leg you arranged to be provided. You know, he never cared about having one before."

Brian laughed. "Before Greta, you mean."

"She is an amazing individual, isn't she?"

"My take on the relationship is that he needed someone to share things with. Greta needed someone who would listen. They found their someone in each other."

Kenneth drank from his cup thoughtfully. "You're right, Brian. He was determined to walk down the red carpet for her. He had the antique ring, which is probably quite valuable, in his pocket and I doubt he'd have taken no for an answer."

"This has been quite an event and although you're not familiar with the story about the estate sale and Mary Ludwig, I can tell you, legacies have been carried out here."

"I'd like to hear the story some time."

"Sure. It's one which will change your life just listening to it."

Betty approached her husband. "Sorry to interrupt, but I'm really worn out. Honey, do you mind if we head home?"

Brian took a last drink of his coffee and tossed the cup into the trash can by the counter. "At your service," he said eloquently. Turning to Kenneth, he shook hands. "Thanks for all your help. We'll see you after the holidays and I'll share the story with you."

"Sounds great. Happy Thanksgiving to you both."

"Kenneth," Betty said, "I appreciate you so much for having your friend come to the event. We plan to get with him in January and discuss using the film on PBS."

"I'm glad it worked out."

Betty and Brian waved goodbyes to the others and headed for the car.

Outside, Kat caught up with them. "I'm going with Clay over to his mom's." She hugged Brian first, then Betty. "It turned out awesome, Mum."

Betty hugged her back. "Thanks sweetie. Have fun."

Brian took Betty's hand and they walked slowly to the car. "We have a lot to be thankful for."

"We do indeed," she answered.

Chapter Seventeen

Jared ambled in and found an empty booth at Tim's Diner. He skipped breakfast and only had junk food for lunch. It was nearly four and his stomach thought he had deserted it. He needed to hang on to his cash so he stretched meals out sparingly. There was an ATM close by, so he'd take advantage of it after he ate something.

"Hi there," Sarah said, "you're still in town I see."

"Yep, and I'm hungry."

"Would you like another George's Special?"

"No, I'm on my own dollar this time. How about a cheeseburger and fries?"

"Sure, anything to drink?"

"Just water will do."

"Coming right up."

Jared watched the young waitress tear off the sheet from her order pad and hand it to the cook, who jammed it up onto a stainless steel clip. Sarah zipped around, refilling glasses, picking up empty plates, and wiping down tables. She's sure a hard worker. Wonder why she hangs around this small town.

He heard the sizzle of a hamburger patty being slapped on a hot grill, and cold potato planks being submerged in boiling oil. The smell made his stomach growl.

"Here's your water," Sarah said, placing the tall glass in front of him. "Won't be long, I promise." She smiled and left as quickly as she appeared.

She has a kindness about her that puts a man at ease. Too bad he was just passing through. Jared had a number of too bads in the past week. The biggest one was the sale of his parent's house falling through. If it had worked out, he and Gus would be moving in soon. Here it is the day before Thanksgiving, and I'm alone in a diner. It was too bad he argued with his half-brother and stormed out. Gus tried to help him. It was definitely too bad his own parents didn't care to communicate with him. But that was their bad, sort of.

"Cheeseburger, fries and a coke," Sarah announced, setting the tray down in front of Jared.

"I didn't order a coke," he corrected her.

"Tim told me it's included with the meal."

Jared looked at her skeptically, yet accepted the welcomed drink. "Thank you, and Tim."

"Enjoy, and if you need anything else, let me know. Oh, and there are free refills on the drink."

"Double thanks," he replied, squeezing ketchup over the fries and dousing them with salt. He was so hungry.

Sarah retreated from his booth, but had a feeling Jared was hungry for more than physical food. He seemed needy in a way a burger and fries could never fill him. Silently, she prayed for God to provide this young man with what he really needed.

***

"Momma," Bree called from the kitchen, "It's pouring down rain."

Blanca followed the sound of her daughter's voice and heard loud pummeling on the roof. "I can't remember a Thanksgiving when it rained this much," she said, giving Bree a good morning hug. "I love the sound."

"I can't either, but it won't be fun driving to the church in it. We better leave a little earlier than we planned."

"You're right, honey. One thing for sure, no matter if it rains or the sun is blazing, the church holiday dinner will see a crowd."

"Momma?" Bree said, turning serious.

"What, Sweetie?"

"I'm really thankful to have you as my mother. But, I feel badly for all those orphans we saw in the villages."

Touched by her daughter's compassion, Blanca felt tears welling. "I know, I feel the same. That's one reason we try to help at the community Thanksgiving meal when the church invites the homeless, orphans and elderly. Let's think of this as our village and be part of helping those whom God puts in our path today."

Bree smiled. "Thanks, you always brighten my day. I love the idea the pastor's wife came up with, to pack meals for those who were homebound and can't attend. There's a whole team of volunteers ready to deliver them."

"I know, and the best part is the volunteers plan to spend a little time with each one. I'm thrilled about our estate sale friends volunteering to show up and be part of the festivities."

"I know. Kat said she and Clay would deliver meals." Bree took her cup with her as she prepared to begin her morning routine. "Okay, I'm first in the shower."

Blanca smiled. She placed a small book on the table and poured tea into the cup Bree had set out for her. "You go. I'm gonna read my devotional and sip my cup of tea."

***

Gus waited for his mom to answer and on the third ring he heard her confident voice.

"Good afternoon, Ruby Orlov speaking."

"It's just me," he sighed, "Gus."

"I'm sorry, dear; I didn't look at the caller ID. Any word from Jared?"

"No, he hasn't called."

"You would think with it being Thanksgiving he would let one of us know he's okay."

Gus knew the tone. She seemed more concerned Jared hadn't eased her mind than if he was in trouble or even hurt. Suddenly he felt guilty thinking in such a way.

"He probably just needs time to sort things out and decide on a direction for his future. He's not a kid you know."

"Yes, I'm aware of his age Gus. It's Thanksgiving after all. Families should be together."

"Mom, we haven't been together as a family on Thanksgiving in three years. I was actually surprised when you invited me over for dinner."

He realized his mother hadn't responded when the silence continued.

"Mom, are you there?"

Her voice softened a bit.

"Yes, I'm here. You're coming aren't you?"

"I plan to be there."

"Good. I made your favorite dessert."

Gus could taste the combined flavors of coconut, pineapple and cherries already.

"I'll be over at eleven. Do you want me to bring anything?"

"No. But would you wear a dress shirt? It makes the day more special."

"I'll wear anything you want for some of your ambrosia. See you soon."

Gus hung up the phone. He wondered if she had some motive for the dressing up a bit thing. I hope she hasn't invited anyone to dinner. He loved his mother but she liked putting on airs at times. Theirs was definitely a fractured family. His stepdad, Vic, sidestepped a lot allowing her to run things. Gus figured out a long time back why his parents divorced. His mom preferred to make all the decisions and dad resented it. Even when he died a year after they split up, she handled all the arrangements. Maybe that's the reason I never cared to get serious about anyone.

Gus checked his closet to see if he even had a decent shirt to wear, and sure enough, a clean, blue-checked fit the bill. He took it out and hung it on the doorframe.

He wondered what Jared would be doing today and felt saddened at the thought he might be alone or sick. Gus picked up the phone and pressed speed dial for Jared. Voice mail. He left his half-brother a message to return the call, then hung up. He tried. Gus certainly couldn't force him to reconnect, but he wished Jared would call and at least let him know his whereabouts.

***

Jake sat with Annie in the coffee shop, discussing the film event. It was early and they planned to meet up with Ron and Rita about eleven and help feed the homeless. Jake thought an early morning coffee with Annie would be fun. They found a table in the corner after ordering a Latte for her and black coffee for him.

"I was so moved by the film and how it emphasized the past of the two stars. It made me realize how much people need people. It's not good to be alone and not have someone to share your joys and sorrows with."

"I know." Jake agreed. "Although the film wasn't what I expected."

Annie looked at him inquisitively. "What did you think it would be like? They said it was a documentary."

Jake stared out the window at the rain. "I'm not sure, but I know I wasn't expecting the sadness of Greta's younger life. Her dad took his own life and left her to deal with it. That would be really hard. She never found happiness."

"It was a different time then and women had few options other than to become a maid, schoolteacher, or marry."

"I just think how emotional it was for her. Losing both her parents in a short time and not having a place of safety."

"You had wonderful parents who made sure you and your brother wouldn't have to worry about the future. It was hard on both of you when your mom passed away, but you've found ways to cope and get through it."

She noticed his eyes misting over. "Wasn't it sweet when Clarence proposed to Greta?"

Jake couldn't help but smile. "He's got style and she has humor. I liked when she said they would have to get married soon because they weren't getting any younger."

They both laughed.

Annie finished the last of her latte and set the cup down. "You're wrong you know."

"Wrong about what?"

"Greta did find happiness. I saw it in her eyes."

Jake grinned.

"Thanks for inviting me to be here this week."

"The week's just begun. We've enjoyed a Thanksgiving meal, a great event, and today we'll become servants and help feed those less fortunate."

"I know," Annie said, "this is what Thanksgiving is really about. Being grateful for what we have and giving back."

Jake extended his hands toward Annie. "I'm glad you're here."

She folded her fingers over his. "Being with you makes me happy."

The moment was broken as an excited, boisterous group came through the door.

"I think they're the cue for us to leave."

Annie nodded her head as Jake helped her from the booth.

The rain had stopped. I'll give Ron a call and let him know we'll meet them at his place and ride together."

She tucked her small umbrella under one arm and they headed out to the car. "Sounds like the plan of an organized man."

Chapter Eighteen

The succulent aroma of roasted turkey and cornbread dressing filled the entire church. It wafted through the hall as Emily and Seth followed their noses to the dining room. They spotted Blanca and Bree by the counter, in white aprons, hair nets and plastic gloves.

"Wow," Emily called out. "This is one big holiday feast."

Blanca looked up and smiled broadly. "We call it, 'The Feast of the Grateful'."

"Very appropriate," Seth commented. "We're here to help. We await your instructions. The others should arrive any time now."

"You can begin by tying on an apron and getting a hairnet and gloves from over there," Blanca said, swinging an arm toward the cupboard."

A gray-haired gentleman appeared out of nowhere, approaching Seth from behind.

"Good morning, I'm Pastor Roman," he said, shaking hands with both Seth and Emily.

Seth noticed a large group of people who seemed to show up instantaneously. He presumed them to be church members. Coming down the hall were the Davis brothers, Ron and Jake, accompanied by Rita and Annie. The other folks from the estate sale group followed; Betty and Brian, Kat and Clay, plus Lane and Sheila.

Emily laughed. "I guess the gang's all here. We should suit up and prepare to be servants."

"Amen to being servants," said Pastor Roman in a loud voice.

***

Jared couldn't figure out why he was still in Blanco. He should have left a couple days ago, but something held him here. He sat in his car with both hands wrapped around the cardboard cup filled with hot coffee from the small coffee shop up the street. Tim's Diner was closed today, as was ninety-five percent of the town. He tried to imagine his parents having a big dinner, probably invited Gus too. Would they talk about me? Sure.

A tap on the passenger side window rescued him from his thoughts.

He unlocked the door.

"Hop in, Sarah. What are you doing out so early on Thanksgiving?"

She slid into the passenger seat and closed the door.

"I ran to Walgreens to pick up marshmallows for my mom. She makes great ambrosia."

Jared suddenly felt choked up. The blood seemed to drain from his head.

"Are you okay? You look a little gray."

He quickly composed himself, a little ashamed that something as simple as a dessert name would shake him. He remembered well, his mom's ambrosia and how she knew he loved it. "I'm fine, just a little caffeine deprived," he said, taking a swallow of his coffee.

"I was heading back home and saw your car. I thought you left for parts unknown."

"That was my intention, but for some reason I'm still here." He feigned a laugh to shrug off his melancholy.

"Would you like to join me and my family for dinner about

noon?"

Jared turned his head toward her in surprise. "Shouldn't you check with your mom before inviting a strange man to dinner?"

She laughed. "You're no stranger, I know your name and where you're from. Besides, George likes you."

"I didn't say 'stranger', I said 'strange'. Wouldn't you agree?"

"Sure, but in a good way. My mom will be happy to add one more plate for dinner."

Jared thought for a minute. "Okay, if you're sure she won't mind."

"I'm positive. I live two lights north, take a left and it's the 5th house on the right, 423 Haywood." She opened the door and stepped out. "I need to get those marshmallows home," she called out, walking briskly to her car. "See you at noon."

Jared liked her smile. Two lights north, take a left and it's the 5th house on the right. 423 Haywood.

He watched her drive off then decided to seek out the laundromat on the corner. He could at least throw a couple things in and change to a clean shirt and jeans. Washing up in the restroom wouldn't hurt him a bit either. He saved his empty cup and started the car. Thanksgiving might turn out well after all.

His phone ring startled him and he answered without looking to see who it was. His half-brother's voice seemed surprised to hear him.

"Jared?"

"Yeah, Gus, how you doing?"

"I'm good. I thought I'd end up in your voice mail again. I've called twice. Didn't you get my message to call?"

"Sorry, the phone went dead and I had to search my car for the charger."

"Where are you?"

"North of San Antonio."

"That's pretty evasive. Mind being more specific? I've been worried. You took off without our having a civil conversation. I didn't cause the house to go off the market you know."

"Yeah. I needed to distance myself from all that. I was at a breaking point."

Gus took a deep breath hoping he could bring Jared around to coming back.

"Mom actually is preparing a Thanksgiving meal and invited me over. Get this, she even asked me to wear a dress shirt. She keeps asking if I've heard from you. I know she really wants you there too."

Silence.

"Jared, you there?"

"I'm here. I need some breathing room, Gus. I apologize for storming out like a kid having a tantrum, but maybe this all happened for a reason. Right now I feel free to find something. I'm not sure exactly what, but I feel I'm close."

"I don't think I understand but would you at least tell me where you are?"

"I'm not too far, but it's not important to know where. You can call me if you need me."

"Mom and Vic put money in your account."

"Why?"

"She said you're her son and she wasn't going to have you sleeping in your car."

Jared laughed loudly. "That's what I've been doing."

It was Gus's turn to laugh. "And you had money you didn't know about. Go get a room or rent a place."

"Guess I should pay better attention to my checking account. I will. Thanks for calling and letting me know."

"Happy Thanksgiving."

"Same to you, Gus."

Jared pressed end on the phone and continued staring at it. Something deep inside of him wished he'd told Gus where he was. Why? There was nothing stopping him from hitting redial. Yes there was, his mother's stubborn streak running through his soul. No point in having him come out and trying to convince Jared to return. Their mother would insist he do whatever possible to make it happen. The question on his mind as he placed the phone in his back pocket was, "Why won't his mother do it herself? She could have called."

***

Lane and Sheila plopped onto the sofa.

"I'm bushed," sighed Lane.

Sheila looked at her husband and smiled. "I'm worn out too, but it was a wonderful afternoon. Even with the thunderstorm, people swarmed the church. Serving them and talking with each of them really brought the sunshine indoors."

Lane put his arm around his wife and kissed her hair.

"You smell like cornbread dressing."

"You're so funny." Sheila snuggled closer. "Just think, next week there'll be three of us. I'm so excited we get to foster little Mary Dee. My heart breaks thinking of how she lost her parents in the car wreck which could have ended her short life if she'd been with them."

Lane's brow wrinkled. "She's so young. At only two I doubt she'll remember them. I'm praying we can fill her with so much love she'll respond and depend on us. I know it'll take time, she'll miss them."

"We have God to help us so we're not alone," Sheila commented.

"Absolutely, and when the time comes where we can adopt her, she'll be ours."

***

Jared expressed his appreciation to Sarah's parents for having him over on such short notice and had complimented her mother on the delicious Thanksgiving meal. It was good and he was sincere. He had to excuse himself right after dessert or break down in front of them all. His mind just wouldn't let go of his own family who were having dinner today and of his not being there with them.

He got in his car and headed to the highway. Where should he go? Everyone here was friendly and because he knew there was some money in his account, he could look for an apartment and try settling here. But do I want to?

***

George Banks had eaten too much turkey and dressing. It could have been dessert. In any case, he was stuffed worse than the turkey. Walking it off seemed the best way to solve the problem. He spotted the young man, Jared, pulling in to the coffee shop, so he figured that boy might need company. He picked up his pace and soon entered the almost empty shop. He ordered a cup of decaf, paid the pretty girl at the counter and walked up behind Jared.

"Hi there, young man. Happy Thanksgiving."

Jared, startled, turned to see George approaching his booth.

"Happy Thanksgiving to you as well. What are you doing away from your family?"

The old man slid onto the Naugahyde seat and placed his cup on the table.

George patted his midsection and laughed. "Figured I'd walk off some of what I put on at the feast."

Jared grinned. "I probably should do the same. Sarah invited me over to her place and I definitely had more than my share. Her mom's a great cook."

"She is indeed. So are you leaving Blanco?"

"I'm undecided. I like this town, but I feel like I haven't found whatever I'm looking for."

"Do you believe in God?"

Jared looked straight into the elderly man's silver blue eyes. "I suppose I do, why?"

"Well, my way a thinkin' is He has a plan laid out for His children. It's up to us to get to know Him and find out what His plan is. Maybe you're looking for it."

"How do I find out?"

"Best way I know is to have a talk with Him."

"Talk with God?"

"Sure, He likes when those He loves give Him a call."

Jared looked serious. "How do I know He loves me?"

"For one thing, you're alive. If He didn't love ya, you'd not be a sittin' here. For another, His only Son, Jesus Christ, died on the cross for you."

Silence.

"Listen, there was a time when I strayed off the path and it took me losing part of my arm to wake up and realize God had work for me to do. My work might seem small to some but He gives me people to talk with and the words to give out."

"People like me?"

"Could be, Son. You look like you need a little direction and maybe I can help." George reached into his shirt pocket and pulled out a small New Testament. He saw Jared eyes widen a bit. "I never leave home without it. He tore off a corner of his napkin, opened to a section and placed the paper between its pages. He handed it to Jared. "Spend a little time reading the passages I marked. You might find what you're looking for there."

Jared opened to the place indicated. 1 John 4. "Thank you, George. I will read it later, but don't you need this back tonight?"

"I have extras and I have my own copy at home."

"Thanks again. I'll read it tonight."

***

Emily was still excited over how much she enjoyed serving so many needy people today. She prepared a cup of tea for herself and coffee for Seth.

"Honey," she asked, "did you notice all the senior citizens in the crowd we served? When they first arrived their faces looked haggard. Once the meal was in progress and we were all talking with them, they perked up and smiles grew on their faces. I think they enjoyed the social part as much as the food."

"You're right; I think that's what Betty discovered with Greta and Clarence. We weren't created to be alone in this world."

Emily removed her shoes and sat in the recliner across from her husband. She engaged the foot rest to relieve her aching feet. "No, we need each other," she replied as her eyelids slowly closed.

Seth rose from his chair and knelt down by Emily, tenderly massaging her right foot. He put just enough pressure to work out the soreness from being on her feet most the day. He looked up at his wife.

"I know I need you by my side," he said in a hushed voice.

"Uh huh," she managed to utter before drifting off.

He stood and scooped her up and wrapped her arms around his neck. Seth carried her to their room, thanking God for this beautiful gift.

***

Jared decided to get a room at the motel outside of town rather than sleep in his car. He wanted to read the Bible passages George told him about. He was also pretty tired of the cramped quarters his Charger offered.

After settling into the sparse accommodations, Jared took a hot shower and plugged his phone in to charge. The bed was decently comfortable and had a good number of pillows. He plumped them behind his head and stretched out his full length. He had stopped to refill his thermos with coffee so he felt content. Jared reached for the small New Testament and turned to the first marked section George wanted him to read. A long sip of coffee tasted delicious and for only a moment he wished he were enjoying it with Sarah. She was different. He didn't think about her in a romantic way, although she was attractive. Sarah seemed to read him and that unnerved Jared a bit. He sure didn't want her getting inside his head. He was just passing through.

Jared looked at the heading on the page George had placed a scrap of paper. 1 John 4. It seemed odd to begin reading a book near the end, but he guessed George knew what he was doing, so he began.

As he read each verse he felt pulled in like quicksand. He reached verses nine and ten and something inside of him jumped. Must be the strong coffee. He continued and this time he read verses nine and ten out loud.

"This is how God showed His love among us: He sent His one and only Son into the world that we might live through Him. This is love;

not that we loved God, but that He loved us and sent his Son as an atoning sacrifice for our sins." Wow, this is what the pastor in that church was saying.

Jared reached for his coffee and this time, took a gulp. His hand was shaking.

He continued down to the last verse. "And He has given us this command; Whoever loves God must also love his brother." Gus, I'm sorry I blew up at you and walked out. I do love you.

Jared replaced the paper scrap between the pages and closed the small book. He sat back against the pillows and closed his eyes.

"God, my name is Jared Orlov and I just now discovered some things in this book George loaned me. You must know who he is because he sure knows You. Anyway, this stuff about how we should love each other because You command it and how You loved us first, is pretty direct. I'm not sure about most of this but this business about relying on the love You have for me is pretty serious. I want the love this book talks about. Can you help me out here?"

He sat in silence, waiting, hoping to hear something from God. He believed in God and knew how the world began in seven days. But this love stuff was heavy and Jared wanted to make sure he understood it. Silence. Maybe God didn't hear me.

Jared swung his feet over the side of the bed and reached for his phone, unplugging it from the charger. He needed to talk to Gus but wasn't sure if his half-brother had the answer he was looking for. Who am I kidding; I don't even know the questions I should be asking.

Suddenly Kat's face popped into his mind. She would know the questions and the answers. He hadn't thought about her for some time, so why would he now? Could God have put her name in his thoughts? She wouldn't give him the time of day, of that he was sure.

Chapter Nineteen

Emily and Seth poured over the plans for the renovation of Mary's house, soon to be known as Texas Tribute B & B. A tribute to Mary's Legacy of loving others and wanting to leave a bit of herself behind.

"Do you think we'll be ready to open in the spring?"

Seth frowned a bit leaving a furrow between his brows. "I'm believing it'll happen, as long as we stay on track." He pointed to the back area of the house as it was shown on the blue prints. "This is where we'll do the legacy up big."

Emily smiled. "I'm excited and can't wait. I'm working on the landscaping and asked Sheila to meet with me. She's familiar with the gardening Bertha did when she and Mary first moved in."

"Sheila will enjoy it, but with the fostering in process, will she have time?"

"It's mostly photos, plans, and sketches, so I can meet at her place since she's right next door."

"Sounds like you have it covered. Later, we'll need to begin looking for a chef and a hostess."

"Seth," Emily said in a subdued voice, "how will all this affect our life in England? I love the wedding venue we created and want to be involved, but renovations here are important too."

Leaning over, Seth placed an arm around his wife. "Honey, we can work it out. You know how in nursing you learned to triage?"

"Yes, of course."

"That's what we'll do in our situation. We take the most urgent thing and treat it, then move to the next. Besides, the wedding season is months away, so we have time to work on that."

"You always have the solution."

"Not always," he answered with a kiss on her nose. "Now, how about we have some of that leftover turkey casserole, and relax."

Emily stood, touseled his hair and headed to the freezer. "Coming right up my love."

***

Gus sat anxiously in his living room, watching the clock and driveway at the same time. Since the call from Jared earlier, time seemed to drag. Jared wanted to see him because he needed to talk and hoped Gus could help him with something. Maybe he wants to move back here and work at the garage. He probably needs money. Jared sounded a bit strange when he called. It's been two hours. Gus had no idea where he was coming from so he couldn't tell when he'd arrive.

A sound in the drive caught his ear. A car. Has to be Jared. Gus hurried to the door and spotted the black Charger pulling in. This time Jared didn't turn it around to face the street. Maybe that means he's done running away.

He watched his half-brother exit the car and slowly amble toward the porch. There was something different about him; the way he carried himself perhaps. A bit more relaxed, free maybe. Gus wasn't quite sure how to read him, but it didn't matter. Here he was at the door and Gus was anxious to find out what had transpired since he raced out of the yard two weeks ago.

"Hey there," Gus greeted his half-brother as he opened the door.

"How ya doin'?"

Jared pulled Gus to him with both hands and presented a hearty hug. "I'm good for the first time in a long while."

Gus noticed the smile Jared wore as they made their way into the house. "You seem like a new man. What happened, you win the lottery?"

Jared laughed. "I don't waste money on that stuff. No, I feel good on the inside for a change."

"Sit down here at the table. Want some coffee?"

"Sounds great, but I really want to run something by you and see if you can help."

Gus poured coffee into two mugs, handing one to Jared as he sat across from him. "What can I help you with? A job? You're welcome back at the garage anytime."

"Well, maybe, but there's something else I need to take care of. Before I get to it though, I'd like to tell you what happened to me during Thanksgiving."

Gus took a long sip of his coffee and leaned in. "I'm all ears."

Jared ran his finger around the rim of his mug before meeting Gus's eyes. "Okay, here goes. I had Thanksgiving dinner with a girl who works at a diner in Blanco."

"Ah, so there's a girl involved. Not sure I can help in that department."

"It's not her, although she's nice and I hope I can get to know her better. She invited me to eat with her family so I accepted. Afterward, this old guy, George, met up with me and gave me a Bible. He said to read a section he marked so I did and it changed me."

Gus was shocked but tried to stay calm so Jared would keep talking. He'd never heard his half-brother share anything like this before. "How did it change you?"

"I never realized I was loved so much. The way I read it was God loved me before I was born and because He loves me I should show love to others because I'm His child. I guess my way of showing love to people is different than what God has in mind."

"What do you mean?"

Jared gulped some of his coffee. "The way I treated you for one thing. I'm sorry about blaming you for Mom's house not selling, running off and not letting anyone know where I was."

"Hey, you were upset. We all were. It's not a big deal."

"That's what I thought too, until I read God's view of love. People who God loves should be kind and loving toward others, without making excuses for behavior. That's what I've always done, made excuses."

"I understand."

"Anyway, there's more."

"I'm listening."

"I treated Kat horribly. You remember, the college girl?"

"Of course, how could I forget? The San Marcos episode which caused chaos."

"There's that of course. Yeah. But I need to speak to her, to apologize for my behavior, and that's where I need your help."

"Wait a minute, I'm not getting involved in that situation. The one time I saw her at my shop was enough. Besides, I doubt I'd be able to do any good."

"Gus, please. The Lord is in my heart and I have only good intentions. I know if I try to get in touch with her she'll freak out. Since the fiasco at the pizza place I don't dare try seeing her on my own. I owe her and her family an apology."

"What are your expectations from apologizing? A relationship of some kind?"

"No, not at all. From what George told me, if I've harmed anyone I should try to make amends if at all possible. Like I said earlier, the girl in Blanco is someone I'd like to know better, but I won't attempt it until I've done everything I can to make things right with Kat, you, and especially Mom and Dad. I discovered they still put money in my account even though I disappeared. You were still there for me over the phone. I behaved badly. My hope is to find a decent job and make something of myself before I ruin anyone else's life."

Gus sat in silence, mulling over all Jared expressed. The look on Jared's face was sincere and genuine. He really had changed.

"Okay, give me a day or two and I'll see what I can do. No promises though."

"Good enough, thanks."

"So do you want a job?"

Jared grinned sheepishly. "It's a beginning. I'm hoping to find a trade school and learn something so I can make a decent living."

"Sounds like a plan. One I'll support you in, just as I know Mom and Vic will too."

"Speaking of, I'd like to go see them tonight. Would you check with them for me?"

"No, I think you should make the call yourself."

Jared sat quietly. "You're right." He stood, took out his phone and went into his old room. "I'll be back in a few minutes."

Gus nodded and made his way outside to give his brother some space. Thank You, Lord, for bringing him back to us, now help me find the girl so he can put it all behind him.

***

Jared sat on the edge of the bed and pressed the phone buttons for his mom. He waited.

"Hello?" Ruby Orlov answered on the third ring.

"Hi, Mom, it's me, Jared."

The sound of crying wracked the phone. He waited.

"Is it really you?"

"Yes, Mom, I'm sorry I missed Thanksgiving with you, Dad, and Gus. I'd like to stop by today if it's okay."

Ruby spoke slowly, carefully trying to keep from crying again. "Of course, Jared, yes, please come by."

"I'll be there in forty-five minutes. See you then."

He hung up the phone, inhaled deeply and stood. Jared just then realized his eyes were moist and his heart was beating fast. Thank You, Lord.

When he left his room and headed toward the door, Gus was coming in from outside.

"Hey, I'm going to Mom's and I'll be back later if that's okay with you."

Gus hugged his half-brother. "I'm glad you're back. Hope all goes well over there. I'll look forward to having some company tonight. It's been kinda lonely around here."

Jared smiled as he hugged Gus back and bounded down the steps to his Charger. "See you later," he said, waving as he pulled the car out.

Gus felt a weight fall off his shoulders. I don't have to play middleman anymore. He opened the door and went in whistling, "Tis the season to be jolly, fa la la la la."

***

Ruby paced the living room while her husband sat quietly

clicking the channels on the TV remote.

"He should pull in any minute now." She pulled the curtain a bit on the window.

"Come sit down," Victor said, keeping his eyes on the screen. "You traipsing back and forth won't get Jared here any quicker."

"I can't sit, I'm too excited."

"You mean nervous. You're too nervous."

Ruby stopped midway between the window and her husband. "I'm excited. I haven't seen him in forever and now he wants to stop by. Just like that — he wants to stop by."

"Like I said, you're nerv...."

"Vic, puulease," she declared with emphasis on please.

He turned the volume up two numbers. "Okay, dear."

The sound of a car caused them both to turn their heads toward the door.

"He's here. Now let him do the talking, Victor."

Her husband nodded his head in agreement.

She stood in front of the door and waited for Jared to ring the bell. Silence. Ruby dared not look out the window now. She turned to Victor with a what-do-I-do look, and he responded with a shrug. She waited.

Footsteps.

Ruby threw the door open, feasting her eyes on her wayward son. Immediately, tears sprung to her cheeks as she pulled him into her arms.

"I've missed you so," she sobbed.

Jared stroked his mother's hair and patted her back. "I've missed you too, Mom."

She backed up a little. "You're so thin, come, I have plenty of leftovers. I'll heat up some turkey and dressing."

"Is there any ambrosia left?"

Ruby looked him in the eye. "Of course, now let's go inside so we can talk. Your dad is anxious to see you."

Jared wasn't so sure.

***

Lane and Sheila sat comfortably at home watching the news. Lane shook his head at the newscast showing Black Friday shoppers from the previous day, fighting and mauling each other.

"I can't believe the craziness of people fighting over who was in line first or who made it through the door first on Black Friday. The day before they were giving thanks for all God provided them and the very next day they scramble to buy more."

Sheila nodded. "I know, and it's sad they forget what's really important. Like our little girl who's coming next week. I'm so excited, Lane, aren't you?"

He looked into his wife's beautiful hazel eyes. "I can't wait. I want to give her love and protection so she'll know we care about her. Poor little girl, losing both parents in the wreck, and not having any other family to take her is horrible."

"Since she's not quite two, let's pray we can help her love us. Then when she's older there will be time enough to tell her about her mom and dad. The caseworker said she'll provide us with all she has."

"I can't wait to see her eyes on Christmas morning. She will never go without love. I don't mean toys and things. I mean the love of God, Mary's legacy of love, and our hearts overflowing with it."

Sheila scooted over closer to her husband and took his hand. "I heard that a legacy is like planting a tree others will enjoy sitting under. Mary's legacy is the tree."

Lane squeezed her hand then put his arm around her. "It's exactly that."

***

Kat was excited when Clay picked her up for a drive downtown to view the Christmas lights along the Riverwalk. It was always a magical time. They parked and maneuvered the steps down from the street level in the mist which began just as they exited the car.

She hung on to his hand as they carefully meandered among tourists as well as other locals. "This was a great idea. The lights are gorgeous and it's not too crowded."

Clay patted her hair, now damp to her forehead. "I'm sorry I didn't have an umbrella in the car. Are you sure you want to keep going?"

"I'm fine. Unless a downpour arrives I'll survive."

"Tell you what, there's a Starbucks in the Marriott Hotel lobby. Let's duck in, grab a cup of coffee and maybe the rain will let up. Besides, I want to talk about something."

Kat looked at Clay, wondering what was on his mind. "Sounds good, how far is it?"

"I think it's on the other side of the river. We can cross on the bridge a little further down."

They picked up their pace as the sky turned from mist to steady light rain. Both began laughing at their predicament as they hurried across the small foot bridge and took cover under a store awning.

Kat brushed her now wet hair from her face. "Maybe we should wait a bit." She shivered a little.

Clay put his arms around her. "I really am sorry."

"I'm fine, really."

A middle-aged couple approached. They were protected by a

large blue umbrella. Stopping, the woman looked at Kat, and pulled a small folded umbrella from her shopping bag.

"Here, Sweetie, you can have this," she said, handing the flowered rain gear to Kat. "My husband, bless his heart, bought our large one so I stuck this in my bag."

"Oh my goodness, thank you so much." Kat opened it up with a touch on the handle. "Bless you, ma'am, and you too sir."

Clay acknowledged his appreciation to the couple as they strolled down the walkway, the man's arm around his wife's waist and holding the umbrella over them both.

"That was generous of them," Clay said, guiding Kat toward the hotel and a hot cup of coffee.

Ten minutes into their stroll, Kat spotted the Starbucks icon. "There it is," she pointed.

"Not a minute too soon," Clay said, relieved.

***

"I'm curious," Kat said. Her hands were wrapped around the hot cardboard cup. "What did you want to talk about?"

"Us."

She looked him in the eyes. "Working with you on films will be awesome. I'm thrilled to finally know what it is I want to do that will make a difference for other people."

"I mean I want to talk about us — not work. I would like to know how you feel about me. "There've been times when I thought you cared for me and other times I think you feel I'm a big brother. I'd like to know where I stand."

Kat stared down at her coffee unsure of how to respond. Did she even know how she felt toward Clay? Looking up at his expression, it was obvious he would like them to have a closer relationship. She sipped the hot liquid slowly to provide time to choose her words carefully.

"Clay, you're very dear to me." She immediately regretted her response. His face faded to ash. "I mean I've grown fond of you since we've spent so much time together on the film."

He sighed.

"I'm sorry. I'm not saying what I mean. I don't know how to express my feelings for you."

Clay watched her fumble for words and felt badly. He shouldn't have put her in such an awkward position. "Just tell me if you want us to get closer. I want to date you, not become your big brother." He stopped talking and smiled.

"Let's ask God to guide us. My future is in His hands and if we are meant to be together as you want, then I desire it too. We can date, I'd like that."

This time Clay's sigh was relief. "I won't argue with that." He finished his coffee and looked out the window. "I think the rain stopped."

Kat turned. "Yes, now let's go take in the holiday lights."

He stood and pulled her chair back as she got up. Gathering their napkins and cups, they deposited them in the trash can. They walked side by side, holding hands as "Joy to the World" started playing throughout the lobby.

Kat began singing along and Clay joined in with his melodic voice. Passersby stared but some started singing and smiling.

Clay looked at her warmly. "See, already you're making a difference in people's lives."

Chapter Twenty

Emily sealed the last envelope and placed a holiday postage stamp in the upper right corner. "There," she stated with satisfaction, "I have them all finished."

Seth looked up from his newspaper. "Finished with what?"

"Addressing the invitations to our estate sale group. I think they'll be surprised, don't you?"

"Without a doubt. I think all of us enjoying dinner on the Riverwalk barge is a great way to bring us all together one final time this year."

"Thank you for arranging everything," she said, walking to where Seth sat at the table. "Want more coffee?"

"I'm good. I'll take those to the post office in the morning if you want me to."

Emily leaned over to plant a kiss on her husband's cheek. "You're such a dear. I love you."

"Do you think Annie will accept the invitation and show up with Jake? I got the feeling they might be more than just friends."

"I don't know, but I like her a lot. She has a compassionate heart and is very friendly."

"Hence the nickname, Nurse Heartie." Seth chuckled at the sound of it. "It fits her though."

Emily set the envelopes on the table.

Looking at the stack of envelopes, Seth commented. "Mary's

legacy is traveling a lot of paths. It's hard to believe all that's transpired in the past year."

Emily sat down. "I can't help but wonder where our lives will be next year. God has done so much already with reconciliations, new love, hope, and healing."

"That's how God works." Seth placed his hand on top of the invitations. "Each person here has walked a difficult path and may still have more ahead. The great thing about it is they don't have to travel alone."

She stood and bent to hug him. "You're so wise. I'm blessed to be married to you."

"The feeling is mutual my dear," he responded, hugging her with one arm. "Right now though, let's drive over to King William and check out some things at the house."

"Sounds like a great idea. Maybe we can stop by the garden center and look at landscaping plants for the B & B."

Seth smiled. "You're always on my wavelength. I'd like to look at an arbor too. Remember the one in Essex?"

"I'll never forget it. We were married beneath its beauty."

He gave her a long glance. "We better get moving."

Emily winked at him as she headed for the door.

***

Blanca locked her car and was halfway up the stairs when she heard singing coming from within the house. She thought it was a CD or the radio but as soon as she entered the kitchen she realized it was Rosie singing in Spanish. Blanca made her way to the back of the house when Rosie appeared. They both stopped in their steps and looked at each other.

"You have a beautiful voice. I had no idea you were a singer."

349

Rosie laughed. "Oh, I just enjoy singing when I'm alone. It gives me heart thumps," she said, tapping her chest.

"It certainly gave me heart thumps when I walked in. Your voice touched me deep inside. I love "10,000 Reasons" and the Spanish version is beautiful, but you took it over the top."

"Gracias, dear friend, you're so kind. Carlos taught it to me."

Blanca swallowed hard at the mention of her late husband's name. "He did love that song." Before tears formed at the memory of his deep voice, Blanca turned.

"I'll make some apple cider, would you like some?"

"Yes, it sounds perfect."

"Bree should be home soon. If she's up to getting the Christmas tree out of the storage shed, we could decorate it this evening."

Rosie clapped her hands together as she followed Blanca to the kitchen. "It'll be fun having Christmas with friends."

Blanca turned to face Rosie. "We're family now."

A tear slid silently down Rosie's cheek. She reached out and hugged Blanca. "Yes."

***

Jake Davis had mixed feelings about being back home in Mesquite. He enjoyed the time spent with his brother, Ron, and the festivities during Thanksgiving week. Having Annie with him for it all made things even better. But, she had to go back to work at the hospital and he needed to return to his job at the hotel in the morning.

He remembered how Annie squeezed his hand during the film event when Clarence proposed to Greta. Was she trying to drop a hint? He doubted it. Annie was one to speak her mind. Then again, she certainly wouldn't propose to him. Jake wasn't ready for marriage though. He wanted to spend time with Annie, enjoy making her smile and hearing her laugh. Jake felt comfortable with her, even though she was a little older than him.

The phone rang. He saw Annie's name on the caller ID.

"Hi," he said, picking up the phone, "I was just thinking about you."

"Hello, Jake. I hope I'm not interrupting dinner."

He laughed. "I'm still full from the Mexican food we had at lunch on the way home so no dinner for me."

"I wanted to tell you again how much I enjoyed the week with you in San Antonio. Your brother's girlfriend was such a sweet hostess, allowing me to stay with her. If you'll give me her mailing information, I want to send her a thank you note."

"You made the week special for me. Thanks for going with me. I'll get Rita's info and give you a call back."

"When are you planning to move into your mom's home? If I know in advance maybe I can get off work and help you."

"I'm thinking about waiting until January. The holidays are hectic at work and I need time to sort through Mom's things in the house."

"That makes sense. Just remember I'm happy to help if you need it. I'll even bring food while you're working."

"You know the secret password: food."

She laughed. "One thing my mom taught me is to learn to cook well."

"A wise mother."

"I'll let you go. I hope you get enough rest before going back to work."

" Thanks, you too."

Jake hung up the phone, her voice still sweet to his ears.

***

Gus returned from getting a half dozen breakfast tacos and put on a pot of coffee. He wondered how things went between Jared and his parents last night. It was late when he came home and Gus didn't want to seem nosy so he stayed in bed. He figured if his brother wanted to talk he'd knock on his door, but Jared went right to his room. Maybe he'll feel like talking this morning. He heard the shower turn off so he set out a couple plates and waited for Jared and the coffee.

"Morning brother." Jared greeted Gus with a smile.

"Same to you. Hungry? I ran over to Taco Cabana and picked up some potato, egg, and bacon tacos."

"You're a mind reader. Thanks," he said, pulling out a chair and taking a seat. He put two tacos on his plate and wolfed down the first.

"How'd things go?" Gus poured the finished coffee into their mugs.

"I think I made amends. I apologized to them both. Mom cried and she even apologized for a couple things."

"What did your Dad say or do?"

Jared was quiet for a moment, sipping the Texas Pecan coffee.

"How did he respond?" Gus asked, concerned.

"I'm not totally sure. On the surface he was okay, but he asked me a few questions that caused me to think he expects more."

"What do you mean?"

"He wants to know how I'll make it up to Mom. He said the situation required more than words. You know, he's right."

"What do you plan to do?"

"Not sure just yet. I told him I would see what the Lord wants me to do and it seemed to satisfy him for now."

"Maybe you should talk to someone."

"That's what I'm doing now. Talking to you."

Gus finished eating his second taco, took a drink of coffee and set down the mug.

"Well, this is how I see it. The best way to show both of them you've changed is to make better choices. Finish college or find a trade. Stay out of trouble and be part of the family."

Jared looked at Gus. "You're right and I hope to work with you at the shop until I can get into a school of some kind. I don't want to take any more money from them so I need a job."

"I can use your help and pay you a salary. You can stay here for now."

"Thanks, Gus. I don't deserve it, but I'm grateful. One more thing."

"What?"

"Have you been able to contact Kat or find out how to get in touch with her family yet?"

"I have a lead but haven't acted on it yet."

The brothers stared at each other for a moment.

"My intention is honorable. I only want to make things right."

Gus nodded and reached for the last taco.

"I'll try later today."

"Thanks, and by the way, I'll work hard and earn every penny you pay me."

***

Rita settled in with Pekoe on her lap. Her intention was to read a while then go to bed. The week had been busy, fun and tiring. Pekoe kneaded her paws against her thigh, loving private time with Rita.

She stroked the kitten's fur and leaned back in the recliner. She missed having Annie here. It was nice not being alone over the holiday and Rita was thankful for friends.

She looked at the ring sparkling on her finger and immediately Ron's face appeared in her mind. She had a wedding to plan and only five months to pull everything together.

Pekoe looked up at her and rolled her head against Rita for more affection.

Rita asked in a baby voice. "You haven't gotten much attention this past week, have you?" Pekoe responded by licking her arm and curling back down in Rita's lap.

"We all need attention, "Sweetie. Thanks for the reminder. Tomorrow I'll give Kat a call and see how she's doing."

The phone startled her. The caller ID revealed only a number. She answered.

"Hi, I don't know if you remember me. I'm Gus from the auto shop and I fixed a car for a woman you know."

"Oh, yes," Rita answered, "but how did you get my number?"

"From my paperwork for the car repair."

"Of course. How can I help you? Do I owe you more money?"

Gus laughed. "No, definitely not. I would like to talk to you about something really important though. Would you have a few minutes to listen?"

"I suppose. Sure, go ahead."

Rita listened as Gus recounted the situation with Jared and Kat. Her feelings grew a little hostile remembering the fear and pain Jared caused her friend. Gus begged her to listen to the whole story before commenting, so she held it in.

"Jared has changed because of an encounter with the Lord," Gus

354

said with passion. "I've seen the change in him. He is trying desperately to make amends with people he's wronged and only wants to apologize to Kat and her family."

"So why are you telling me this?" Rita interrupted.

"I'm hoping you will try to set something up where Jared could meet with them."

"Whoa, that's asking a lot."

"I don't know who else to ask. We can't contact them directly. Please?"

Silence.

"I promise you, Jared wants only to apologize. No excuses."

Speaking slowly, Rita began. "I'm not sure I'll be able to convince Kat or her dad to meet with him, but I will explain your request and get back to you."

"That's all I'm asking, thank you."

Rita hung up the phone and exhaled. She couldn't believe the conversation that just took place, nor her agreement to try and arrange a meeting. What was I thinking? She glanced at the book on her side table, then at Pekoe purring on her lap. She sighed. No reading tonight. She got up, carefully placing her furry friend onto the seat. Pekoe stretched, turned toward the back of the cushion and resumed her nap.

I can catch the bus if I hurry. I'm sure Kat will bring me home. I really need to get a car.

***

Brian, Betty and Kat were in the middle of a game of Scrabble, with Betty looking up a questionable word Brian had thrown out there, when the phone rang. Kat took the call and was surprised to hear Rita's voice.

"Kat, I'm on the bus heading to your house. There's something important I need to talk to you and your parents about."

"What's wrong? Are you okay?"

"I'm fine, I just wanted you to know I'll be there within the hour and hope I'm not interrupting your evening."

"No, of course not, we're just quibbling over a word my Dad used in Scrabble. Of course, come on over."

"Great, I'll see you in a bit."

Kat put the phone down and shared the conversation with Betty and Brian.

"She was very mysterious."

Brian pondered what was said. "Did she sound upset?"

"No, just a little anxious maybe. She said nothing was wrong, but then why the quick trip over here to discuss something? Maybe she and Ron are having trouble."

"Well, we'll have to wait and see."

Betty put the dictionary down and frowned at her husband. "Okay, you can use Muzjiks. The Scrabble dictionary says Muzjiks are Russian peasants. How in the world did you know this?"

Brian laughed. "I read a lot," he said, adding up his points.

Betty stood, promising to come right back after putting on a pot of tea. "Tea always helps so I'll get a pot of Chai started. I know Rita enjoys it."

"That's sweet of you, Mum." Kat said.

"We love Rita and whatever is on her mind can be helped by a cup of spicy tea."

***

Greta rested on her bed thinking about so many things her mind whirled. Here she was, starring in a film and having her life displayed

356

for all to see. It was exciting, but at her age would anyone who viewed it really care about an old woman?

A picture of Clarence crossed her mind. In her wildest dreams she would never have imagined marrying at the age of 97. Marriage! She remembered they agreed to do it on December 30 because neither wanted to wait until next year. Ha, who knows if one or both of us will be around next year.

The Director, Mr. Cavanaugh, assured them their wedding would be lovely and held in the small chapel if the weather was too bad for the garden. Greta hoped for good weather so they could say their vows in the secluded bower. She could almost hear Clarence whisper her name as she drifted off.

***

Kenneth Cavanaugh looked at the room layout for Mt. Laurel. He tried to figure a way to give Greta and Clarence accommodations which would work best for them. He had to follow rules, but he wanted them to be happy too. They were each very independent, but enjoyed being together. He had a thought and wanted to run it by his work crew and see if it was a possibility. The more he thought about it, the more excited he became. Kenneth would take the drawings home and go over it with Jewel and see what she thought first. Her creativity was invaluable to him.

***

Brian sat in his recliner and stared at Rita in disbelief. "He wants to do what?"

Rita shuddered a bit at the tone in Mr. Hills voice. She knew he wouldn't want to have Jared anywhere near him or his daughter.

"His brother said Jared had changed because of Scriptures he read and now he feels strongly about making things right with people he mistreated in his past."

Brian stood defiantly. "He can make it right with God, but I don't want him near any of my family."

Kat rose from the sofa and went to her father's side.

"Dad, I'm okay with it. Really I am. If the Lord has changed and forgiven him, we can do no less."

Brian looked into the moistened eyes of his daughter. She was sincere and the love of the Lord was in her heart.

"Please, Dad. I'll go with Rita tomorrow over to Gus's garage and meet with him."

Rita interjected part of her conversation with Gus.

"He wants to apologize to all of you, not just Kat. He said Jared realizes now how hurting one can affect many others."

Betty spoke softly. "I agree with what the boy wants to do. He can't harm any of us. I believe he should be accountable for his actions and the best way is for him to face all of us."

Brian reluctantly agreed. "Okay, we'll go in the morning but one wrong move from him and I'm calling the cops. I hope the change in him is real."

"I'll call him back and let him know. He mentioned ten o'clock, is that okay?"

Brian nodded. "I'm going upstairs. I want to do some praying."

"Goodnight, Mr. Hills," Rita called after him.

Turning to Kat, Rita asked for a ride home.

"Sure, let's go," she said, picking up her messenger bag. "I'll be right back, Mum."

Chapter Twenty-One

The small office smelled metallic and seemed to Kat to be claustrophobic. She had stayed outside when she brought Rita out to pick up her friend's car. So much had happened since then. Right now her senses were high and she wanted this meeting to be over with. Glancing at her dad she felt certain he had the same thoughts. He stood stiffly while Betty sat in the oak chair beside him.

Gus thanked Rita for arranging the group to meet, then in turn thanked the Hills for agreeing. Jared nodded in their direction, looking each of Kat's family in the eye.

"I'm just a mediator here," Gus finally announced. "Jared wants to express some feelings and thoughts, so I wanted to provide a place for us all to feel comfortable in. Jared, this is what you asked of me, so I'll turn things over to you."

"Thanks, Gus. I appreciate you more than I can say." Turning to the others, he began. "My life has been one of rebellion I suppose. I always seemed to make bad choices and refuse to accept accountability for them. I've alienated my parents over my idiotic actions and have no reason for them to stand by me." He swallowed hard, fighting emotions he didn't want to expose.

"Kat, the way I treated you was inexcusable. I can't even imagine all you went through and I certainly deserved the tongue-lashing you gave me at the pizza place."

Jared paused and looked straight at Brian.

"Mr. Hills, please forgive me for the pain and suffering I caused you and your family."

He glanced at Betty and nodded, then looked back at Brian.

"If you wanted to punch me out, I'd stand and take it. I'm not trying to get into your life; I only hope to convince you of my regret over my actions."

Brian allowed his hands to relax. He waited a moment before speaking. "You have no idea how many times I've wanted to do just that, but the Lord restrained me. My daughter is the most important person in my life besides the Lord and my wife. If anything would have harmed her during your tirade, I'm not sure I would have been able to hold back."

Jared hung his head and tears streaked his face.

Betty spoke for the first time. "Your brother told us you have changed because of an encounter with Jesus. Would you like to share your experience?"

The young man sat up straight and a glowing expression came over him.

"I would, thank you. I first should tell you what happened beforehand." Jared started with the flare-up when he discovered his parents' house didn't sell and his blow-up with Gus. He let it all out. "Thanksgiving was a turning point for me. I'll never be able to thank George enough for showing me how much Jesus loves me. It was at that point where I understood what loving someone really meant. That's how I knew I had to make things right with those I've wronged."

Betty's throat seemed to swell with tears. "I believe you," she finally managed to say.

"I do too," Kat said softly, and added, "I forgive you."

The sob buried in Jared's throat broke loose.

Brian took four steps toward Jared and extended his hand. "I hold no animosity toward you son. If Christ forgives you, so do I."

Jared shook Brian's hand and in an emotion-packed voice said, "Thank you, Sir."

***

Betty picked up the phone. "Hi, Emily, it's good to hear from you. How's Seth?"

"He's fine and absorbed in the plans for the King William house. I was wondering if you would like to visit over a cup of tea. I have something I'd like to talk with you about."

"Sounds like a great way to have a fun conversation, when?"

"Well, I'm not sure about the fun part, but maybe in an hour at the coffee shop? They do serve tea of course."

"Emily, is something wrong?"

"I'll tell you about it when I see you. Don't say anything to Brian, okay?"

"He's not here so that's not an issue. Now you really have me worried."

"I'll see you in a bit. Don't worry."

Emily ended the call, a little regretful of sharing this with her friend, but friends need each other when some situations come into a person's life. Betty and Emily had grown close since their double wedding last June and with her being older, Emily needed to confide in her.

She found Seth in his study pouring over blueprints. "I'm meeting Betty for a cup of tea and girl talk. I'll be back in a couple hours. Can I bring you something?" She moved to kiss his cheek but he turned and kissed her first.

"How about one of their honeybuns?" He smiled at his wife.

"I'll see if they have any for my honey." She turned to go, then spun around and looked at Seth. Her heart wanted to tell him but she couldn't get the words out.

Seth looked up. "Did you forget something?"

"Just to say I love you."

"I love you more." Seth watched as she left the room, staring even when she was out of sight. A sudden uneasiness came over him. He rose from his desk and walked to the window. Peering through the vertical blinds he kept his eyes on her as she pulled out of the driveway. I love you more.

***

Emily arrived at the coffee shop first and found a table in the corner away from the main stream of people lining up to order. She would wait until Betty walked in and they could order together. Jingle Bells played cheerfully over the speakers and the shop was decked out for the holidays. The thought of the Riverwalk dinner passed through her mind and she wished for a happier feeling. No matter what, Emily decided, I will smile and enjoy the special event she and Seth planned for their group. Who knows what next week will bring. God knows though and I can get through whatever lies ahead.

She spotted Betty at the door and waved her over. Watching her friend's troubled face made her sad. Maybe I shouldn't burden her with my troubles.

"I'm sorry I took so long. Kat called and I went over some things with her. Have you ordered yet?"

"No, and I haven't been here long so don't fret. Let's get our tea and we can sit here out of the way."

Together they slipped into the growing line. Neither said much until they reached the counter.

"Will this be together or on one ticket?" The barista said, giving them a boyish grin.

"One," Emily responded quickly before Betty could object. "My treat," she said, giving Betty a short hug, "I invited you."

They returned to the cozy corner with their hot beverages and settled quietly.

Betty carefully took a sip of her cranberry spiced tea. "Delicious."

Emily wrapped her hands around her cardboard cup. "I found a lump."

Betty looked up at her friend and saw the furrows on her forehead and immediately her stomach dropped. "You found a what?"

"I did my self-exam in the shower this morning and I found a lump." Emily lifted her cup to take a drink, but set it back down. "I'm a nurse, I know what a lump is."

"I believe you," Betty reassured her friend, "I just wanted to make sure I understood correctly. Have you told Seth?"

"No, I needed time to process things, but I felt I needed to share it with a friend."

Betty reached her hand across the table and squeezed Emily's tightly. "Thanks for trusting me with something so important. I'm here for you. Can we pray about this right now?"

"I'd like that, thank you."

Hands joined, both women bowed their heads. Betty's voice softly sent a call for help from the sanctuary. "Lord, help Emily as she makes choices and decides what the next step will be. You alone know what's in the lump she found this morning. We want it to be nothing, but no matter what the outcome, she can lean on you. Give her guidance and be with Seth as she shares this with him later. Show both of them Your healing hand. Amen."

"Amen," Emily echoed as they squeezed hands and resumed their drinks. Emily pulled a tissue from her purse and dabbed her eyes. She watched Betty do the same.

They both laughed.

Betty spoke first. "Laughter is the best medicine."

"You stole my line. Speaking of lines, I better get in one and order a honeybun to go. Seth asked me to bring him one."

***

Kenneth Cavanaugh wore his biggest grin when he sat down with Greta and Clarence in his office. "I have some great news for you both, concerning your future accommodations here at Mt. Laurel."

"I don't understand what you mean, future accommodations." Clarence said.

Kenneth began explaining his idea. "Right now you each have a nice living space which is perfect for one person but too small for a couple. I came up with an idea I think will provide enough room where you can be a married couple and yet still have your own independence."

Greta looked at the director and then at Clarence. "Who said we needed more space?"

Kenneth was surprised at her question. "I-I just assumed after you marry you both would want to share living quarters. You do, right?"

Clarence nodded his head and looked at Greta. Sure, I'd like her close to me instead of on the opposite end of the hall." He looked at his future bride. "Don't you?"

Greta sat quietly and contemplated both men's questions. "I

supposed I never thought about any changes. It's not like we have to take a taxi to see each other."

"I would like to share what I had in mind and then you can tell me if you like the idea or want to leave things as they are."

The couple sat waiting for more information.

"So long as it doesn't cost a fortune," Greta said. "My money has to stretch until I die. Who knows, I might live another ten years or so."

Clarence patted her hand which rested on the arm of the Cherrywood chair. "My dear, I hope you and I both do. We're getting' a late start and I want to get to know more of your charming ways." He winked at the director.

Kenneth laughed. "This is what I'm proposing. Clarence, the space next to yours is vacant and has the same layout as Greta's current rooms. The cost is the same as well. I worked out a way to create a door in each room to make those two adjoining units. You would each have your privacy when you want it but togetherness when you leave the doors open. It would become the Hartman Suite. The name was my wife's idea."

Greta thought for a moment. "I'm keeping my name."

Kenneth puckered his lips and wrinkled his brows. "Hmm, I guess we'll have to rethink the name. Other than that are there other comments or questions?"

Once again Greta spoke up. "Will the suite cost us more?"

Clarence turned to his future bride. "If it does, I'll cover the extra."

"No, neither of you will have an increase. I want you both to think about it and decide. I can walk us down there so Greta can look at the room she'd move to, and I'll show you how the conversion will look."

Greta and Clarence both agreed and stood to follow the director down the hall. Clarence put his arm around her and gave her a squeeze.

She protested slightly but was secretly pleased. "Watch it, we're not married yet."

Clarence and Kenneth both chuckled.

"Let's head down there. Clarence, do you plan to carry your bride over the threshold?"

Now Greta laughed. "He'd drop me and we'd both get carried away on stretchers."

**

Seth heard the car pull in and knew Emily was home. His heart seemed to beat louder in his chest. He remained on the sofa and waited.

"Hi honey, I'm back, and I have your honeybun." Emily called out from the kitchen.

"I'm in here reading the paper."

She walked slowly to the living room and sat down next to her husband, handing him the white bag containing his sweet snack. After an exchange of soft kisses she leaned back. "I want to talk to you about something, Seth."

He waited for the proverbial other shoe to drop. "Okay." Putting his arm around Emily he spoke caringly. "Whatever it is we can handle it together."

Tears welled and her throat seemed to close, but somehow she said those four words. "I found a lump."

Fear gripped Seth's heart and voice. He turned her by the shoulders to face him. Seeing tears stream down her cheeks, Seth pulled her into his arms, rocking her back and forth. "I'm sorry baby, but we'll get things started and find out what needs to be done. I knew you were troubled about something."

Emily eased back from his embrace. "I should have told you first. I'm sorry. I called Betty and talked it through. I guess I needed girl time to wrap my head around this. I just found the lump this morning."

"It's okay. I love you and I'm not letting some little lump rob us of happiness. We'll get an appointment and have you looked at. When we know what we're dealing with we can figure out what the next step is." He looked his wife in the eye. "Trust me; I'll be with you through whatever we have to do. God brought you into my life and He will keep you there."

They sat huddled together quietly and rested in their love for each other.

Chapter Twenty-Two

The Riverwalk downtown was ablaze in Christmas colors. Every tree was dressed with multicolored twinkling lights. Barges carrying tourists up and down the river were decked out in wreaths and strings of lights wound around the railing and music for the holidays echoed around each bend.

Seth and Emily arrived early to make sure their dinner barge was on time. He was pleased to see a green tablecloth and red napkins on the table. He waited for the estate sale group to find their agreed upon meeting place. He spotted Blanca, her daughter, Bree, along with their new resident, Rosie, heading his way, waving. They were followed by Lane and Sheila. He greeted them one by one and ushered them to benches to wait.

Emily nudged Seth. "Here come Jake and Annie with Ron and Rita. I'm so happy they were able to make it."

Seth beckoned the foursome toward their area. When they were within earshot he called out, "Glad you could get away. It's good to see all of you again."

Ron reached for a handshake as they approached. "Traffic was heavy, but we still managed to arrive on time."

Emily and Annie hugged and moved to a nearby bench with the others.

The boat pilot took Seth aside. "You and your party of thirteen may begin boarding if they're all here. The restaurant will begin bringing the salads and appetizers in ten minutes. Once everyone is served, we'll leave the dock for a fifteen-minute boat ride and then return to dock for the main course. Once served, it's a forty-five minute excursion down and around the river before docking for dessert which you'll enjoy during a short fifteen-minute jaunt."

"Thanks for the information. We have four who should be here any minute."

Betty and Brian, as if on cue, called to Seth. "We're here, don't leave without us."

Seth laughed. "We'll be boarding in a few minutes so you're right on time. Where are Kat and Clay?"

"She texted me saying they were five minutes out. Traffic was bad."

"Great. That accounts for everyone."

They waited and talked when finally the two late arrivals appeared, seemingly breathless.

Kat apologized and Clay explained trying to find a parking spot. "It's crazy out there," he said, waving his arm toward the street on the upper level.

"It's the Christmas season, what can I say?" Seth reasoned, hugging Kat and giving Clay a firm handshake.

The boat pilot unhooked the velvet cord to the boat entry. "Time to board, folks. Watch your step."

As each of Seth's guests stepped carefully into the boat, the pilot assisted them. Seth made sure the ladies found their seats first before taking his own next to Emily.

"This is all so elegant," Emily commented, "You did an excellent job arranging everything, my dear."

Seth did a little bow. "Glad you're pleased. I hope the others enjoy it too."

Waiters began bringing trays of beverages, salads, and hot appetizers on board.

"It's all so festive," Annie said, "and the Riverwalk is beautiful."

"Have you been down here before?" Brian asked.

"Not on the barge. I came with friends once and we only walked around. This is so special. Thank you, Seth, for inviting me."

"You're welcome. I'm happy you and Jake both could attend."

The waiters disappeared and the boat pilot readied the barge engine. "Here we go; ya'll enjoy your food while I give you a bit of history on a few of the buildings along the way. We'll return to the dock for the main course in about 15 minutes."

***

The short river ride ended and they docked for dinner and set off once again for the longer tour. People dining alongside the river waved to the estate sale group as they slipped around bends and made their way up the route.

The boat pilot, whose name was Scout, pointed out Marriage Island, a small islet in the middle of the river, where hundreds are married each year.

Ron nudged Rita. "We might think about having our wedding there next April."

Rita smiled as she gazed at the tall cypress tree on the islet. "It would be a lovely setting. Let's check into it."

Ron gave her a hug and turned back to the salmon he was enjoying. "You're planning the wedding, remember?"

She laughed. "Of course. I just made a mental note to call the city and get the details."

Brian was seated next to Lane on his right with Betty on his left.

"Any word on when that little one arrives?"

Lane set down his fork and dabbed his lips with the red napkin. "Yes, they're bringing her on the fifteenth."

Betty excitedly commented, "I know you're both overjoyed and we can't wait to meet her too. Her name is Mary Dee, correct?"

Sheila jumped into the conversation. "Yes, that's how I knew this precious girl was from God. Her mother's name was Mary and the father was David. Our son's name was David and we planned to name our adopted girl Mary."

Brian put both hands together then pointed upward. "Yes, she truly is a gift from God. We're happy for you."

Scout maneuvered around the islet to move the barge down the other side and continued his monologue.

Rosie listened and found Scout's account of the history of the Riverwalk interesting as she enjoyed seeing the Mexican colonial-designed buildings the barge was passing. San Antonio was a lovely place and she was so happy to have accepted Blanca's offer to move in with her and Bree. But, she couldn't get the recent conversation she had with her son, Roland, out of her mind. *How can I just up and leave Blanca after she opened her home to me?* Ro had asked her to move to the east coast and be close to him. When he told her he'd be getting out of the service and had a good job in cyber security lined up, she was surprised, but felt good knowing he wanted her there.

Rosie pulled herself back to the present when she heard Mariachis on the side of the river. Diners had been serenaded and everyone in the area showed their appreciation. It made her smile. Thoughts of seeing Ro after four years made her smile. *But how will I tell Blanca?*

***

Jared placed a call to Sarah to let her know he was on his way up for a short visit. He knew she'd be working at the diner so he left a message. He bought her a holiday corsage. Her church was planning a Christmas cantata and he wanted her to have it. The glossy leaves in it would reflect on her green eyes. He was fond of Sarah but hesitant to show it. His life had been so chaotic and less than desirable. Thanks to George, he understood the right kind of love the Bible describes. Maybe now he would have a chance with Sarah. I hope so. She deserves someone better than the person I used to be.

***

Sarah finished her work at the diner, bid Tim goodbye and headed out to finish her Christmas shopping at the antique store. She had seen a few vintage items for her parents and asked the owner to hold them with a small deposit. Her recent paycheck made it possible to pick them up today.

She hopped into her jeep and was about to call her mom when she noticed a message. It was from Jared.

"Hi Sarah, it's me, Jared. I've taken care of my family business and thought I'd drive up to see you this evening. I have something for you. I should be there about eight."

She hit redial and waited.

"Sarah, good to hear from you. I hope it's okay for me to come up."

"I was surprised to get your message. It'll be nice to see you again. I wondered if you would come back."

Jared wanted to tell her everything but decided to wait and do it in person. If he was to have any kind of meaningful relationship with her, it would have to be built on honesty. That would need to be done face-to-face.

"I had to get some unfinished business handled, that's all. Now I can move forward."

"I'm happy for you, Jared."

"Thanks, where can I meet you?"

"I'll be at home. I'm doing a little Christmas shopping right now."

"Sounds like fun. See you soon."

"Drive carefully," she cautioned.

Jared laughed. "I've toned down my driving."

***

Scout pulled out from the dock after servers brought desserts and beverages to the group. He shared over the loudspeaker how he enjoyed their company and hoped they had a great experience.

Jake spoke up. "I did for sure. This was my first time on the barge and it was interesting and fun. I love your humor."

Everyone applauded while Scout laughed. "Wish my wife enjoyed it as much."

Annie turned to Jake. "I have enjoyed myself a lot. I'm glad we came."

He smiled. Her face glowed in the reflection of the holiday lights. "We'll have to make San Antonio a regular thing."

"I'd like that," she said softly.

Betty watched as Emily and Seth talked to each other and noticed Emily wore a smile. Is it real or one for the occasion? She felt Emily was strong and secure in her faith, but she was a woman. No woman wants to discover a lump. Thankfully, Seth will be there to support her.

What about women facing such news alone? Betty knew there were many thousands in just such a position. An idea struck her but now wasn't the time to explore it. After the holidays she would get with Brian, Kat, and Clay. Perhaps the four of them would expand their subjects for the documentaries.

***

As soon as the barge docked, Seth stood and handed Scout the envelope containing a generous tip he had prepared in advance.

"We appreciate your effort in successfully making our holiday event memorable."

Scout accepted the gift and shook hands vigorously. "Thank you. I enjoy what I do."

"It's obvious because you do it well."

Seth stepped carefully onto the walkway and waited for the rest. He and Scout stood opposite each other, helping the guests, one by one, to disembark. When everyone made it safely off, Seth gathered them around.

"Thank you all for being here tonight. Emily and I wish you a Merry Christmas and hope you'll remember the reason we celebrate the holiday. Let's all keep CHRIST in Christmas."

Each of the group hugged and exchanged handshakes, thanking Emily and Seth before heading to their vehicles. The couple stood, watching their friends fade into the crowd of tourists and locals along the Riverwalk. When the last one disappeared, Seth put his arm around Emily.

"I think the evening was a success, don't you?"

She leaned on her husband, enjoying their closeness. "Yes, it couldn't have turned out better."

"Let's stroll down the river awhile before we leave."

Emily tilted her face up and smiled. "You're such a romantic."

"What can I say? I love my wife and being with her makes me happy."

They joined hands and made a path through the maze of people milling around, talking, until they passed a store front window and Seth paused. "Let's go in here a minute."

Emily followed her husband into the store.

"Wait here a second, okay?" he asked as they entered.

"Sure, I'll look for this year's tree ornament."

Emily browsed the section filled with creative decorations, mentally selecting one for their second Christmas together as husband and wife, but nothing seemed to express what she felt. Tomorrow perhaps she'd look online.

Seth returned to where she waited, wearing a huge smile. "Just found a special gift for someone I love."

She saw the sparkle in his eyes and knew he had bought her something special. She tiptoed to give him a quick kiss. "You're so sneaky, but I love you. I already have your present."

"Now who's sneaky?"

He held his bag in one hand and took Emily's in the other. "How about heading home for a cozy evening and happy talk?"

"I can't think of a better way to end a beautiful evening."

Chapter Twenty-Three

Clarence woke up with searing pain in his leg. Not the ghost pain he used to have after losing the other one years ago, but the kind which seemed to set his body on fire. He laid there until it became unbearable. He pressed the call button by his bed. Before long, Josie, his favorite nurse arrived to check on him.

"Clarence?" she asked in her most cheerful voice. "You rang for help? What's going on?"

"I'm not sure. My leg, feels like it's on fire."

"Let's take a look," she said, uncovering his leg.

She placed her hand gently over the red area on his calf, feeling the heat radiating from it.

"There's definitely something going on. I'll let the director know and we'll get the doctor to check it out."

"Thanks. I can't get down now; I'm getting married on the thirtieth."

"I know, Clarence, and we'll get you fixed up in time."

Josie left the room to talk to the director. She found Mr. Cavanaugh carrying a cup of coffee to his office.

"Good morning, Sir. I was just in to see Clarence and he has inflammation in his good leg. I think the doctor should check him out."

"Good morning, Josie. Certainly, put a call in to come as soon as possible." Kenneth unlocked his office door, entered and set his cup on the corner of his desk. "I'll go down and talk to Clarence."

"Thanks. He reminded me of his wedding date."

Kenneth laughed. "We're gonna make sure he doesn't miss it."

After the nurse left, he took a sip of the steaming coffee and made his way to visit with Clarence. As he walked the short distance to Clarence's room, the director prayed it was nothing serious. He approached the closed door and knocked softly.

No response.

Kenneth eased the door open and was shocked to see Clarence shivering so badly the bed shook. He quickly grabbed an extra blanket from the foot of the bed and threw it over Clarence. "What's the matter, my friend?"

Clarence looked at him but his gaze seemed confused. The shaking continued. Kenneth pulled out his phone and called 911. He explained the situation and was relieved EMS would arrive quickly to transport the patient to the hospital.

Josie entered the room just as the director finished giving information to the operator. She took one look at Clarence and knew this was serious.

"He wasn't like this when I left him. I contacted the doctor and he's on his way. Should I call him back and have him go directly to the hospital?"

"Yes, tell him to meet the ambulance at the emergency room. When the medics arrive escort them here."

Josie left and Kenneth stayed with Clarence. *Please, Lord, bring him through this.*

***

Greta heard a commotion in the hallway and threw on her robe. She opened the door and Nurse Josie grabbed Greta by the hand.

"My dear, Clarence is being transported to the hospital. Come with me and you can see him before he's loaded in the ambulance."

"What?" Greta uttered in disbelief. "He was fine last night, what happened?"

"We're not sure. I'll explain later. We need to hurry before they leave." She tugged on Greta's arm, gently pulling her alongside.

Greta felt the chilly morning air and saw the stretcher with her fiancé tucked under a sheet. She pulled her hand from Josie and scurried to his side.

"Clarence, what's going on? You can't get sick, we're getting married soon."

Still shivering, he looked at her but didn't respond.

The medic gently moved Greta back. "Please, ma'am, we need to go."

The director appeared behind Greta, assuring her Clarence would be fine and they would keep her informed after they examined him. "Let's go in before you get sick in this cool, damp air," he urged.

Greta allowed herself to be escorted back inside as the ambulance drove off, but she turned her head to watch until they disappeared around the bend. Her heart was heavy and tears were ready to flow.

"Why don't we get some of that good coffee you like?" Kenneth suggested.

She nodded.

He kept patting Greta's shoulder as they walked into the dining area where some residents, having heard the ruckus, had gathered. Concerned looks from each of them told Kenneth he needed to make an announcement and settle everyone's nerves. He seated Greta, promising to bring her coffee right away.

Kenneth stood in the front of the room and asked for their attention.

"I know you're wondering what happened," he began.

"Who died?" someone called out.

Immediately chatter took over. Kenneth called loudly to restore order. "No one has died!" he assured them. "Mr. Hartman woke this morning with an inflamed leg and as a precaution we had him transported to the hospital for tests. That's all. They will give him medication and before you know it he'll be back with us." He turned to look at Greta, "And—we'll be having a wedding." He smiled at Greta with his last words.

Sighs of relief were heard in the room and the residents seemed satisfied. Kenneth went to the breakfast bar and prepared a cup of coffee for Greta as well as him, and returned to where he left her. He sat opposite Greta, placing the coffee in front of her.

"I promise, I'll let you know right away when I hear from the hospital."

She looked at the director and nodded, unable to think of anything to say.

"Have a sip of your coffee. You'll feel better."

Greta stared at the cup.

Kenneth's heart broke seeing her this way. "Okay, go get dressed and I will personally drive you to the hospital so we can find out first hand what's going on."

Immediately, she lifted her head and life returned to her eyes. She stood and smiled for the first time.

"Thank you, Mr. Cavanaugh. I won't be long."

Kenneth watched her move more quickly than he'd ever observed. He decided to call the hospital and let them know they were on the way.

***

Blanca knew Rosie had something on her mind. Since the Riverwalk dinner she seemed preoccupied and restless, but Blanca didn't want to pry. She hoped Rosie would open up and share whatever she was feeling. Then this morning she asked Blanca if they could talk tonight.

Bree was at the library so dinner would be light for just Rosie and Blanca. She had stopped and picked up a pizza, something rare in their house. When Blanca walked in, Rosie was watching the news.

"I'm home and I brought us a mixed pizza; cheese on one side and pepperoni on the other. How does that sound?"

"I can smell it in here. I love cheese." She rose from the sofa and met Blanca in the kitchen. "It looks delicious," she said, as Blanca opened the box. "I'll get some plates."

"Would you grab a couple of glasses too? I'll get the pitcher of tea from the refrigerator."

Once settled at the table and enjoying their food, Rosie took a sip of tea and cleared her throat. "I wanted to speak with you about where I'm headed."

"Headed?" Blanca said, surprised. "What do you mean?"

"I received a call from my son, Ro last week."

"How wonderful," Blanca said, "how is he?"

"Ro is fine and excited. He is getting out of the service and already has a great job lined up."

"I'm so happy for him—and you. I suppose you'll be going to visit him soon?"

"That's what I want to talk with you about. The other night on the Riverwalk, I couldn't get him off my mind. I'm not getting any

380

younger and he's the only family I have. I thought about all the years he has been gone due to military service and how much I've missed being with him. Now that he'll be in one place I can see him often. There's just one thing--"

Blanca stared at her friend for a moment. "What?"

"He has asked me to come live with him now that he's settled stateside."

"Move? Oh no, we're just getting close and we love you."

Rosie felt her eyes moisten. "I care deeply about you and Bree too, but you each have your own purpose and calling in life. She'll be leaving soon for Mexico and you have plans for serving God. I need to find mine."

"I understand, but can we pray about this for a while? Maybe wait until after the first of the year?"

Rosie hesitated. "Ro wants me to come for Christmas."

Blanca threw her hand over her mouth in shock. "Christmas? That's just two days away?"

She reached in her pocket and pulled out an envelope. "He sent me the plane ticket and money."

Blanca got up and rushed to Rosie's side, hugging her tightly. "I can't believe this. I understand being with your son for Christmas, but moving to the east coast so quickly?"

Rosie returned the embrace and felt humbled to be cared about so deeply. "I'm sorry to cause you distress, especially right before the holiday. I only know it's something I need to do."

Blanca took a deep breath. Okay, how about this. You pack what you need for a couple weeks and go. Pray during the time you're there and see if it's where you feel God truly wants you; if so, I'll ship the rest of your things."

Relief spread through Rosie. I promise I'll be praying. Thank you for understanding and for the generosity you've shown to me."

"I know Carlos would want you to be happy and it's why I've tried to make that happen. I'll be here for you and you'll always have a home here."

The two women embraced once again.

"Let me clean up the kitchen," Rosie said, "You've worked hard and should rest."

"Sounds good to me. I'll jump in the shower and later we can either watch a Christmas movie or talk, whichever you like."

Rosie began clearing the table. "It's a Wonderful Life, is on tonight."

"Jimmy Stewart it is then." Blanca said as she headed to the bathroom.

***

Sheila watched as Mary Dee sat on Lane's lap and he pushed the buttons on her musical player. She could see the sparkle in the two-year-old's eyes and the adoration in Lane's. Finally having this precious toddler in their home was from God, of this much Sheila was sure. For now they were fostering her but with the intent of adopting as soon as possible. She belongs here with us.

Lane laughed every time Mary Dee giggled when the different silly songs played. He looked at his wife and his heart was full. They had waited so long for this child and now she was theirs—well almost theirs. He couldn't wait for Christmas morning and seeing her unwrap the gifts from last Christmas—when the daughter they thought was theirs was denied them. He was happy for the mother though. She changed her mind and wanted to keep her baby. Lane began praying for them when his disappointment almost crushed him and Sheila. He prayed they would be happy, healthy, and the mother would raise her to love the Lord. It helped him when he was hurting. Now God has brought this beautiful child into our lives. He hugged her tightly until she squirmed. He put her down and watched as Mary Dee toddled over to Sheila.

Sheila took her tenderly in her arms. "Would you like some apple juice?"

"I don't want juice."

"How about a glass of milk?"

"Bwown milk."

"You mean chocolate milk?"

Sheila saw an impatient frown form on Mary's face.

"I want bwown milk."

Sheila laughed. She put Mary Dee down and stood, taking the child's small hand in hers. "Okay little one, let's go get some bwown milk." She turned to Lane. "Papa, would you like to have bwown milk with us?"

He rose from his chair. "I'd love some."

***

Kenneth and Greta sat nervously in the ER waiting area. He tried to assure Greta that Clarence would be fine, but inside doubt nagged. The man was nearing the century mark and his body wasn't strong.

"Mr. Cavanaugh?"

Kenneth looked up and the facility doctor was coming toward him. "Yes, how's Clarence?"

Dr. Bergstrum kept a solemn face. "He has cellulitis in his leg and it's septic. I've ordered tests to make sure it hasn't affected his bones. We have him on antibiotics and medications to aid in his recovery. I won't kid you; he's not out of the woods. His white blood count was extremely high and we are doing everything possible to bring it down."

"How long will you keep him?"

"I'm moving him to ICU where he'll stay until we see improvement in the leg. We want to make sure he doesn't have to lose it."

Greta stood. "Doctor, may I see him? We're supposed to be married on the 30th."

Dr. Bergstrum looked at the old woman in front of him and his heart melted. "Ma'am, I'll escort you to him myself." He put his elbow out for her and after she slipped her arm around it, they walked slowly to the ER triage room.

***

Bree came in quietly, not wanting to wake her momma or Rosie. After studying at the library she had finished her Christmas shopping and ran into her friend, Diego. They stopped at the coffee shop and talked for hours.

Diego was happy for her about going to the mission field in Mexico. She shared her thoughts with him more than she did with anyone. He was interested in what she'd be doing and all the details of the trip. He was a good friend. She thought once they might become more than friends but now her future was taking her down a different path. She wanted to follow in her father's footsteps and when the pastor offered her the chance to go she couldn't turn it down.

The house was dark except for a lamp by the sofa. Her momma always left it on when she went to bed if Bree wasn't home. It's like God saying, I'll leave the light on for you.

She went to her room and prepared for bed. After crawling under the cool sheet and pulling the quilt up, she reached for her dad's journal on the bedside table. Reading it before falling asleep comforted her. It was as if they were having a conversation and she was learning things about him unknown to her until now. Her bookmark held the place where he had tried to end his life by jumping into the river. A chaplain spotted him and dove in, saving her dad's life.

She spotted a small note next to the river entry. It was difficult to read but after straining her eyes a bit, she couldn't believe what she read. Her dad noted that later after he accepted Jesus Christ as his Savior, he was baptized in the same river which almost ended his life. She looked up the Scripture he jotted in the margin. Romans 6:4 We were therefore buried with him through baptism into death in order that, just as Christ was raised from the dead through the glory of the Father, we too may live a new life.

Bree sat up in bed and a wonderful connection to dad filled her mind. He has a new life now and I'm about to begin a new one as well. "Thank you, Daddy," she whispered. Turning out the light, she hugged the journal to her and snuggled down in bed. "Good night, Daddy."

***

Greta was shocked at the condition she found her soon-to-be groom. He laid still, an IV in each arm and a blood pressure cuff inflating. Dr. Bergstrum assured her he was doing well in spite of how he looked.

"Easy for you to say," Greta snapped, "You're not a hundred years old."

The doctor smiled at her spunk. "He's not yet either. Trust me, we're taking very good care of him."

She leaned against the bed railing and spoke his name. Immediately Clarence opened his eyes and grinned.

"I'm sorry, please don't worry. I promised I'd put a ring on your finger and the Lord will get me well enough to do it."

She laughed in spite of her anguish over his condition. "You better. I spent money on a dress I'll never wear again."

He laughed a bit then coughed.

"We better let him rest now," the doctor urged. "Perhaps Mr. Cavanaugh can bring you back in a couple of days. Mr. Hartman will feel better by then."

Kenneth guided Greta out of the room and back to the car.

"All my life I've waited for a man like Clarence. I don't have much time left and now—"

"Hush," he said, driving out of the parking lot, "He will pull through and I'll see to it your dress doesn't go to waste."

Greta rode the rest of the trip back to Mt. Laurel in silence.

Chapter Twenty-Four

Christmas Day

"Church was beautiful today, wasn't it, Seth?"

"Indeed. I enjoyed the dinner after the service and hearing how God is working in people's lives."

"I know. Then receiving updates from our estate sale group gave me such a wonderful feeling of hope. Even Clarence is making small strides of improvement."

"That's great news for sure. I think Greta's Christmas is better knowing he's making progress." Seth stretched his feet onto the coffee table. "I love being home with my wife, Christmas music playing and having her open a special gift." He handed her a small box wrapped in silver paper with a tiny bell attached to a red bow.

She sat down beside him and held the package in her hands. Is this what you hid from me on the Riverwalk?"

"Yep."

Emily carefully untied the bow and slipped it from the wrapping. One side at a time, she undid the folds of paper until a box revealed the contents. "A Willow Tree figurine," she said in a high pitch happy voice. She tenderly pulled it from the Styrofoam and the card said simply, Together.

"Together," Seth emphasized. "Together we'll get through whatever God allows into our lives."

Emily set the couple figurine down on the coffee table and buried her head against her husband's chest. After a cluster of tears were dried, she looked him in the eyes. "Together Forever," she promised.

"Now it's your turn." She rose and brought out a package from under the small tree and placed it on his lap as she took her seat beside him.

The sky blue paper floated puffy clouds. The little tag had two words printed on it. Our future.

Seth gave her a questioning look and proceeded to open the box. As he lifted the lid he let out a loud shout of excitement. He carefully pulled the tiny blue and white cap out. The word Daddy, was embroidered over the brim. He turned to his wife. "You're sure?"

She nodded. "Positive."

"Boy?"

She laughed. "We won't know the gender for a while, but I asked the Lord for a son for you. If it's a girl, we'll just have to try again."

He wrapped his arms around Emily and kissed her forehead, cheeks, nose and lips. "You've just made my Christmas the happiest I've ever had. I love you."

***

December 30th

The hospital staff and Dr. Bergstrum gathered with Kenneth and his wife, Betty, Brian and Kat, to witness the marriage between Clarence and Greta. He still would not be released but insisted the wedding go on.

Greta stood next to his bed in a satin, ivory-colored dress which Betty found for her in a consignment shop. The bride held a lovely bouquet Clarence had Brian pick up for him. Kenneth held the ring, waiting for the right moment to give to the groom to slip on his wife's finger. Kenneth's wife, Jewel, handed Greta the gold band for Clarence. Vows were exchanged and Clarence kissed his bride.

"Sorry I can't carry you over the threshold, my dear."

"Don't worry, I'm spending the night here with you. They're bringing a bed in for me. It's a good thing they moved you out of ICU. There's not much privacy there."

Dr. Bergstrum laughed along with the others. "You two lovebirds enjoy your day. The TV has programming on the screen and the nurse can help you find something to watch."

"Greta, here's your overnight case and a change of clothes. I'll be happy to help you out of your gown if you like," Betty offered.

"Are you kidding? I want to get my money's worth. I'll probably fall asleep in it watching the television."

The afternoon flew by as nurses stopped in to congratulate the newlyweds. Some brought flowers and candy while others left cards. Clarence dozed off several times. Staff moved a bed in for Greta and she promptly occupied it. She enjoyed reading the cards and knowing at last they were married. "Mrs. Clarence Hartman," she said out loud.

"What did you say, dear?" Clarence said from a drowsy state.

"I said I am now Mrs. Clarence Hartman."

"Sounds pretty good to me," he whispered as he fell asleep.

Greta gazed over at her husband. Her heart was full. "Thank You, Lord," she said, laying her head on the pillow. She wished Clarence goodnight but fell asleep before speaking it.

***

News of Emily's pregnancy spread through the estate sale group. Each one called, sent a text, stopped by, or mailed a card, expressing their excitement over the coming baby due in the fall.

Betty and Emily talked after the Hartman wedding. "Do you plan

389

to go back to Essex?"

"I haven't figured out that part yet. Right now I'm concerned about getting the lump checked. I have an appointment right after the New Year. Once I know what's going on with that, I can make better decisions. Besides, Seth is gung ho about getting the King William house remodeled and transformed into the Bed & Breakfast. I have a big part in making that happen."

"Are the caretakers able to handle the wedding venues?"

"I doubt they could do all the work but it doesn't begin until June, so we have time to work things out."

Betty felt she may have added more stress on Emily by bringing it up so she changed the subject. "You better promise to let me know first if the baby is a boy or girl."

"I promise."

***

At home, Brian and Betty changed into comfortable clothes and joined each other in the living room. "Want some popcorn?" Betty asked before getting settled in the recliner.

"Not really. I just want to relax and talk about some things."

"What things?"

"The new year ahead. Since I'm resigning from Boeing and helping you with the film business, we should probably work out where we're headed with it."

"Oh, honey, I'm glad you brought it up. The night we were having dinner on the Riverwalk, I had an idea. Want to hear it?"

"I'm all ears."

"Before I get to it, I wanted to tell you how happy I am. Just six months ago we were getting married in England and beginning a new life together. I remember flying back and feeling on top of the clouds

390

in love with you."

Brian motioned for her to come and sit on his lap. "We were on top of the clouds," he said as she sat down. He embraced his wife. "I am still there."

The End

Special Recipes by Rita, Betty, and Annie

In Legacy's Path, several great dishes were mentioned. Rita developed her take on a slow-cooker chili recipe with a secret ingredient and she shares it with you here.

Kat's mom, Cassie had a special recipe for stuffed manicotti and Betty offered to work with Kat and teach her how to make it. You'll love it, too.

Betty includes a recipe for her very own mouth-watering pot roast, so jot down the ingredients and get cooking.

With the story set in San Antonio, Texas, Emily had to include her version of Texas Sheet Cake, which her husband, Seth, could never pass up.

Rita's Secret Ingredient Chili

1 tablespoon vegetable oil
1 large white onion chopped
2 cloves garlic, minced
2 pounds ground beef
2 (14.5 ounce) can peeled & diced tomatoes (including juice)
3 (8 ounce cans) tomato sauce
½ cup beef broth
2 tablespoons chili powder
1 teaspoon granulated sugar
2 teaspoons smoked paprika
2 teaspoons cocoa powder (the secret ingredient)
2.5 teaspoons ground cumin
½ teaspoon ground coriander; Salt & pepper to taste
2 (15 ounce) can dark red kidney beans (drained & rinsed)

Instructions:

- Heat olive oil in a large, deep non-stick skillet over medium-high heat. Add onion and saute 3 minutes, then add garlic and saute 30 seconds. Pour onions into a slow cooker (6-7 quart).
- Return skillet to medium-high heat, add beef and cook, stirring occasionally until beef has browned. Drain most of fat from beef, leaving 2 tablespoons in with beef for flavor. Pour browned beef into slow cooker.
- Stir in diced tomatoes, tomato sauce, beef broth, chili powder, cumin, paprika, cocoa powder, sugar, coriander and season mixture with salt and pepper to taste.
- Cover with lid and cook on low for 5-6 hours.
- Stir in kidney beans and allow to heat through, about 2 minutes. Serve warm with desired toppings. Makes 8 servings.

Kat's Mom's Stuffed Manicotti

4 manicotti
1 (16 ounce can diced tomatoes
¼ cup white wine vinegar
2 tablespoons tomato paste
½ teaspoon dried basil, crushed
¼ teaspoon dried oregano, crushed
½ pound hamburger
¼ cup yellow onion, chopped
1 clove garlic, minced
½ (10 ounce) package frozen chopped spinach, thawed and well-drained
2 tablespoons parmesan cheese

Instructions:

- Cook manicotti according to package directions. Drain. Rinse with cold water and drain. In saucepan, combine undrained tomatoes, wine vinegar, tomato paste, basil and oregano. Cook uncovered, 5 minutes or until slightly thickened. Set aside.
- In skillet, cook meat, onion, and garlic until meat is browned. Drain. Stir in spinach, parmesan, ¼ teaspoon salt, and ¼ cup of the tomato mixture.
- Divide meat mixture among manicotti. Place each filled manicotti in shallow individual baking dish. Spoon tomato mixture on top. Cover with foil and freeze. Makes 4 single servings.
- To bake: Place covered manicotti in oven at 375 degrees for 50 minutes or until hot.

Betty's Perfect Pot Roast

1 three-pound very lean beef bottom round roast
½ teaspoon salt and ½ teaspoon pepper
½ teaspoon garlic powder
1 cup cola
½ cup chili sauce
1 tablespoon Worcestershire sauce

Instructions:

- Preheat oven to 325 degrees. Coat a roasting pan with cooking spray and place roast in pan.
- Season roast with salt, pepper and garlic powder.
- In a small bowl, combine remaining ingredients and pour over roast.
- Cover with foil and roast 2 ½ - 3 hours, or until roast is tender.
- Slice and serve topped with sauce from pan.

Serves 7-9, (maybe fewer if they love melt-in-the-mouth pot roast).

Emily's Texas Sheet Cake

2 cups flour
2 cups sugar
1 stick margarine
½ cup shortening
4 tablespoons cocoa
1 cup water
½ cup buttermilk
2 eggs
1 teaspoon baking soda
1 teaspoon vanilla

Instructions:

- Combine sugar and flour in a bowl.
- In pan, combine margarine, cocoa, shortening and water. Bring to a rapid boil, then add the sugar and flour mixture. Mix well.
- Add all other ingredients and mix well again. Pour into a large, well-greased, floured sheet pan and bake at 400 degrees for 30 minutes.

Icing:

1 stick margarine
4 tablespoons cocoa
6 tablespoons milk
1 box powdered sugar
1 teaspoon vanilla

- Boil margarine, cocoa, and milk until thick.
- Add all other ingredients and mix well.
- Spread over cake while both are still hot.

About the Author

June Chapko is an avid journal writer and lover of estate sales. She enjoys helping others discover treasures of the past and the legacy of their future. June has written several Bible studies, many devotionals, and has been published in Mature Living, Quilt World and other publications. Her first novel, The Estate Sale, was published in 2018. She is a certified teacup indulgent, never passing up a chance to add to her collection. She also loves reading and quilting.

A wife, mother, grandmother and great-grandmother, June is also a member of American Christian Fiction Writers and Advanced Writers and Speakers Association. She and her husband, Nick, and Shih Tzu puppy, Chai, reside in San Antonio, Texas.

Made in the USA
Middletown, DE
27 November 2019

79532241R00243